Sophie Kinsella is an ~~international~~ writer and former financial journalis~~t~~. She is the author of the number-one bestsellers *Can You Keep A Secret?*, *The Undomestic Goddess*, *Remember Me?*, *Twenties Girl*, *I've Got Your Number* and *Wedding Night* as well as the hugely popular Shopaholic novels, the first of which has become the Hollywood movie *Confessions of a Shopaholic*. Her new novel is *Shopaholic to the Stars*. She lives in London with her husband and children.

Visit the global Sophie Kinsella website at www.sophiekinsella.co.uk for Sophie's latest news, videos and competitions, and join her at www.facebook.com/SophieKinsellaOfficial.

'A laugh-a-minute read'
Glamour

'Witty and hilarious'
Cosmopolitan

'Brilliant . . . Funny, romantic and believable'
Heat

'Never has a character with a personality
disorder been more appealing'
Marie Claire

'You won't have to shop around to find a
more winning protagonist'
Ireland on Sunday

'Hilarious'
OK!

'Expect to laugh. A lot'
Company

'I almost cried with laughter'
Daily Mail

'A sure-fire, laugh-out-loud hit'
Sun

'High-octane, laugh-a-minute entertainment'
Woman & Home

THE SHOPAHOLIC SERIES

Starring the unforgettable Becky Bloomwood,
shopper extraordinaire . . .

The Secret Dreamworld of a Shopaholic

(also published as *Confessions of a Shopaholic*)

Meet Becky – a journalist who spends all her time
telling people how to manage money, and all her leisure
time spending it. But the letters from her bank manager
are getting harder to ignore. Can she ever escape this
dream world, find true love . . . and regain the use of
her credit card?

Shopaholic Abroad

Becky's life is peachy. Her balance is in the black – well,
nearly – and now her boyfriend has asked her to move to
New York with him. Can Becky keep the man *and* the
clothes when there's so much temptation around
every corner?

Shopaholic Ties the Knot

Becky finally has the perfect job, the perfect man and, at
last, the perfect wedding. Or rather, *weddings* . . . How has
Becky ended up with not one, but two big days?

Shopaholic & Sister

Becky has received some incredible news. She has a
long-lost sister! But how will she cope when she realizes
her sister is not a shopper . . . but a skinflint?

Shopaholic & Baby

Becky is pregnant! But being Becky, she decides to shop around – for a new, more expensive obstetrician – and unwittingly ends up employing Luke's ex-girlfriend! How will Becky make it through the longest nine months of her life?

Mini Shopaholic

Times are hard, so Becky's Cutting Back. She has the perfect idea: throw a budget-busting birthday party. But her daughter Minnie can turn the simplest event into chaos. Whose turn will it be to sit on the naughty step?

Shopaholic to the Stars

Becky is in Hollywood and her heart is set on a new career – she's going to be a stylist to the stars! But in between choosing clutch bags and chasing celebrities, Becky gets caught up in the whirlwind of Tinseltown.
Has Becky gone too far this time?

Shopaholic to the Rescue

Becky is on a major rescue mission! Hollywood was full of surprises, and now she's on a road trip to Las Vegas to find out why her dad has mysteriously disappeared, help her best friend Suze and *maybe* even bond with Alicia Bitch Long-legs. She comes up with her biggest, boldest, most brilliant plan yet – can she save the day?

OTHER BOOKS

Sophie Kinsella's hilarious, heart-warming
standalone novels

Can You Keep a Secret?

Certain she's going to die in a plane crash, Emma blurts out her
deepest, darkest secrets to the sexy stranger next to her. But it's OK,
because she'll never have to see him again . . . will she?

The Undomestic Goddess

Samantha works all hours, has no home life and thrives on adrenalin.
Then one day it all falls apart. She finds herself a new life as
housekeeper in a country house. Will her old life ever catch up with
her? And if it does, will she want it back?

Remember Me?

What if you woke up and your life was perfect? Somehow Lexi's
life has fast-forwarded three years, and she has everything she's ever
wanted – the job, the house, the man. Or does she? What went on in
those missing years, and can she cope when she finds out the truth?

Twenties Girl

Lara has always had an overactive imagination. But even she finds
it hard to believe when the ghost of her great aunt Sadie shows up,
asking for her help. Is Lara losing her mind? Or could two girls from
different times end up helping each other?

I've Got Your Number

First Poppy loses her engagement ring – a priceless heirloom – and
then she misplaces her phone. The only alternative seems to be to
take a mobile she finds in a bin. Little knowing that she's picked up
another man in the process . . .

Wedding Night

Lottie is determined to get married. And Ben seems perfect – they
have history, he's gorgeous and he's willing to do it now. They'll iron
out their little differences later. All that's left to do is seal the deal.
But their families have different plans . . .

THE UNDOMESTIC GODDESS

Sophie Kinsella

BLACK SWAN

THE UNDOMESTIC GODDESS
A BLACK SWAN BOOK : 9780552153140

Originally published in Great Britain by Bantam Press
a division of Transworld Publishers

PRINTING HISTORY
Bantam Press edition published 2005
Black Swan edition published 2006

21

Set in 11/13pt Melior by
Falcon Oast Graphic Art Ltd.

Black Swan Books are published by Transworld Publishers,
61–63 Uxbridge Road, London W5 5SA,
a division of The Random House Group Ltd,
in Australia by Random House Australia (Pty) Ltd,
20 Alfred Street, Milsons Point, Sydney, NSW 2061, Australia,
in New Zealand by Random House New Zealand Ltd,
18 Poland Road, Glenfield, Auckland 10, New Zealand
and in South Africa by Random House (Pty) Ltd, Isle of Houghton,
Corner Boundary Road & Carse O'Gowrie, Houghton 2198, South Africa.

Penguin Random House is committed to a sustainable future for
our business, our readers and our planet. This book is made from
Forest Stewardship Council® certified paper.

Printed and bound in Great Britain by Clays Ltd, St Ives plc

ACKNOWLEDGEMENTS

I am incredibly grateful to the many people who have gone out of their way to help me with this book. To Emily Stokely, domestic goddess extraordinaire, for teaching me how to bake bread. To Roger Barron, for being so generous with his time and giving me a wonderful insight into the world of corporate law (not to mention his Jo Malone expertise!). And especially to Abigail Townley, for acting as legal plot consultant, allowing me to shadow her, and patiently answering a million dumb questions.

Thank you to the endlessly supportive Patrick Plonkington-Smythe, Larry Finlay, Laura Sherlock, Ed Christie, Androulla Michael, Kate Samano, Judith Welsh and all the fabulous people at Transworld. To my wonderful agent Araminta Whitley, whose enthusiasm for this book has known no bounds, and to Lizzie Jones, Lucinda Cook, Nicki Kennedy and Sam Edenborough. To Valerie Hoskins, Rebecca Watson and Brian Siberell. Thanks as ever to the members of the Board and to all my boys, big and small.

These acknowledgements would not be complete, of course, without a mention of Nigella Lawson, whom I've never met – but whose books should be required reading for all undomestic goddesses.

To Linda Evans

ONE

Would you consider yourself stressed?

No. I'm not stressed.

I'm . . . busy. Plenty of people are busy. It's the way the world is. I have a high-powered job, my career is important to me and I enjoy it.

OK. So sometimes I do feel a bit tense. Kind of pressured. But I'm a lawyer in the City, for God's sake. What do you expect?

My handwriting is pressing so hard into the page, I've torn the paper. Dammit. Never mind. Let's move on to the next question.

On average, how many hours do you spend in the office every day?

~~14~~

~~12~~

~~8~~

It depends.

Do you exercise regularly?

~~I regularly go swimming~~

~~I occasionally go swim~~

9

I am intending to begin a regular regime of swimming. When I have time. Work's been busy lately, it's a blip.

Do you drink 8 glasses of water a day?
> ~~Yes~~
> ~~Someti~~
> No.

I put down my pen and clear my throat. Across the room, Maya looks up from where she's rearranging all her little pots of wax and nail varnish. Maya is my beauty therapist for the day. She has long dark hair in a plait with one white streak woven through it, and a tiny silver stud in her nose.

'Everything all right with the questionnaire?' she says in her soft voice.

'I did mention that I'm in a bit of a hurry,' I say politely. 'Are all these questions absolutely necessary?'

'We like to have as much information as possible to assess your beauty and health needs,' she says in soothing yet implacable tones.

I glance at my watch. Nine forty-five.

I don't have time for this. I really do not have the time. But it's my birthday treat and I promised Aunt Patsy.

To be more accurate, it's *last* year's birthday treat. Aunt Patsy gave me the gift voucher for an 'Ultimate De-stress Experience' just over a year ago. She's my mother's sister and has major worries about women with careers. Every time I see her she grasps my shoulders and peers at my face with an anxious frown, and in the card that came with the voucher she wrote 'Make Some Time For Yourself, Samantha!!!'

Which I did fully intend to do. But we had a couple of busy patches at work and somehow a year went by without my finding a spare moment. I'm a lawyer with Carter Spink, and just at the moment things are pretty hectic. It's a blip. It'll get better. I just have to get through the next couple of weeks.

Anyway, then Aunt Patsy sent me *this* year's birthday card – and I suddenly realized the voucher was about to expire. So here I am, on my twenty-ninth birthday. Sitting on a couch in a white towelling robe and surreal paper knickers. With a half-day window. Max.

Do you smoke?
   No.

Do you drink alcohol?
   Yes.

Do you eat regular home-cooked meals?
   I look up, a bit defensive. What does that have to do with anything? What makes home-cooked meals superior?
   I eat a nutritious, varied diet, I write at last.
   Which is absolutely true.
   Anyway, everyone knows the Chinese live longer than we do – so what could be more healthy than to eat their food? And pizza is Mediterranean. It's probably *more* healthy than a home-cooked meal.

Do you feel your life is balanced?
   ~~Yes.~~
   ~~N~~
   Yes.

11

'I'm done,' I announce, and hand the pages back to Maya, who starts reading through my answers. Her finger is travelling down the paper at a snail's pace. Like we've got all the time in the world.

Which she may well have. But I seriously have to be back in the office by one.

'I've read your answers carefully,' Maya gives me a thoughtful look, 'and you're obviously quite a stressed-out woman.'

What? Where does she get that from? I specifically put on the form, I am *not* stressed out.

'No I'm not.' I give her a relaxed, see-how-unstressed-I-am smile.

Maya looks unconvinced. 'Your job is obviously very pressured.'

'I thrive under pressure,' I explain. Which is true. I've known that about myself ever since . . .

Well, ever since my mother told me, when I was about eight. *You thrive under pressure, Samantha.* Our whole family thrives under pressure. It's like our family motto or something.

Apart from my brother Peter, of course. He had a nervous breakdown. But the rest of us.

I love my job. I love the satisfaction of spotting the loophole in a contract. I love the adrenaline rush of closing a deal. I love the thrill of negotiation, and arguing, and making the best point in the room.

I suppose, just occasionally, I do feel as though someone's piling heavy weights on me. Like big concrete blocks, one on top of the other, and I have to keep holding them up, no matter how exhausted I am . . .

But then everyone probably feels like that. It's normal.

'Your skin's very dehydrated.' Maya is shaking her

head. She runs an expert hand across my cheek and rests her fingers underneath my jaw, looking concerned. 'Your heart rate's very high. That's not healthy. Are you feeling particularly tense at the moment?'

'Work's pretty busy right now,' I shrug. 'It's just a blip. I'm fine.' *Can we get on with it?*

'Well.' Maya gets up. She presses a button set in the wall and gentle pan-pipe music fills the air. 'All I can say is, you've come to the right place, Samantha. Our aim here is to de-stress, revitalize and detoxify.'

'Lovely,' I say, only half listening. I've just remembered, I never got back to David Elldridge about that Ukrainian oil contract. I meant to call him yesterday. Shit.

'The aim of the Green Tree Centre is to provide a haven of tranquillity, away from all your day-to-day worries.' Maya presses another button in the wall, and the light dims to a muted glow. 'Before we start,' she says softly, 'do you have any questions?'

'Actually, I do.' I lean forward.

'Good!' She beams. 'Are you curious about today's treatments, or is it something more general?'

'Could I possibly send a quick email?' I say politely. Maya's smile freezes on her face.

'Just quickly,' I add. 'It won't take two secs—'

'Samantha, Samantha . . .' Maya shakes her head. 'You're here to relax. To take a moment for yourself. Not to send emails. It's an obsession! An addiction! As evil as alcohol. Or caffeine.'

For goodness' sake, I'm not *obsessed*. I mean, that's ridiculous. I check my emails about once every . . . thirty seconds, maybe.

The thing is, a lot can change in thirty seconds.

'And besides, Samantha,' Maya goes on, 'do you see a computer in this room?'

'No,' I reply, obediently looking around the dim little room.

'This is why we ask that you leave all electronic equipment in the safe. No mobile phones are permitted. No little computers.' Maya spreads her arms. 'This is a retreat. An escape from the world.'

'Right.' I nod meekly.

Now is probably not the time to reveal that I have a BlackBerry hidden in my paper knickers.

'So, let's begin.' Maya smiles. 'Lie down on the couch, under a towel. And please remove your watch.'

'I need my watch!'

'It's another addiction.' She clicks her tongue reprovingly. 'You don't need to know the time while you're here.'

She turns away discreetly and with reluctance I take off my watch. Then, a little awkwardly, I arrange myself on the couch, trying to avoid squashing my precious BlackBerry.

I did see the rule about no electronic equipment. And I did surrender my Dictaphone. But three hours without a BlackBerry? I mean, what if something came up at the office? What if there was an emergency?

And it doesn't even make logical sense. If they really wanted people to relax, they would let them *keep* their BlackBerries and mobile phones, not confiscate them.

Anyway, she'll never see it under my towel.

'I'm going to begin with a relaxing foot rub,' says Maya, and I feel her smoothing some kind of lotion over my feet. 'Try to clear your mind.'

I stare dutifully up at the ceiling. Clear my mind. My mind is as clear as a transparent . . . glass . . .

What am I going to do about Elldridge? I should have got back to him. He'll be waiting for a response.

What if he tells the other partners I was lax? What if it affects my chances of partnership?

I feel a clench of alarm. Now is not the time to be leaving anything to chance.

'Try to let go of all your thoughts . . .' Maya is chanting. 'Feel the release of tension . . .'

Maybe I could send him a very quick email. Underneath my towel.

Surreptitiously I reach down and feel the hard corner of my BlackBerry. Gradually I inch it out of my paper knickers. Maya is still massaging my feet, totally oblivious.

'Your body is growing heavy . . . your mind should be emptying . . .'

I edge the BlackBerry up onto my chest until I can just see the screen underneath the towel. Thank goodness this room is so dim. Trying to keep my movements to a minimum, I furtively start typing an email with one hand.

'Relaax . . .' Maya is saying soothingly. 'Imagine you're walking along a beach . . .'

'Uh huh . . .' I murmur.

David, I'm typing. *Re ZFN Oil contract. I read through amendments. Feel our response should be*

'What are you doing?' says Maya, suddenly alert.

'Nothing!' I say, hastily shoving the BlackBerry back under the towel. 'Just . . . er . . . relaxing.'

Maya comes round the couch and looks at the bump in the towel where I'm clutching the BlackBerry.

'Are you hiding something?' she says in disbelief.

'No!'

From under the towel the BlackBerry emits a little bleep. Damn.

'I think that was a car,' I say, trying to sound casual. 'Outside in the street.'

Maya's eyes narrow. 'Samantha,' she says in slow, ominous tones. 'Do you have a piece of electronic equipment under there?'

I have the feeling that if I don't confess she'll rip my towel off anyway.

'I was just sending an email,' I say at last and sheepishly produce the BlackBerry.

'You workaholics!' She grabs it out of my hand in exasperation. 'Emails can *wait*. It can all *wait*. You just don't know how to relax!'

'I'm not a workaholic!' I retort indignantly. 'I'm a lawyer! It's different!'

'You're in denial.' She shakes her head.

'I'm *not*! Look, we've got some big deals on at the firm. I can't just switch off! Especially not right now. I'm . . . well, I'm up for partnership at the moment.'

As I say the words aloud I feel the familiar stabbing of nerves. Partner of one of the biggest law firms in the country. The only thing I've ever wanted, ever.

'I'm up for partnership,' I repeat, more calmly. 'They make the decision tomorrow. If it happens, I'll be the youngest partner in the whole history of the firm. Do you know how big a deal that is? Do you have any idea—'

'Anyone can take a couple of hours out,' interrupts Maya. She puts her hands on my shoulders. 'Samantha, you're incredibly nervy. Your shoulders are rigid, your heart's racing . . . it seems to me you're right on the edge.'

'I'm fine.'

'You're a bundle of jitters!'

'I'm not!'

'You have to *decide* to slow down, Samantha.' She looks at me earnestly. 'Only you can decide to change your life. Are you going to do that?'

'Er . . . well . . .'

I stop with a squeak of surprise, as from inside my paper knickers there comes a judder.

My mobile phone. I shoved it in there along with the BlackBerry and turned it onto 'vibrate' so it wouldn't make a noise.

'What's that?' Maya is gaping at my twitching towel. 'What on earth is that . . . . quivering?'

I *can't* admit it's a phone. Not after the BlackBerry.

'Erm . . .' I clear my throat. 'It's my special . . . er . . . love toy.'

'Your what?' Maya looks taken aback.

The phone judders inside my pants again. I have to answer. It might be the office.

'Um . . . you know, I'm reaching a bit of an intimate moment right now.' I give Maya a significant look. 'Maybe you could, uh . . . leave the room?'

Suspicion snaps through Maya's eyes.

'Wait a moment!' She peers again. 'Is that a phone under there? You smuggled in a *mobile phone as well*?'

Oh God. She looks furious.

'Look,' I say, trying to sound apologetic, 'I know you've got your rules and everything, which I do respect, but the thing is, I *need* my mobile.' I reach under the towel for the phone.

'*Leave it!*' Maya's cry takes me by surprise. 'Samantha,' she says, making an obvious effort to keep calm, 'if you've listened to a single word I've said, you'll switch the phone off right now.'

The phone vibrates again in my hand. I look at the caller ID and feel a twist in my stomach. 'It's the office.'

'They can leave a message. They can wait.'

'But—'

'This is your own time.' She leans forward and

clasps my hands earnestly. '*Your own time.*'

God, she really doesn't get it, does she? I almost want to laugh.

'I'm an associate at Carter Spink,' I explain. 'I don't *have* my own time.' I flip the phone open and an angry male voice bites down the line.

'Samantha, where the hell are you?'

I feel an inward clutch. It's Ketterman. The head of our corporate department. He must have a Christian name, I suppose – but no one ever calls him anything except Ketterman. He has black hair and steel glasses and grey gimlet eyes and when I first arrived at Carter Spink I actually used to have nightmares about him.

'The Fallons deal is back on. Get back here now. Meeting at ten thirty.'

Back *on*?

'I'll be there as soon as I can.' I snap the phone shut and give Maya a rueful glance. 'Sorry.'

I'm not *addicted* to my watch.

But obviously I rely on it. You would too, if your time was measured in six-minute segments. For every six minutes of my working life, I'm supposed to bill a client. It all goes on a computerized time sheet, in itemized chunks.

11.00–11.06 Drafted contract for Project A
11.06–11.12 Amended documentation for Client B
11.12–11.18 Consulted on point for Agreement C

When I first started at Carter Spink it freaked me out slightly, the idea that I had to write down what I was working on, every minute of the day. I used to think: What if I do nothing for six minutes? What am I supposed to write down then?

11.00–11.06 Stared aimlessly out of window
11.06–11.12 Daydreamed about bumping into
George Clooney in street
11.12–11.18 Attempted to touch nose with tongue

But the truth is, you get used to it. You get used to measuring your life in little chunks. And you get used to working. All the time.

If you're a lawyer at Carter Spink, you don't sit around. You don't stare out of the window or daydream. Not when every six minutes of your time is worth such a lot. Put it this way: if I let six minutes tick away without achieving anything, I've wasted the firm £50. Twelve minutes: £100. Eighteen minutes: £150.

Like I say, lawyers at Carter Spink don't sit around.

TWO

As I arrive at the office, Ketterman is standing by my desk, looking at the mess of papers and files strewn everywhere with an expression of distaste.

Truthfully, I don't have the most pristine desk in the world. In fact . . . it's a bit of a tip. But I am totally intending to tidy it up, and sort out all the piles of old contracts on the floor. As soon as I have some time.

'Meeting in ten minutes,' he says, looking at his watch. 'I want the draft financing documentation ready.'

'Absolutely,' I reply, trying to stay calm. But just his presence is giving me the jitters.

Ketterman is unnerving at the best of times. He emanates scary, brainy power like other men emanate aftershave. But today is a million times worse, because Ketterman is on the decision panel. Tomorrow he and thirteen other partners are holding a big meeting to decide on who will become a new partner.

Tomorrow I discover whether I've made it or whether my life has been one big useless failure. No pressure, or anything.

'The draft documentation is right here . . .' I reach

into a pile of folders and pull out what feels like a box file with an efficient flourish.

It's an old box of Krispy Kreme doughnuts.

Hastily I shove it in the bin. 'It's definitely here somewhere . . .' I scrabble frantically and locate the correct file. Thank God. 'Here!'

'I don't know how you can work in this shambles, Samantha.' Ketterman's voice is thin and sarcastic, and his eyes entirely without humour.

'At least everything's to hand!' I attempt a little laugh, but Ketterman looks stony. Flustered, I pull out my chair, and a pile of letters which I'd forgotten about falls in a shower to the floor.

'You know, the old rule was that desks were completely cleared every night by six.' Ketterman's voice is steely. 'Perhaps we should reintroduce it.'

'Maybe!' I try to smile, but Ketterman is making me more and more nervous.

'Samantha!' A genial voice interrupts us and I look round in relief to see Arnold Saville approaching along the corridor.

Arnold is my favourite of the senior partners. He's got woolly grey hair which always seems a bit wild for a lawyer, and a flamboyant taste in ties. Today he's wearing a bright-red paisley affair, with a matching handkerchief in his top pocket. He greets me with a broad smile, and I smile back, feeling myself relax.

I'm sure Arnold's the one who's rooting for me to be made partner. Just as I'm equally sure Ketterman will be opposing it. Arnold is the maverick of the firm; the one who breaks the rules; who doesn't care about irrelevant things like messy desks.

'Letter of appreciation about you, Samantha.' Arnold beams and holds out a sheet of paper. 'From the chairman of Gleiman Brothers, no less.'

I take the headed sheet in surprise and glance down the handwritten note. '. . . *great esteem . . . her services always professional . . .*'

'I gather you saved him a few million pounds he wasn't expecting,' Arnold twinkles. 'He's delighted.'

'Oh yes.' I colour slightly. 'Well, it was nothing. I just noticed an anomaly in the way they were structuring their finances.'

'You obviously made a great impression on him.' Arnold raises his bushy eyebrows. 'He wants you to work on all his deals from now on. Excellent, Samantha! Very well done.'

'Er . . . thanks.' I glance at Ketterman, just to see if by any remote chance he might look impressed. But he's still wearing his impatient frown.

'I also want you to deal with this.' Ketterman plonks a file on my desk. 'I need a due diligence review in forty-eight hours.'

Oh, bloody hell. My heart sinks as I look at the heavy folder. It'll take me hours to do this.

Ketterman's always giving me extra bits of mundane work he can't be bothered to do himself. In fact, all the partners do it. Even Arnold. Half the time they don't even tell me, just dump the file on my desk with some illegible memo and expect me to get on with it.

'Any problems?' His eyes are narrowing.

'Of course not,' I say in a brisk, can-do, potential-partner voice. 'See you at the meeting.'

As he stalks off I glance at my watch. Ten twenty-two. I have precisely eight minutes to make sure the draft documentation for the Fallons deal is all in order. I open the file and scan the pages swiftly, checking for errors, searching for gaps. I've learned to read a lot faster since I've been at Carter Spink.

In fact, I do everything faster. I walk faster, talk

faster, eat faster . . . have sex faster . . .

Not that I've had much of that lately. But a couple of years ago I dated a senior partner from Berry Forbes. He was called Jacob and worked on huge international deals, and he had even less time than me. By the end, we'd honed our routine to about six minutes, which would have been quite handy if we were billing each other. (Although obviously we weren't.) He would make me come – and I would make him come. And then we'd check our emails.

Which is practically simultaneous orgasms. So no one can say that's not good sex. I've read *Cosmo*, I know these things.

Anyway, then Jacob was made a huge offer and moved to Boston, so that was the end of it. I didn't mind very much.

To be totally honest, I didn't really fancy him.

'Samantha?' A voice interrupts my thoughts. It's my secretary, Maggie. She only started a few weeks ago and I don't know her very well yet. 'You had a message while you were out. From Joanne?'

'Joanne from Clifford Chance?' I look up, my attention grabbed. 'OK. Tell her I got the email about clause four, and I'll call her about it after lunch—'

'Not that Joanne,' Maggie interrupts. 'Joanne your new cleaner. She wants to know where you keep your vacuum-cleaner bags.'

I look at her blankly. 'My what?'

'Vacuum-cleaner bags,' repeats Maggie patiently. 'She can't find them.'

'Why does the vacuum cleaner need to go in a bag?' I say, puzzled. 'Is she taking it somewhere?'

Maggie peers at me as though she's not sure if I'm joking.

'The bags which go *inside* your vacuum cleaner,'

she says carefully. 'To collect the dust? Do you have any of those?'

'Oh!' I say, quickly. 'Oh, *those* bags. Er . . .'

I frown thoughtfully, as though the solution is on the tip of my tongue. The truth is, I can't even visualize my vacuum cleaner. Have I ever actually seen it? I know it was delivered, because the porter signed for it.

'Maybe it's a Dyson,' suggests Maggie. 'They don't take bags. Is it a cylinder or an upright?' She looks at me expectantly.

I have no idea what she's talking about. Not that I'm going to admit this.

'I'll sort it,' I say in a businesslike manner, and start gathering my papers together. 'Thanks, Maggie.'

'She had another question.' Maggie consults her paper. 'How do you switch on your oven?'

For a moment I continue gathering my papers, as though I haven't quite heard. Obviously I know how to switch on my own oven.

'Well. You turn the, er . . . knob,' I say at last, trying to sound nonchalant. 'It's pretty clear, really . . .'

'She said it has some weird timer lock.' Maggie frowns thoughtfully. 'Is it gas or electric?'

OK, I think I might terminate this conversation right now.

'Maggie, I really need to make a call,' I say regretfully, gesturing at the phone.

'So what shall I tell your cleaner?' Maggie persists. 'She's waiting for me to call back.'

'Tell her to . . . leave it for today. I'll sort it out.'

As Maggie leaves my office I reach for a pen and memo pad.

1. How switch on oven?
2. Vacuum-cleaner bags – buy

I put the pen down and massage my forehead. I really don't have time for this. I mean, vacuum bags. I don't even know what they look like, for God's sake, let alone where to buy them—

A sudden brainwave hits me. I'll order a new vacuum cleaner. That'll come with a bag already installed, surely.

'Samantha.'

'What? What is it?' I give a startled jump and open my eyes. Guy Ashby is standing at my door.

Guy is my best friend in the firm. He's six foot three with olive skin and dark eyes, and normally he looks every inch the smooth, polished lawyer. But this morning his dark hair is rumpled and there are shadows under his eyes.

'Relax.' Guy smiles. 'Only me. Coming to the meeting?'

He has the most devastating smile. It's not just me, everyone noticed it, the minute he arrived at the firm.

'Oh. Er . . . yes I am.' I pick up my papers, then add carelessly, 'Are you OK, Guy? You look a bit rough.'

He broke up with his girlfriend. They had bitter rows all night and she's walked off for good . . .

No, she's emigrated to New Zealand . . .

'All-nighter,' he says, wincing. 'Fucking Ketterman. He's inhuman.' He yawns widely, showing the perfect white teeth he had fixed when he was at Harvard Law School.

He says it wasn't his choice. Apparently they don't let you graduate until you've been OK'd by the cosmetic surgeon.

'Bummer.' I grin in sympathy, then push back my chair. 'Let's go.'

I've known Guy for a year, ever since he joined the corporate department as a partner. He's intelligent, and funny, and works the same way I do, and we just somehow . . . click.

And yes. It's possible that some kind of romance would have happened between us if things had been different. But there was a stupid misunderstanding, and . . .

Anyway. It didn't. The details aren't important. It's not something I dwell on. We're friends – and that's fine by me.

OK, this is exactly what happened.

Apparently Guy noticed me pretty much the first day at the firm, just like I noticed him. And he was interested. He asked if I was single. Which I was.

This is the crucial part: I was single. I'd just split up with Jacob. It would have been perfect.

I try not to think too often about how perfect it would have been.

But Nigel MacDermot, who is a stupid, stupid, *thoughtless* behind-the-times moron, told Guy I was attached to a senior partner at Berry Forbes.

Even though I was single.

If you ask me, the system is majorly flawed. It should be clearer. People should have engaged signs, like toilets. Taken. Not taken. There should be no ambiguity about these things.

Anyway, I didn't have a sign. Or if I did, it was the wrong one. There was a slightly embarrassing few weeks where I smiled a lot at Guy – and he looked awkward and started avoiding me, because he didn't want to a) break up a relationship or b) have a three-some with me and Jacob.

I didn't understand what was going on, so I backed off. Then I heard on the grapevine he'd started going out with a girl called Charlotte who he'd met at some weekend party. A month or two later we worked together on a deal, and got to know each other as friends – and that's pretty much the whole story.

I mean, it's fine. Really. That's the way it goes. Some things happen – and some things don't. This one obviously just wasn't meant to be.

Except deep down, right inside . . . I still believe it was.

'So,' says Guy as we walk along the corridor to the meeting room. 'Partner.' He cocks an eyebrow.

'Don't say that!' I hiss in horror. He'll totally jinx it.

'Come on. You know you've made it.'

'I don't know anything.'

'Samantha, you're the brightest lawyer in your year. And you work the hardest. What's your IQ again, 600?'

'Shuddup.' I stare at the pale-blue carpet and Guy laughs.

'What's 124 times 75?'

'Nine thousand, three hundred,' I say grudgingly.

This is the *one* thing that irritates me about Guy. Since I was about ten years old, I've been able to do big sums in my head. God knows why, I just can. And everyone else just goes 'Oh cool,' and then forgets about it.

But Guy keeps on about it, pitching sums at me like I'm a circus performer. I know he thinks it's funny – but it actually gets a bit annoying.

One time I told him the wrong number on purpose. But then it turned out he actually needed the answer, and he put it in a contract and the deal nearly got wrecked as a result. So I haven't done that again.

'You haven't practised in the mirror for the firm's website?' Guy adopts a pose with his finger poised thoughtfully at his chin. 'Ms Samantha Sweeting, Partner.'

'I haven't even thought about it,' I say, rolling my eyes with disdain.

This is a slight lie. I've already planned how to do my hair for the photo. And which of my black suits to wear. And this time I'm going to smile. In the photo on my Carter Spink web page, I look way too serious.

'I heard your presentation blew their socks off,' says Guy more seriously.

My disdain vanishes in a second. 'Really?' I say, trying not to sound too eager. 'You heard that?'

'And you put William Griffiths right on a point of law in front of everybody?' Guy folds his arms and regards me humorously. 'Do you ever make a mistake, Samantha Sweeting?'

'Oh, I make plenty of mistakes,' I say lightly. 'Believe me.'

Like not grabbing you and telling you I was single, the very first day we met.

'A mistake isn't a mistake,' Guy pauses, 'unless it can't be put right.' As he says the words, his eyes seem to twist more deeply into mine.

Or else they're just squiffy after his night of no sleep. I was never any good at reading the signs.

I should have done a degree in that, instead of law. It would have been a lot more useful. Bachelor of Arts (Hons) in Knowing When Men Fancy You And When They're Just Being Friendly.

'Ready?' Ketterman's whiplash voice behind us makes us both jump and I turn to see a whole phalanx of soberly suited men, together with a pair of even more soberly suited women.

'Absolutely.' Guy nods at Ketterman, then turns back and winks at me.

Or maybe I should just take a course in telepathy.

THREE

Nine hours later we're all still in the meeting.

The huge mahogany table is strewn with photo-copied draft contracts, financial reports, note-pads covered in scribbles, polystyrene coffee cups and Post-its. Take-out boxes from lunch are littering the floor. A secretary is distributing fresh copies of the draft agree-ment. Two of the lawyers from the opposition have got up from the table and are murmuring intently in the break-out room. Every meeting room has one of these: a little side area where you go for private conver-sations, or when you feel like breaking something.

The intensity of the afternoon has passed. It's like an ebb in the tide. Faces are flushed around the table, tempers are still high, but no one's shouting any more. The clients have gone. They reached agreement at about four o'clock, shook hands and sailed off in their shiny limos.

Now it's up to us, the lawyers, to work out what they said and what they actually meant (and if you think these are the same thing, you might as well give up law now) and put it all into a draft contract in time for the meeting tomorrow.

When they'll probably begin shouting some more.

I rub my dry face and take a gulp of cappuccino, before realizing I've picked up the wrong cup – the stone-cold cup from four hours ago. Yuck. *Yuck*. And I can't exactly spit it out all over the table.

I swallow the revolting mouthful with a grimace. The fluorescent lights are flickering in my eyes and I feel drained. My role in all of these mega deals is on the finance side – so it was me who negotiated the loan agreement between our client and PGNI Bank. It was me who rescued the situation when some black hole of debt turned up in a subsidiary company. And it was me who spent about three hours this afternoon discussing the use of one single, stupid phrase in clause 29(d).

The phrase was 'best endeavours'. The opposition wanted to use 'reasonable efforts'. We won, but I can't feel my usual triumph. All I know is, it's seven nineteen, and in eleven minutes I'm supposed to be halfway across town, sitting down to dinner with my mother and brother Daniel.

I'll have to cancel. My own birthday dinner.

Even as I think the thought, I can hear the outraged voice of my oldest school friend Freya ringing in my mind.

They can't make you stay at work on your birthday!

I cancelled on her too, last week, when we were supposed to be going to a comedy club. The deal was due to be signed the next morning and I didn't have any choice.

What she doesn't understand is, the deadline comes first, end of story. Prior engagements don't count, birthdays don't count. Holidays are cancelled every week. Across the table from me is Clive Sutherland from the corporate department. His wife had twins

30

this morning and he was back at the table by lunchtime.

'All right, people.' Ketterman's voice commands immediate attention.

Ketterman is the only one here who isn't red-faced or weary-looking or even jaded. He looks as machine-like as ever; as polished as he did this morning. When he gets angry, not a hair goes out of place. He just exudes a silent, steely fury.

'We have to adjourn.'

What? My head pops up.

Other heads have popped up too; I can detect the hope around the table. We're like school kids sensing a disturbance during the maths test, not daring to move in case we land a double detention.

'Until we have the documentation from Fallons, we can't proceed. I'll see you all tomorrow, here at nine a.m.' He sweeps out, and as the door closes, I exhale. I was holding my breath, I realize.

Clive Sutherland has already bolted for the door. People are already on their mobile phones all over the room, discussing dinner, films, uncancelling arrangements. There's a joyful lift to the proceedings. I have a sudden urge to yell 'Yippee!'

But that wouldn't be partner-like.

I gather up my papers, stuff them into my briefcase and push back my chair.

'Samantha. I forgot.' Guy is making his way across the room. 'I have something for you.'

As he hands me a simple white package, I feel a ridiculous rush of joy. A birthday present. He's the only one in the whole company who remembered my birthday. I can't help glowing as I undo the cardboard envelope.

'Guy, you really shouldn't have!'

31

'It was no trouble,' he says, clearly satisfied with himself.

'Still!' I laugh. 'I thought you'd—'

I break off abruptly as I uncover a corporate DVD in a laminated case. It's a summary of the European Partners presentation we had the other day. I mentioned that I'd like a copy.

I turn it over in my hands, making sure my smile is completely intact on my face before I look up. Of course he didn't remember my birthday. Why would he? He probably never even knew it.

'That's . . . great,' I say at last. 'Thanks!'

'No problem.' He's picking up his briefcase. 'Have a good evening. Anything planned?'

I can't tell him it's my birthday. He'll think – He'll realize—

'Just . . . a family thing.' I smile. 'See you tomorrow.'

Anyway. The main thing is, I got away. I'm going to make dinner after all. And I shouldn't even be too late!

As my taxi edges through the traffic on Cheapside, I quickly rifle in my bag for my new make-up bag. I nipped into Selfridges in my lunch-hour the other day, when I realized I was still using the old grey eyeliner and mascara I bought for my graduation six years ago. I didn't have time for a demonstration, but I asked the girl at the counter if she could just quickly sell me everything she thought I should have.

I didn't really listen as she explained each item, because I was on the phone to Elldridge about the Ukrainian contract. But the one thing I do remember is her insistence I should use something called 'Bronzer Powder'. She said it might give me a glow and stop me looking so dreadfully—

Then she stopped herself. 'Pale,' she said at last. 'You're just a bit . . . pale.'

I take out the compact and huge blusher brush, and start sweeping the powder onto my cheeks and forehead. Then, as I peer at my reflection in the mirror, I stifle a laugh. My face stares back at me, freakishly golden and shiny. I look ridiculous.

I mean, who am I kidding? A City lawyer who hasn't been on holiday for two years doesn't have a tan. Or even a glow. I might as well walk in with beads in my hair and pretend I've just flown in from Barbados.

I look at myself for a few more seconds, then take out a cleansing wipe and scrub the bronzer off until my face is white again, with shades of grey. Back to normal. The make-up girl kept mentioning the dark shadows under my eyes, too.

Thing is, if I *didn't* have shadows under my eyes, I'd probably get fired.

I'm wearing a black suit, as I always do. My mother gave me five black suits for my twenty-first birthday, and I've never really broken the habit. The only item of colour about me is my bag, which is red. Mum gave that to me as well, two years ago.

At least, she gave me a black one. But for some reason – maybe the sun was shining or I'd just closed some fantastic deal, I can't remember – I had a brainstorm and exchanged it for a red one. I'm not sure she's ever forgiven me.

I free my hair from its elastic band, quickly comb it out, then twist it back into place. My hair has never exactly been my pride and joy. It's mouse colour, medium length, with a medium wave. At least, it was last time I looked. Most of the time it lives screwed up into a knot.

'Nice evening planned?' says the taxi driver, who's been watching me in his mirror.

'It's my birthday, actually.'

'Happy birthday!' He twinkles at me. 'You'll be partying, then. Making a night of it.'

'Er . . . kind of.'

My family and wild parties don't exactly go together. But even so, it'll be really great for us to see each other and catch up. It doesn't happen very often.

It's not that we don't want to see each other. It's just we all have very busy careers. There's my mother, who's a barrister. She's quite well known, in fact. She started her own chambers ten years ago and last year she won an award for Women In Law. And then there's my brother Daniel, who is thirty-six and Head of Investment at Whittons. He was named last year as one of the top deal-makers in the City.

There's also my other brother, Peter, but like I said, he had a bit of a breakdown. He lives in France now, and teaches English at a local school and doesn't even have an answering machine. And my dad, of course, who lives in South Africa with his third wife. I haven't seen much of him since I was three. But that's OK. My mother's got enough energy for two parents.

I glance at my watch as we speed along the Strand. Seven forty-two. I'm starting to feel quite excited. How long is it since I even *saw* Mum? It must be . . . Christmas. Six months ago.

We come to a halt outside the restaurant and I pay the taxi driver, adding a large tip.

'Have a great evening, love!' he says. 'And happy birthday!'

'Thanks!'

As I hurry into the restaurant, I'm looking all around for Mum or Daniel, but I can't spot either of them.

'Hi!' I say to the maître d'. 'I'm meeting Ms Tennyson.'

That's Mum. She disapproves of women taking the name of their husband. She also disapproves of women staying at home, cooking, cleaning, or learning to type, and thinks all women should earn more than their husbands because they're naturally brighter.

The maître d' leads me to an empty table in the corner and I slide onto the suede banquette.

'Hi!' I smile at the waiter who approaches. 'I'd like a Buck's Fizz, a gimlet and a martini, please. But don't bring them over until the other guests arrive.'

Mum always drinks gimlets. And I've no idea what Daniel's on these days, but he won't say no to a martini.

The waiter nods and disappears, and I shake out my napkin, looking all around at the other diners. Maxim's is a pretty cool restaurant, all wenge floors and steel tables and mood lighting. It's very popular with lawyers, in fact Mum has an account here. Two partners from Linklaters are at a distant table, and I can see one of the most renowned libel lawyers in London at the bar. The noise of chatter, corks popping and forks against oversized plates is like the huge roar of the sea, with occasional tidal waves of laughter making heads turn.

As I scan the menu I suddenly feel ravenous. I haven't had a proper meal for a week, and it all looks so yummy. Glazed foie gras. Lamb with spiced houmous. And on the specials board is chocolate-mint soufflé with two homemade sorbets. I just hope Mum can stay long enough for pudding. She has this habit of coming to dinner and then whizzing off halfway through the main course. I've heard her say plenty of times that half a dinner party is enough for anybody. The trouble is, she's not really interested in food. Nor in anyone less intelligent than her. Which rules out most people.

But Daniel will stay. Once my brother starts on a bottle of wine, he feels obliged to see it through to the end.

'Miss Sweeting?' I look up to see the maître d' approaching, holding a mobile phone. 'I have a message. Your mother has been held up at her chambers.'

'Oh.' I try to hide my disappointment. But I can hardly complain. I've done the same thing to her enough times. 'So . . . what time will she be here?'

The maître d' looks at me silently for a few moments. I think I see a flash of pity.

'I have her here on the telephone. Her secretary will put her through . . . Hello?' he says into the phone. 'I have Ms Tennyson's daughter.'

'Samantha?' comes a crisp, precise voice in my ear. 'Darling, I can't come tonight, I'm afraid.'

'You can't come at *all*?' My smile falters. 'Not even . . . for a drink?'

Her chambers is only five minutes away, in Lincoln's Inn Fields.

'Far too much to do. I have a very big case on and I'm in court tomorrow . . . No, get me the other file,' she adds to someone in her office. 'These things happen,' she resumes. 'But have a nice evening with Daniel. Oh, and happy birthday. I've wired three hundred pounds to your bank account.'

'Oh, right,' I say after a pause. 'Thanks.'

'Have you heard about the partnership yet?'

'Not yet.' I can hear her tapping her pen on the phone.

'How many hours have you put in this month?'

'Um . . . probably about two hundred . . .'

'Is that enough? Samantha, you don't want to be passed over. There will be younger lawyers coming up behind. Someone in your position could easily go stale.'

'Two hundred is quite a lot,' I try to explain. 'Compared to the others—'

'You have to be *better* than the others!' Her voice cuts across mine as though she's in a court room. 'You can't afford for your performance to slip below excellent. This is a *crucial time* – Not *that* file!' she adds impatiently to whoever it is. 'Hold the line, Samantha—'

'Samantha?'

I look up in confusion from the phone to see a girl in a powder-blue suit approaching the table. She's holding a gift basket adorned with a bow, and has a wide smile.

'I'm Lorraine, Daniel's PA,' she says in a sing-song tone I suddenly recognize. 'He couldn't make it tonight, I'm afraid. But I've got a little something for you – plus he's here on the phone to say hello.'

She holds out a lit-up mobile phone. In total confusion, I take it and press it to my other ear.

'Hi, Samantha,' comes Daniel's businesslike drawl. 'Look, sweets, we're on a mega deal. I can't be there.'

I feel a plunge of total dismay. *Neither* of them is coming?

'I'm really sorry, babe,' Daniel's saying. 'One of those things. But have a great time with Mum, won't you?'

I swallow several times. I can't admit she blew me out too. I can't admit that I'm sitting here all on my own.

'OK!' Somehow I muster a breezy tone. 'We will!'

'I've transferred some money to your account. Buy

something nice. And I've sent some chocolates along with Lorraine,' he adds proudly. 'Picked them out myself.'

I look at the gift basket Lorraine is proffering. It isn't chocolates, it's soap.

'That's really lovely, Daniel,' I manage. 'Thanks very much.'

'*Happy Birthday to You . . .*'

There's sudden chorusing behind me. I swivel round to see a waiter carrying over a cocktail glass. A sparkler is fizzing out of it and 'Happy Birthday Samantha' is written in caramel on the steel tray, next to a miniature souvenir menu signed by the chef. Three waiters are following behind, all singing in harmony.

After a moment, Lorraine awkwardly joins in. '*Happy Birthday to You . . .*'

The waiter puts the tray down in front of me, but my hands are full of phones.

'I'll take that for you,' says Lorraine, relieving me of Daniel's phone. She lifts it to her ear, then beams at me. 'He's singing!' she says, pointing to the receiver encouragingly.

'Samantha?' Mum is saying in my ear. 'Are you still there?'

'I'm just . . . they're singing Happy Birthday . . .'

I put the phone on the table. After a moment's thought, Lorraine puts the other phone carefully down on the other side of me.

This is my family birthday party.

Two cell phones.

I can see people looking over at the singing, their smiles falling a little as they see I'm sitting on my own. I can see the pity in the faces of the waiters. I'm trying to keep my chin up, but my cheeks are burning with embarrassment.

Suddenly the waiter I ordered from earlier appears at the table. He's carrying three cocktails on a tray and looks at the empty table in slight confusion.

'Who is the martini for?'

'It was supposed to be for my brother . . .'

'That would be the Nokia,' says Lorraine helpfully, pointing at the mobile phone.

There's a pause – then, with a blank, professional face, the waiter sets the drink down in front of the phone, together with a cocktail napkin.

I want to laugh – except there's a stinging at the back of my eyes and I'm not quite sure I can. He places the other cocktails on the table, nods at me, then retreats. There's an awkward pause.

'So anyway . . .' Lorraine retrieves Daniel's mobile phone and pops it into her bag. 'Happy birthday – and have a lovely evening!'

As she tip-taps her way out of the restaurant, I pick up the other phone to say goodbye – but Mum's already rung off. The singing waiters have melted away. It's just me and a basket of soap.

'Did you wish to order?' The maître d' has re-appeared at my chair. 'I can recommend the risotto,' he says kindly. 'Some nice salad, perhaps? And a glass of wine?'

'Actually,' I force myself to smile, 'I'll just get the bill, thanks.'

It doesn't matter.

The truth is, we were never all going to make a dinner. It was a fantasy idea. We shouldn't even have tried. We're all busy, we all have careers, that's just the way my family is.

As I stand outside the restaurant, a taxi pulls up right in front of me and I quickly stick my hand out.

The rear door opens and a tatty beaded flip-flop emerges, followed by a pair of cut-off jeans, an embroidered kaftan, familiar tousled blonde hair . . .

'Stay here,' she's instructing the taxi driver. 'I can only be five minutes.'

'*Freya?*' I say in disbelief. She wheels round and her eyes widen.

'Samantha! What are you doing on the pavement?'

'What are *you* doing here?' I counter. 'I thought you were going to India.'

'I'm on my way! I'm meeting Lord at the airport in about . . .' She looks at her watch. 'Ten minutes.'

She pulls a guilty face, and I can't help laughing. I've known Freya since we were both seven years old and starting boarding school together. On the first night she told me her family were circus performers and she knew how to ride an elephant and walk the tightrope. For a whole term I believed her and heard stories about her exotic circus life. Until her parents arrived to pick her up and turned out to be a pair of accountants from Staines. Even then she was unabashed, and said they *used* to be circus performers.

She has bright blue eyes and freckled skin, permanently tanned from her travels. Right now her nose is peeling slightly, and she has a new earring, right at the top of her ear. She has the whitest, most crooked teeth I've ever seen, and when she laughs one corner of her top lip rises.

'I'm here to gatecrash your birthday dinner.' Freya's eyes swivel to the restaurant in suspicion. 'But I thought I was late. What happened?'

'Well . . .' I hesitate. 'The thing was . . . Mum and Daniel . . .'

'Left early?' As she peers at me Freya's expression changes to one of horror. 'Didn't turn *up*? Jesus Christ, the *bastards*. Couldn't they just for *once* put you first instead of their frigging . . .' She breaks off, breathing hard. 'Sorry. I know. They're your family. Whatever.'

Freya and my mum don't exactly get on.

'It doesn't matter,' I say, with a rueful shrug. 'Really. I've got a pile of work to get through anyway.'

'*Work?*' She stares at me. 'Now? Are you serious? Doesn't it ever *stop?*'

'We're busy at the moment,' I say defensively. 'It's just a blip.'

'There's always a blip! There's always a crisis! Every year you put off doing anything fun—'

'That's not true.'

'Every year you tell me it'll get better soon. But it never does!' Her eyes are burning with concern. 'Samantha, what happened to your life?'

I stare back at her for a few moments, cars roaring along behind me on the street. I'm not sure how to reply. To be honest, I can't remember what my life used to be like.

'I want to be a partner of Carter Spink,' I say at last. 'That's what I want. You have to make sacrifices.'

'And what happens when you make partner?' she persists. 'Does it get easier?'

I shrug evasively. The truth is I haven't thought beyond making partner. It's like a dream. Like a shiny ball in the sky.

'You're twenty-nine years old, for Christ's sake!' Freya gestures with a bony, silver-ringed hand. 'You should be able to do something spontaneous once in a while. You should be seeing the world!' She grabs my arm. 'Samantha, come to India. Now!'

'Do what?' I give a startled laugh. 'I can't come to *India!*'

'Take a month off. Why not? They're not going to

41

fire you. Come to the airport, we'll get you a ticket . . .'

'Freya, you're crazy. Seriously.' I squeeze her arm. 'I love you, but you're crazy.'

Slowly, Freya's grip on my arm loosens. 'Same,' she says. 'You're crazy, but I love you.'

Her mobile starts ringing, but she ignores it. Instead, she's rummaging in her embroidered bag. At last she produces a tiny, intricately worked silver perfume bottle, haphazardly wrapped in a piece of purple shot silk.

'Here.' She thrusts it at me.

'Freya,' I turn it over in my fingers, 'it's amazing.'

'I thought you'd like it.' She pulls her mobile out of her pocket. 'Hi!' she says impatiently into it. 'Look, Lord, I'll be there, OK?'

Freya's husband's full name is Lord Andrew Edgerly. Freya's nickname for him started as a joke and just kind of stuck. They met five years ago on a kibbutz and got married in Las Vegas. Technically, this makes her Lady Edgerly – but nobody can quite get their heads round this idea. Least of all the Edgerlys.

'Thanks for coming. Thanks for this.' I hug her. 'Have a fabulous time in India.'

'We will.' Freya is climbing back into her taxi. 'And if you want to come out, just let me know. Invent a family emergency . . . anything. Give them my number. I'll cover for you. Whatever your story is.'

'Go,' I say, laughing, and give her a little push. 'Go to India.'

The door slams, and she sticks her head out of the window.

'Sam . . . good luck for tomorrow.' She seizes my hand and meets my eyes, suddenly serious. 'If it's really what you want, then I hope you get it.'

'It's what I want more than anything else.' As I look

at my oldest friend, all my calculated nonchalance disappears. 'Freya – I can't tell you how much I want it.'

'You'll get it. I know it.' She kisses my hand, then waves goodbye. 'And don't go back to the office! Promise!' she shouts indistinctly as her taxi roars off into the traffic.

'OK! I promise!' I yell back. I wait until she's disappeared, then stick my hand out for a taxi.

'Carter Spink, please,' I say as it pulls up.

I was crossing my fingers. Of course I'm going back to the office.

I arrive home at eleven o'clock, exhausted and brain-dead, having got through only about half of Ketterman's file. Bloody Ketterman, I'm thinking, as I push open the main front door of the 1930s mansion block where I live. Bloody Ketterman. Bloody . . . bloody . . .

'Good evening, Samantha.'

I nearly jump a mile. It's Ketterman. Right there, standing in front of the lifts, holding a bulging brief-case. For an instant I'm transfixed in horror. What's he doing here?

Have I gone crazy and started hallucinating senior partners?

'Someone told me you lived here.' His eyes glint through his spectacles. 'I've bought number 32 as a pied-à-terre. We'll be neighbours during the week.'

No. Please tell me this is not happening. He *lives* here?

'Er . . . welcome to the building!' I say, trying as hard as I can to sound like I mean it. The lift doors open and we both get in.

Number 32. That means he's only two floors above me.

I feel like my headmaster has moved in. How will I ever feel relaxed again? Why did he have to choose *this* building?

As we rise up in silence I feel more and more uncomfortable. Should I make small talk? Some light, neighbourly chit-chat?

'I made some headway on that file you gave me,' I say at last.

'Good,' he says shortly, and nods.

So much for the small talk. I should just cut to the big stuff.

Am I going to become a partner tomorrow?

'Well . . . good night,' I say awkwardly as I leave the lift.

'Good night, Samantha.'

The lift doors close and I emit a silent scream. I cannot live in the same building as Ketterman. I'm going to have to move.

I'm about to put my key in the lock when the door to the opposite flat opens a crack.

'Samantha?'

My heart sinks. As if I haven't had enough this evening. It's Mrs Farley, my neighbour. She has silver hair and three little dogs and an insatiable interest in my life. But she is very kind and takes in parcels for me, so I basically let her poke and pry at will.

'Another delivery arrived for you, dear,' she says. 'Dry-cleaning this time. I'll just fetch it for you.'

'Thanks,' I say gratefully, swinging my door open. A small pile of junk leaflets is sitting on the doormat and I sweep them aside, onto the bigger pile building up at the side of my hallway. I'm planning to recycle them when I get a moment. It's on my list.

'You're late home again.' Mrs Farley is at my side, holding a pile of polythene-covered shirts. 'You girls

44

are so busy!' She clicks her tongue. 'You haven't been home before eleven this week!'

This is what I mean by an insatiable interest. She probably has it all logged somewhere in a little book.

'Thanks very much.' I make to take my dry-cleaning, but to my horror Mrs Farley pushes past me into the flat, exclaiming, 'I'll carry it in for you!'

'Er ... excuse the ... er ... mess,' I say as she squeezes past a pile of pictures propped against the wall. 'I keep meaning to put those up ... and get rid of the boxes ...'

I steer her hastily into the kitchen, away from the pile of takeaway menus on the hall table. Then I wish I hadn't. On the kitchen counter is a stack of old tins and packets, together with a note from my new cleaner, all in capitals:

DEAR SAMANTHA

1. ALL YOUR FOOD IS PAST ITS SELL-BY-
   DATES, SHOULD I THROW AWAY?
2. DO YOU HAVE ANY CLEANING MATERIALS
   E.G. BLEACH? COULD NOT FIND ANY.
3. ARE YOU COLLECTING CHINESE FOOD
   CARTONS FOR ANY REASON? DID NOT
   THROW THEM AWAY, JUST IN CASE.

YOUR CLEANER JOANNE

I can see Mrs Farley reading the note. I can practically *hear* the clucking going on in her head. Last month she gave me a little lecture on did I have a slow cooker, because all you needed to do was put in your chicken and vegetables in the morning and it didn't take five minutes to slice a carrot, did it?

I really wouldn't know.

'So . . . thanks.' I hastily take the dry-cleaning from Mrs Farley and dump it on the hob, then usher her out to the front door, aware of her swivelling, inquisitive eyes. 'It's really kind of you.'

'It's no trouble.' She gives me a beady look. 'Not wishing to interfere, dear, but you know, you could wash your cotton blouses *very* well at home, and save on all that money.'

I look at her blankly. If I did that I'd have to dry them. And iron them.

'And I *did* just happen to notice that one of them came back missing a button,' she adds. 'The pink and white stripe.'

'Oh right,' I say. 'Well . . . that's OK. I'll send it back. They won't charge.'

'You can pop a button on yourself, dear!' says Mrs Farley, sounding shocked. 'It won't take you two minutes. You must have a spare button in your work box?'

My what?

'I don't have a work box,' I explain as politely as I can. 'I don't really *do* sewing.'

'You can sew a simple button on, surely!' she exclaims.

'No,' I say, a bit rankled at her expression. 'But it's no problem. I'll send it back to the dry-cleaners.'

Mrs Farley looks appalled. 'You really can't sew a button on? Your mother never taught you?'

I stifle a laugh at the thought of my mother sewing on a button. 'Er, no. She didn't.'

'In my day,' says Mrs Farley, shaking her head, 'all well-educated girls were taught how to sew on a button, darn a sock and turn a collar.'

None of this means anything to me. *Turn a collar*. It's gibberish.

'Well, in my day we weren't,' I reply politely. 'We were taught to study for our exams and get a career worth having. We were taught to have opinions. We were taught to use our *brains*,' I can't resist adding.

Mrs Farley looks me up and down for a few moments.

'It's a shame,' she says at last, and gives me a sympathetic pat on the arm.

I'm trying to keep calm, but the tensions of the day are rising inside me. I've worked for hours, I've had a non-existent birthday, I feel bone-tired and hungry . . . and now this old woman's telling me to sew on a *button*?

'It's not a shame,' I say tightly.

'All right, dear,' says Mrs Farley in pacifying tones, and heads across the hallway to her flat.

Somehow this goads me even more.

'How is it a shame?' I demand, stepping out of my doorway. 'How? OK, maybe I can't sew on a button. But I can restructure a corporate finance agreement and save my client thirty million pounds. That's what I can do.'

Mrs Farley regards me from her doorway. If anything she looks more pitying than before. 'It's a shame,' she repeats, as though she didn't even hear me. 'Goodnight, dear.' She closes the door and I emit a squeal of exasperation.

'Did you never *hear* of feminism?' I cry at her door.

But there's no answer.

Crossly I retreat into my own flat, close the door and pick up the phone. I speed-dial the local wood-fired pizza company and order my usual: a capricciosa and a bag of Kettle Chips. I pour myself a glass of wine-box wine out of the fridge, then head back into the sitting room and flick on the telly.

A *work box*. What else does she think I should have? A pair of knitting needles? A loom?

I sink down onto the sofa with the remote and flick through the TV channels, peering vaguely at the images. News ... a French film ... some animal documentary ...

Hang on. I stop flicking, drop the remote and settle back on the cushions.

The Waltons.

Ultimate comfort viewing. Just what I need.

It's a final, wrap-up kind of scene. The family's gathered round the table; Grandma's saying grace.

I take a swig of wine and feel myself start to unwind. I've always secretly loved *The Waltons*, ever since I was a kid. I used to sit in the darkness when everyone else was out and pretend I lived on Walton's Mountain too.

And now it's the last scene of all; the one I always wait for: the Walton house in darkness. Lights twinkling; crickets chirping. John Boy talking in voice-over. A whole huge houseful of people. I hug my knees and look wistfully at the screen as the familiar music tinkles to its close.

'Good night, Elizabeth!'

'Good night, Grandma,' I reply aloud. It's not like there's anyone to hear.

'Night, Mary Ellen!'

'Good night, John Boy,' I say in unison with Mary Ellen.

'Good night.'

'Night.'

'Night.'

FOUR

I wake with my heart pounding, half on my feet, scrabbling for a pen and saying out loud, 'What? What?'

Which is pretty much how I always wake up. I think it runs in the family or something. We're all nervy sleepers. Last Christmas at Mum's house I crept into the kitchen at about three a.m. for a drink of water – to find Mum in her dressing gown reading a court report, and Daniel swigging a Xanax as he checked the Hang Seng on TV.

I totter into the bathroom and stare at my pale reflection. This is it. All the work, all the studying, all the late nights . . . it's all been for this day.

Partner. Or not partner.

Oh God. Stop it. Don't think about it. I head into the kitchen and open the fridge. Dammit. I'm out of milk.

And coffee.

I *must* find myself a food-delivery company. And a milkman. I reach for a biro and scrawl '47. Food delivery/milkman?' at the bottom of my 'TO DO' list.

My 'TO DO' list is written on a piece of paper pinned up on the wall, and is a useful reminder of things I'm intending to do. It's a bit yellowing now, actually – and the ink at the top of the list has become so faint I can barely read it. But it's a good way to keep myself organized.

I should really cross off some of the early entries, it occurs to me. I mean, the original list dates from when I first moved into my flat, three years ago. I must have done some of this stuff by now. I pick up a pen and squint at the first few faded entries.

1. Find milkman
2. Food delivery – organize?
3. How switch on oven?

Oh. Right.

Well, I really *am* going to get all this delivery stuff organized. At the weekend. And I'll get to grips with the oven. I'll read the manual and everything.

I scan quickly down to newer entries, around two years old.

16. Sort out milkman
17. Have friends over?
18. Take up hobby??

The thing is, I *am* meaning to have some friends over. And take up a hobby. When work is less busy.

I look down to even later entries – maybe a year old – where the ink is still blue.

41. Go on holiday?
42. Give dinner party?
43. MILKMAN??

I stare at the list in slight frustration. How can I have

done *nothing* on my list? Crossly I throw my pen down and turn on the kettle, resisting the temptation to rip the list into bits.

The kettle has come to the boil and I make myself a cup of weird herbal tea I was once given by a client. I reach for an apple from the fruit bowl – only to discover it's gone all mouldy. With a shudder, I throw the whole lot into the bin, and nibble a few Shreddies out of the packet.

The truth is, I don't care about the list. There's only one thing I care about.

As I arrive at the office, I'm determined I'm not going to acknowledge this is any kind of special day. I'll just keep my head down and get on with my work.

But as I travel up in the lift, three people murmur 'Good luck'. Then I walk along the corridor – and a guy from Tax grasps me meaningfully on the shoulder.

'Best of luck, Samantha.'

How does he know my name?

I head hurriedly into my office and close the door, trying to ignore the fact that through the glass partition I can see people talking in the corridor and glancing at me.

I really shouldn't have come in today. I should have feigned a life-threatening illness.

Anyway, it's fine. I'll just start on some work, like any other day. I open Ketterman's file, find my place and start reading through a document on a five-year-old share transfer.

'Samantha?'

I look up. Guy is at my door, holding two coffees. He puts one down on my desk.

'Hi,' he says. 'How are you doing?'

'Fine,' I say, turning a page in a businesslike manner.

'I'm fine. Just . . . normal. In fact, I don't know what all the fuss is.'

Guy's amused expression is flustering me slightly. I flick over another page to prove my point – and somehow knock the entire file to the floor.

Thank God for paperclips.

Red-faced, I retrieve the file off the floor, shove all the papers back inside and take a sip of coffee.

'Uh huh.' Guy nods gravely. 'Well, it's a good thing you're not nervous or jumpy or anything.'

'Yes,' I say, refusing to rise, 'isn't it?'

'See you later.' He lifts his coffee cup as though toasting me, then walks off. I look at my watch.

Only eight fifty-three. I'm not sure I can bear this.

Somehow I get through the morning. I finish up on Ketterman's file and make a start on my report. I'm halfway through the third paragraph when Guy appears at my office door again.

'Hi,' I say without looking up. 'I'm fine, OK? And I haven't heard anything.'

Guy doesn't reply.

At last I lift my head. He's right in front of my desk, just looking down at me, with the strangest expression I've ever seen. It's like a mixture of affection and pride and excitement, all squashed together under a poker-straight face.

'I should not be doing this,' he murmurs. He leans in closer. 'You did it, Samantha. You're a partner. You'll hear officially in an hour.'

A white dazzling heat shoots across my chest. For an instant I can't breathe.

I made it. I *made* it.

'You didn't hear it from me, OK?' Guy's face creases briefly in a smile. 'Well done.'

'Thanks . . .' I manage.

'I'll see you later. Congratulate you properly.' He turns and strides away, and I'm left staring unseeingly at my computer.

I made partner.

Oh my God. *Oh my God.* Oh my GOD!

I take out a hand mirror and glance at my own exhilarated reflection. My cheeks are bright pink. I'm feeling a terrible urge to leap to my feet and cry out 'YES!' I want to dance about and scream. How do I survive an hour? How can I just sit here calmly? I can't possibly concentrate on Ketterman's report.

I stand up and walk over to my filing cabinet, purely for something to do. I open a couple of drawers at random, and close them again. Then, as I swivel round, I notice my desk, crammed with papers and files, with a teetering pile of books on my computer terminal.

Ketterman's right. It is a bit of a disgrace. It doesn't look like a partner's desk.

I'll tidy it up. This is the perfect way to spend an hour. 12.06–1.06: Office administration. We even have a code for it on the computer time sheet.

I had forgotten how much I loathe and detest tidying.

All sorts of things are turning up as I sift through the mess on my desk. Company letters . . . contracts which need to be filed . . . old invitations . . . memos . . . a Pilates pamphlet . . . a CD which I bought three months ago and thought I'd lost . . . last year's Christmas card from Arnold, which depicts him in a woolly reindeer costume . . . I smile at the sight, and put it into the 'things to find a place for' pile.

There are tombstones, too – the engraved, mounted pieces of perspex we get at the end of a big deal. And

. . . oh God, half a Snickers bar I obviously didn't finish eating at one time or another. I dump it in the bin and turn with a sigh to another pile of papers.

They shouldn't give us such big desks. I can't believe how much stuff is on here.

Partner! shoots through my mind, like a glittering firework. *PARTNER!*

Stop it, I instruct myself sternly. Concentrate on the task in hand. As I pull out an old copy of *The Lawyer* and wonder why on earth I was keeping it, some paper-clipped documents fall to the floor. I reach for them, and run my gaze down the front page, already reaching for the next thing. It's a memo, from Arnold.

Re Third Union Bank.
Please find attached debenture for Glazerbrooks Ltd. Please attend to registration at Companies House.

I peer at it without great interest. Third Union Bank are Arnold's client, and I've only dealt with them once. The deal is a loan for fifty million pounds to Glazerbrooks and all I have to do is register it within twenty-one days at Companies House. It's just another of the mundane jobs that partners are always dumping on my desk. Well not any more, I think with a surge of determination. In fact, I think I'll delegate this to someone else, right now. I glance automatically at the date.

Then I look again. It's dated May 26th.

Five weeks ago? That can't be right.

Puzzled, I flip quickly through the papers, looking to see if there's been a typo. There *must* be a typo— But the date is consistent throughout. May 26th.

May 26th?

I sit, frozen, staring at the document. Has this thing been on my desk for *five weeks*?

But . . . it can't. I mean . . . it couldn't. That would mean—

It would mean I'd missed the deadline.

I swallow hard. I have to be reading this wrong or something. I can't have made such a basic mistake. I cannot possibly have failed to register a charge before the deadline. I always register charges before the deadline.

I close my eyes, trying to calm down. I have to be getting the wrong end of the stick. It's the excitement of being partner. It's addled my brain. OK. Let's look at this again, carefully.

I open my eyes and look at the memo – but it says exactly the same thing as before. Attend to registration. Dated May 26th, in black and white. Which would mean I've exposed our client to an unsecured loan. Which would mean I've made about the most elementary mistake a lawyer can make.

My happy glow has gone. There's a kind of iciness about my spine. I'm trying desperately to remember if Arnold said anything about the deal to me. I can't even remember him mentioning it. But then – why would he? It's one simple loan agreement. The kind of thing we do in our sleep. He would have assumed I'd carried out his instructions. He would have trusted me.

Oh Jesus.

I leaf through the pages again, more quickly, searching desperately for some let-out. Some clause that will have me exclaiming 'Oh, of *course*!' in relief. But it's not there. As I clutch the document I feel dizzy. How could this have happened? Did I even notice this? Did I sweep it aside, meaning to do it later? I can't remember. I can't bloody *remember*.

What am I going to do? A wall of panic hits me as I take in the consequences. Third Union Bank has lent Glazerbrooks fifty million pounds. Without the charge being registered, this loan – this multi-million-pound loan – is unsecured. If Glazerbrooks went bust tomorrow, Third Union Bank would go to the back of the queue of creditors. And probably end up with nothing.

'Samantha!' says Maggie at the door, and I jump a mile high. Instinctively I plant my hand over the memo, even though she's not looking at it; even though she wouldn't realize the significance, anyway.

'I just heard!' she says in a stage whisper. 'Guy let it slip! Congratulations!'

'Um . . . thanks!' Somehow I force my lips into a smile.

'I'm just getting a cup of tea. D'you want one?'

'That'd be . . . great. Thanks.'

Maggie disappears and I bury my head in my hands. I'm trying to keep calm, but inside is a great well of terror. I have to face it. I've made a mistake.

I have made a mistake.

What am I going to do? My whole body is tensed up in fright, I can't think straight—

Then suddenly Guy's words from yesterday ring in my ears, and I feel an almost painful flood of relief. *A mistake isn't a mistake unless it can't be put right.*

Yes. The point is, I can put this right. I can still register a charge.

It will be excruciating. I'll have to tell the bank what I've done – and Glazerbrooks – and Arnold – and Ketterman. I'll have to have new documentation drawn up. And, worst of all, live with everyone knowing I've made the kind of stupid, thoughtless error a trainee would make.

It might mean an end to my partnership, runs through my mind, and for an instant I feel sick.

But there's no other option. I have to put the situation right.

Quickly I log on to the Companies House website and enter a search for Glazerbrooks. As long as no other charge has been registered in the meantime, it will all come to the same thing . . .

I stare at the page in disbelief.

No.

It can't be.

A charge of £50 million was entered last week by some company called BLLC Holdings. Our client has been bumped down the creditors' queue.

My mind is helter-skeltering. This isn't good. It's not good. I have to talk to someone quickly. I have to do something about this now, before any more charges are made. I have to . . . to tell Arnold.

But just the thought paralyses me with horror.

I can't do it. I just can't go out and announce I've made the most basic, elementary error and put £50 million of our client's money at risk. What I'll do is . . . is start sorting out the mess first, before I tell anyone here. Have the damage limitation underway. Yes. I'll call the bank first. The sooner they know, the better.

'Samantha?'

'What?' I practically leap off my chair.

'You're nervy today!' Maggie laughs and comes towards the desk with a cup of tea. 'Feeling on top of the world?' She twinkles at me.

For an instant I honestly have no idea what she's talking about. My world has reduced to me and my mistake and what I'm going to do about it.

'Oh! Right. Yes!' I try to grin back and surreptitiously wipe my damp hands on a tissue.

57

'I bet you haven't come down off your high yet!' She leans against the filing cabinet. 'I've got some champagne in the fridge, all ready.'

'Er . . . great! Actually, Maggie, I've really got to get on . . .'

'Oh.' She looks hurt. 'Well, OK. I'll leave you.'

As she walks out I can see indignation in the set of her shoulders. She probably thinks I'm a total cow. But every minute is another minute of risk. I have to call the bank. Immediately.

I search through the attached contact sheet and find the name and number of the guy at Third Union. Charles Conway.

This is the man I have to call. This is the man whose day I have to disturb and admit that I've totally messed up. With trembling hands I pick up my phone. I feel as though I'm psyching myself up to dive into a noxious swamp full of leeches.

For a few moments I just sit there, staring at the keypad. Willing myself to do it. At last, I reach out and dial the number. As it rings, my heart begins to pound.

'Charles Conway.'

'Hi!' I say, trying to keep my voice steady. 'It's Samantha Sweeting from Carter Spink. I don't think we've met.'

'Hi, Samantha.' He sounds friendly enough. 'How can I help?'

'I was phoning on a . . . a technical matter. It's about . . .' I can hardly bear to say it. 'Glazerbrooks.'

'Oh, you've heard about that,' says Charles Conway. 'News travels fast.'

The room seems to shrink. I grip the receiver more tightly.

'Heard . . . what?' My voice is higher than I'd like. 'I haven't heard anything.'

'Oh! I assumed that's why you were calling.' He pauses, and I can hear him ordering someone to look the damn thing up on Google. 'Yes, they called in the receivers today. That last-ditch attempt to save themselves obviously didn't work . . .'

He's still talking but I can't hear him. I feel light-headed. Black spots are dancing in front of my eyes.

Glazerbrooks is going bust. They'll never draw up the new documentation now. Not in a million years.

I won't be able to register the charge.

I can't put it right.

I've lost Third Union Bank fifty million pounds.

I feel like I'm hallucinating. I want to gibber in panic. I want to thrust down the phone and run, very fast.

Charles Conway's voice suddenly hits my consciousness.

'It's a good thing you phoned, as it happens.' I can hear him tapping at a keyboard in the background, totally unconcerned. 'You might want to double-check that loan security.'

For a few moments I can't speak.

'Yes,' I say at last, my voice hoarse. I put down the receiver, shaking all over. I think I might throw up.

I've fucked up.

I have fucked up so big, I can't . . .

I can't even . . .

Barely knowing what I'm doing, I push back my chair. I have to get out. Away.

FIVE

I walk through reception on auto-pilot. Out onto the sunny crowded lunchtime street, one foot in front of the other, just another office worker walking along.

Except I'm different. I've just lost my client fifty million pounds.

Fifty million. It's like a drum beat in my head.

I don't understand how it happened. I don't understand. My mind keeps turning it over. Over and over, obsessively. How could I have not seen . . . how could I have overlooked . . .

I never even saw the document. I never even clocked it for an instant. It must have been put on my desk, then covered up with something else. A file, a pile of contracts, a cup of coffee.

One error. One mistake. The only mistake I've ever made. I want to wake up and find this is all a bad dream, it happened in a movie, it happened to some-one else. It's a story I'm listening to in the pub, agog, thanking my lucky stars it wasn't me . . .

But it was me. It is me. My career is over. The last person at Carter Spink who made a mistake like this was Ted Stephens in 1983, who lost a client ten million pounds. He was fired on the spot.

And I've lost five times that.

My breaths are getting shorter; my head is dizzy; I feel like I'm being smothered. I think I could be having a panic attack. I sit down on a bench and wait to feel better.

OK, I'm not feeling better. I'm feeling worse.

Suddenly I jump in terror as my mobile phone vibrates in my pocket. I pull it out and look at the caller ID. It's Guy.

I can't talk to him. I can't talk to anybody. Not right now.

A moment later, the phone tells me a message has been left. I lift the phone to my ear and press '1' to listen.

'Samantha!' Guy sounds jovial. 'Where are you? We're all waiting with the champagne to make the big partnership announcement!'

Partnership. I almost want to burst into tears. But . . . I can't. It's too big for that. I thrust my phone in my pocket and get to my feet again. I begin to walk faster and faster, weaving through the pedestrians, ignoring the strange looks I'm getting. My head is pounding and I have no idea where I'm going. But I just can't stop.

I walk for what seems like hours, my head in a daze, my feet moving blindly along the pavement. The sun is beating down, and the pavements are dusty and after a while my head starts to throb. At some point my mobile starts to vibrate again, but I ignore it.

At last, when my legs are starting to ache, I slow down and come to a halt. My mouth is dry; I'm totally dehydrated. I need some water. I look up, trying to get my bearings. Somehow I seem to have reached Paddington Station, of all places.

Numbly, I turn my steps towards the entrance and walk inside. The place is noisy and crowded with travellers. The fluorescent lights and air conditioning and the blaring announcements make me flinch. As I'm making my way to a kiosk selling bottled water, my mobile vibrates again. I pull it out and look at the display. I have fifteen missed calls and another message from Guy. He left it about twenty minutes ago.

I hesitate, my heart beating with nerves, then press '1' to listen to it.

'Jesus Christ, Samantha, what *happened*?'

He doesn't sound jovial any more, he sounds totally stressed. I feel prickles of dread all over my body.

'We know,' he's saying. 'OK? We know about Third Union Bank. Charles Conway called up. Then Ketterman found the paperwork on your desk. You have to come back to the office. Now. Call me back.'

He rings off, but I don't move. I'm paralysed with fright.

They know. They all know.

The black spots are dancing in front of my eyes again. Nausea is rising up inside me. The entire staff of Carter Spink knows I messed up. People will be calling each other. Emailing the news in horrified glee. *Did you hear . . .*

As I'm standing there, something catches the corner of my eye. A familiar face is just visible through the crowd. I turn my head and squint at the man, trying to place him – then feel a fresh jolt of horror.

It's Greg Parker, one of the senior partners. He's striding along the concourse in his expensive suit, holding his mobile phone. His brows are knitted together and he looks concerned.

'So where *is* she?' His voice travels across the concourse.

Panic hits me like a lightning bolt. I have to get out of his line of vision. I have to hide. Now. I edge behind a vast woman in a beige mac and try to cower down so I'm hidden. But she keeps wandering about, and I keep having to shuffle along with her.

'Did you want something? Are you a beggar?' She suddenly turns and gives me a suspicious look.

'No!' I say in shock. 'I'm . . . er . . .'

I can't say 'I'm hiding behind you.'

'Well, leave me alone!' She scowls and stalks off towards Costa Coffee. My heart is hammering in my chest. I'm totally exposed in the middle of the concourse. Greg Parker has stopped striding now. He's standing about fifty yards away, still talking on his mobile phone.

If I move, he'll see me. If I stay still . . . he'll see me.

Suddenly the electronic Departures display board renews itself with fresh information. A group of people who have been gazing up at it all pick up their bags and newspapers and head towards platform nine.

Without thinking twice I join the throng. I'm hidden in their midst as we sweep towards platform nine, through the open barriers. I get on the train along with everyone else, walking swiftly down the carriage as far as I can.

The train pulls out of the station and I sink into a seat, opposite a family all wearing London Zoo T-shirts. They smile at me – and somehow I manage to smile back. I feel totally, utterly unreal.

'Refreshments?' A wizened man pushing a trolley appears in the carriage and beams at me. 'Hot and cold sandwiches, teas and coffees, soft drinks, alcoholic beverages?'

'The last, please.' I try not to sound too desperate. 'A double. Of . . . anything.'

* * *

No one comes to check my ticket. No one bothers me. The train seems to be some sort of express. Suburbs turn into fields, and the train is still rattling along. I've drunk three small bottles of gin, mixed with orange juice, tomato juice and a chocolate yoghurt drink. The chunk of icy fright in my stomach has thawed. I feel weirdly distanced from everything.

I have made the biggest mistake of my career. I have quite possibly lost my job. I will never be a partner.

One stupid mistake.

The London Zoo family have opened packets of crisps and offered me one and invited me to join in their game of Travel Scrabble. The mother even asked me if I was travelling for business or fun?

I couldn't bring myself to answer.

My heart-rate has gradually subsided, but I have a bad, throbbing headache. I'm sitting with a hand over one eye, trying to block out the light.

'Ladies and gentlemen . . .' The conductor is crackling over the loudspeaker. 'Unfortunately . . . rail works . . . alternative transport . . .'

I can't follow what he's saying. I don't even know where I'm headed. I'll just wait for the next stop, get out of the train and take it from there.

'That's not how you spell raisin,' London Zoo mother is saying to one of the children, when the train suddenly starts to slow down. I look up to see that the train is pulling into a station. Lower Ebury. Everybody is gathering up their stuff and getting off.

Like an automaton I get up too. I follow the London Zoo family off the train and out of the station, and look around. I'm standing outside a tiny, twee country station, with a pub called The Bell over the road. The road bends round in both directions, and I can glimpse fields in the distance. There's a coach standing on the side of the road, and all of the passengers from the train are piling onto it.

London Zoo mother has turned round and is gesturing at me. 'You need to come this way,' she says helpfully. 'If you want the bus to Gloucester? The big station?'

The thought of getting on a coach makes me want to heave. I don't want the bus to anywhere. I just want a painkiller. My head feels like my skull is about to split open.

'Er . . . no thanks. I'm fine here, thanks.' I smile as convincingly as I can and, before she can say anything else, start walking down the road, away from the coach.

I have no idea where I am. None.

Inside my pocket, my phone suddenly vibrates. I pull it out. It's Guy. Again. This must be the thirtieth time he's rung. And every time he's left a message telling me to call him back; asking if I've got his emails.

I haven't got any of his emails. I was so freaked out, I left my BlackBerry on my desk. My phone is all I have. It vibrates again and I stare at it for a few moments. Then, my stomach clenched with nerves, I lift it to my ear and press Talk.

'Hi.' My voice is scratchy. 'It's . . . it's me.'

'Samantha?' His incredulous voice blasts down the line. 'Is that *you*? Where *are* you?'

'I don't know. I had to get away. I . . . I went into shock . . .'

'Samantha, I don't know if you got my messages. But . . .' He hesitates. 'Everyone knows.'

'I know.' I lean against an old crumbling wall and squeeze my eyes shut, trying to block out the pain. 'I know.'

'How did it *happen*?' He sounds as shocked as I feel. 'How the hell did you make a simple error like that? I mean, Christ, Samantha—'

'I don't know,' I say numbly. 'I just . . . didn't see it. It was a mistake—'

'You never make mistakes!'

'Well, I do now!' I feel tears rising and fiercely blink them down. 'What's . . . what's happened?'

'It's not good.' He exhales. 'Ketterman's been having damage-limitation talks with Glazerbrooks' lawyers and talking to the bank . . . and the insurers, of course.'

The insurers. The firm's professional indemnity insurance. I'm suddenly gripped by an almost exhilarating hope. If the insurers pay up without making a fuss, maybe things won't be as bad as I thought.

But even as I feel my spirits lift I know I'm like some desperate traveller seeing the mirage through the haze. Insurers never cough up the whole amount. Sometimes they don't cough up anything. Sometimes they pay up but raise their premiums to unfeasible levels.

'What did the insurers say?' I gulp. 'Will they . . .'

'They haven't said anything yet.'

'Right.' I wipe my sweaty face, screwing myself up to ask the next question. 'And what about . . . me?'

Guy is silent.

As his meaning hits me I feel myself swaying as though I'm going to faint. There's my answer. I open my eyes to see two small boys on bikes staring at me.

'It's over, isn't it?' I'm trying to sound calm but my voice is wobbling out of control. 'My career's over.'

'I . . . I don't know that. Listen, Samantha, you're freaked out. It's natural. But you can't hide. You have to come back.'

66

'I can't.' My voice rises in distress. 'I can't face everyone.'

'Samantha, be rational!'

'I can't do it! I can't! I need some time . . .'

'Saman—' I flip my phone shut.

I feel faint. My head is bursting. I have to get some water. But the pub doesn't look open, and I can't see any shops.

I totter along the road until I reach a pair of tall carved pillars decorated with lions. Here's a house. I'll ring the bell and ask for a painkiller and a glass of water. And ask if there's a hotel near by.

I push open the wrought-iron gates and crunch over the gravel towards the heavy, oak front door. It's a rather grand house, made out of honey-coloured stone, with steep gables and tall chimneys and two Porsches on the drive. I raise a hand and tug the bell pull.

There's silence. I stand there for a while, but the whole house seems dead. I'm about to give up and trudge back down the drive, when all of a sudden the door swings open.

There before me is a woman with blonde, lacquered hair to her shoulders and long, dangly earrings. She has lots of make-up, long silk trousers in a weird shade of peach, a cigarette in one hand and a cocktail in the other.

'Hello.' She drags on her cigarette and looks at me a bit suspiciously. 'Are you from the agency?'

SIX

I have no idea what this woman's talking about. My head's hurting so much, I can barely look at her, let alone take in what she's saying.

'Are you all right?' She peers at me. 'You look terrible!'

'I've got a rather bad headache,' I manage. 'Could I possibly have a glass of water?'

'Of course! Come in!' She waves her cigarette in my face and beckons me into a huge, impressive hall with a vaulted ceiling. 'You'll want to see the house, anyway. *Eddie?*' Her voice rises to a shriek. 'Eddie, another one's here! I'm Trish Geiger,' she adds to me. 'You may call me Mrs Geiger. This way . . .'

She leads me into a luxurious maple kitchen and tries a few drawers, apparently at random, before crying 'Aha!' and pulling out a plastic box. She opens it to reveal about fifty assorted bottles and packets of tablets, and starts rootling about with her lacquered fingernails.

'I've got Aspirin . . . paracetamol . . . ibuprofen . . . *very* mild valium . . .' She holds up a livid red pill.

'This one's from America,' she says brightly. 'Illegal in this country.'

'Um . . . lovely. You've got . . . lots of painkillers.'

'Oh, we love pills in this house,' she says, giving me a sudden, rather intense look. 'Love them. *Eddie!*' She hands me three green tablets and, after a few attempts, locates a cupboard full of glasses. 'Here we are. They'll zap any headache.' She runs me some iced water from the fridge. 'Drink that up.'

'Thanks,' I say, swallowing the tablets down with a wince. 'I'm so grateful. My head's just so painful. I can barely think straight.'

'Your English is very good.' She gives me a close, appraising look. 'Very good indeed!'

'Oh,' I say, thrown. 'Right. Well, I'm English. That's . . . you know, probably why.'

'You're *English*?' Trish Geiger seems galvanized by this news. 'Well! Come and sit down. Those'll kick in, in a minute. If they don't we'll get you some more.'

She sweeps me out of the kitchen and back through the hall. 'This is the drawing room,' she says, pausing by a door. She gestures around the large, grand room, dropping ash on the carpet. 'As you'll see, there's quite a lot of hoovering . . . dusting . . . silver to be kept clean . . .' She looks at me expectantly.

'Right.' I nod. I have no idea why this woman is telling me about her housework, but she seems to be waiting for a reply.

'That's a beautiful table,' I offer at last, gesturing at a shiny mahogany side table.

'It needs polishing.' Her eyes narrow. 'Regularly. I do notice these things.'

'Of course.' I nod again, bemused.

'We'll go in here.' She's leading me through another huge, grand room into an airy glassed conservatory furnished with opulent teak sunloungers, frondy plants and a well-stocked drinks tray.

'Eddie! Come in here!' She bangs on the glass and I look up to see a man in golfing slacks walking over the well-manicured lawn. He's tanned and affluent looking, probably in his late forties.

Trish is probably in her late forties, too, I think, glimpsing her crow's feet as she turns away from the window. Although something tells me she's going for thirty-nine and not a day older.

'Lovely garden,' I say.

'Oh.' Her eyes sweep over it without much interest. 'Yes, our gardener is very good. Has all sorts of ideas. Now, sit down!' She makes a flapping motion with her hands and, feeling a little awkward, I sit down on a lounger. Trish sinks into a basket chair opposite and drains her cocktail.

'Can you make a good Bloody Mary?' she asks abruptly.

I stare at her, bewildered.

'No matter.' She drags on her cigarette. 'I can teach you.'

She can *what*?

'How's your head?' she demands and carries on before I'm able to reply. 'Better? Ah, here's Eddie!'

'Greetings!' The door opens and Mr Geiger comes into the conservatory. He doesn't look quite as impressive close up as he did striding over the lawn. His eyes are a little bloodshot, and he has the beginnings of a beer belly.

'Eddie Geiger,' he says, holding out his hand jovially. 'Master of the house.'

'Eddie, this is . . .' Trish looks at me in surprise. 'What's your name?'

'Samantha,' I explain. 'I'm so sorry to bother you,

but I had the most terrible headache . . .'

'I gave Samantha some of those prescription painkillers,' puts in Trish.

'Good choice.' Eddie unscrews a Scotch bottle and pours himself a drink. 'You should try the red pills. Lethal!'

'Er . . . right.'

'Not literally, of course!' He gives a sudden, short burst of laughter. 'We're not trying to poison you!'

'Eddie!' Trish slaps him with a jangle of bracelets. 'Don't scare the girl!'

They both turn to survey me. Somehow I get the feeling a reply is expected.

'I'm very grateful, really.' I manage a half-smile. 'You've been very kind, letting me trespass on your evening.'

'Her English is good, isn't it?' Eddie raises his eyebrows at Trish.

'She's English!' says Trish triumphantly, as though she's pulled a rabbit out of a hat. 'Understands everything I say!'

I am really not getting something here. Do I *look* foreign?

'Shall we do the tour of the house?' Eddie turns to Trish.

My heart plummets. People who give tours of their houses should be abolished. The thought of trailing round, trying to find different things to say about each room, is unbearable. I just want to sit here and wait for the pills to kick in.

'Really, it's not necessary,' I begin. 'I'm sure it's absolutely beautiful—'

'Of course it's necessary!' Trish stubs out her cigarette. 'Come on.'

As I get up my head swims, and I have to clutch on

to a yucca plant to steady myself. The pain in my head is starting to ebb, but I feel light-headed and kind of weirdly detached from reality. This all feels like a bit of a dream.

OK, this woman cannot have a life. All she seems interested in is housework. As we trail round one splendid room after another she keeps pointing out things which need special dusting and showing me where the Hoover is kept. Now she's telling me about the washing machine, of all things.

'It seems . . . very . . . efficient,' I say, as she seems to be waiting for a compliment.

'We do like fresh linen *every* week. Well ironed, of course.' She gives me a sharp look.

'Of course.' I nod, trying to hide my bewilderment. 'Good idea.'

'Now upstairs!' She sweeps out of the kitchen.

Oh God. There's more?

'You come from London, Samantha?' says Eddie Geiger as we head up the stairs.

'That's right.'

'And you have a full-time job there?'

He's only asking to be polite — but for a few moments I can't bring myself to answer. Do I have a job?

'I did,' I say at last. 'To be honest . . . I don't know what my situation is at the moment.'

'What sort of hours did you work?' Trish wheels round, as though suddenly interested in the conversation.

'All hours.' I shrug. 'I'm used to working all day and into the night. Through the night, sometimes.'

The Geigers look absolutely stunned at this

revelation. People just have no idea what the life of a lawyer is like.

'You used to work *through the night*?' Trish seems stupefied. 'On your own?'

'Me and the other staff. Whoever was needed.'

'So you come from . . . a big set-up?'

'One of the biggest in London.' I nod.

Trish and Eddie are darting glances at each other. They really are the weirdest people.

'Well, we're *far* more relaxed, you'll be glad to hear!' Trish gives a short little laugh. 'This is the master bedroom . . . the second bedroom . . .'

As we walk down the corridor she opens and closes doors and shows me four-poster beds and hand-made drapes, until my head swims even more. I don't know what was in those pills, but I'm feeling weirder by the minute.

'The green bedroom . . . As you will know, we don't have children or pets . . . Are you a smoker?' Trish suddenly demands, inhaling on her own cigarette.

'Um . . . no. Thanks.'

'Not that we mind, either way.'

We descend a small flight of stairs and I grab the wall to keep myself steady, but it seems to run away in a tangle of wallpaper flowers.

'Are you all right?' Eddie catches me as I'm about to topple on the floor.

'I think those painkillers were a bit strong,' I mumble.

'They *are* a bit vicious.' Trish gives me a considering look. 'You haven't drunk any *alcohol* today, have you?'

'Er . . . well, yes . . .'

'Aaah.' She pulls a face. 'Well, it's all right as long as you don't start *hallucinating*. Then we'd have to call a doctor. And . . . here we are!' she continues, and opens the last door with a flourish. 'The staff accommodation.'

All the rooms in this house are huge. This one is about the size of my flat, with pale walls and stone mullioned windows overlooking the garden. It has the plainest bed I've seen yet in this house, vast and square and made up with crisp white bedlinen.

I fight a sudden, almost overwhelming urge to lie down on it, nurse my head and sink into oblivion.

'Lovely,' I say politely. 'It's a gorgeous room.'

'Good!' Eddie smacks his hands together. 'Well, Samantha, I'd say you've got the job!'

I look back at him through my daze.

Job?

What job?

'Eddie!' snaps Trish. 'You can't just offer her the job! We haven't finished the interview!'

Interview?

Did I miss something?

'We haven't even given her a full job description!' Trish is still laying into Eddie. 'We haven't been through any of the details!'

'Well, go through the details, then!' retorts Eddie. Trish shoots him a look of fury and clears her throat.

'So, Samantha,' she says in formal tones, 'your role as full-time housekeeper will comprise—'

'I'm sorry?' I stare at her.

Trish clicks her tongue in exasperation. 'Your role as full-time housekeeper,' she says, more slowly, 'will comprise all cleaning, laundry and cooking. You will wear a uniform and maintain a courteous and respectful . . .'

My role as—

These people think I'm applying to be their *housekeeper*?

For a moment, I'm too dumbfounded to speak.

'. . . full board and lodging,' Trish is saying, 'and four weeks holiday a year.'

'What's the salary?' says Eddie with interest. 'Are we paying her more than the last girl?'

For a moment I think Trish might murder him, there and then.

'I'm so sorry, Samantha!' Before I can even open my mouth she's dragged Eddie out of the room and bangs the door, whereupon a furious, muted argument breaks out.

I look around the room, trying to gather my wits.

They think I'm a housekeeper. A housekeeper! This is ridiculous. I have to put them right. I have to explain the misunderstanding.

Another wave of wooziness engulfs me and I sit down on the bed. Then, before I can stop myself, I lie back on the cool white cover and close my eyes. It's like sinking into a cloud.

I don't want to get up. I do not want to get up from this bed. It's a haven.

It's been a long day. A long, exhausting, painful nightmare of a day. I just want it to be over.

'Samantha, I'm sorry about that.' I open my eyes and struggle up to see Trish coming back in, followed by a pink-faced Eddie. 'Before we continue, did you have any questions about the post?'

I stare back at her, my head swirling like a merry-go-round.

This is the moment where I have to explain there's been a big mistake. That I'm not a housekeeper, I'm a lawyer.

But nothing comes out of my mouth.

I don't want to leave. I want to lie on this bed and fall into oblivion.

I could stay here one night, flashes through my brain. *Just one night. I could sort out the misunderstanding tomorrow.*

'Um . . . would it be possible to start tonight?' I hear myself saying.

'I don't see why not—' begins Eddie.

'Let's not jump ahead of ourselves,' Trish interrupts crisply. 'We have had *quite* a few promising applicants for this post, Samantha. Several quite dazzling. One girl even had a diploma in French cordon bleu cookery!'

She drags on her cigarette, giving me a pointed look. And something inside me stiffens, like an automatic reflex. I can't help it. It's bigger than me, bigger even than my desire to crash out on the soft white bed.

Is she suggesting . . .

Is she implying that I might not *get* this job?

I regard Trish silently for a few moments. Somewhere, down inside my befuddled state of shock, I can feel a tiny flicker of the old Samantha returning. I can feel my ingrained ambition lifting its head and sniffing the air. Rolling back its sleeves and spitting on its hands. I can beat some French-cordon-bleu-cookery girl.

I have never failed an interview in my life.

I'm not about to start now.

'So.' Trish looks at her list. 'You're experienced in all forms of laundry?'

'I won a laundry prize at school,' I reply with a modest nod. 'That's really what started me on my career.'

'Goodness!' Trish looks taken back. 'And you're cordon bleu trained?'

'I trained under Michel de la Roux de la Blanc.' I pause gravely. 'His name obviously speaks for itself.'

'Absolutely!' says Trish, glancing uncertainly at Eddie.

We're sitting in the conservatory again. Trish is firing a series of questions at me which sound like they come from a 'How To Hire Your Housekeeper' pamphlet. And I'm answering every single one with total confidence.

Deep down in my brain I can hear a little voice calling out, 'What are you doing? Samantha, what the hell are you DOING?'

But I'm not listening. I don't want to listen. Somehow I've managed to block out real life, the mistake, my ruined career, the whole nightmare of a day . . . everything else in the world except this interview. My head is still spinning and I feel like I might keel over any moment – but inside is a focused little kernel of determination. *I'm going to get this job.*

'Could you give us a sample menu?' Trish lights another cigarette. 'For a dinner party, say?'

Food . . . Impressive food . . .

Suddenly I remember Maxim's, the night before. The souvenir birthday menu.

'I'll just consult my notes.' I unzip my bag and surreptitiously scan the Maxim's menu. 'For a formal dinner, I would serve . . . er . . . seared foie gras with an apricot glaze . . . lamb with spiced houmous . . . followed by chocolate-mint soufflé with two home-made sorbets.'

Take *that*, cordon bleu girl.

'Well!' Trish looks astounded. 'I must say, that's very impressive.'

'Marvellous!' Eddie looks like he's salivating.

'Seared foie gras! You couldn't knock some up for us now?'

Trish shoots him an annoyed look. 'I'm assuming you have a reference, Samantha?'

A reference?

'We *will* need a reference.' Trish begins to frown.

'My referee is Lady Freya Edgerly,' I say, in sudden inspiration.

'*Lady* Edgerly?' Trish's eyebrows rise and a pink tinge starts slowly creeping up her neck.

'I have been associated with Lord and Lady Edgerly for many years.' I nod. 'I know Lady Edgerly will vouch for me.'

Trish and Eddie are both staring at me, agog. Maybe I should add some housekeeperly detail.

'A lovely family,' I embellish. 'Quite a job it was, keeping the manor house clean. And . . . polishing Lady Edgerly's tiaras.'

Shit. I've gone a step too far with the tiaras.

But to my amazement, not a note of suspicion crosses either face.

'You cooked for them, did you?' enquires Eddie. 'Breakfasts and so forth?'

'Naturally. Lord Edgerly was very fond of my signature dish, Eggs Benedict.' I take a sip of water.

I can see Trish pulling what she clearly imagines are cryptic faces at Eddie, who is surreptitiously nodding back. They might as well have 'Let's Have Her!' tattooed on their foreheads.

'One final thing.' Trish takes a deep drag on her cigarette. 'You will be answering the phone when Mr Geiger and myself are out. Our image in society is very important. Please would you demonstrate how you will do it.' She nods at a phone on a nearby table.

They cannot be serious. Except . . . I think they are.

'You should say, "Good afternoon, the Geiger residence",' prompts Eddie.

Obediently I get up. Ignoring my giddy head as best I can, I walk across and lift the receiver.

'Good afternoon,' I say in my most charming, head-school-prefect tones. 'The Geiger residence. How may I help?'

Eddie and Trish look like all their Christmases have come at once.

SEVEN

I wake the next morning to an unfamiliar, smooth white ceiling above me. I stare at it for a few moments in bewilderment, then lift my head a little. The sheets make a strange rumpling sound as I move. What's going on? My sheets don't sound anything like that.

But of course. They're the Geigers' sheets.

I sink comfortably back into my pillows – until another thought strikes me.

Who are the Geigers?

I screw up my face, trying to remember. I feel as though I'm both hungover and still drunk. Snatches of yesterday are vivid in my mind, amidst a dense fog. I'm not sure what's real and what's a dream. I came on the train . . . yes . . . I had a headache . . . Paddington Station . . . walking out of the office . . .

Oh God. Oh please, no.

With a sickening whoosh the whole nightmare is back in my brain. I feel as if someone's punched me in the solar plexus. The memo. Third Union Bank. Fifty million pounds. Asking Guy if I had a job left . . .

His silence.

I lie very still for a while, letting it all sink in again.

My career is wrecked. I have no chance of partnership. I probably have no job. Everything is over as I knew it.

At last I push back the covers and get out of bed, feeling weak and spacey. I didn't have anything to eat yesterday, I suddenly realize, apart from those few Shreddies in the morning.

This time yesterday I was in my kitchen, getting ready for work, blissfully unaware of what was going to happen. In another world — in a parallel universe to this one — I would be waking up today a partner of Carter Spink. I'd be surrounded by messages of congratulation. My life would be complete.

I squeeze my eyes tight shut, trying to escape the thoughts starting to float into my mind. Sickening, if-only thoughts. If I'd seen the memo earlier . . . If I had a tidier desk . . . If Arnold hadn't given that piece of work to me . . .

But there's no point. Ignoring my throbbing head, I walk to the window. What happened, happened. All I can do is deal with it. As I stare out onto the garden, I feel utterly surreal. Until this moment my whole life has been mapped out to the hour. Through exams, holiday internships, the rungs of the career ladder . . . I thought I knew exactly where I was headed.

And now I find myself in a strange room in the middle of the countryside. With my career in ruins.

Plus . . . there's something else. Something's nagging at me. A final piece of the jigsaw still missing in my dazed brain. It'll come to me in a minute.

I lean my forehead against the cool, soothing glass and watch a man on the distant horizon walking his dog. Maybe things are salvageable. Maybe it's not all as bad as I thought. Did Guy actually *say* I'd lost my job? I have to call him and find out just how bad it is. I take a deep breath and run my hands through my tangled hair. God, I flipped out yesterday. When I consider the way I acted, running out of the office, jumping on a train . . . I was really on another planet. If it weren't for the Geigers being so understanding—

My train of thought halts abruptly.

The Geigers.

Something about the Geigers. Something I'm not remembering . . . something that's ringing slight alarm bells . . .

I turn round and focus on a blue dress hanging on the wardrobe door. Some kind of uniform, with piping. Why would there be a—

The alarm bells are getting louder. They're starting to clang wildly. It's coming back to me like some kind of terrible, drunken dream.

Did I take a job as a housekeeper?

For an instant I cannot move. Oh Jesus. What have I done? What have I *done*?

My heart starts to thump as I take in my situation properly for the first time. I am staying in a strange couple's house under completely false pretences. I've slept in their bed. I'm wearing one of Trish's old T-shirts. They even gave me a toothbrush, after I invented a 'suitcase stolen on the train' story. The last thing I remember before crashing out is hearing Trish gloating on the phone. 'She's English!' she was saying. 'Yes, speaks English perfectly! *Super* girl. Cordon bleu trained!'

I'll have to tell them it was all lies.

There's a rapping at my bedroom door and I jump in fright.

'Samantha? May I come in?'

'Oh! Um . . . yes!'

The door opens and Trish appears, wearing pale-pink exercise clothes with a diamanté logo. She's fully made up, and is wearing some very strong scent which is already choking me.

'I've made you a cup of tea,' she says, handing me the mug with a formal smile. 'Mr Geiger and I would like you to feel very welcome in our house.'

'Oh!' I swallow nervously. 'Thanks.'

Mrs Geiger, there's something I need to tell you. I'm not a housekeeper.

Somehow the words don't make it out of my mouth.

Trish's eyes have narrowed as though she's already regretting her kind gesture.

'Don't think you'll be getting this every day, of course! But since you weren't feeling well last night . . .' She taps her watch. 'Now you'd better get dressed. We'll expect you down in ten minutes. We only have a light breakfast as a rule. Toast, coffee and whatnot. Then we can discuss the other meals of the day.'

'Er . . . OK,' I say feebly.

She closes the door and I put the tea down. Oh fuck. What am I going to do? What? What?

OK. Calm down. Prioritize. I need to call the office. Find out exactly how bad the situation is. With a spasm of apprehension I reach inside my bag for my mobile phone.

The display is blank. The battery must have run out.

I stare at it in frustration. I must have been so spaced out yesterday I forgot to charge it. I pull out my charger, plug it into the wall and attach the phone. At once it starts charging up.

I wait for the signal to appear . . . but it doesn't. There's no bloody signal.

I feel a thrust of panic. How am I going to call the office? How am I going to do *anything*? I cannot exist without my mobile phone.

Suddenly I remember passing a telephone on the

landing. It was on a table in a little window bay. Maybe I could use that. I open my bedroom door and look up and down the corridor. No one's about. Cautiously I creep into the bay and lift the receiver. The dial tone rings calmly in my ear. I take a deep breath – then dial the direct line for Arnold. It isn't nine yet, but he'll be in.

'Arnold Saville's office,' comes the cheerful voice of Lara, his secretary.

'Lara,' I say nervously, 'it's Samantha. Samantha Sweeting.'

'*Samantha?*' Lara sounds so gobsmacked, I wince. 'Oh my God! What happened? Where *are* you? Everyone's been—' She draws herself up.

'I . . . I'm out of London right now. Can I talk to Arnold?'

'Of course. He's right here.' She disappears briefly into chirpy Vivaldi, before the line clears again.

'Samantha.' Arnold's friendly, assured voice booms down the line. 'My dear girl. You've got yourself in a pickle, haven't you?'

Only Arnold could describe the loss of a client's fifty million pounds as a 'pickle'. In spite of everything, a tiny half-smile comes to my lips. I can just picture him, in his waistcoat, his woolly eyebrows knitting together.

'I know,' I say, trying to match his understated tones. 'It's . . . not great.'

'I'm obliged to point out that your hasty departure yesterday did not help matters.'

'I know. I'm so sorry. I just panicked.'

'Understandable. However, you left a bit of a mess behind.'

Underneath Arnold's jolly veneer I can detect unfamiliar levels of stress. Arnold never gets stressed.

Things must be really bad. I want to fall to the floor in a grovelling heap, crying 'I'm so sorry!' But that wouldn't help anyone. I've already been un-professional enough.

'So – what's the latest situation?' I'm trying to sound composed. 'Is there anything the receivers can do?'

'I think it unlikely. They say their hands are tied.'

'Right.' It's like a hammer blow to the stomach. So that's it. The fifty million is gone for good. 'And the insurers?'

'That is the next step, of course. The money will be recovered eventually, I'm sure. But not without com-plications. As I think you will appreciate.'

'I know,' I whisper.

For a few moments neither of us speaks. There's no good news, I realize with a dull ache of compre-hension. There's no silver lining. I've fucked up, end of story.

'Arnold,' I say, my voice quivering, 'I have no idea how I could have made such a . . . a *stupid* mistake. I don't understand how it happened. I don't even remember seeing the memo on my desk—'

'Where are you now?' Arnold breaks in.

'I'm . . .' I look helplessly out of the window. 'To be honest, I don't even know exactly where I am. But I can come in. I'll come back now.' My words come tumbling out. 'I'll get on the first train . . . I'll only be a few hours.'

'I don't think that's a good idea.' There's a new edge to Arnold's voice which pulls me up.

'Have I . . . have I been fired?'

'It hasn't been addressed yet.' He sounds testy. 'There have been slightly more pressing matters to consider, Samantha.'

'Of course.' I feel the blood rush back into my head.

'I'm sorry. I just . . .' My throat is thickening. I close my eyes, trying to keep control of myself. 'I've been with Carter Spink all my working life. All I ever, ever wanted was . . .'

I can't even say it.

'Samantha, I know you're a very talented lawyer.' Arnold sighs. 'No one is in any doubt of that.'

'But I made a mistake.'

I can hear tiny crackles down the line; my own pulse beating in my ears.

'Samantha, I'll do everything I can,' he says at last. 'I might as well tell you now, a meeting has been arranged this morning to discuss your fate.'

'And you don't think I should come in?' I bite my lip.

'It might do more harm than good at the moment. Stay where you are. Leave the rest to me.' Arnold hesitates, his voice a little gruff. 'I'll do my best, Samantha. I promise.'

'I'll be waiting,' I say quickly. 'Thank you so much.' But he's gone. Slowly I put down the phone.

I have never felt so powerless in my life. I have a sudden vision of them all, sitting gravely round a conference table. Arnold. Ketterman. Maybe even Guy. Deciding whether to give me a break.

I have to think positive. There's still a chance. If Arnold is on my side, others will be too . . .

'*Super* girl.'

I jump at the sound of Trish's approaching voice. 'Well, of course I'll check her references, but Gillian, I am a *very* good judge of character. I'm not easily fooled—'

Trish rounds the corner, holding a mobile to her ear, and I quickly move away from the telephone.

'Samantha!' she says in surprise. 'What are you

doing? Still not dressed? Buck up!' She heads off again and I scuttle back to my room. I close the door and stare at myself in the mirror.

I suddenly feel a bit bad.

In fact, I feel really bad. How are the Geigers going to react when I tell them I'm a total fraud? That I'm not a trained cordon bleu housekeeper at all, I just wanted a place to stay for the night?

I have a sudden image of them bundling me furiously out of the house. Feeling totally used. Maybe they'll even call the police. Have me arrested. Oh God. This could get really nasty.

But I mean, it's not like I have any other option. It's not like I could actually . . .

Could I?

I pick up the blue uniform and finger it, my mind whirling round and round.

They've been pretty kind, putting me up. It's not like I'm doing anything else right now. It's not like I have anywhere else to go. Maybe it'll even take my mind off things, doing a little light housework . . .

Abruptly I come to a decision.

I'll busk it for a morning. It can't be that hard. I'll make their toast and dust the ornaments or whatever. I'll think of it as my little thank-you to them. Then as soon as I hear from Arnold I'll find a convincing excuse to leave. And the Geigers will never know I wasn't a proper housekeeper.

Hurriedly I put on my uniform and run a comb through my hair. Then I stand to face myself in the mirror.

'Good morning, Mrs Geiger,' I say to my reflection. 'And . . . er . . . how would you like the drawing room dusted?'

OK. It'll be fine.

* * *

As I walk down the stairs, the Geigers are both standing at the bottom, looking up at me. I have never felt more self-conscious in my life.

I'm a housekeeper. I have to behave like a housekeeper.

'Welcome, Samantha!' says Eddie as I arrive down in the hall. 'Sleep all right?'

'Very well, thank you, Mr Geiger,' I reply demurely.

'That's good!' Eddie rocks back and forth on the soles of his feet. He seems just a little awkward. In fact, they both seem awkward. Underneath the make-up, the tans, the expensive clothes, there seems just a hint of uncertainty about the Geigers.

I walk over to a bench seat and straighten a cushion, trying to look as though I know what I'm doing.

'You'll be wanting to get to know your new kitchen!' says Trish brightly.

'Of course!' I say with a confident smile. 'I'm looking forward to it!'

It's only a kitchen. It's only one morning. I can do this.

Trish leads the way into the vast, maple kitchen, and this time I look around more carefully, trying to take in the details. There's a huge, hob-type thing set into the granite counter to my left. A bank of ovens built into the wall. Everywhere I look I can see shiny chrome gadgets plugged into sockets. Racks of saucepans and implements of all descriptions are hanging overhead in a jumble of stainless steel.

I have not one single clue what anything is.

'You'll want to get it the way you like it, of course,' says Trish, gesturing around. 'Just change anything you like. Knock it into shape. You're the professional!'

They're both looking at me expectantly.

'Absolutely,' I say in a businesslike way. 'Obviously I have my own . . . um . . . systems. That shouldn't be there, for example.' I point randomly at some gadget. 'I'll have to move it.'

'Really?' Trish looks fascinated. 'Why's that?'

There's a momentary beat of silence. Even Eddie looks interested.

'Kitchen . . . ergonomic . . . theory,' I improvise. 'So, you'd like toast for breakfast?' I add quickly.

'Toast for both of us,' says Trish. 'And coffee with skimmed milk.'

'Coming up.' I smile, feeling slight relief.

I can make toast. Once I've worked out which of these things is the toaster.

'So, I'll just bring that through in a moment,' I add, trying to chivvy them out. 'Would you like to eat in the dining room?'

There's a small crash from the hall.

'That'll be the newspaper,' says Trish. 'Yes, you may serve breakfast in the dining room, Samantha.' She hurries out, but Eddie loiters in the kitchen.

'You know, I've changed my mind.' He gives me a jovial smile. 'Forget the toast, Samantha. I'll have your famous Eggs Benedict. You whetted my appetite last night!'

Last night? What did I say last—

Oh Jesus. Eggs Benedict. My famous signature dish as beloved by Lord Edgerly.

What was I *thinking*?

I don't even know what Eggs Benedict *are*.

'Are you . . . sure that's what you want?' I manage in a constricted voice.

'I wouldn't miss your speciality!' Eddie rubs his stomach appreciatively. 'It's my favourite breakfast. The best Eggs Benedict I've ever tasted were at the

Carlyle in New York, but I'll take a bet yours are even better!'

'I don't know about that!' Somehow I summon a bright smile.

Why the fuck did I say I could cook Eggs Benedict? OK . . . keep calm. It must be simple enough. Eggs and . . . something.

Eddie leans against the granite counter with an expectant look. I have a nasty suspicion he's waiting for me to start cooking. Hesitantly I get down a gleaming pan from the rack, just as Trish bustles in with the newspaper. She eyes me with bright curiosity.

'How will you be using the asparagus steamer, Samantha?'

Shit.

'I just wanted to . . . examine it. Yes.' I nod briskly, as though the pan has confirmed my suspicions, then carefully hang it back on the rack again.

I'm feeling hotter and hotter. I have no idea even how to begin. Do I crack the eggs? Boil them? Throw them against the wall?

'Here are the eggs.' Eddie plonks a huge box on the counter and lifts the lid. 'Should be enough there, I'd imagine!'

I stare at the rows of brown eggs, feeling a little light-headed. What do I think I'm doing? I can't make bloody Eggs Benedict. I can't make these people breakfast. I'm going to have to come clean.

I turn round and take a deep breath.

'Mr Geiger . . . Mrs Geiger . . .'

'*Eggs?*' Trish's voice cuts across mine. 'Eddie, you can't have eggs! Remember what the doctor said!' She looks at me, eyes narrowed. 'What did he ask you for, Samantha? Boiled eggs?'

'Er . . . Mr Geiger ordered Eggs Benedict. But the thing is—'

'You're not eating Eggs Benedict!' Trish practically shrieks at Eddie. 'It's full of cholesterol!'

'I'll eat what I like!' Eddie protests.

'The doctor gave him an eating plan.' Trish is dragging furiously on her cigarette. 'He's already had a bowl of cornflakes this morning!'

'I was hungry!' says Eddie, defensive. 'You had a chocolate muffin!'

Trish gasps as though he's hit her. Small red dots appear on her cheeks. For a few moments she seems unable to speak.

'We will have a cup of coffee each, Samantha,' she announces at last in dignified tones. 'You may serve it in the lounge. Use the pink china. Come along, Eddie.' And she sweeps out before I can say anything else.

As I look around the empty kitchen I'm not sure if I want to laugh or cry. This is ridiculous. I can't carry on with this charade. I have to go and tell the truth. Now. I walk decisively out of the kitchen into the hall. Then I come to a halt. Behind the closed door of the sitting room I can hear the shrill, indistinct voice of Trish angrily berating Eddie, interspersed with his defensive rumbles.

Hastily I back away again into the kitchen and switch the kettle on. It might be easier just to make the coffee.

Ten minutes later I've arranged a silver tray with a pink coffee pot, pink cups, creamer, sugar, and a sprig of pink flowers I snipped from a hanging basket outside the kitchen window. I'm rather proud of it, if I say so myself.

91

I approach the sitting-room door, put the tray down on the table in the hall and knock cautiously.

'Come in!' Trish calls.

As I enter, she's sitting in a chair by the window, holding a magazine at a rather artificial angle. Eddie is on the other side of the room, examining a wooden carving.

'Thank you, Samantha.' Trish inclines her head graciously as I pour out the coffee. 'That will be all for the moment.'

I feel as though I've stumbled into some weird Merchant Ivory costume drama, except the costumes are pink yoga wear and golfing sweaters.

'Er . . . very good, Madam,' I say, playing my part. Then, without meaning to, I bob a curtsey.

There's a staggered pause. Both Geigers just gape at me in astonishment.

'Samantha, did you just . . . *curtsey*?' says Trish at last.

I stare back, frozen.

What was I thinking? Why did I curtsey? She'll think I'm taking the piss. Housekeepers don't bloody curtsey. This isn't Gosford Park.

They're still goggling at me. I have to say something.

'The Edgerlys liked me to curtsey.' My face is prickling all over. 'It's a habit I got into. I'm sorry, Madam, I won't do it again.'

Trish's head is leaning further and further over, her eyes all screwed up. She's squinting at me as though she's trying to make me out.

She must realize I'm a fake, she *must*.

'I like it,' she pronounces at last, and nods her head in satisfaction. 'Yes, I like it. You can curtsey here, too.'

What?

I can do *what*?

This is the twenty-first century. And I am being asked to curtsey to a woman called Trish?

I take a breath to protest – then close it again. It doesn't matter. It's not real. I can curtsey for a morning.

EIGHT

As soon as I'm out of the room, I dash upstairs, along
the corridor and into my bedroom to check my mobile.
But it's only half charged up and I have no idea
where I'm going to find a signal. If Trish could
get one, I must be able to. I wonder what network she's
on—

'Samantha?'

Trish's voice rises from the ground floor.

'Samantha?' She sounds annoyed. Now I can hear
her footsteps coming up the stairs.

'Madam?' I hurry along the corridor.

'There you are!' She frowns slightly. 'Kindly do *not*
disappear to your room whilst on duty. I don't want to
have to be calling you like that.'

'Er . . . yes, Mrs Geiger,' I say. As we arrive down in
the hall my stomach flips over. Beyond Trish, I can see
The Times lying on the table. It's open at the business
pages and a headline reads GLAZERBROOKS
CALLS IN RECEIVERS.

My eyes run down the text as Trish starts rootling
around in a huge white Chanel bag – but I can't see any
mention of Carter Spink. Thank God for that. The PR

department must have managed to keep a lid on the story.

'Where are my keys?' Trish sounds fretful. 'Where *are* they?' She rummages more and more violently in her Chanel bag. A gold lipstick goes flying through the air and lands at my feet. 'Why do things *disappear*?'

I pick up the lipstick and hand it to her. 'Do you remember where you lost them, Mrs Geiger?'

'I didn't *lose* them.' She inhales sharply. 'They've been stolen. It's obvious. We'll have to change all the locks. Our identities will be taken.' She clutches her head. 'This is what these fraudsters do, you know. There was a huge article about it in the *Mail*—'

'Is this them?' I've suddenly noticed a Tiffany key fob glinting on the window sill. I pick it up and hold out the bunch of keys.

'Yes!' Trish looks utterly amazed. 'Yes, that's them! Samantha, you're marvellous! *How* did you find them?'

'It was no trouble.' I shrug modestly.

'Well! I'm very impressed!' She gives me a significant look. 'I will be telling Mr Geiger.'

'Yes, Madam,' I say, trying to inject the right note of overwhelmed gratitude into my voice. 'Thank you.'

'Mr Geiger and I will be going out in a minute,' she continues, producing a scent spray and spritzing herself. 'Kindly prepare a light sandwich lunch for one o'clock, and get on with the downstairs cleaning. We'll talk about dinner later.' She swivels round. 'I might tell you, we were both very impressed by your seared foie gras menu.'

'Oh . . . um . . . good!'

It's fine. I'll be gone by dinner time.

'*Now*.' Trish pats her hair one final time. 'Come in the drawing room a moment, Samantha.'

I follow her into the room and over to the fireplace.

'Before I go out and you start dusting in here,' Trish says, 'I wanted to show you the arrangement of the ornaments.' She gestures to a row of china figurines on the mantelpiece. 'This can be tricky to remember. For some reason, cleaners never get it right. So kindly *pay attention.*'

Obediently, I turn with her to face the mantelpiece.

'It's very important, Samantha, that these china dogs face each other.' Trish points to a pair of King Charles spaniels. 'Do you see? They don't face out. They face *each other.*'

'Each other,' I echo, nodding. 'Yes. I see.'

'And the shepherdesses face very slightly *out.* You see? They face *out.*'

She's speaking slowly and clearly, as though I have the IQ of a rather thick three-year-old.

'Out,' I repeat dutifully.

'Now have you got that?' Trish looks at me intently. 'Let's see. Which way do the china dogs go?' She lifts an arm to block my view of the mantelpiece.

I don't believe it. She's testing me.

'The china dogs,' she prompts. 'Which way?'

Oh God, I cannot resist this.

'Er . . .' I ponder hard for a few moments. 'They face . . . out?'

'*Each other!*' Trish cries in exasperation. 'They face *each other!*'

'Oh right,' I say apologetically. 'Yes. Sorry. I've got that now.'

Trish has closed her eyes and is holding two fingers to her forehead as though the stress of stupid help is too much to bear.

'Never mind,' she says at last. 'We'll try again tomorrow.'

'I'll take the coffee tray out,' I suggest humbly. As I pick it up I glance again at my watch. Ten twelve. I wonder if they've started the meeting.

This morning is going to be unendurable.

By eleven thirty I'm a nervous wreck. My mobile's charged up and I've finally found a signal in the kitchen, but it hasn't rung. And there are no messages. I've checked it every minute.

I've stacked the dishwasher and, after about fifty attempts, managed to turn it on. And I've dusted the china dogs with a tissue. Other than that all I've done pretty much is pace up and down the kitchen.

I gave up on the 'light sandwich lunch' almost straight away. I sawed away for what seemed like hours at two loaves of bread – and ended up with ten huge, wonky slices, each one more misshapen than the last, lying in a sea of crumbs. God knows what I did wrong. There must have been something wrong with the knife.

All I can say is, thank God for *Yellow Pages* and caterers. And American Express. It's only going to cost me £45.50 to provide Trish and Eddie with a 'gourmet sandwich lunch' from Cotswold Caterers. I would have paid twice that. To be honest, I would probably have paid ten times that.

Now I'm just sitting on a chair, my hand clasped tightly over my mobile in my pocket.

I'm desperately willing it to ring.

At the same time I'm utterly terrified that it will.

All of a sudden I can't bear the tension any more. I need something to relieve it. *Anything.* I wrench open the door of the Geigers' enormous fridge and pull out a bottle of white wine. I pour myself a glass and take an enormous, desperate gulp. I'm about to take another when I feel a tingling on the nape of my neck.

As if . . . I'm being watched.

I swivel round and nearly jump out of my skin. There's a man at the kitchen door.

He's tall and broad, and deeply tanned, with intense blue eyes. His wavy hair is golden brown with bleached-blond tips. He's wearing old jeans and a torn T-shirt and the muddiest boots I've ever seen.

His eyes run doubtfully over the ten wonky, crumbly bread slices on the side, then on to my glass of wine.

'Hi,' he says at last. 'Are you the new cordon bleu cook?'

'Er . . . yes! Absolutely.' I smooth my uniform down. 'I'm the new housekeeper, Samantha. Hello.'

'I'm Nathaniel.' He holds out his hand and after a pause I take it. His skin is so hard and rough, it's like shaking a piece of tree bark. 'I do the garden for the Geigers. You'll be wanting to talk to me about vegetables.'

I look at him uncertainly. Why would I want to talk to him about vegetables?

As he leans against the door frame and folds his arms, I can't help noticing how massive and strong his forearms are. I've never *seen* a man with arms like that before. Not in real life.

'I can supply pretty much anything,' he continues. 'Seasonal, of course. Just tell me what you want.'

'Oh, *vegetables*,' I say, suddenly realizing what he means. 'For cooking. Er . . . yes. I'll be wanting some of those. Definitely.'

'They told me you trained with some Michelin-starred chef?' He gives a small frown. 'I don't know what kind of fancy stuff you use, but I'll do my best.' He produces a small, mud-stained notebook and a pencil. 'Which brassicas do you like to use?'

Brassicas?

What are brassicas?

They must be some kind of vegetable. I search my mind frantically but all I can see is an image of brassieres, waving on a washing line.

'I'd have to consult my menus,' I say at last with a businesslike nod. 'I'll get back to you on that one.'

'But just generally.' He looks up. 'Which do you use most? So I know what to plant.'

Oh God. I daren't risk naming a single vegetable in case I get it totally wrong.

'I use . . . all sorts, really.' I give him an airy smile. 'You know how it is with brassicas. Sometimes you're in the mood for one . . . sometimes another!'

I'm really not sure how convincing that sounded. Nathaniel looks baffled.

'I'm about to order leeks,' he says slowly. 'What variety do you prefer? Albinstar or Bleu de Solaise?'

I stare back at him, my face prickling. I didn't catch either of those.

'The . . . um . . . first one,' I say at last. 'It has very tasty . . . qualities.'

Nathaniel puts down his notebook and surveys me for a moment. His attention shifts to my wine glass again. I'm not sure I like his expression.

'I was just about to put this wine in a sauce,' I say hastily. With a nonchalant air, I take a saucepan down from the rack, put it on the hob and pour the wine in. I shake in some salt, then pick up a wooden spoon and stir it.

Then I dart a glance at Nathaniel. He's just staring at me with something approaching incredulity.

'Where did you say you trained?' he says.

I feel a twinge of alarm. He's not stupid, this man.

'At . . . cordon bleu school.' My cheeks are growing rather hot. I shake more salt into the wine and stir it briskly.

'You haven't turned the hob on,' Nathaniel observes.

'It's a cold sauce,' I reply, without lifting my head. I keep stirring for a minute, then put down my wooden spoon. 'So. I'll just leave that to . . . marinate now.'

At last I look up. Nathaniel is still leaning against the doorframe, calmly watching me. There's an expression in his blue eyes which makes my throat tighten.

He knows.

He knows I'm a fake.

Please don't tell the Geigers, I silently transmit to him. *Please. I'll be gone soon.*

'Samantha?' Trish's head pops round the door and I start nervously. 'Oh, you've met Nathaniel! Did he tell you about his vegetable garden?'

'Er . . . yes.' I can't look at him. 'He did.'

'*Mar*vellous!' She drags on a cigarette. 'Well, Mr Geiger and I are back now, and we'd like our sandwiches in twenty minutes.'

I feel a jolt of shock. Twenty minutes? But it's only ten past twelve. The caterers aren't coming till one o'clock.

'Would you like a drink first?' I suggest desperately.

'No thanks!' she says. 'Just the sandwiches. We're both rather famished, actually, so if you could hurry up with them . . .'

'Right.' I swallow. 'No problem!'

I automatically bob a curtsey as Trish disappears and hear a kind of snorting sound from Nathaniel.

'You curtsey,' he says.

'Yes, I curtsey,' I say defiantly. 'Anything wrong with that?'

Nathaniel's eyes rest again on the misshapen bread slices lying on the bread board.

'Is that lunch?' he says.

'No, that's not lunch!' I snap, flustered. 'And please could you get out of my kitchen? I need a clear space to work in.'

He raises his eyebrows.

'See you around then. Good luck with the sauce.' He nods his head towards the pan of wine.

As he closes the kitchen door behind him I whip out my phone and speed-dial the caterers. But they've left their machine on.

'Hi,' I say breathlessly after the bleep. 'I ordered some sandwiches earlier? Well, I need them *now*. As soon as you can. Thanks.'

Even as I put the phone down I realize it's fruitless. The caterers are never going to turn up in time. The Geigers are waiting.

Determination rises in me.

OK. I can do this. I can make a few sandwiches.

Quickly I pick up the two least wonky of my bread slices. I pick up the bread knife and start cutting off the crusts until they're about an inch square but presentable. There's a butter dish on the side and I gouge some out with a knife. As I spread it on the first slice the bread tears into two pieces.

Fuck.

I'll patch them together. No one'll notice.

I fling open a cupboard door and frantically root through pots of mustard . . . mint sauce . . . strawberry jam. Jam sandwiches it is. An English classic. I hastily smother one piece of bread with jam, spread some more butter on the other, and sandwich the two together. Then I stand back and look at it.

It's a total disaster. Jam is oozing out of the cracks. It still isn't completely square.

I've never seen a more revolting sandwich in my life.

I cannot possibly serve this to the Geigers.

Slowly I put the knife down in defeat. So this is it. Time for my resignation. As I stare at the jammy mess I feel strangely disappointed in myself. I would have thought I could last a morning.

A knocking sound breaks me out of my reverie. I whip round to see a girl in a blue velvet hairband peering through the kitchen window.

'Hi!' she calls. 'Did you order sandwiches for twenty?'

It all happens so fast. One minute I'm standing there looking at my botch of jam and crumbs. The next, two girls in green aprons are trooping into the kitchen with plate after plate of professionally made sandwiches.

Clean-cut, white and brown sandwiches, stacked in neat pyramids, garnished with sprigs of herbs and slices of lemon. They even have little handwritten paper flags describing the fillings.

Tuna, mint and cucumber. Smoked salmon, cream cheese and caviar. Thai chicken with wild rocket.

'I'm *so* sorry about the numbers mix-up,' the Sloaney girl in the hairband says as I sign for them. 'It honestly looked like a twenty. And we don't often get an order for sandwiches for just two people . . .'

'It's fine!' I say, edging her towards the door. 'Really. Whatever. Just put it on my card.'

The door finally closes and I look around the kitchen, totally dazed. I've never *seen* so many sandwiches. There are plates of them everywhere. On every surface. I've even had to put some on the cooker.

'Samantha?' I can hear Trish approaching.

'Um . . . hold on!' I hurry to the door, trying to block her view.

'It's already five past one,' I can hear her saying a little sharply. 'And I did ask *most* clearly for . . .'

Her voice trails off into silence as she reaches the kitchen door, and her whole face sags in astonishment. I turn and follow her gaze as she surveys the endless plates of sandwiches.

'My goodness!' At last Trish finds her voice. 'This is . . . this is very impressive!'

'I wasn't sure what fillings you'd prefer,' I say. 'Obviously next time I won't make quite so many . . .'

'Well!' Trish appears totally at a loss. She picks up one of the little flags and reads it out loud. 'Rare beef, lettuce and horseradish.' She looks up in astonishment. 'I haven't bought any beef for weeks! Where did you find it?'

'Er . . . in the freezer?'

I looked in the freezer earlier. The amount of food crammed into it would probably feed an entire small African country for a week.

'Of course!' Trish clicks her tongue. 'Aren't you clever!'

'I'll put a selection on a plate for you,' I suggest. 'And bring it out to the conservatory.'

'*Mar*vellous. Nathaniel!' Trish raps on the kitchen window. 'Come in and have a sandwich!'

I stop dead. No. Not him again.

'We don't want to waste them, after all.' She arches her eyebrows. 'If I did have a criticism, Samantha, it would be that you were a *little* profligate. Not that we're *poor*,' she adds suddenly. 'It isn't *that*.'

'Er . . . no, Madam.'

'I don't like to talk about money, Samantha.' Trish

lowers her voice a little. 'It's very vulgar. However—'

'Mrs Geiger?'

Nathaniel has appeared in the kitchen doorway again, holding a muddy garden spade.

'Have one of Samantha's delicious sandwiches!' exclaims Trish, gesturing around the kitchen. 'Just look! Isn't she clever?'

There's total silence as Nathaniel surveys the end-less mounds of sandwiches. I can't bring myself to meet his eye. My face is tingling all over. I feel I could be losing my grip on sanity here. I'm standing in a kitchen in the middle of nowhere. In a blue nylon uniform. Masquerading as a housekeeper who can magically make sandwiches out of thin air.

'Extraordinary,' says Nathaniel at last.

I finally risk looking up. He's gazing at me, his brow deeply furrowed as if he really can't make me out.

'That didn't take you long,' he says, a slight question in his voice.

'I'm pretty quick when I want to be.' I give him a bland smile.

'Samantha's wonderful!' says Trish, biting greedily into a sandwich. 'And such a tidy worker! Look at this immaculate kitchen!'

'Cordon bleu training,' I say modestly.

'Oh!' Trish has shoved another sandwich in her mouth and is practically swooning. 'This Thai chicken is divine!'

Surreptitiously I pick up one from the pile and bite into it.

Bloody hell, that's good. Though I say it myself.

By half past two the kitchen is empty. Trish and Eddie devoured over half the sandwiches, and have now gone out. Nathaniel is back in the garden. I'm pacing up and down, fiddling with a spoon, looking at the clock every thirty seconds.

Arnold will call soon. It's been hours.

I can't think about anything else. My mind has narrowed down to a one-track tunnel and all I care about is what's at the end.

I look out of the window at a small brown bird pecking at the ground, then turn away and sink into a chair, staring down at the table, running my thumb nail obsessively round the fine grain of the polished wood.

I made one mistake. One. People are allowed to make one mistake in life. It's in the rules.

Or maybe it's not. I just don't know.

Suddenly I feel my mobile vibrate and my whole chest seems to explode in painful fright. I grab the phone out of my uniform pocket with a suddenly trembling hand.

The caller ID tells me it's Guy. I take a deep breath, then press OK.

'Hi, Guy?' I try to speak confidently, but my voice sounds tiny and scared to my own ears.

'Samantha? Is that you?' Guy's voice rushes out in an urgent torrent. 'Where the hell *are* you? Why aren't you here? Didn't you get my emails?'

'I haven't got my BlackBerry,' I say, taken aback. 'Why didn't you call?'

'I tried! You didn't answer. Then I was in meetings but I've been sending you emails all morning . . . Samantha, where on earth *are* you? You should be here at the office! Not hiding out, for Christ's sake!'

A huge shock reverberates through my body. Hiding out?

'But . . . but Arnold said don't come in! He said it would be best! He told me to stay away and he would do what he could . . .'

'Do you have any idea how this *looks*?' Guy cuts across me. 'First you freak out, then you disappear from view. People are saying you're unhinged, you've had a breakdown . . . there's a rumour you've skipped the country . . .'

As the truth hits me, I feel a hot, choking panic. I can't believe how wrong I've played this. I can't believe how stupid I've been. What am I doing still sitting in this kitchen, miles from London?

'Tell them I'm coming straight in,' I stammer. 'Tell Ketterman I'll be there at once . . . I'm getting on a train . . .'

'It might be too late.' Guy sounds heavy and reluctant. 'Samantha, all sorts of stories are going round.'

'Stories?' My heart is thudding so hard I can barely say the word. 'What . . . what stories?'

I can't take all this in. I feel like my car has suddenly lurched off the road and I can't stop it. I thought everything was under control. I thought I was doing the right thing, staying here, letting Arnold plead my case.

'Apparently people have said you're unreliable,' Guy says at last. 'That this isn't the first time. That you've made errors before.'

'*Errors?*' I leap to my feet, my voice as sharp as though I've been scalded. 'Who's saying that? I've never made any errors! What are they talking about?'

'I don't know. I wasn't in the meeting. Samantha – think back carefully. Have you made any other mistakes?'

Think back carefully?

I stare at the mobile in shock and disbelief. He doesn't believe me?

'I've never made any mistakes,' I say, trying and failing to keep my voice level. 'None. Never! I'm a good lawyer. I'm a *good* lawyer.' To my dismay I realize tears are pouring down my cheeks. 'I'm steady! You *know* that, Guy.'

There's a tense little silence.

The unsaid is there between us. Like a conviction. I did make a mistake.

'Guy, I don't know how I didn't see the Glazerbrooks documentation.' My words tumble out faster and faster. 'I don't know how it happened. It doesn't make any sense. I know my desk is messy but I have my systems, for God's sake. I don't miss things like that. I just don't—'

'Samantha, calm down.'

'How can I calm down?' I almost yell. 'This is my life. My *life*. I don't have anything else!' I wipe the tears away from my cheeks. 'I'm not losing this. I'm coming in. Now.'

I cut the phone dead and get to my feet, bubbling with panic. I should have gone back. I should have gone back straight away, not wasted time here. I don't know what times the trains will be but I don't care. I have to get out of here.

I grab a piece of paper and a pencil, and scrawl,

Dear Mrs Geiger,

I am afraid I must resign as your housekeeper. Whilst I have enjoyed my time

Come on. I haven't got time to write any more, I have to leave now. I put the paper down on the table and head for the door. Then I stop.

I can't leave the letter unfinished in the middle of a sentence. It'll bug me for the rest of the day.

*Whilst I have enjoyed my time with you, I feel I would
like a fresh challenge. Many thanks for your kindness.*

Yours sincerely,

Samantha Sweeting.

I put the pen down and push my chair back with a
scrape. As I reach the door my mobile vibrates again.

Guy, I instantly think. I reach for it and am already
flipping it open when I see the caller ID. It's not Guy.

It's Ketterman.

Something cold seems to grip my spine. As I stare at
his name I feel real fear in a way I never have before.
Childish, nightmarish fear. Every instinct in my body
is telling me not to answer.

But too late. My phone's already open. Slowly I lift
it up to my ear.

'Hello.'

'Samantha. John Ketterman here.'

'Right.' My voice is scratchy with nerves. 'Hello.'

There's a long pause. I know this is my moment to
speak. But I'm paralysed by terror; my throat feels
wadded with cotton wool. No words seem adequate.
Everyone knows how much Ketterman despises
apologies and excuses and explanations.

'Samantha, I'm ringing to tell you that your contract
with Carter Spink has been terminated.'

I feel all the blood drain from my face.

'A letter is on its way to you giving the reasons.' His
tone is distant and formal. 'Gross negligence com-
pounded by your subsequent unprofessional
behaviour. Your P45 will be sent to you. Your pass has
been disabled. I don't expect to see you at the Carter
Spink offices again.'

He's going too fast. This is all happening too fast.

'Please don't . . .' My voice comes blurting out in desperation. 'Please give me another chance. I made one mistake. One.'

'Lawyers at Carter Spink don't make mistakes, Samantha. Nor do they run away from their mistakes.'

'I know it was wrong to run away. I know.' I'm shaking all over. 'But it was such a shock. I wasn't thinking straight . . .'

'You've disgraced the reputation of the firm and yourself.' Ketterman's voice sharpens as though he, too, might be finding this difficult. 'You have lost fifty million pounds of a client's money through your own negligence. And subsequently absconded with no explanation. Samantha, you cannot have expected any other outcome, surely.'

There's a long silence. My forehead is pressed hard against the heel of my hand. I try to focus on breathing. In and out. In and out.

'No,' I whisper at last.

It's over. It's really over.

Ketterman starts on a pre-prepared speech about meeting with the human resources department but I don't listen. The room is swimming around me and I'm struggling for breath.

It's over. My entire career. Everything I've worked for since I was twelve years old. All gone. Everything ruined. In twenty-four hours.

At last I realize Ketterman has disappeared from the line. I get to my feet and stagger over to the shiny fridge. I look greenish-grey in its reflection. My eyes are huge, burning holes.

I don't know what to do. I don't know where to start. For a long time I just stand there, staring at my own face until it doesn't make sense any more, until the features blur and move around.

I've been fired. The phrase echoes round my mind. *I've been fired.* I could collect the dole. The thought sends a painful snort through my nose. I imagine myself with the men from *The Full Monty.* Standing in the unemployment queue, moving my hips back and forth to 'Hot Stuff'.

Suddenly I hear the sound of a key in the front door. My eyes snap into focus and I move away from the fridge.

I can't be found like this. I can't face any probing; any sympathy. Otherwise I'm afraid I might just collapse into sobs and never stop.

Distractedly I reach for a cloth and start sweeping it in meaningless circles over the table. Then I glimpse my note to Trish, still lying on the table. I grab it, crumple it and throw it in the bin. Later. I'll do it later. I feel as though I can barely speak, right now, let alone give a convincing resignation speech.

'There you are!' Trish comes tripping into the kitchen on her high-heeled clogs, holding three bursting shopping bags. 'Samantha!' She stops at the sight of me. 'Are you all right? Is your headache back?'

'I'm . . . fine.' My voice shakes a little. 'Thanks.'

'You look *dreadful*! Goodness me! Have some more pills!'

'Really . . .'

'Go on! I'll have some too, why not?' she adds gaily. 'Now, sit down, and I'll make *you* a cup of tea!'

She plonks the bags down and switches on the kettle, then rootles around for the green painkillers.

'These are the ones you like, aren't they?'

'Um, I'd rather just have an aspirin,' I say quickly. 'If that's OK.'

'Are you quite sure?' She runs me a glass of water and gives me a couple of aspirin. 'Now, you just sit there. Relax. Don't even *think* of doing anything else! Until it's time to make the supper,' she adds as an afterthought.

'You're very kind,' I manage.

As I say the words I have the dim realization that I mean them. Trish's kindness may be a bit warped, but it's real.

'Here we are.' Trish puts a cup of tea down and scrutinizes me for a few moments. 'Are you *home*-sick?' She sounds triumphant, as though she's cracked the mystery. 'Our girl from the Philippines did get rather blue from time to time, but I used to say to her, Cheer up Manuela!' Trish pauses thoughtfully. 'Then I found out her name was Paula. Extraordinary.'

'I'm not homesick,' I say, gulping my tea.

My mind is beating like a butterfly's wings. What am I going to do?

Go home.

But the thought of returning to that flat, with Ketterman living two floors above, makes me sick. I can't face him. I can't do it.

Phone Guy. He'll have me to stay. They have that huge house in Islington with all those spare rooms. I've stayed the night before. Then I'll . . . sell my flat. Find a job.

What job?

'This will cheer you up.' Trish's voice breaks my thoughts. She pats the shopping bags with suppressed glee. 'After your *stunning* performance at lunch . . . I've been shopping. And I've got a surprise for you! This will make your day!'

'A surprise?' I look up, bewildered, as Trish starts producing packets from the bag.

111

'Foie gras . . . chick peas . . . shoulder of lamb . . .' She hefts a joint of meat onto the table and looks at me expectantly. Then she clicks her tongue at my bewildered expression. 'It's *ingredients*! Your dinner-party menu! We'll eat at eight, if that's OK?'

NINE

It'll be all right.

If I say it often enough to myself, it must be true.

I know I need to call Guy. I've opened my phone several times to do it. But each time, humiliation has stopped me. Even though he's my friend; even though he's the person closest to me in the company. I'm the one who's fired. I'm the one in disgrace. And he's not.

At last I sit up and rub my cheeks, trying to get my spirits back. Come on. This is *Guy*. He'll want to hear from me. He'll want to help. I flip open my phone and dial his direct line. A moment later I hear footsteps clopping along the wooden floor of the hall.

Trish.

Seamlessly I shut the phone, pocket it and reach for a clump of broccoli.

'How are you getting on?' Trish's voice greets me. 'Making progress?'

As she enters the kitchen she looks a little surprised to see me still sitting in the exact same spot she left me. 'Everything all right?'

'I'm just . . . assessing the ingredients,' I improvise. 'Getting the feel of them.'

Just then another blonde woman appears round the door, next to Trish. She's wearing diamanté sunglasses on her head and regards me with avid interest.

'I'm Petula,' she announces. 'How do you do.'

'Petula's just eaten some of your sandwiches,' puts in Trish. 'She thought they were *marvellous*.'

'And I've heard about the foie gras with an apricot glaze!' Petula raises her eyebrows. 'Very impressive!'

'Samantha can cook anything!' boasts Trish, pink with pride. 'She trained with Michel de la Roux de la Blanc! The master himself!'

'So how exactly will you be glazing the foie gras, Samantha?' asks Petula with interest.

The kitchen is silent. Both women are waiting, agog.

'Well.' I clear my throat several times. 'I expect I'll use the . . . usual method. The word "glaze" obviously comes from the transparent nature of the . . . er . . . finish . . . and complements the . . . gras. Foie,' I amend. 'De gras. The . . . blend of the flavours.'

I am making absolutely no sense here, but neither Trish nor Petula seems to have noticed. In fact they both seem totally impressed.

'Where on earth did you find her?' says Petula to Trish in what she clearly imagines to be a discreet undertone. 'My girl is *hopeless*. Can't cook *and* doesn't understand a word I say.'

'She just applied out of the blue!' Trish murmurs back, still flushed with pleasure. 'Cordon bleu! English! We couldn't believe it!'

They both eye me as though I'm some rare animal with horns sprouting out of my head.

I can't bear this any more.

'Shall I make you some tea and bring it through to the conservatory?' I say desperately.

'No, we're popping out to have our nails done,' says Trish. 'I'll see you later, Samantha.'

There's an expectant pause. Suddenly I realize Trish is waiting for my curtsey. I start to prickle all over in embarrassment. Why did I curtsey? *Why* did I curtsey?

'Very good, Mrs Geiger.' I bow my head and make an awkward bob. When I look up, Petula's eyes are like saucers.

As the two women leave, I can hear Petula hissing, 'She *curtseys*? She *curtseys* to you?'

'It's a simple mark of respect,' I hear Trish replying airily. 'But very effective. You know, Petula, you should really try it with your girl . . .'

Oh God. What have I started?

I wait until the sound of tapping heels has completely disappeared. Then, moving into the larder to be on the safe side, I flip open my phone and repeat dial Guy's number. After three rings he answers.

'Samantha.' He sounds guarded. 'Hi. Have you—'

'It's OK, Guy.' I squeeze my eyes shut briefly. 'I've spoken to Ketterman. I know.'

'Oh Christ, Samantha.' He exhales hard. 'I'm so sorry this has happened. *So* sorry . . .'

I cannot stand his pity. If he says anything else I might just burst into tears.

'It's fine,' I say, cutting him off. 'Really. Let's not talk about it. Let's just . . . look forward. I have to get my life on track.'

'Jesus, you're focused!' There's a note of admiration in his voice. 'You don't let anything faze you, do you?'

I push my hair back off my face. It feels dry and unloved, and full of split ends.

'I just have to . . . get on with things.' Somehow I keep my voice even and steady. 'I need to get back to London.

But I can't go home. Ketterman bought a flat in my building. He *lives* there.'

'Yes, I heard about that.' I can hear the wince in Guy's voice. 'That's unfortunate.'

'I just can't face him, Guy.' I feel the threat of tears again, and force myself to take a few deep breaths. 'So . . . I was wondering. Could I come and stay with you for a while? Just for a few days?'

There's silence. I wasn't expecting silence.

'Samantha, I'd love to help,' says Guy at last. 'But I'll have to check it with Charlotte.'

'Of course,' I say, a little taken aback.

'Just stay on the line for a sec. I'll call her.'

The next moment I've been put on hold. I sit waiting, listening to the tinny harpsichord music, trying not to feel discomfited. It was unreasonable to expect him to say yes straight away. Of course he has to clear it with his girlfriend.

At last Guy comes on the line again. 'Samantha, I'm not sure it's possible.'

I feel a slam of disbelief. 'Right.' I try to smile; to sound natural, as though this is no big deal. 'Well, never mind. It doesn't matter.'

'Charlotte's very busy right now . . . we're having some work done to the bedrooms . . . it's just not a good time . . .'

He sounds halting, as if he wants to get off the line. And suddenly it hits me. This isn't about Charlotte. This is all just a big excuse. He doesn't want to be near me. It's as though my disgrace is contagious; as though his career might get blighted, too.

Yesterday I was his best friend. Yesterday, when I was about to become a partner, he was hanging around my desk, full of smiles and quips. And today he doesn't want to know.

I know I should stay quiet, keep my dignity, but I just can't contain myself. 'You don't want to be associated with me, do you?' I burst out.

'Samantha!' His voice is defensive. 'Don't be ridiculous.'

'I'm still the same *person*. I thought you were my friend, Guy.'

'I am your friend! But you can't expect me to . . . I have Charlotte to consider . . . we don't have that much space . . . Look, call me in a couple of days, maybe we can meet up for a drink . . .'

'Really, don't worry.' I try to control my voice. 'I'm sorry to have bothered you.'

'Wait!' he exclaims. 'Don't go! What are you going to do?'

'Oh, Guy.' I manage a little laugh. 'Like you really care.'

I switch off my phone, light-headed with disbelief. Everything's changed. Or maybe he hasn't changed. Maybe this is what Guy was always like and I just never realized it.

I stare down at the tiny display of my phone, breathing hard, watching the seconds tick by. Wondering what to do next. When it suddenly vibrates in my hand, I nearly jump out of my skin. *Tennyson*, my display reads.

Mum.

I feel a clutch of apprehension inside. I guess she's heard. I guess I should have known this was coming. I could go and stay with her, it occurs to me. How weird. I didn't even think of that before. I open up the phone and take a deep breath.

'Hi, Mum.'

'Samantha.' Her voice pierces my ear with no preamble. 'How long were you going to leave it exactly

117

before you told me about your debacle? I have to find out about my own daughter's disgrace from an *Internet joke*.' She utters the words with revulsion.

'An Internet joke?' I echo faintly. 'What do you mean?'

'You didn't know? Apparently in certain legal circles the new term for fifty million pounds is "a Samantha". Take it from me, I was not amused.'

'Mum, I'm so sorry—'

'At least the story has been contained within the legal world. I've spoken to Carter Spink and they assure me that it won't be going further. You should be grateful for that.'

'I . . . I suppose so.'

'Where are you?' She cuts across my faltering words. 'Where are you right now?'

I'm standing in a larder, surrounded by packets of cereal.

'I'm . . . at someone's house. Out of London.'

'And what are your plans?'

'I don't know.' I rub my face. 'I need to . . . get myself together. Find a job.'

'A job,' she says scathingly. 'You think any top law firm is going to touch you now?'

I flinch at her tone. 'I . . . I don't know. Mum, I've only just heard about being fired. I can't just—'

'You can. Thankfully, I have acted for you.'

She's *acted* for me?

'What do you—'

'I've called in all my favours. It wasn't an easy job. But the senior partner at Fortescues will see you tomorrow at ten.'

I stare at the phone in disbelief.

'You've organized me a job interview?'

'Assuming all goes well, you will enter at senior associate level.' Her voice is crisp. 'You're being given this chance as a personal favour to me. As you can imagine, there are . . . reservations. So if you want to progress, Samantha, you are going to have to perform. You're going to have to give this job every hour you have.'

'Right.' I shut my eyes, my thoughts whirling. I have a job interview. A fresh start. It's the solution to my nightmare.

Why don't I feel more relieved? More happy?

'You will have to give more than you did at Carter Spink,' Mum continues in my ear. 'No slacking. No complacency. You will have to prove yourself *doubly*. Do you understand?'

'Yes,' I say automatically.

More hours. More work. More late nights.

It's almost as if I can feel the concrete blocks being loaded on to me again. More and more of them. Heavier and heavier.

'I mean, no,' I hear myself saying. 'No. I don't want that. I don't want it. I can't . . . it's too much . . .'

The words come out of my mouth all by themselves. I wasn't planning them; I've never even thought them before. But now they're out in the air they somehow feel . . . true.

'I'm *sorry*?' Mum's voice is sharp. 'Samantha, what on earth are you saying?'

'I don't know.' I'm kneading my forehead, trying to make sense of my own confusion. 'I was thinking . . . I could take a break, maybe.'

'A break would finish your legal career.' Her voice snaps dismissively. '*Finish* it.'

'I could do something else.'

'You wouldn't last more than two minutes in anything else!' She sounds affronted. 'Samantha, you're a *lawyer*. You've been trained as a *lawyer*.'

119

'There are other things in the world than being a lawyer!' I cry, rattled.

There's an ominous silence.

'Samantha, if you're having some kind of break-down—'

'I'm not!' My voice rises in distress. 'Just because I question my life, it doesn't mean I'm having a break-down! I never *asked* you to find me another job. I don't know what I want. I need a bit of time to . . . to think.'

'You will be at that job interview, Samantha.' Mum's voice is like a whip. 'You will be there tomorrow at ten o'clock.'

'I won't!'

'Tell me where you are! I'm sending a car straight away.'

'No! Leave me alone.'

I switch off my phone, come out of the larder and almost savagely throw it down onto the table. My face is burning. Tears are pressing hotly at the back of my eyes. The phone starts vibrating angrily on the table but I ignore it. I'm not going to answer it. I'm not going to talk to anyone. I'm going to have a drink. And then I'm going to cook this bloody dinner.

I slosh some white wine into a glass and take several gulps. Then I address myself to the pile of raw ingredients waiting on the table.

I can cook. I can cook this stuff. Even if everything else in my life is in ruins, I can do this. I have a brain, I can work it out.

Without delay I rip the plastic covering off the lamb. This can go in the oven. In some kind of dish. Simple. And the chick peas can go in there too. Then I'll mash them and that will make the houmous.

I open a cupboard and pull out a whole load of gleaming baking dishes and trays. I select a baking tray

120

and scatter the chick peas onto it. Some bounce onto the floor but I don't care. I grab a bottle of oil from the counter and drizzle it over the top. Already I'm feeling like a cook.

I shove the tray into the oven and turn it on full blast. Then I plonk the lamb in an oval dish and shove that in too.

So far so good. Now all I need to do is leaf through all Trish's recipe books and find instructions for seared foie gras with an apricot glaze.

OK, there wasn't a single recipe for seared foie gras with an apricot glaze. The closest I've found is one for apricot and raspberry flan. Maybe I can amend it.

'Rub fat into flour till it produces breadcrumbs,' I read.

That makes no sense, for a start. Breadcrumbs? Out of butter and flour?

I stare at the page blindly, my mind in turmoil. I have just turned down what may be my only opportunity to start over. I don't even understand why I did it. I'm a lawyer. That's what I *am*. What else am I going to do? What's happened to me?

Oh God. Why is smoke coming out of the oven?

By seven o'clock I'm still cooking.

At least I think that's what I'm doing. Both ovens are roaring with heat. Pots are bubbling on the hob. The electric whisk is whirring busily. I've burnt my right hand twice, taking things out of the oven. Eight recipe books are open around the kitchen, one drenched in spilled oil and another in egg yolk. I'm puce in the face, sweating hard, and trying every so often to run my hand under cold water.

I've been going for three hours. And I haven't yet

made anything that could actually be eaten. So far I've discarded a collapsed chocolate soufflé, two pans of burnt onions, and a saucepan of congealed apricots that made me feel sick just to look at them.

I can't work out what's going wrong. I haven't got *time* to work out what's going wrong. There's no scope for analysis. Every time there's a disaster I just dump it and start again.

The Geigers, meanwhile, have no idea. They're drinking sherry in the drawing room. They think everything is going splendidly. Trish tried to come into the kitchen about half an hour ago but I managed to head her off.

In less than an hour she and Eddie are going to be sitting down at the table expecting a gourmet meal. Shaking out their napkins with anticipation; pouring out their mineral water.

A kind of frenzied hysteria has come over me. I know I cannot do this. But somehow I can't give up either. I keep thinking a miracle will happen. I'll pull it all together. I'll manage it somehow—

Oh God, the gravy's bubbling over.

I shove the oven door shut, grab a spoon and start stirring it. It looks like revolting lumpy brown water. Frantically I start searching in the cupboards for something to chuck in. Flour. Cornflour. Something like that. This'll do. I grab a small pot and shake in vigorous amounts of the white powder, then wipe the sweat off my brow. OK. What now?

Suddenly I remember the egg whites, still whisking up in the food mixer. I grab the recipe book, running my finger down the page. I changed the dessert course to pavlova after I chanced upon the line in a recipe book: 'Meringues are so easy to make.'

So far so good. What next? 'Form the stiff meringue

mixture into a large circle on your baking parchment.'

I peer at my bowl. *Stiff* meringue mixture? Mine's liquid.

It has to be right, I tell myself feverishly. It has to be. I followed the instructions. Maybe it's thicker than it looks. Maybe once I start pouring it out, it'll stiffen up by some weird culinary law of physics.

Slowly I start to pour it onto the tray.

It doesn't stiffen up. It spreads in a white oozing lake and starts dripping off the tray onto the floor in big splodges.

Something tells me this is not going to make White Chocolate Pavlova for eight.

A splodge lands on my foot and I give a frustrated cry. I feel near tears. Why didn't it work? I followed the sodding recipe and everything. A pent-up rage is rising up inside me: rage at myself, at my defective crappy egg whites, at cookery books, at cooks, at food . . . And most of all at whoever wrote that meringues were 'so easy to make'.

'They're not!' I hear myself yelling. 'They're bloody not!' I hurl the book across the kitchen, where it smashes against the kitchen door.

'What the hell—' a male voice exclaims in surprise.

The next minute the door flies open and Nathaniel is standing there, his legs like tree trunks in jeans, his hair glinting in the evening sun. A rucksack is hefted over his shoulder; he looks like he's on his way home. 'Is everything OK?'

'It's fine,' I say, rattled. 'Everything's fine. Thank you. Thank you so much.' I make a dismissive motion with my hand, but he doesn't move.

'I heard you were cooking a gourmet dinner tonight,' he says slowly, looking around at the mess.

'Yes. That's right. I'm just in the . . . most complex

stage of the . . . um . . .' I glance down at the hob, and give an involuntary scream. 'Fuck! The gravy!'

I don't know what's happened. Brown bubbles are expanding out of my gravy saucepan, all over the cooker and down the sides onto the floor. It looks like the porringer in the story of the magic pot that wouldn't stop making porridge.

'Get it off the heat, for God's sake!' exclaims Nathaniel. He snatches up the pan and moves it. 'What on earth is in that?'

'Nothing!' I say. 'Just the usual ingredients . . .'

Nathaniel has noticed the little pot on the counter. He grabs it and stares at it incredulously. '*Baking soda?* You put baking soda in gravy? Is that what they taught you at—' He breaks off and sniffs the air. 'Hang on. Is something burning?'

I watch helplessly as he opens the bottom oven, grabs an oven glove with a practised air and hauls out a baking tray covered in what look like tiny black bullets.

My chick peas. I forgot all about them.

'What are *these* supposed to be?' he says incredulously. 'Rabbit droppings?'

'They're chick peas,' I retort. My cheeks are flaming but I lift my chin, trying to regain some kind of dignity. 'I drizzled them in olive oil and put them in the oven so they could . . . melt.'

Nathaniel stares at me. '*Melt?*'

'Soften,' I amend hurriedly.

Nathaniel puts down the tray and folds his arms.

'Do you know *anything* about cooking?' he says.

Before I can answer there's the most almighty BANG from the microwave.

'Oh my God!' I shriek in terror. 'Oh my *God*! What was that?'

Nathaniel is peering through the glass door. 'What the hell was in there?' he demands. 'Something's exploded.'

My mind races frantically. What on earth did I put in the microwave? It's all a blur.

'The eggs!' I suddenly remember. 'I was hardboiling the eggs for the canapés.'

'In the *microwave*?' he expostulates.

'To save time!' I practically yell back. 'I was being efficient!'

Nathaniel yanks the plug of the microwave from the wall socket and turns round, his face working with disbelief. 'You know bugger all about cooking! This is all a bluff! You're not a housekeeper. I don't know what the hell you're up to—'

'I'm not up to anything!' I reply, in shock.

'The Geigers are good people.' He faces me square on. 'I won't have them exploited.'

He suddenly looks really aggressive. Oh God. What does he think? That I'm some kind of confidence trickster?

'Look . . . please.' I rub my sweaty face. 'I'm not trying to rip anyone off. OK, I can't cook. But I ended up here because of . . . a misunderstanding.'

'A misunderstanding?' He gives a suspicious frown.

'Yes,' I say, a little more sharply than I meant to. I sink down onto a chair and massage my aching lower back. I hadn't realized how exhausted I was. 'I was running away from . . . something. I needed a place to stay for the night. The Geigers assumed I was a housekeeper. And then next morning I felt bad. I thought I'd do the job for a morning. But I'm not planning to stay. And I won't take any money from them, if that's what you're thinking.'

There's silence. At last I look up. Nathaniel is

leaning against the counter, his huge arms folded. His wary frown has eased a little. He reaches into his rucksack and takes out a bottle of beer. He offers it to me and I shake my head.

'What were you running from?' he says, cracking the bottle open.

I feel a painful wrench inside. I cannot face telling the whole dreadful story.

'It was . . . a situation.' I look down.

He takes a slug of beer. 'A bad relationship?'

For a moment I'm silenced. I think back over all my years at Carter Spink. All the hours I gave them; everything I sacrificed. Finished in a three-minute phone call.

'Yes,' I say slowly. 'A bad relationship.'

'How long were you in it?'

'Seven years.' To my horror I can feel tears seeping out of the corners of my eyes. I have no idea where they came out of the corners of my eyes. I have no idea where they came from. 'I'm sorry,' I gulp. 'It's been quite a stressful day.'

Nathaniel tears off a square of kitchen towel from the wallmounted roll behind him, and hands it to me.

'If it was a bad relationship, you're well out of it,' he says calmly. 'No point staying. No point looking back.'

'You're right.' I wipe my eyes. 'Yes. I just have to decide what to do with my life. I can't stay here.' I reach for the bottle of Creme de Menthe which was supposed to go in the mint-chocolate soufflé, pour some into a handy egg cup and take a gulp.

'The Geigers are good employers,' says Nathaniel with a tiny shrug. 'You could do worse.'

'Yeah.' I raise a half-smile. 'Unfortunately I can't cook.'

He puts his bottle of beer down and wipes his mouth. His hands look scrubbed clean, but I can still see the traces of earth ingrained around his nails; in the seams of his weatherbeaten skin.

'I could speak to my mum. She can cook. She could teach you the basics.'

I look at him in astonishment, almost laughing. 'You think I should *stay*? I thought I was supposed to be a confidence trickster.' I shake my head, wincing at the taste of the Creme de Menthe. 'I have to go.'

'Shame.' He shrugs. 'It would have been nice to have someone around who speaks English. And makes such great sandwiches,' he adds, totally deadpan.

I can't help smiling back. 'Caterers.'

'Ah. I wondered.'

A faint rapping at the door makes us both look up.

'Samantha?' Trish's voice outside is hushed and urgent. 'Can you hear me?'

'Er . . . yes?' I call back, my voice a little strangled.

'Don't worry, I won't come in. I don't want to disturb anything! You're probably at a very *crucial* stage.'

'Kind of . . .'

I catch Nathaniel's eye and a sudden wave of hysteria rises through me.

'I just wanted to ask,' Trish continues, 'if you will be serving any kind of *sorbet* between the courses?'

I look at Nathaniel. His shoulders are shaking with silent laughter. I can't stop a tiny snort escaping. I clamp my hand desperately over my mouth, trying to get control of myself.

'Samantha?'

'Er . . . no,' I manage at last. 'There won't be any sorbet.'

Nathaniel has picked up one of my pans of burnt onions. He mimes taking a spoonful and eating it. *Yummy*, he mouths. Tears are streaming from my eyes. I'm almost asphyxiating, trying to keep quiet.

'Well! See you later!'

Trish tip-taps away and I collapse into helpless laughter. I've never laughed so hard in my life. My ribs hurt; I'm coughing; I almost feel like I'll be sick.

At last I somehow calm down, wipe my eyes and blow my runny nose. Nathaniel's stopped laughing too, and is looking around the bombshelled kitchen.

'Seriously,' he says, 'what are you going to do about this? They're expecting a fancy dinner.'

'I know.' I feel a fresh wave of hysteria and fight it down. 'I know they are. I'll just have to . . . think of something.'

There's silence in the kitchen. I can see Nathaniel curiously eyeing the white splodges of meringue on the floor.

'OK.' I exhale with a little shudder and push back my damp hair. 'I'm going to rescue the situation.'

'You're going to rescue the situation.' He looks disbelieving.

'In fact I think this might solve everyone's problems.' I get to my feet and start busily sweeping packets into the bin. 'First I need to clear up the kitchen a bit . . .'

'I'll help.' Nathaniel stands up. 'This I have to see.'

Companionably, we empty pans and pots and packets into the bin. I scrub all the smeared surfaces while Nathaniel mops up the meringue.

'How long have you worked here?' I ask as he rinses out the mop in the sink.

'Three years. I worked for the people who lived here before the Geigers, the Ellises. Then Trish and Eddie moved in a couple of years ago and kept me on.'

I digest this. 'Why did the Ellises move? It's such a beautiful house.'

'The Geigers made them an offer they couldn't refuse.' Nathaniel's mouth is twitching with . . . is that *amusement*?

'What?' I say, intrigued. 'What happened?'

'Well . . .' He puts the mop down. 'It was fairly comical. The house was used as a location in a BBC period drama. Two weeks after it was aired, Trish and Eddie arrived on the doorstep waving a cheque. They'd seen it on television, decided they wanted it and tracked it down.'

'Wow.' I laugh. 'So presumably they paid over the odds.'

'God knows what they paid. The Ellises would never say.'

'Do you know how the Geigers made all their money?' I know I'm being nosy, but it's nice to delve into someone else's life for a moment. Forget about my own.

'They built up a road-haulage company from nothing and sold it off. Made a packet.' He starts mopping up the final patch of meringue.

'And how about you? Before the Ellises?' I tip the congealed apricots down the waste disposal with a shudder.

'I was working at Marchant House,' Nathaniel replies. 'It's a stately home, near Oxford. Before that, university.'

'University?' I say, my ears pricking up. 'I didn't know—'

I halt, reddening. I was about to say 'I didn't know gardeners went to university.'

'I did natural sciences.' Nathaniel gives me a look which makes me think he knew exactly what I was thinking.

I open my mouth to ask him where and when he

was at university – then on second thoughts, close it and switch the waste disposal on. I don't want to start getting into details, going down the 'Do we know anyone in common?' road. Right now, I could do without remembering the particulars of my life.

At last the kitchen looks a bit more normal. I pick up the egg cup, drain the rest of the Creme de Menthe and take a deep breath.

'OK. Show time.'

'Good luck.' Nathaniel raises his eyebrows.

I open the kitchen door to see Trish and Eddie loitering in the hall, holding their sherry glasses.

'Ah, Samantha! Everything ready?' Trish's face is all lit up with anticipation, and I feel a huge twinge of guilt for what I'm about to do.

But I can't see any other way.

I take a deep breath and put on my best breaking-bad-news-to-a-client face. 'Mr and Mrs Geiger,' I look from one face to the other, making sure I have their attention, 'I am devastated.'

I close my eyes and shake my head.

'Devastated?' echoes Trish nervously.

'I have done my best.' I open my eyes. 'But I'm afraid I cannot work with your equipment. The dinner I created was not up to my own professional standards. I could not allow it out of the kitchen. I will of course reimburse all your costs – and offer my resignation. I will leave in the morning.'

There. Done. And no casualties.

I can't help glancing at Nathaniel, standing in the doorway of the kitchen. He shakes his head with a tiny smile, and gives me the thumbs up.

'*Leave?*' Trish stares at me in consternation, her blue eyes practically bulging out of their sockets. 'You can't leave! You're the best housekeeper we've ever had! Eddie, *do* something!'

'Mrs Geiger, after tonight's performance, I feel I have no choice,' I say. 'To be frank, the dinner was inedible.'

'That wasn't your fault!' she says wildly. 'It was *our* fault! We'll order you new equipment at once.'

'But—'

'Just give us a list of what you need. Spare no expense! And we'll give you a pay rise!' She's suddenly gripped by a new idea. 'How much do you want? Name your price!'

This conversation is really not going the way I planned.

'Well . . . we never actually discussed pay . . .' I look down, a little embarrassed.

'*Eddie!*' Trish rounds on him savagely. 'This is *your* fault! Samantha's leaving because you're not paying her enough!'

'I didn't say that—' I begin helplessly.

'And she needs new kitchen pots and pans. From the best place.' She digs Eddie in the ribs with her elbow and mutters, 'Say something!'

'Ah . . . Samantha.' Eddie clears his throat awkwardly. 'We'd be very happy if you would consider staying with us. We've been delighted with your performance and whatever your salary expectations are . . . we'll match them.' Trish digs him in the ribs again. 'Exceed them.'

'And healthcare,' adds Trish.

They're both gazing at me with a kind of eager hope.

I glance over at Nathaniel, who cocks his head as though to say 'Why not?'

The strangest feeling is coming over me. Three people. All telling me they want me within the space of ten minutes.

I could stay. It's as simple as that.

I can't cook, a little voice reminds me. *I can't clean. I'm not a housekeeper.*

But I could learn. I could learn it all.

The silence is growing in tension. Even Nathaniel is watching me closely from the door.

'Well . . . OK.' I feel a smile coming to my lips. 'OK. If you want me to . . . I'll stay.'

Later that night, after we've all eaten a Chinese take-away, I take out my mobile phone, call my mother's office and wait till I'm put through to voicemail.

'It's all right, Mum,' I say. 'You don't need to call in any favours. I've got a job.' And I put the phone down.

It's like a string has been cut.

I feel free.

TEN

The only thing is, now I actually have to be a housekeeper.

The next morning I set my alarm early and arrive downstairs in the kitchen before seven, in my overall. The garden is misty and there are no sounds, except a couple of magpies chacking at each other on the lawn. I feel as though I'm the only person awake in the world.

As quietly as I can I empty the dishwasher and put everything away in the cupboards. I straighten the chairs under the table. I make a cup of coffee. Then I look around at the gleaming granite counters.

My domain.

It doesn't feel like my domain. It feels like someone else's scary kitchen.

So . . . what do I do now? I feel twitchy, just standing here. I should be occupied. My gaze falls on an old copy of the *Economist* in the magazine rack by the table and I pick it up. I flip through, and start reading an interesting piece on international monetary controls, sipping my coffee.

Then, as I hear a sound from upstairs, I hastily put

it down again. Housekeepers aren't supposed to read articles on international monetary controls. I should be bustling around, making jam or something.

Except there's already a cupboard full of jam. And I don't know how to make it anyway.

What else? What do housekeepers *do* all day? As I survey the kitchen again it looks perfectly clean to me. I could get the breakfast, it occurs to me. But not until I know what they want . . .

Then all of a sudden I remember yesterday morning. Trish made me a cup of tea.

Maybe today I'm supposed to make *her* a cup of tea! Maybe they're waiting upstairs, tapping their fingers impatiently, saying 'Where's the damn tea?'

Quickly I boil the kettle and make a teapot full. I put it on a tray with cups and saucers and, after a moment's thought, add a couple of biscuits. Then I head upstairs, venture along the silent corridor to Trish and Eddie's bedroom . . . and stop outside the door.

Now what?

What if they're asleep and I wake them up?

I'll knock quietly, I decide. Yes. A short, discreet, housekeeperly knock.

I lift a hand to knock – but the tray's too heavy to hold in one hand and there's an alarming chinking as the whole thing starts tilting sideways. In horror, I grab it just before the teapot slides off. Sweating, I put the whole lot on the ground, raise a hand and knock very quietly, then pick up the tray again.

There's no answer. What do I do now?

Hesitantly I tap again.

'Eddie! Stop that!' Trish's raised voice filters faintly through the door.

Oh God. Why can't they hear me?

I'm hot all over. This tray is bloody heavy. I can't stand outside their room with a cup of tea all morning. Shall I just retreat?

I'm about to turn round and creep away. Then determination comes over me. No. Don't be so feeble. I've made the tea and I'll give it to them. Or at least I'll offer it to them. They can always tell me to go away.

I grip the tray tightly and bang the corner hard against the door. They *have* to have heard that.

After a moment, Trish's voice rises up. 'Come in!'

I feel a swell of relief. It's fine. They're expecting me. I knew they would be. Somehow I turn the door knob whilst balancing the tray against the door. I push the door open and walk into the room.

Trish looks up from the bed, where she's sprawled on the pillows, alone. She's wearing a silky nightie, her hair is dishevelled and make-up is smudged about her eyes. For a moment she looks startled to see me.

'Samantha,' she says sharply. 'What do you want? Is everything all right?'

I have an immediate, horrible feeling I've done the wrong thing. My gaze doesn't move from hers, but my peripheral vision starts to register a few details in the room. I can see a book called *Sensual Enjoyment* on the floor. And a bottle of musk-scented massage oil. And . . .

A well-worn copy of *The Joy of Sex*. Right by the bed. Open at 'Turkish Style'.

OK. So they weren't expecting tea.

I swallow, trying to keep my composure, desperately pretending I haven't seen anything.

'I . . . brought you a cup of tea,' I say, my voice cracking with nerves. 'I thought you might . . . like one.'

Do not look at *The Joy of Sex*. Keep your eyes *up*.

Trish's face relaxes.

'Samantha! You treasure! Put it down!' She waves an arm vaguely at the bedside table.

I'm just starting to move towards it when the bathroom door opens and Eddie emerges, naked except for a pair of too-tight boxer shorts, displaying a quite staggeringly hairy chest.

Jesus.

Somehow I manage not to drop the entire tray on the floor.

'I'm . . . I'm sorry,' I stammer, backing away. 'I didn't realize . . .'

'Don't be silly! Come *in*!' exclaims Trish gaily, who now seems completely reconciled to me being in her bedroom. 'We're not *prudish*.'

OK, I'm really wishing they were. Cautiously I edge towards the bed, stepping over a mauve lace bra. I find a place for the tray on Trish's bedside cabinet by pushing aside a photo of her and Eddie sitting in a jacuzzi, holding up glasses of champagne.

I pour out the tea as fast as I can and hand a cup to each of them. I cannot look Eddie in the eye. In what other job do you see your boss naked?

Only one other occupation springs immediately to mind. Which isn't that encouraging.

'Well . . . I'll go now,' I mumble, head down.

'Don't rush off!' Trish sips her tea with relish. 'Mmm. Now you're here, I wanted to have a little chat! See where we *are* with things.'

'Er . . . right.' Her nightie is gaping and I can see the edge of her nipple. I hastily look away and find myself catching the eye of the bearded guy in *The Joy of Sex* as he contorts himself.

Without meaning to I have a sudden vision of Trish and Eddie in the exact same position.

No. Stop it.

I can feel my face flaming with embarrassment. What kind of surreal weirdness is this, that I am standing in the bedroom of two people, pretty much strangers to me, being practically *shown* how they have sex? And they don't seem remotely bothered . . .

And then it comes to me. Of course. I'm staff. I don't count.

'So, is everything all right, Samantha?' Trish puts her cup down and gives me a beady look. 'You've got your routine sorted? All under control?'

'Absolutely.' I grope for a competent-sounding phrase. 'I'm pretty much . . . on top of everything.' Aaargh. 'I mean . . . getting to grips with it all.'

Aaaargh.

'Good!' she exclaims. 'I knew it! You don't need mollycoddling! You know your way around a house!'

'I should say so!'

Trish beams back and takes a sip of tea. 'I expect you'll be tackling the laundry today.'

The laundry. I hadn't even thought about the laundry.

'Only I'd like you to change the sheets when you make the beds,' she adds.

Make the beds?

That hadn't occurred to me either.

I feel a twinge of slight panic. Not only am I not remotely 'on top of everything', I don't have a clue what 'everything' is.

'Obviously I have my own . . . er . . . established routine,' I say, trying to sound casual. 'But it might be an idea if you give me a list of duties.'

'Oh.' Trish looks a little irritated. 'Well, if you really think you need it.'

'And I, Samantha, must go through your terms and

137

conditions later on,' says Eddie. He's standing in front of the mirror, holding a dumb-bell. 'Let you know what you've got yourself into.' He guffaws, then with a slight grunt lifts the weight above his head. His stomach is rippling with the effort. And not in a good way.

'So . . . I'll get on with . . . things.' I start backing towards the door, my eyes fixed on the floor.

'See you later, then, at breakfast.' Trish gives me a cheery little wave from the bed. 'Ciao ciao!'

I cannot keep up with Trish's mood shifts. We seem to have lurched straight from employer–employee to people-enjoying-a-luxury-cruise-together.

'Er . . . bye then!' I say, matching her chirpy tone. I bob a curtsey, step over her bra again and exit the room as quickly as I can.

Breakfast is a bit of a nightmare. It takes me three failed attempts before I realize how you're supposed to cut a grapefruit in half. You'd think they'd make it clearer. They could draw guidelines round them, or have perforations, or something. Meanwhile the milk for the coffee boils over – and when I plunge down the cafetière, the coffee explodes everywhere. Luckily Trish and Eddie are so busy arguing about where to go on their next holiday, they don't seem to notice what's going on in the kitchen. Or hear my shrieks.

On the plus side, I really think I'm getting the hang of the toaster.

When they've finished, I stack the dirty dishes in the dishwasher and am desperately trying to remember how I made it work yesterday, when Trish comes into the kitchen.

'Samantha, Mr Geiger would like to see you in his study,' she says. 'To discuss your pay and conditions. Don't keep him waiting!'

138

'Er . . . very good, Madam.' I curtsey, then smooth down my uniform and head out into the hall. I approach the door of Eddie's study and knock twice.

'Come in!' comes a jovial voice. As I walk in, Eddie is sitting behind his desk: a huge affair of mahogany and tooled leather with an expensive-looking laptop. He's fully clothed by now, thank God, in tan trousers and a sports shirt, and the whole room smells of aftershave.

'Ah, Samantha. Ready for our little meeting?' Eddie gestures to an upright wooden chair and I sit down. 'Here we are! The document you've been waiting for!'

With a self-important air he hands me a folder marked HOUSEKEEPER'S CONTRACT. I open it up to find a title sheet on cream vellum paper printed to look like an old scroll. Printed in an ornate, medieval-style font are the words

CONTRACT OF AGREEMENT
Between Samantha Sweeting and
Mr and Mrs Edward Geiger,
this 2nd day of July in the year of our Lord
two thousand and four.

'Wow,' I say in surprise. 'Did a . . . lawyer draw this up?'

I cannot imagine any lawyer I know drawing up a contract in Disney-medieval lettering. Let alone putting it all in a fake scroll.

'I didn't need a lawyer.' Eddie chuckles knowingly. 'I'm not playing at that game. Charge you an arm and a leg, those guys will, just for a bit of fancy Latin. Take it from me, Samantha, these things are simple enough to draw up if you've half a brain.' He gives me a wink.

'I'm sure you're right,' I say at last. I turn over

139

the title sheet and run my eyes down the printed clauses.

Oh my God. What *is* this gibberish? I have to bite my lip as I take in phrases here and there.

. . . Samantha Sweeting (to be known hereafter as the PLAINTIFF) . . .

The plaintiff? Does he even know what a plaintiff is?

. . . Insofar, notwithstanding the provision of culinary services, in a manner which shall be deemed, prima facie, to include yet not exclude light snacks and beverages . . .

My lips are clamped together. I must not laugh.

Pursuant to the aforetaining, ipso facto, all parties will retain the aforementioned rights beyond reasonable doubt.

What? *What?*

The whole thing is a total nonsensical mish-mash. Bits of legal jargon soldered together in meaningless, would-be-impressive phrases. I scan the rest of the page, desperately keeping a straight face, trying to think of a suitable response.

'Now, I know it looks frightening!' says Eddie, mis-interpreting my silence. 'But don't be intimidated by all these long words. It's quite simple, really! Did you have a chance to look at the pay?'

My eye flicks to the figure quoted in bold under 'Weekly Salary'. It's slightly less than I charged per hour as a lawyer.

'It seems extremely generous,' I say after a pause. 'Thank you very much, Sir.'

'Is there anything you don't understand?' He beams jovially. 'Just say!'

Where do I start?

'Um . . . this bit.' I point to *Clause 7: Hours.* 'Does this mean I have the whole weekend off? Every weekend?'

'Of course.' Eddie seems surprised. 'We wouldn't expect you to give up your weekends! Unless it's a special occasion, in which case we'll pay you extra . . . you'll see in Clause 9 . . .'

I'm not listening. Every weekend free. I can't get my head around this idea. I don't think I've had a totally free weekend since I was about twelve.

'That's great.' I look up, unable to stop myself smiling. 'Thanks very much!'

'Didn't your previous employers give you weekends off?' Eddie looks taken aback.

'Well, no,' I say truthfully. 'Not really.'

'They sound like slave-drivers! You'll find us far more reasonable!' He beams. 'Now, I'll leave you alone for a while to study the agreement before you sign.'

'I've pretty much read it—' I halt as Eddie raises a hand in reproof.

'Samantha, Samantha, Samantha,' he says in avuncular tones, shaking his head. 'I'm going to give you a little tip which will stand you in good stead in life. Always read legal documents *very carefully.*'

I stare back at him for a few moments, my nose twitching with the effort of staying deadpan.

'Yes, Sir,' I say at last. 'I'll try to remember that.'

As Eddie disappears from the room, I look down at the contract again, rolling my eyes. I pick up a pencil and automatically start correcting the text, rephrasing, scoring out and adding queries in the margin.

Then, abruptly I stop myself.

What the hell am I doing?

I grab a rubber and hastily erase all my amendments. I reach for a biro and turn to the bottom of the
page, where a cartoon owl in lawyer's garb is pointing
to a dotted line.

Name: Samantha Sweeting.
Occupation:

I hesitate for a moment, then put 'Domestic Help'.

As I write the words I have a fleeting blink of
incredulity. I'm really doing this. I'm really taking this
job, miles away from my former life in every sense.
And no one knows what I'm doing.

I have a sudden flash on my mother's face, on the
expression she'd have if she knew where I was right
now . . . if she could see me in my uniform . . . She
would *flip*. I'm almost tempted to call her up and tell
her what I'm doing.

But I'm not going to. And I haven't got time to think
about it. I have laundry to do.

It takes me two trips to bring down all the washing to
the laundry room. I dump the overflowing baskets
on the tiled floor and look at the hi-tech washing
machine. This should be simple enough.

I'm not exactly experienced in this area. At home I
send everything except underwear to the dry-cleaners.
But that doesn't mean I *can't* do it. It's just a question
of using my brain. Experimentally I open the door of
the machine and at once an electronic display starts
flashing at me. WASH? WASH?

Immediately I feel flustered. *Obviously* I want you
to wash, I feel like snapping back. Just give me a
chance to get the bloody clothes in.

142

I take a deep breath. Stay calm. One thing at a time. First step: fill the machine. I pick up a bundle of clothes – then stop myself.

No. First step: sort the clothes. Feeling pleased with myself for having thought of this, I start sorting out the dirty clothes into piles on the floor, consulting the labels as I go.

Whites 40.

Whites 90.

Wash inside out.

Wash colours separately.

Wash with care.

Wash with GREAT CARE.

By the end of the first basket I'm totally bewildered. I've made about twenty different piles on the floor, most consisting of only one item. This is ridiculous. I can't put on twenty washes. It'll take all week.

What am I supposed to do? How am I supposed to make sense of all this? Frustration is rising inside me. And slight panic. I've been in here for fifteen minutes now, and I haven't even started.

OK ... let's just be rational. People do washing every day, all over the world. It cannot be that hard. I'll just have to mix and match a bit.

I pick up a bundle of clothes from the floor and shove it into the drum. Then I open a nearby cupboard and find myself gazing at a whole array of washing powders. Which one? My mind is teeming with words familiar only from TV ads. *Spotless whites. Whiter-than-white. Non-biological. Washing machines last longer with Calgon.*

I don't want this washing machine to last longer. I just want it to wash the bloody clothes.

At last I grab a packet covered in pictures of white T-shirts, shake some powder into the little tray at the top and some into the drum for good measure. I close the door firmly. Now what?

WASH? the machine is still flashing at me. WASH?

'Er . . . yes!' I say. 'Wash them.' I jab randomly at a button.

ENTER PROGRAM? it flashes back.

Program?

My eyes dart about for clues and I spot a manual tucked behind a spray bottle. I grab it and start leafing through.

The half-load option for small washes is only available for pre-wash programs A3–E2 and super rinse programs G2–L7 not including H4.

What?

Come on. I have a degree from Cambridge. I know Latin, for God's sake. I can work this out. I flip to another page.

Programs E5 and F1 exclude spin cycle UNLESS button 'S' is depressed for five seconds before commencing OR ten seconds during program in case of E5 (non-wool).

I can't cope. My exam on international corporate litigation was a million times easier than this. OK, let's forget the manual. Let's just use common sense. I briskly press at the key pad in my best competent-housekeeper manner.

PROGRAM K3? the machine flashes at me. PROGRAM K3?

I don't like the sound of program K3. It sounds sinister. Like a cliff-face or secret government plot.

'No,' I say aloud, jabbing at the machine. 'I want something else.'

YOU HAVE CHOSEN PROGRAM K3 it flashes back.

'But I don't want program K3!' I say, flustered. 'Give me something else!' I'm pressing all the buttons, but it's ignoring me. I can hear water surging into the machine, and a green light comes on.

K3 COMMENCING, flashes the display. HEAVY DUTY UPHOLSTERY PROGRAM.

Heavy duty? *Upholstery?*

'Stop it,' I say under my breath, and start banging all the buttons. 'Stop!' I kick the machine in desperation. '*Stop!*'

'Everything all right?' comes Trish's voice from the kitchen and I leap away from the machine, smoothing my hair down.

'Er . . . fine! Fine!' I plaster on a professional smile as she appears at the door. 'Just . . . getting some washing on.'

'Well done.' She holds out a stripy shirt to me. 'Now, Mr Geiger needs a button sewn on this shirt, if you would be so kind . . .'

'Absolutely!' I take it from her with an inward gulp.

'And here's your list of duties!' She hands me a sheet of paper. 'It's by no means complete, but it should get you *started . . .*'

As I run my eyes down the endless list, I feel a bit faint.

Make beds . . . sweep and clean front steps . . . arrange flowers . . . polish all mirrors . . . store cupboards tidy . . . laundry . . . clean bathrooms daily . . .

'Now there's nothing here that should present you with a problem, is there?' adds Trish.

'Er . . . no!' My voice is a little strangled. 'No, it should all be fine!'

'But make a stab at the ironing *first*,' she continues firmly. 'There is quite a lot, I'm afraid, as you'll have seen. It does tend to mount *up* rather . . .' For some reason, Trish is looking upwards. With slight foreboding, I follow her gaze. There, above us, is a mountain of crumpled shirts hanging on a wooden drying rack. At least thirty.

As I stare up at them, I feel wobbly. I can't iron a shirt. I've never used an iron in my life. What am I going to do?

'I expect you'll whip through these in no time!' she adds gaily. 'The ironing board's just there,' she adds with a nod.

'Um, thanks!' I manage.

The important thing is to look convincing. I'll get the ironing board out, wait till she leaves ... then come up with a new plan.

I reach for the ironing board, trying to look matter-of-fact, as if I do this all the time. I tug briskly at one of the metal legs, but it won't move. I try another one with no luck. I'm pulling harder and harder, till I'm hot with the effort, but the bloody thing won't budge. How am I supposed to open it up?

'It's got a catch,' Trish says, watching me in surprise. 'Underneath.'

'Ah. Of course!' I flash her a smile, then grope around, desperately prodding and pressing, until with no warning the whole thing expands into a sliding triangle of legs. It slithers out of my grasp and promptly sinks down to a two-foot height, where it clicks shut.

'Right!' I give a flustered laugh. 'I'll just ... adjust that, then.'

I lift the board up and attempt to slide the legs along – but they won't shift. My cheeks are burning as I grapple endlessly with the board, turning it this way and that. *How the fuck does this thing work?*

'Actually, on second thoughts,' I say casually, 'I quite like a low ironing board. I'll just leave it as it is.'

'You can't iron down *there*!' Trish says with an astonished laugh. 'Just pull the lever! It needs quite a sharp tug . . . I'll show you.'

She takes the board from me, and in two movements has adjusted it to exactly the right height. 'I expect you're used to a different model,' she adds wisely as she clicks it shut. 'They all have their own little tricks.'

'Absolutely!' I say, seizing on this excuse in relief. 'Of course! I'm far more used to working with a . . . a . . . a Nimbus 2000.'

Trish peers at me in surprise. 'Isn't that the broomstick out of Harry Potter?'

Fuck.

I knew I'd heard it somewhere.

'Yes . . . it is,' I say at last, my face flaming. 'And also a well-known ironing board. In fact, I think the broomstick was named . . . er . . . *after* the ironing board.'

'Really?' Trish looks fascinated. 'I never knew that!' To my horror she leans expectantly against the door and lights a cigarette. 'Don't mind me!' she adds, her voice muffled. 'Just carry on!'

Carry on?

'There's the iron,' she adds with a gesture. 'Behind you.'

'Er . . . great! Thanks!' I take the iron and plug it in, as slowly as possible, my heart banging in fright. I cannot do this. I need a way out. But I can't think of one. My brain is totally blank.

'I expect the iron's hot enough now!' says Trish helpfully.

'Right!' I give her a sick smile.

I have no choice. I'm going to have to start ironing. I reach for one of the shirts overhead, and spread it out awkwardly on the ironing board, playing for time. I don't even know where to start.

'Mr Geiger doesn't like his collars *over*-starched,' remarks Trish.

Over-what? My eyes swing around wildly and land on a bottle labelled Spray Starch.

'Right!' I swallow, trying to hide my panic. 'Well, I'll probably . . . come to the starching stage . . . in a minute . . .'

Unable to believe what I'm doing, I pick up the iron. It's far heavier than I imagined and emits a terrifying cloud of steam. Very gingerly, I start lowering it towards the cotton fabric. I have no idea which bit of the shirt I'm aiming for. I think my eyes might be shut.

Suddenly there's a trilling from the kitchen. The phone. Thank God . . . thank God . . . thank God . . .

'Oh, who's *that*?' says Trish, frowning. 'Sorry, Samantha. I should get this . . .'

'That's fine!' My voice is shrill. 'No worries! I'll just get on . . .'

As soon as Trish is out of the room I put the iron down with a crash and bury my head in my hands. I must have been mad. This isn't going to work. I'm not made to be a housekeeper. The iron puffs steam in my face and I give a little scream of fright. I switch it off and collapse against the wall. It's only nine twenty and I'm already a total wreck.

And I thought being a lawyer was stressful.

ELEVEN

By the time Trish comes back into the kitchen I'm a little more composed. I can do this. Of course I can. It's not quantum physics. It's *housework*.

'Samantha, I'm afraid we're going to *desert* you for the day,' says Trish, looking concerned. 'Mr Geiger is off to golf and I'm going to see a *very* dear friend's new Mercedes. Will you be all right on your own?'

'I'll be fine!' I say, trying not to sound too joyful. 'Don't you worry about me. Really. I'll just get on with things . . .'

'Is the ironing done already?' She glances at the laundry room, impressed.

Done? What does she think I am, Wonder Woman?

'Actually, I thought I'd leave the ironing for now and tackle the rest of the house,' I say, trying to sound matter-of-fact. 'That's my normal routine.'

'Absolutely.' She nods vigorously. 'Whatever suits you. Now, I won't be here to answer any questions, I'm afraid, but Nathaniel will!' She beckons out of the door. 'You've met Nathaniel, haven't you?'

'Oh,' I say as he walks in, wearing ripped jeans, his hair dishevelled. 'Er . . . yes. Hi, again.'

This is a bit weird. Seeing him this morning, after all the dramas of last night. As he meets my eye there's just the faintest twitch of a smile at his mouth.

'Hi,' he says. 'How's it going?'

'Great!' I say lightly. 'Really well.'

'Nathaniel knows *all* there is to know about this house,' puts in Trish, who is doing her lipstick. 'So if you can't find anything . . . need to know how a door unlocks or whatever . . . he's your man.'

'I'll bear that in mind,' I say. 'Thanks.'

'But Nathaniel, I don't want you *disturbing* Samantha,' adds Trish, giving him a severe look. 'Obviously she has her own established routine.'

'Obviously,' says Nathaniel, nodding gravely. As Trish turns away he shoots me an amused glance and I feel my colour rise.

What's that supposed to mean? How does he know I don't have a routine? Just because I can't cook, it doesn't follow I can't do *anything*.

'So you'll be OK?' Trish picks up her handbag. 'You've found all the cleaning stuff?'

'Er . . .' I look around uncertainly.

'In the laundry room!' She disappears for a moment, then comes out, holding a gigantic blue tub full of cleaning products, and dumps it on the table. 'There you are! And don't forget your Marigolds!' she adds merrily.

My what?

'Rubber gloves,' says Nathaniel. He takes a huge pink pair out of the tub and hands them to me with a little bow.

'Yes, thank you,' I say with dignity. 'I knew that.'

I have never worn a pair of rubber gloves in my life. Trying not to flinch, I slowly pull them onto my hands.

Oh my God. I've never felt anything quite so squelchy and rubbery and . . . *revolting*. I have to wear these all *day*?

'Toodle-oo!' calls Trish from the hall, and the front door bangs shut.

'Right!' I say. 'Well . . . I'll get on.'

I wait for Nathaniel to leave, but he leans against the table and looks at me quizzically. 'Do you have any idea how to clean a house?'

I'm starting to feel quite insulted here. Do I *look* like someone who can't clean a house?

'Of course I know how to clean a house.' I roll my eyes.

'Only I told my mum about you last night.' He gives a sudden smile, as though remembering the conversation, and I gaze at him suspiciously. What did he say? 'Anyway,' Nathaniel looks up, 'she's willing to teach you cooking. And I said you'd probably need cleaning advice too—'

'I do not need cleaning advice!' I retort. 'I've cleaned houses loads of times. In fact, I need to get started.'

'Don't mind me.' Nathaniel shrugs.

I'll show him. In a businesslike manner I pick a can out of the tub and spray it onto the counter. There. Who says I don't know what I'm doing?

'So you've cleaned lots of houses,' says Nathaniel, watching me.

'Yes. Millions.'

The spray has solidified into crystalline little grey droplets. I briskly rub them with a cloth – but they won't come off. Shit.

I look more closely at the can. 'DO NOT USE ON GRANITE'. *Shit.*

'Anyway,' I say, hastily putting the cloth down to hide the droplets, 'you're in my way.' I grab a feather duster from the blue tub and start brushing crumbs off the kitchen table. 'Excuse me . . .'

'I'll leave you then,' says Nathaniel, his mouth twitching again. He looks at the feather duster. 'Don't you want to be using a dustpan and brush for that?'

I look uncertainly at the feather duster. What's wrong with this one? Anyway, what is he, the duster police?

'I have my methods,' I say, lifting my chin. 'Thank you.'

'OK.' He grins. 'See you.'

I'm not going to let him faze me. I'm perfectly capable of cleaning this house. I just need . . . a plan. Yes. A time sheet, like at work.

As soon as Nathaniel's gone I grab a pen and piece of paper and start scribbling a list for the day. I have an image of myself moving smoothly from task to task, brush in one hand, duster in the other, bringing order to everything. Like Mary Poppins.

9.30–9.36   Make beds
9.36–9.42   Take laundry out of machine and put in dryer
9.42–10.00   Clean bathrooms

I get to the end and read it over with a fresh surge of optimism. This is better. This is more like it. At this rate I should be done easily by lunchtime.

9.36 Fuck. I cannot make this bed. Why won't this sheet lie flat?

9.42 And why do they make mattresses so *heavy*?

9.54 This is sheer torture. My arms have never ached

so much in my entire life. The blankets weigh a ton, and the sheets won't go straight and I have no idea how to do the wretched corners. How do chamber-maids do it? How?

10.30 At last. A whole hour of hard work and I have made precisely one bed. I'm already way behind. But never mind. Just keep moving. Laundry next.

10.36 No. Please, no.

I can hardly bear to look. It's a total disaster. Everything in the washing machine has gone pink. Every single thing.

What *happened*?

With trembling fingers I pick out a damp cashmere cardigan. It was cream when I put it in. It's now a sickly shade of candy floss. I knew K3 was bad news. I *knew* it—

Keep calm. There must be a solution, there must be. My eye starts flicking frantically over cans of products stacked on the shelves. Stain Away . . . Vanish. There has to be a remedy . . . I just need to think . . .

10.42 OK, I have the answer. It may not totally work – but it's my best shot.

11.00 I've just spent £852 replacing all the clothes in the machine as closely as possible. Harrods personal-shopping department were very helpful, and will send them all tomorrow, Express Delivery. I just hope to heaven Trish and Eddie won't notice that their wardrobe has magically regenerated.

Now I just have to dispose of all the pink clothes. And get through the rest of the list.

11.06 And . . . oh. The ironing. What am I going to do about that?

11.12 Right. I've looked in the local paper and I have a solution to that, too. A girl from the village will collect it, iron it all overnight at three pounds a shirt, and sew on Eddie's button.

So far this job has cost me nearly a thousand pounds. And it's not even midday.

11.42 I'm doing fine. I'm doing well. I've got the Hoover on, I'm cruising along nicely—

Shit. What was that? What just went up the Hoover? Why is it making that grinding noise?

Have I *broken* it?

11.48 How much does a Hoover cost?

12.24 My legs are in total agony. I've been kneeling on hard tiles, cleaning the bath, for what seems like hours. There are little ridges where the tiles have dug into my knees, and I'm boiling hot and the cleaning chemicals are making me cough. All I want is a rest. But I have to keep moving. I can't stop for a moment. I am *so* behind . . .

12.30 What is wrong with this bleach bottle? Which way is the nozzle pointing, anyway? I'm turning it round in confusion, peering at the arrows on the plastic . . . why won't anything come out? OK, I'm going to squeeze it really, really hard—

Fuck. That nearly got my eye.

12.32 FUCK. What has it done to my HAIR?

By three o'clock I am utterly knackered. I'm only halfway down my list and I can't see myself ever making it to the end. I don't know how people clean houses. It's the hardest job I've ever done, ever.

I am not moving smoothly from task to task like

Mary Poppins. I'm darting from unfinished job to unfinished job like a headless chicken. Right now I'm standing on a chair, cleaning the mirror in the drawing room. But it's like some kind of bad dream. The more I rub, the more smeary it gets.

I keep catching glances of myself in the glass. I have never looked more dishevelled in my life. My hair is sticking out wildly, with a huge grotesque streak of greeny-blonde where I splashed the bleach. My face is bright red and sheeny, my hands are pink and sore from scrubbing and my eyes are bloodshot.

Why won't it get clean? Why?

'Get clean!' I cry, practically sobbing in frustration. 'Get clean, you bloody . . . bloody . . .'

'Samantha.'

Abruptly I stop rubbing, to see Nathaniel standing in the doorway, looking at the smeary glass. 'Have you tried vinegar?'

'*Vinegar?*' I stare at him in suspicion.

'It cuts through the grease,' he adds. 'It's good on glass.'

'Oh. Right.' I put my cloth down, trying to regain my cool. 'Yes, I knew that.'

Nathaniel shakes his head. 'No you didn't.'

I look at his adamant face. There's no point pretending any more. He knows I've never cleaned a house in my life.

'You're right,' I admit at last. 'I didn't.'

As I get down off the chair I feel wobbly with fatigue. I grip the mantelpiece for a moment, trying to get my head straight.

'You should have a break,' says Nathaniel firmly. 'You've been at it all day, I've seen you. Did you have any lunch?'

'No time.'

I sink down onto a chair, feeling suddenly too drained to move. Every single muscle in my body is in pain, including muscles I never even knew I had. I feel like I've run a marathon. Or swum the Channel. And I still haven't polished the woodwork or beaten the mats.

'It's . . . harder than I thought,' I say at last. 'A lot harder.'

'Uh huh.' He nods, looking more closely at me. 'What happened to your hair?'

'Bleach,' I say shortly. 'Cleaning the loo.'

He gives a muffled snort of laughter but I don't look up. To be honest, I'm beyond caring.

'You're a hard worker,' he says. 'I'll give you that. And it'll get easier—'

'I can't do it.' The words come out before I can stop them. 'I can't do this job. I'm . . . hopeless.'

'Sure you can.' He rifles in his rucksack and produces a can of Coke. 'Have this. You can't work on no fuel.'

'Thanks,' I say, taking it gratefully. I crack open the can and take a gulp, and it's the most delicious thing I've ever tasted. I take another greedy slurp, and another.

'The offer still stands,' he adds after a pause. 'My mother will give you lessons if you like.'

'Really?' I wipe my mouth, push back my sweaty hair and look up at him. 'She'd . . . do that?'

'She likes a challenge, my mum.' Nathaniel gives a little smile. 'She'll teach you your way around a kitchen. And anything else you need to know.' He glances quizzically towards the smeary mirror.

I feel a sudden burn of humiliation and look away. I don't want to be useless. I don't want to need lessons. That's not who I am. I want to be able to do this on my own, without asking assistance from anyone.

But I have to get real. The truth is, I need help.

Apart from anything else, if I keep on going like today I'll be bankrupt in two weeks.

I turn back to Nathaniel.

'That would be great,' I say humbly. 'I really appreciate it. Thanks.'

TWELVE

I wake up on Saturday, heart pounding, and leap to my feet, my mind racing with everything I have to do . . .

And then it stops, like a car screeching to a halt. For a moment I can't move. Then, hesitantly, I sink back into bed, overcome by the weirdest, most extraordinary feeling I've ever experienced.

I have nothing to do.

No contracts to go over, no emails to reply to, no emergency meetings at the office. Nothing.

I wrinkle my brow, trying to remember the last time I had nothing to do. But I'm not sure I can. It seems like I've *never* had nothing to do, ever since I was about seven. I get out of bed, walk to the window and stare out at the early-morning, translucent blue sky, trying to get my head around my situation. It's my day off. No one has any hold over me. No one can call me up and demand my presence. This is my own time. *My own time.*

As I stand there at the window, contemplating this fact, I start to feel a weird feeling inside. Light and giddy, like a helium balloon. I'm free. A smile of exhilaration spreads across my face as I meet the eyes of my own reflection in the glass. For the first time ever, I can do whatever I like.

I check the time – and it's only seven fifteen a.m. The whole day stretches before me like a clean sheet of paper. What shall I do? Where do I *start*? I can feel a fresh bubble of joy rising inside me, until I want to laugh out loud.

I'm already sketching out a timetable for the day in my head. Forget six-minute-segments. Forget hurrying. I'm going to start measuring time in *hours*. An hour for wallowing in the bath and getting dressed. An hour for lingering over breakfast. An hour for reading the paper, cover to cover. I'm going to have the laziest, most indolent, most enjoyable morning I've ever had in my adult life.

As I head into the bathroom, I can feel muscles twinging with pain all over my body. Muscles I never even knew I had. They really should market house-cleaning as a workout. I run a deep warm bath and slosh in some of Trish's bath oil, then step into the scented water and lie back happily.

Delicious. I'm just going to stay here for hours and hours and hours.

I close my eyes, letting the water lap my shoulders, and let time waft past in great swathes. I think I even fall asleep for a while. I have never spent so long in a bath in my entire life.

At last I open my eyes, reach for a towel and get out again. As I'm starting to dry myself off I reach for my watch, just out of curiosity.

Seven thirty a.m.

What?

I was only fifteen minutes?

I feel a flash of astonishment. How on earth can I have only taken fifteen minutes? I stand, dripping, in

159

indecision for a moment, wondering if I should get back in again and do it all again, more slowly.

But no. That would be too weird. It doesn't matter. So I had my bath too quickly. I'll just make sure I take my time properly over breakfast. Really *enjoy* it.

At least I have some clothes to put on. Trish took me out last night to a shopping centre a few miles away, so I could stock up on underwear and shorts and summer dresses. She told me she'd leave me to it — then ended up bossing me about and picking every-thing out for me . . . and somehow I ended up with not a single item in black.

I cautiously put on a pink slip dress and pair of sandals, and look at myself. I've never worn pink before in my life. But to my amazement I don't look too bad! Apart from the huge streak of bleach in my hair. I'm going to have to do something about that.

As I make my way along the corridor, there's no sound from the Geigers' bedroom. I move silently past the door, feeling suddenly awkward. It'll be a bit strange, being in their house all weekend, with nothing to do. I'd better go out later. Get out of their way.

The kitchen is as silent and gleamy as ever, but it's starting to feel slightly less intimidating. I know my way around the kettle and the toaster, if nothing else, and I've found a whole stash of jams in the larder. I'll have toast for breakfast, with orange and ginger marmalade, and a nice cup of coffee. And I'll read the paper from cover to cover. That'll take me to about eleven o'clock and then I can think about what else to do.

I find a copy of *The Times* on the doormat, and bring it back to the kitchen just as my toast is popping up.

This is the life.

I sit by the window, crunching toast, sipping coffee

160

and leafing through the paper in a leisurely way. At last, after devouring three slices, two cups of coffee and all the Saturday sections, I stretch my arms in a big yawn and glance at the clock.

I don't believe it. It's only seven fifty-six.

What is wrong with me? I was supposed to take *hours* over breakfast. I was supposed to be sitting there all morning. Not get everything finished in twenty minutes flat.

OK . . . never mind. Let's not stress about it. I'll just chill out in some other way.

I put my crockery in the dishwasher and wipe away my toast crumbs. Then I sit down at the table again and look about. I wonder what to do next. It's too early to go out yet.

Abruptly I realize I'm tapping the table with my fingernails. I stop myself and stare down at my hands for a moment. This is ridiculous. I'm having my first true day off in about ten years. I should be *relaxed*. Come on, I can think of something nice to do, surely.

What do people do on days off? My mind scrolls through a series of images from TV. I could make another cup of coffee? But I've already had two. I don't really feel like another one. I could read the paper again? But I have an almost photographic memory. So re-reading things is a bit pointless.

My gaze drifts outside to the garden, where a squirrel is perched on a stone pillar, looking around with bright eyes. Maybe I'll go outside. Enjoy the garden and the wildlife and the early-morning dew. Good idea.

Except the trouble with early-morning dew is it gets all over your feet. As I pick my way over the damp grass, I'm already wishing I hadn't put on open-toed sandals. Or that I'd waited till later for my little stroll.

The garden is a lot bigger than I'd appreciated. I walk down the lawn towards an ornamental hedge where everything seems to finish, only to realize there's a whole further section beyond it, with an orchard at the end, and some sort of walled garden to my left.

It's a stunning garden. Even I can see that. The flowers are vivid without being garish, every wall is covered with some beautiful creeper or vine, and as I walk towards the orchard I can see little golden pears hanging from the branches of trees. I don't think I've ever seen an actual pear growing on a tree before in my life.

I walk through the fruit trees towards a huge, square, brown patch of earth with plants growing in serried rows. These must be the vegetables. I prod one of them cautiously with my foot. It could be a cabbage or a lettuce. Or the leaves of something growing underground, maybe.

To be honest, it could be an alien. I have no idea.

I wander round a bit longer, then sit down on a mossy wooden bench and look at a nearby bush covered in white flowers. Mm. Pretty.

Now what? What are people supposed to *do* in their gardens?

I feel I should have something to read. Or I should be calling someone. My fingers are itching to move. I look at my watch. Still only eight sixteen. Oh God.

Come on, I can't give up yet. I'll just sit here for a bit and enjoy the peace. I lean back, get myself comfortable on the bench and watch a little bird pecking the ground nearby for a while.

Then I look at my watch again. Eight seventeen.

I can't do this.

I can't do nothing all day. It's going to drive me crazy. I'll have to go and buy another paper from the village shop. If they've got *War and Peace*, I'll buy that too. I get up and am starting to head briskly back across the lawn when a bleep from my pocket makes me stop still.

It's my mobile. It's received a text. Someone's just texted me, early on a Saturday morning. I pull out my mobile and look at it, feeling edgy. I haven't had any contact with the outside world for over a day.

I know there are other texts in my phone – but I haven't read any of them. I know there are messages in my voicemail – but I haven't listened to a single one. I don't want to know. I'm blocking it all out.

I finger my mobile, telling myself to put it away. But now my curiosity has been sparked. Someone texted me just a few seconds ago. Someone, somewhere has been holding a mobile phone, punching in a message to me. I have a sudden vision of Guy, in his off-duty chinos and blue shirt. Sitting at his desk, frowning as he texts.

Apologizing.

Giving me some news. Some kind of development I couldn't have guessed at yesterday—

I can't help it. Despite it all, I feel a sudden flicker of hope. As I stand there on the early-morning lawn, I can feel my mental self being dragged out of this garden, back to London, back to the office. A whole day has gone on there without me. A lot can happen in twenty-four hours. Things can change. Everything could have turned out positive in some way.

Or ... become even worse. They're suing me. They're prosecuting me.

The tension is rising inside me. I'm gripping my phone more and more tightly. I have to know. Good or bad. I flip open the phone and find the text. It's from a number I don't even recognize.

Who? Who on earth is texting me?

Feeling a little sick, I press OK to read.

hi samantha, nathaniel here.

Nathaniel?

Nathaniel?

My relief is so huge, I laugh out loud. Of course! I gave him my mobile number yesterday for his mother. I scroll down to read the rest of the message.

if you're interested, mum could start cooking
lessons today. nat.

Cooking lessons. I feel a spark of delight. That's it. The perfect way to fill the day. I press Reply and quickly text:

would love to. thanks. sam.

I send it with a little smile. This is fun. A minute or two later, the phone bleeps again.

what time? is 11 too early? nat

I look at my watch. Eleven o'clock is still two and a half hours away.

Two and a half hours with nothing to do except read the paper and avoid Trish and Eddie. I press Reply.

shall we make it 10? sam

At five to ten I'm ready in the hall. Nathaniel's

mother's house is apparently tricky to find, so the plan is to meet here and he'll walk me over. As I check my reflection in the hall mirror, I wince. The streak of bleach is as obvious as ever. I push my hair backwards and forwards a few times – but I can't hide it. Maybe I could walk along with my hand carelessly positioned at my head, as if I'm thinking hard. I attempt a few casual, pensive poses in the mirror.

'Is your head all right?'

I swivel round in shock to see Nathaniel at the open door, wearing a plaid shirt and jeans.

'Er . . . fine,' I say, my hand still glued to my head. 'I was just . . .'

Oh, there's no point. I bring my hand down from my hair and Nathaniel regards the streak for a moment.

'It looks nice,' he says. 'Like a badger.'

'A *badger*?' I say, affronted. 'I don't look like a badger.'

I glance in the mirror for quick reassurance. No. I don't.

'Badgers are beautiful creatures,' says Nathaniel with a shrug. 'I'd rather look like a badger than a stoat.'

Hang on. Since when was my choice between badger or stoat? I don't even know how we got onto this conversation.

'Perhaps we should go,' I say with dignity. I pick up my bag and give one last glance in the mirror as I reach for the door.

OK. Maybe I look a little bit like a badger.

The summer air is already warming up outside, and as we walk down the gravel drive I sniff appreciatively. There's some sort of nice flowery smell going on which I definitely recognize . . .

'Honeysuckle and jasmine!' I exclaim in sudden

recognition. I have the Jo Malone bath oil at home.

'Honeysuckle on the wall.' Nat points to a tangle of pale-yellow flowers on the old, golden stone. 'Put it in a year ago.'

I peer up at the delicate flowers with interest. That's what honeysuckle looks like?

'There's no jasmine around here, though,' he says, curiously. 'Can you smell it?'

'Er . . .' I spread my hands vaguely. 'Maybe not.'

I don't think I'll mention Jo Malone bath oil at this point. Or, in fact, any point.

As we turn out of the drive I realize this is the first time I've been out of the Geigers' grounds since I arrived here – apart from the shopping trip with Trish, when I was too busy scrabbling for her Celine Dion CD to notice my surroundings. Nathaniel has turned left and is striding easily along the road – but I can't move. I'm gazing at the sight in front of me, my jaw wide open. This village is absolutely *stunning*.

I had no idea.

I look around, taking in the old, honey-coloured stone walls. The rows of ancient cottages with steeply pitched roofs. The little river lined with willow trees. Up ahead is the pub I noticed on the first night, decorated with hanging baskets. I can hear the distant clip-clop of horses' hooves. Nothing jars. Everything is soft and mellow and feels like it's been here for hundreds of years.

'Samantha?'

Nathaniel has finally noticed I'm pinned to the spot.

'I'm sorry.' I hurry to join him. 'It's just such a beautiful place! I didn't realize.'

'It's nice.' I can hear a note of pride in his voice. 'Gets too many tourists, but . . .' He shrugs.

'I had no idea!' We continue walking along the

street, but I can't stop looking around, wide-eyed. 'Look at the river! Look at the little *church*!'

I feel like a child discovering a new toy. I've hardly ever been to the English countryside. We always stayed in London or went abroad. I've been to Tuscany more times than I can remember and I once spent six months in New York when Mum was on secondment there. But I've never been to the Cotswolds in my life.

We walk over the river on an old arched, stone bridge. At the top I stop to look at the ducks and swans.

'It's just gorgeous.' I exhale. 'Absolutely beautiful.'

'Didn't you see any of this as you arrived?' Nathaniel regards me with amusement. 'Did you just appear in a bubble?'

I think back to that panicked, dazed, desperate journey. Getting off the train, my head throbbing, my vision a blur.

'Kind of,' I say at last. 'I wasn't really noticing where I was going.'

We both watch as a pair of swans sail regally under the little bridge. Then I glance at my watch. It's already five past ten.

'We should get going,' I say with a little start. 'Your mother will be waiting.'

'There's no rush,' Nathaniel calls as I hasten down the other side of the bridge. 'We've got all day.' He lopes down the bridge and joins me. 'It's OK. You can slow down.'

He starts walking along the street and I join him, trying to match his relaxed pace. But I'm not used to this easy rhythm. I'm used to striding along crowded pavements, fighting my way, pushing and elbowing.

'So, did you grow up here?' I ask, trying to slow my legs to a saunter.

'Yup.' He swings into a little cobbled lane to the left. 'I came back when my dad got ill. Then he died, and I had to sort things out. Take care of Mum. It's been tough on her. The finances were in a mess . . . everything was in a mess.'

'I'm sorry,' I say awkwardly. 'Do you have any other family?'

'My brother Jake. He came back for a week.' Nathaniel hesitates. 'He runs his own business. Very successful.'

His voice is as easy as ever, but I can detect a thread of . . . something. Maybe I won't ask any more about his family.

'Well, *I'd* live here,' I say with enthusiasm.

Nathaniel gives me a slightly odd look. 'You do live here,' he reminds me.

I feel a tweak of surprise. I suppose he's right. Technically, I do.

I walk on a few paces, trying to process this new thought. I've never lived anywhere except London before, apart from my three years at Cambridge. I've always had an NW postcode. An 0207 number. That's who I am. That's who I . . . was.

But already the old me is feeling more distant. When I think back to myself, even last week, it's as if I'm seeing myself through tracing paper.

Everything I once prized has been destroyed. And I'm still feeling sore and bruised. But at the same time . . . I feel more alive with possibility than I have ever done. My ribcage expands widely as I breathe in the country air and I suddenly feel a wave of optimism; almost euphoria. On impulse, I stop by a huge tree and gaze up into the green-laden branches.

'There's a wonderful Walt Whitman poem about an oak tree.' I lift a hand and tenderly stroke the cool, rough bark. ' "I saw in Louisiana a live-oak growing. All alone stood it and the moss hung down from the branches." '

I glance over at Nathaniel, half expecting him to look impressed.

'That's a beech,' he says, nodding at the tree.

Oh. Right.

I don't know any poems about beeches.

'Here we are.' Nathaniel pushes open an old iron gate and gestures me to go up a stone path towards a little cottage with blue flowered curtains at the windows. 'Come and meet your cooking teacher.'

Nathaniel's mother is nothing like I expected. I was picturing some cosy Mrs Tiggywinkle character with grey hair in a bun and half-moon spectacles. Instead, I'm looking at a wiry woman with a vivid, pretty face. Her eyes are bright blue, with the beginnings of pencil-lines around them. Her greying hair is in plaits either side of her face, she's wearing an apron over jeans, T-shirt and espadrilles, and is vigorously kneading some kind of dough.

'Mum.' Nathaniel grins and pushes me forward into the kitchen. 'Here she is. This is Samantha. Samantha . . . my mum. Iris.'

'Samantha. Welcome.' Iris looks up, and I can see her taking me in, head to foot, as she kneads. 'Just let me finish this.'

Nathaniel gestures to me to sit down, and I cautiously take a seat on a wooden chair. The kitchen is at the back of the house, and is filled with light and sun. Flowers in earthenware jugs are everywhere. There's an old-fashioned range cooker and a scrubbed wooden table and a stable door open to the outside. As I'm wondering whether I should be making conversation, a chicken wanders in and starts scratching at the ground.

'Oh, a chicken!' I exclaim before I can stop myself.

'Yes, a chicken.' I can see Iris looking at me with wry amusement. 'Never seen a chicken before?'

Only in the Waitrose chill counter. The chicken comes pecking towards my open-toe-sandalled feet and I quickly tuck them under my chair, trying to look as though I meant to do that anyway.

'There.' Iris picks up the dough, shapes it efficiently into a round shape on a tray, opens the heavy oven door and pops it in. She washes her floury hands at the sink, then turns to face me.

'So, you want to learn how to cook.' Her tone is friendly but businesslike. I sense this is a woman who doesn't waste words.

'Yes.' I smile. 'Please.'

'Cordon bleu fancy stuff,' chimes in Nathaniel, who's leaning against the range.

'And how much cooking have you done before?' Iris dries her hands on a red-checked towel. 'Nathaniel said none. That can't be right.' She folds the towel and smiles at me for the first time. 'What can you make? What are your basics?'

Her intent blue gaze is making me feel a little nervous. I rack my brains, trying to think of something I can make.

'Well . . . I can . . . I can make . . . um . . . toast,' I say. 'Toast would be my basic.'

'*Toast?*' She looks taken aback. 'Just toast?'

'And crumpets,' I add quickly. 'Teacakes . . . anything that goes in a toaster, really . . .'

'But what about *cooking*?' She drapes the towel over a steel bar on the range and looks at me more carefully. 'What about . . . an omelette? Surely you can cook an omelette.'

I swallow. 'Not really.'

Iris's expression is so incredulous I feel my cheeks flame. 'I never did home economics at school,' I explain. 'I never really learned how to make meals.'

'But your mother, surely . . . or your grand-mother . . .' She breaks off as I shake my head. '*Anyone?*'

I bite my lip. Iris exhales sharply as though taking in the situation for the first time.

'So you can't cook anything at all. And what have you promised to make for the Geigers?'

Oh God.

'Trish wanted a week's worth of menus. So I . . . um . . . gave her one based on this.' Sheepishly I get the crumpled Maxim's menu out of my bag and hand it to her.

'Braised lamb and baby onion assemblé with a fondant potato and goat's cheese crust, accompanied by cardamom spinach puree,' she reads out, in tones of disbelief.

I hear a snort and look up to see Nathaniel in fits of laughter.

'It was all I had!' I exclaim defensively. 'What was I going to say, fishfingers and chips?'

' "Assemblé" is just flannel.' Iris is still perusing the sheet. 'That's souped-up shepherd's pie. We can teach you that. And the braised trout with almonds is straightforward enough . . .' She runs her finger further down the page then at last looks up, a frown creasing her brow. 'I can teach you these dishes, Samantha. But it isn't going to be easy. If you've really never cooked before.' She glances at Nathaniel. 'I'm not sure . . .'

As I see her expression I feel a flicker of alarm. Please don't say she's going to back out.

'I'm a quick learner.' I lean forward. 'And I'll work

hard. I'll do whatever it takes. I really, really want to do this.'

I gaze at her earnestly, trying to convey the message. *Please. I need this.*

'All right,' says Iris at last. 'Let's get you cooking.'

She reaches into a cupboard for a set of weighing scales and I take the opportunity to delve into my bag for a pad of file paper and a pen. As Iris turns round and sees me, she looks bemused.

'What's that for?' She jerks her head at the file paper.

'So I can take notes,' I explain. I write down the date and 'Cooking lesson no. 1', underline it, then look up. Iris is slowly shaking her head.

'Samantha, you're not going to be taking notes,' she says. 'Cooking isn't about writing down. It's about tasting. Feeling. Touching. Smelling.'

'Right.' I nod intelligently.

I must remember that. I quickly uncap my pen and scribble down 'Cooking = all about tasting, smelling, feeling etc.' I cap my pen again and look up. Iris is regarding me with incredulity.

'Tasting,' she says, removing my pen and paper from my hands. 'Not writing. You need to use your senses. Your instincts.'

She lifts the lid off a pot gently steaming on the cooker and dips a spoon into it. 'Taste this.'

Gingerly I take the spoon in my mouth.

'Gravy,' I say at once. 'Delicious!' I add politely.

Iris shakes her head. 'Don't tell me what you think it is. Tell me what you can taste.'

I stare at her, puzzled. This is a trick question, surely.

'I can taste . . . gravy.'

Her expression doesn't change. She's waiting for something else.

'Er . . . meat?' I hazard.

'What else?'

My mind is blank. I can't think of anything else. I mean, it's gravy. What else can you say about gravy?

'Taste it again.' Iris is relentless. 'You need to try harder.'

My face is growing hot as I struggle for words. I feel like the dumb kid at the back who can't do the two times table.

'Meat . . . water . . .' I try desperately to think what else is in gravy. 'Flour!' I say in sudden inspiration.

'Samantha, don't think about identifying the taste. Just tell me what the sensation is.' Iris holds the spoon out a third time. 'Taste it again – and this time close your eyes.'

Close my eyes?

'OK.' I take a mouthful and close my eyes obediently.

'Now. What can you taste?' Iris's voice is in my ear. 'Concentrate on the flavours. Nothing else.'

Eyes tight shut, I block out everything and focus all my attention on my mouth. All I'm aware of is the warm salty liquid on my tongue. *Salt.* That's one flavour. And sweet . . . and . . . there's another taste as I swallow it down . . .

It's almost like colours appearing. First the bright, obvious ones, and then the gentler ones you'd almost miss . . .

'It's salty and meaty . . .' I say slowly, without open-ing my eyes. 'And sweet . . . and . . . and almost fruity? Like cherries?'

I open my eyes, feeling a bit disoriented. Iris is scrutinizing me intently. Behind her I suddenly notice Nathaniel, also watching. At the sight of him, I feel a tad flustered. Tasting gravy with your eyes closed is

173

a fairly intimate thing to do, it turns out. I'm not sure I want anyone watching me.

Iris seems to understand.

'Nathaniel,' she says briskly, 'we're going to need ingredients for all these dishes.' She scribbles a long list and hands it to him. 'Run down and get these for us, love.'

As he leaves the room, she looks at me, a faint smile on her lips. 'That was much better.'

'By George, she's got it?' I say hopefully, and Iris throws back her head in laughter.

'Not yet, sweetie, by a long chalk. Here, get a pinny on.' She hands me a red and white striped apron and I tie it around myself, feeling self-conscious.

'It's so kind of you to help me,' I say hesitantly as she gets out onions and some orange vegetable I don't recognize. 'I'm really grateful.'

'I like a challenge.' Her eyes sparkle at me. 'I get bored. Nathaniel does everything for me. Too much, sometimes.'

'But still. You'd never even met me—'

'I liked the sound of you.' Iris draws down a heavy wooden chopping board. 'Nathaniel told me how you got yourself out of your mess the other night. That took some spirit.'

'I had to do something.' I give her a rueful smile.

'And they offered you a pay rise as a result. Wonderful.' As she smiles, fine lines appear round her eyes like starbursts. 'Trish Geiger is a very foolish woman.'

'I like Trish,' I say, feeling a stab of loyalty.

'So do I.' Iris nods. 'She's been very supportive to Nathaniel. But you must have noticed she has little or no brain.' She sounds so matter-of-fact I want to giggle. I watch as she puts a huge, gleaming pot on the stove, then turns and looks at me, arms folded. 'So you've taken them in completely.'

'Yes.' I smile. 'They have no idea who I am.'

'And who are you?'

Her question takes me completely by surprise. I open my mouth but no words come out.

'Is your name really Samantha?'

'Yes!' I say in shock.

'That was a little blunt.' Iris lifts a hand in acknowledgement. 'But a girl arrives in the middle of the countryside out of nowhere and takes a job she can't do ...' She pauses as though choosing her words. 'Nathaniel tells me you've got out of a bad relationship?'

'Yes,' I mumble, my head bowed. I can feel Iris's shrewd gaze, appraising me.

'You don't want to talk about it, do you?'

'Not really. No. I don't.'

As I look up there's a thread of understanding in her eyes.

'That's fine by me.' She picks up a knife. 'Now let's start. Roll up your sleeves, tie back your hair and wash your hands. I'm going to teach you to chop an onion.'

We spend all weekend cooking.

I learn to slice an onion finely, turn it the other way and produce tiny dice. I learn to chop herbs with a rounded blade. I learn how to rub flour and ground ginger into chunks of meat, then drop it into a spitting-hot, cast-iron pan. I learn that pastry has to be made with quick, cold hands, by an open window. I learn the trick of blanching French beans in boiling water before sautéing them in butter.

A week ago I didn't know what 'sauté' even meant.

In between cooking I sit on the back step with Iris,

watching the chickens scratch in the dirt and sipping freshly brewed coffee accompanied by a pumpkin muffin, or salty, crumbly cheese sandwiched with lettuce in homemade bread.

'Eat and enjoy,' Iris says each time, handing me my share, then shakes her head in dismay as I start eating. 'Not so fast. Take your time! *Taste* the food!'

On Sunday afternoon, under Iris's calm guidance, I make roast chicken with sage and onion stuffing, steamed broccoli, cumin-scented carrots and roast potatoes. As I heave the huge roasting tin out of the oven, I pause for a moment and let the warm, chicken-scented air rise over me. I have never smelt a more homey smell in my life. The chicken is golden; its crisp, crackly skin speckled with the pepper I ground on earlier; the juices still sizzling in the tin.

'Gravy time,' Iris calls from the other side of the kitchen. 'Take the chicken out and put it on the dish . . . and cover it up. We need to keep it warm . . . Now tilt the roasting tin. Can you see those globules of fat, floating on the surface? You need to spoon those out.'

She's finishing the topping on a plum crumble as she speaks. She dots it with butter and pops it into the oven, then seamlessly reaches for a cloth and wipes down the surface. I've watched her all day, moving swiftly and precisely around the kitchen, tasting as she goes, fully in control. There's no sense of panic. Everything happens as it should happen.

'That's right.' She's by my side, watching as I whisk the gravy. 'Keep going . . . it'll thicken in a minute . . .'

I cannot believe I'm making gravy. *Making gravy*.

And – like everything else in this kitchen – it's working. The ingredients are obeying. The mish-mash of chicken juices, stock and flour is somehow turning into a smooth, fragrant liquid.

'Very good!' says Iris. 'Now, pour it into this nice warm jug . . . sieve out any bits . . . see how easy that was?'

'I think you're magic,' I say, bluntly. 'That's why everything works in here. You're a cooking witch.'

'A cooking witch!' She chuckles. 'I like that. Now come on. Pinny off. Time to enjoy what we've made.' She takes off her apron and holds out a hand for mine. 'Nathaniel, have you finished the table?'

Nathaniel has been in and out of the kitchen all weekend, and I've got used to his presence. In fact, I've been so taken up with cooking I've barely noticed him. Now he's laying the wooden table with rush mats, old bone-handled cutlery and soft checked napkins.

'Wine for the cooks,' says Iris, producing a bottle from the fridge and uncorking it. She pours me a glass, then gestures to the table. 'Sit, Samantha. You've done enough for one weekend. You must be shattered.'

'I'm fine!' I say automatically. But as I sink down into the nearest chair, I realize quite how exhausted I am. I close my eyes and feel myself relax for the first time that day. My arms and back are aching from all the chopping and mixing. My senses have been bombarded with smells and tastes and new sensations.

'Don't fall asleep!' Iris's voice jolts me back to the present. 'This is our reward! Nathaniel, love, put Samantha's roast chicken down there. You can carve.'

I open my eyes to see Nathaniel carrying over the serving dish bearing the roast chicken. As I see it again, all crispy golden and succulent, I feel a fresh glow of pride. My first roast chicken. I almost want to take a photo.

'You're not telling me you *made* this?' says Nathaniel in disbelieving tones.

177

Oh, ha ha. He knows full well I made it. But I can't help smiling back.

'Just something I rustled up earlier . . .' I give a careless shrug. 'As we cordon bleu chefs do.'

Nathaniel carves the chicken with expert ease, and Iris dishes out the vegetables. When we're all served she sits down and raises her glass.

'To you, Samantha. You've done splendidly.'

'Thanks.' I smile and am about to sip my wine when I realize the other two aren't moving.

'And to Ben,' Iris adds softly.

'On Sundays we always remember Dad,' Nathaniel explains.

'Oh.' I hesitate, then raise my glass.

'Now.' Iris's eyes glint and she puts her glass down. 'The moment of truth.' She takes a bite of chicken and I watch her chewing. I try to hide my nerves.

'Very good.' She nods at last. 'Very good indeed.'

I can't help a beam spreading across my face. 'Really? It's good?'

Iris lifts her glass to me. 'By George. She's got roast chicken, at any rate.'

I sit in the glow of the evening light, not talking much but eating and listening to the other two chat. They tell me stories about Eddie and Trish, about when they tried to buy the local church and turn it into a guest cottage, and I can't help laughing. Nathaniel outlines his plans for the Geigers' garden and draws a sketch of the avenue of limes he created at Marchant House. When he gets animated he draws more and more quickly, his hand dwarfing the stub of pencil he's using. Iris notices me watching in admiration and points out a watercolour of the village pond, hanging on the wall.

'Ben did that.' She nods towards Nathaniel. 'He takes after his father.'

The atmosphere is so relaxed and easy, so different from any meal I've ever had at home. No one's on the phone. No one's rushing to get anywhere else. I could sit here all night.

As the meal is finally drawing to a close I clear my throat.

'Iris, I just want to say thank-you again.'

'I enjoyed it.' Iris takes a spoonful of plum crumble. 'I always did enjoy bossing people about.'

'But really, I'm so grateful. I don't know what I would have done without you.'

'Next weekend, we'll make lasagne. And gnocchi!' Iris takes a sip of wine and dabs her mouth. 'We'll have an Italian weekend.'

'*Next* weekend?' I stare at her. 'But—'

'You don't think you've finished, do you?' She hoots with laughter. 'I've only just started on you!'

'But . . . I can't take up all your weekends . . .'

'I'm not graduating you yet,' she says with cheerful asperity. 'So you have no choice. Now, what else do you need help with? Cleaning? Washing?'

I feel a twinge of embarrassment. She clearly knows exactly how much of a mess I got myself into yesterday.

'I'm not really sure how to use the washing machine,' I admit at last.

'We'll cover that.' She nods. 'I'll pop up to the house when they're out and have a look at it.'

'And I can't sew on buttons . . .'

'Buttons.' She reaches for a piece of paper and a pencil, and writes it down, still munching. 'Can you hem?'

'Er . . .'

179

'Hemming.' She scribbles it down. 'What about ironing?' She looks up, suddenly alert. 'You must have had to iron. How did you wriggle out of that one?'

'I'm sending it out to Stacey Nicholson,' I confess. 'In the village. She charges three pounds a shirt.'

'Stacey Nicholson?' Iris puts her pencil down. 'That flibbertigibbet?'

'In her ad she said she was an experienced laundress.'

'She's fifteen years old!' Iris pushes back her chair, looking galvanized. 'Samantha, you are *not* paying Stacey Nicholson to do your ironing. You're going to learn how to do it yourself.'

'But I've never—'

'I'll teach you. Anyone can iron.' She reaches into a little side room, pulls out an old ironing board covered in flowery material and sets it up, then beckons me over. 'What do you have to iron?'

'Mr Geiger's shirts, mainly,' I say, nervously joining her at the ironing board.

'All right.' She plugs in an iron and turns the dial. 'Hot, for cotton. Wait for the iron to heat up. No point beginning till it's at the right temperature. Now, I'll show you the right way to tackle a shirt . . .'

She rootles, frowning, in a pile of clean laundry in the little room. 'Shirts . . . shirts . . . Nathaniel, take off your shirt a moment.'

I stiffen. As I glance at Nathaniel I see he has stiffened too.

'Mum!' He gives an awkward laugh.

'Oh, don't be ridiculous, love,' says Iris impatiently. 'You can take off your shirt for a moment. No one's embarrassed. You're not embarrassed, are you, Samantha?'

'Um . . .' My voice is a little grainy. 'Um . . . no, of course not . . .'

'Now, this is your steam.' She presses a button on the iron and a jet of steam shoots into the air. 'Always check your steam compartment has water . . . Nathaniel! I'm waiting!'

Through the steam I can see Nathaniel slowly unbuttoning his shirt. I catch a flash of smooth tanned skin and hastily lower my gaze.

Let's not be adolescent about this. So he's taking off his shirt. It's no big deal.

He tosses the shirt to his mother, who catches it deftly. My eyes are studiously fixed downwards. I'm not going to look at him.

I'm *not* going to look at him.

'Start with the collar . . .' Iris is smoothing the shirt out on the ironing board. 'Now, you don't have to press hard.' She guides my hand as the iron glides over the fabric. 'Keep a smooth touch . . .'

This is ridiculous. I'm an adult, mature woman. I can look at a man with no shirt on without falling to bits. What I'll do is . . . just take a casual peek. Yes. And get this out of my mind.

'Now the yoke.' Iris turns the shirt around on the board and I start pressing again. 'Very good . . . on to the cuffs now . . .'

I lift the shirt-tail to flip it over – and as I do so, accidentally-on-purpose raise my eyes.

Sweet Jesus.

I'm not sure the whole getting-it-out-of-my-mind plan is going to work after all.

'Samantha?' Iris grabs the iron from my hand. 'You're scorching the shirt!'

'Oh!' I come to. 'Sorry. I . . . I lost concentration.'

'Your cheeks seem very flushed.' Iris puts a curious

hand to my cheek. 'Are you all right, sweetie?'

'Must be the . . . um . . . steam.' I start ironing again, my face like a furnace.

Iris starts instructing me again, but I don't hear a word. As I move the iron blindly back and forth, I'm pondering obsessively on a) Nathaniel, b) Nathaniel without his shirt on, c) whether Nathaniel has a girlfriend.

At last I shake out his ironed shirt, perfectly done with all the creases in the right places.

'Very good!' says Iris, applauding. 'After some practice you'll be able to do that in four minutes flat.'

'Looks great,' Nathaniel smiles, holding out a hand. 'Thanks.'

'That's OK!' I manage in a strangled squawk, and hastily look away again, my heart thumping.

Great. Just great. One glimpse of his body and I have a full-blown crush.

I honestly thought I was a bit deeper than that.

THIRTEEN

He doesn't have a girlfriend.

I managed to get that information out of Trish last night, under the guise of asking about all the neighbours. There was some girl in Gloucester, apparently – but that was all over months ago. The way is clear. I just need a strategy.

As I shower and get dressed the next morning, I'm totally fixated by thoughts of Nathaniel. I'm aware I've reverted to the behaviour of a fourteen-year-old adolescent; that next I'll be doodling 'Samantha loves Nathaniel' with a love heart dotting the i. But I don't care. It's not as though being a mature, level-headed professional was working out so great for me.

I brush my hair, looking out at the misty green fields, and feel an inexplicable lightheartedness. I have no reason to feel so happy. On paper, everything is still catastrophic. My high-flying career is over. My family has no idea where I am. I'm earning a fraction of what I used to, for a job which involves picking other people's dirty underwear off the floor.

And yet I can't help humming as I straighten my bed.

My life has changed and I'm changing with it. It's as if the old conventional, monochrome Samantha has faded away into a paper doll. I've thrown her into the water and she's melting away to nothing. And in her place is a new me. A me with possibilities.

I've never gone after a man before. But then, until yesterday I'd never basted a chicken before. If I can do that, I can ask a man out, surely? The old Samantha would have sat back and waited to be approached. Well, not the new Samantha. I've seen the dating shows on TV, I know the rules. It's all about looks and body language and flirty conversation.

I walk over to the mirror and, for the first time since I've arrived here, examine my appearance with an honest, unflinching eye.

At once I regret it. Ignorance was better.

For a start, *how* can anyone look good in a blue nylon overall? I reach for a belt, fasten it around my middle, and hitch up my overall till the skirt is about three inches shorter, like we used to at school.

'Hi,' I say to my reflection, and casually toss back my hair. 'Hi, Nathaniel. Hi, Nat.'

All I need now is lots of black eyeliner badly applied, and I'll be back to my fourteen-year-old self in every single way.

I reach for my make-up bag, and spend about ten minutes alternately applying and removing make-up, until I've got something which looks natural and subtle, yet defined. Or else like I've wasted ten minutes. I have no idea.

Now to the body language. I wrinkle up my forehead, trying to remember the rules from TV. If a woman is attracted to a man, her pupils will dilate. Also, she will unconsciously lean forward, laugh at his jokes and expose her wrists and palms.

Experimentally I lean towards my reflection, holding out my hands as I do so.

I look like Jesus.

I'll try adding a flirty laugh. 'Ha ha ha!' I exclaim aloud. 'You just crack me up!'

Now I look like a cheerful Jesus.

I'm really not sure this is adding to my chances.

I head downstairs, draw back the curtains, letting in the bright morning sunshine, and pick up the post from the doormat. I'm just flicking through *Cotswold Property Magazine* to see how much a house around here costs, when the doorbell rings. A guy in uniform, holding a clipboard, is standing outside, a van behind him in the drive. 'Delivery from Professional Chef's Equipment Direct,' he says. 'Where shall I put the boxes?'

'Oh, right,' I say apprehensively. 'In the kitchen, please. Thanks.'

Professional Chef's Equipment. I guess that would be for me, the Professional Chef. I was kind of hoping it wouldn't arrive for a few more days.

'What's that van, Samantha?' calls Trish, tottering down the stairs in a dressing gown and high-heeled mules. 'Is it flowers?'

'It's the cookery equipment you ordered for me!' Somehow I summon up an enthusiastic tone.

'Oh *good*! At last!' Trish beams at me. 'Now you'll be able to stun us with your cooking! It's roasted sea bream with julienned vegetables tonight, isn't it?'

'Er . . . yes!' I gulp. 'I suppose it is.'

'Mind your backs!'

We both jump aside as two delivery men troop past with boxes stacked high in their arms. I follow them into the kitchen and watch the growing pile in disbelief. How much bloody stuff did the Geigers order?

'Now, we bought you *everything*,' says Trish, as though reading my mind. 'Go on! You can open them! I'm sure you can't wait!'

I fetch a knife and start unpacking the first box, while Trish slits the plastic on another with her razor-nails. Out of the profusion of foam peanuts and bubble wrap, I lift a gleaming, stainless steel . . . something. What on earth is this? I glance quickly at the label on the side of the box. *Savarin Mould.*

'A savarin mould!' I exclaim. 'How marvellous. Just what I wanted.'

'We only got *eight* of those,' says Trish, with concern. 'Is that enough?'

'Er . . .' I look at it helplessly. 'That should be plenty.'

'Now, the saucepans.' Trish has ripped open a box of shiny aluminium pans and holds out one to me expectantly. 'We were told these were the very *best* quality. Would you agree? As a trained chef?'

I look at the pan. It's new and shiny. That's about all I could say.

'Let's just have a look,' I say, trying to sound professional. I heft the saucepan appraisingly, then lift it up, study the bottom, run my finger round the rim and, for good measure, ping the surface with my fingernail. 'Yes, that's a nice quality pan,' I say at last. 'You chose well.'

'Oh, *good*!' Trish beams, delving into another box. 'And look at *this*!' She scatters foam to reveal a weird-shaped gadget with a wooden handle. 'I've never even *seen* one of these! What is it, Samantha?'

I stare at it in silence. What in God's name is that? It looks like a cross between a sieve, a grater and a whisk. I glance quickly at the box for clues, but the label has been torn off.

'What is it?' says Trish again.

Come on. I'm a trained chef. Obviously I know what this is.

'This is used for a highly specialized cooking technique,' I say at last. 'Highly specialized.'

'What do you *do* with it?' Trish is staring, agog. 'Show me!' She thrusts the handle at me.

'Well.' I take the thing from her. 'It's a kind of ... whisking ... circular motion ... keep the wrist light ...' I beat the air briskly a few times. 'Kind of like that. It's difficult to show properly without the ... um ... truffles.'

Truffles? Where did that come from?

'Next time I'm using it, I'll let you know,' I add, and hastily put it down on the counter.

'Oh, do!' Trish looks delighted. 'So what's it called?'

'I've always known it as a ... truffle beater,' I say at last. 'But it could have some other name as well. Why don't I make you a cup of coffee?' I add quickly. 'And I'll unpack everything else later.'

I switch on the kettle, reach for the coffee pot and glance out of the window. Nathaniel is striding across the lawn.

Oh God. Full crush alert. Full, one hundred per cent, old-fashioned adolescent crush.

I cannot take my eyes off him. The sunlight is catching the ends of his tawny hair and he's wearing ancient, faded jeans. As I watch, he picks up some huge sack of something, swings it round easily and throws it onto something which might be a compost heap.

My mind is suddenly filled with a fantasy of him picking me up in exactly the same way. Swinging me round easily in his big strong arms. I mean, I can't be *that* much heavier than a sack of potatoes—

'So, how was your weekend off, Samantha?' Trish breaks my thoughts. 'We barely saw you! Did you go into town?'

'I went to Nathaniel's house,' I reply without thinking.

'Nathaniel?' Trish sounds astonished. 'The *gardener*? Why?'

Immediately I realize my huge mistake. I can't exactly say 'To have cooking lessons.' I stare back at her foolishly for a few moments, trying to fabricate an instant, convincing reason.

'Just . . . to say hello, really . . .' I say at last, aware that I sound tongue-tied. And also that my cheeks are turning pink.

Trish's face suddenly snaps in comprehension and her eyes open very wide, like dinner plates.

'Oh, I *see*,' she says. 'How *adorable*!'

'No!' I say quickly. 'It's not . . . Honestly . . .'

'Don't worry!' Trish cuts me off emphatically. 'I won't say a *word*. I am discretion itself.' She puts a finger to her lips. 'You can rely on me.'

Before I can say anything else she picks up her coffee and heads out of the kitchen. I sit down amidst all the kitchen stuff and packaging, and fiddle with the truffle beater.

That was awkward. But I suppose it doesn't really matter. As long as she doesn't say anything in-appropriate to Nathaniel.

Then I realize I'm being stupid. Of *course* she'll say something inappropriate to Nathaniel. She'll make some oh-so-subtle innuendo. And then who knows what he'll think. This could be really embarrassing. This could ruin everything.

I must go and make the situation quite clear to him. That Trish misunderstood me, and I don't have a crush on him or anything like that.

Whilst, obviously, making it clear that I do.

I force myself to wait until I've done breakfast for Trish and Eddie, tidied the new kitchen equipment away, mixed up some olive oil and lemon zest, and put tonight's sea bream fillets into it, just as Iris taught me.

Then I hitch up my uniform a bit more, add some more eyeliner for luck, and head out into the garden, holding a basket I found in the larder. If Trish wants to know what I'm doing, I'm gathering herbs for cooking.

After walking around the garden for a while I find Nathaniel in the orchard behind the old wall, standing on a ladder, tying some rope round a tree. As I make my way towards him I suddenly start feeling ridiculously nervous. My mouth feels dry – and did my legs just *wobble*?

God, you'd think I'd have some poise. You'd think being a lawyer for seven years would have prepared me a bit better. Ignoring my jitters as best I can, I walk up to the ladder, toss back my hair and smile up at him, trying not to squint in the sun.

'Hi!'

'Hi.' Nathaniel smiles down. 'How's it going?'

'Fine thanks! Much better. No disasters yet . . .'

There's a pause. I suddenly realize I'm gazing a little too hard at his hands as they tighten the rope. 'I was just after some . . . rosemary.' I gesture to my basket. 'If you have any?'

'Sure. I'll cut you some.' He jumps down off the ladder and we start walking along the path towards the herb garden.

It's totally silent, down here away from the house,

apart from the odd buzzing insect and the crunch of gravel on the path. I try to think of something light and easy to say, but my brain is blank.

'It's hot,' I manage at last.

Great.

'Uh huh.' Nathaniel nods, and steps up easily over the stone wall into the herb garden. I try to follow him with a light springing step, and catch my foot on the wall. Ow.

'All right?' Nathaniel turns.

'Fine!' I beam, even though my foot is throbbing with agony. 'Um . . . lovely herbs!' I gesture around the garden in genuine admiration. It's laid out in a hexagonal shape, with little paths between the sections. 'Did you do all this? It's amazing.'

'Thanks. I'm pleased with it.' Nathaniel smiles. 'Anyway. Your rosemary.'

He pulls out a pair of secateurs from an old leather holster-type thing and starts clipping at a dark-green, spiky bush.

My heart starts to thump. I have to say what I've come to say.

'So . . . um . . . it's really weird,' I begin as lightly as I can, fingering the scented leaves of some bushy plant. 'But Trish seems to have got the wrong idea about us! She seems to think we're . . . You know.'

'Ah.' He nods, his face averted.

'Which is obviously . . . ridiculous!' I add with another laugh.

'Mm-hmm.' He clips some more rosemary sprigs and holds them up. 'This enough for you?'

Mm-hmm? That's it? That's all he has to say on the subject?

'Actually, I'd like some more,' I say, and he turns back to the bush. 'So . . . isn't it ridiculous?' I add

190

desperately, trying to prod him into a proper answer.

'Well, of course.' At last Nathaniel looks at me properly, his tanned forehead creased in a frown. 'You won't be wanting to get into anything for a while. Not so soon after a bad relationship.'

I look at him blankly. What on earth—

Oh yes. My bad relationship.

'Right,' I say after a pause. 'Yes, that.'

Dammit.

Why did I invent a bad relationship? What was I *thinking*?

'Here's your rosemary.' Nathaniel puts a fragrant bundle into my arms. 'Anything else?'

'Um . . . yes!' I say quickly. 'Could I have some mint?'

I watch as he moves carefully over the rows of herbs to where mint is growing in large stone containers.

'Actually . . .' I force myself to sound careless. 'Actually, the relationship wasn't *that* bad. In fact, I think I've pretty much got over it.'

Nathaniel looks up, shading his eyes against the sun.

'You've got over a seven-year relationship in a week?'

Now he puts it like that, it does sound a bit implausible. I cast around quickly in my mind.

'I have great reserves of resilience,' I say at last. 'I'm like . . . rubber.'

'Rubber,' he echoes, his expression unreadable.

Was rubber a bad choice of word? No. Come on, rubber is sexy.

Nathaniel adds the mint to the rosemary in my arms. He looks as though he's trying to fathom me out.

'Mum said . . .' He stops, looking awkward.

'What?' I say, a little breathless. They've been talking about me?

'Mum wondered if you'd been . . . badly treated.' He shifts his gaze away. 'You're so tense and twitchy.'

'I'm not tense and twitchy!' I retort at once.

Maybe that was a little tense and twitchy.

'I'm naturally twitchy,' I explain. 'But I wasn't badly treated or anything like that. I was just . . . I always felt . . . trapped.'

The word comes out to my own surprise.

I have a flash of my life at Carter Spink. Practically living at the office, some weeks. Taking piles of work home with me. Answering emails at every hour. Maybe I did feel a little bit trapped.

'But I'm fine now.' I shake back my hair. 'Ready to move on . . . and start a new relationship . . . or something more casual . . . whatever . . . '

A one-night stand would do . . .

I gaze up at him, trying as hard as I can to dilate my pupils, and casually lifting my hand to my ear for good measure. There's a still, tense silence, broken only by the buzzing of insects.

'You probably shouldn't rush into anything new,' Nathaniel says. He moves away without meeting my eye and starts examining the leaves on a shrub.

There's an awkwardness in his back. I feel a rush of blood to my face as it hits me. He's letting me down lightly. He doesn't want to go out with me.

Aargh. This is hideous. Here I am, with my hitched-up skirt and eyeliner, doing all the body language I know, basically just *offering* myself to him . . . And he's trying to let me know he's not interested.

I'm mortified. I have to get away from here. From him.

'You're right,' I say, flustered. 'It's . . . far too soon to think about anything like that. In fact, it would be a terrible idea. I'm just going to focus on my new job.

Cooking and . . . and . . . so forth. I must get on. Thanks for the herbs.'

'Any time,' says Nathaniel.

'Yes. Well. I'll see you.'

Clasping the bundle more tightly, I turn on my heel, step over the wall, managing not to bash my foot this time, and stride back along the gravel path up to the house.

I am *beyond* embarrassed. So much for a whole new Samantha.

That is the last time I ever go after a man, ever. My original strategy of waiting politely, being ignored and then passed over for someone else was a million times better.

Anyway, I don't care. It's for the best, really. Because I *do* have to concentrate on my work. As soon as I get back to the house I set up the ironing board, plug in the iron, turn on the radio and make a nice strong cup of coffee. This is going to be my focus from now on. Getting my tasks for the day done. Not some stupid ridiculous crush on the gardener. I'm being paid to do a job here and I'm going to do it.

By mid morning I've ironed ten shirts, put a load of laundry on and hoovered the conservatory. By lunchtime, I've dusted and hoovered all the downstairs rooms and polished all the mirrors with vinegar. By tea time, I've put on another load of laundry, shredded my vegetables in the food processor, measured out the wild rice to be steamed, and carefully prepared four filo pastry cases for my tartes de fruits, as Iris taught me.

By seven o'clock I've thrown away one lot of burnt filo cases, baked another four, topped them with strawberries and finished them with heated-up apricot jam. I've pan-fried the vegetable shreds in olive oil and garlic till they're soft. I've blanched my French beans. I've put the sea bream in the oven. I've also taken more than a few swigs of vermouth meant for the coulis, but that's neither here nor there.

My face is bright red and my heart is beating fast and I'm moving round the kitchen in a kind of speeded-up reality . . . but I kind of feel OK. In fact, I almost feel exhilarated. Here I am, actually cooking a meal all on my own . . . and I'm just about on top of it! Apart from the mushroom fiasco. But they're safely in the bin.

I've laid the dining table with the best china I could find and put candles in the silver candlesticks. I've got a bottle of Prosecco waiting in the fridge and heated plates waiting in the oven, and I've even put Trish's CD of Enrique Iglesias love songs in the player. I feel like I'm throwing my first-ever dinner party.

With a pleasant flutter in my stomach, I smooth down my apron, push open the kitchen door and call 'Mrs Geiger? Mr Geiger?'

What I need is a big gong.

'Mrs Geiger?' I try again.

There's absolutely no reply. I would have thought they'd be hovering around the kitchen by now. I go back into the kitchen, fetch a glass and a fork, and tinkle one loudly in the other.

Nothing. Where *are* they?

I investigate the rooms on the ground floor, but they're all empty. Cautiously, I start to advance up the stairs.

Maybe they're having a *Joy of Sex* moment. Maybe I should retreat.

'Er . . . Mrs Geiger?' I call hesitantly. 'Dinner's served.'

I can hear voices from the end of the corridor as I take a few more steps forward. 'Mrs Geiger?'

Suddenly a door is violently flung open.

'What's money *for*?' Trish's voice comes shrilling through the air. 'Just tell me that!'

'I don't need to tell you what money's for!' Eddie is yelling back. 'Never have!'

'If you understood *anything*—'

'I understand!' Eddie sounds apoplectic. 'Don't tell me I don't understand!'

Ooooookay. So probably not a *Joy of Sex* moment. I start backing away silently on tiptoe – but it's too late.

'What about *Portugal*?' Trish shrieks. 'Do you remember *that*?' She strides out of the room in a whirl-wind of pink and stops short as she sees me.

'Um . . . dinner's ready,' I mumble, my eyes fixed on the carpet. 'Madam.'

'If you mention *bloody* Portugal one more *bloody* time—' Eddie comes marching out of the room.

'Eddie!' Trish cuts him off savagely, then gives a tiny nod towards me. 'Pas devant.'

'What?' says Eddie, scowling.

'Pas devant les . . . les . . .' She wheels her hands, as though trying to conjure the missing word.

'Domestiques?' I offer awkwardly.

Trish shoots me a flinty look, then draws herself up with dignity. 'I shall be in my room.'

'It's my bloody room too!' says Eddie furiously, but the door has already banged shut.

'Um . . . I've made dinner . . .' I venture, but Eddie stalks to the stairs, ignoring me.

I feel a swell of dismay. If the sea bream isn't eaten soon it'll get all shrivelled.

'Mrs Geiger?' I knock on her door. 'I'm just worried the dinner will spoil—'

'So what?' comes back her muffled voice. 'I'm not in the mood for eating.'

I stare at the door in disbelief. I've spent all bloody day cooking dinner for them. It's all ready. The candles are lit, the plates are in the oven. They can't just not eat it.

'You *have* to eat!' I cry out, and Eddie stops, halfway down the stairs. The bedroom door opens, and Trish looks out in astonishment.

'What?' she says.

OK. Play this one carefully.

'Everyone has to eat,' I improvise. 'It's a human need. So why not discuss your differences over a meal? Or put them on hold! Have a glass of wine and relax and agree not to mention . . . er . . . Portugal.'

As I say the word, I can feel hackles rising.

'I'm not the one who mentioned it,' growls Eddie. 'I thought the subject was closed.'

'I only mentioned it because you were so *insensitive* . . .' Trish's voice is rising and she brushes a sudden tear from her eye. 'How do you think *I* feel, being your . . . trophy wife?'

Trophy?

I must not laugh.

'Trish.' To my astonishment, Eddie is hurrying up the stairs as fast as his paunch will allow. 'Don't you *ever* say that.' He grips her shoulders and looks her fiercely in the eye. 'We've always been a partnership. You know that. Ever since Sydenham.'

First Portugal, now Sydenham. One day I have to sit Trish down with a bottle of wine and get her entire life history out of her.

'I know,' whispers Trish.

She's gazing up at Eddie as though no one else exists, and I suddenly feel a little pang. They really are in love. I can see the antagonism slowly melting away. It's like witnessing a chemical reaction in a test-tube.

'Let's go and eat,' says Eddie finally. 'Samantha was right. We should have a nice meal together. Sit down and talk it over.'

He glances at me and I beam back in relief. Thank God for that. The sea bream will still be just about OK . . . I just need to put the sauce in a jug . . .

'All right, let's.' Trish sniffs. 'Samantha, we'll be out to dinner tonight.'

My smile freezes on my face. What?

'Don't worry about cooking for us,' puts in Eddie, giving me a jovial pat. 'You can have a night off!'

What?

'But . . . I've cooked!' I say quickly. 'It's done!'

'Oh. Well, never mind.' Trish makes a vague flapping gesture. 'Eat it yourself.'

No. No. They cannot do this to me.

'But it's all ready for you downstairs! Roasted fish . . . and julienned vegetables . . .'

'Where shall we go?' says Trish to Eddie, not listening to a word. 'Shall we try and get in at the Mill House?'

As I stand there in stupefaction, she disappears into the bedroom, followed by Eddie. The door closes and I'm left on the landing.

My dinner party's ruined.

When they've roared out of the drive in Eddie's Porsche, I go into the dining room and slowly clear everything up. I put away the crystal glasses and fold up the napkins and blow out the candles. Then I head back into the kitchen and look for a moment at all my dishes, set out ready for action. My sauce, still bubbling away on the hob. My carved-lemon-slice garnishes. I was so proud of everything.

Anyway, there's nothing I can do about it.

My sea bream are looking pretty sorry for themselves, but I put one onto a plate and pour myself a glass of wine. I sit at the table, cut myself a piece and raise it to my mouth. Then I put my knife and fork down without even tasting it. I'm not hungry.

A whole wasted day. And tomorrow I've got to do it all over again. The thought makes me feel like sinking my head down onto my arms and never looking up again.

What am I doing here?

I mean, really. What am I doing? Why am I not walking out right now and getting on a train back to London?

As I'm slumped there I become aware of a faint tapping at the open door. I look up to see Nathaniel leaning on the door frame, holding his rucksack. I feel a flash of embarrassment, as I remember this morning's encounter. Without quite meaning to I swivel my chair away slightly and fold my arms.

'Hi,' I say with a tiny 'If you think I'm interested in you, you're *much* mistaken' shrug.

'I thought I'd come and see if you needed any help.' His eyes travel around the kitchen, at the dishes of untouched food. 'What happened?'

'They didn't eat it. They went out to dinner.'

Nathaniel stares at me for a moment, then closes his eyes briefly and shakes his head. 'After you spent all day cooking for them?'

'It's their food. Their house. They can do what they like.'

I'm trying to sound careless and matter-of-fact. But I can still feel the disappointment, heavy inside me. Nathaniel puts down his rucksack, strides over to the cooker and inspects the sea bream. 'Looks good.'

'It looks like congealed, overcooked fish,' I correct him.

'My favourite.' He grins, but I'm not in the mood to smile back.

'Have some, then.' I gesture at the dish. 'No one else is going to eat it.'

'Well then, shame to waste it.' He helps himself to everything, piling his plate ludicrously high, then pours himself a glass of wine and sits down opposite me at the table.

For a moment neither of us speaks. I'm not even looking at him.

'To you.' Nathaniel raises his wine-glass. 'Congratulations.'

'Yeah, right.'

'Seriously, Samantha.' He waits patiently until I drag my eyes up from the floor. 'Whether they ate it or not, this is a real achievement. I mean, bloody hell.' His mouth twists humorously. 'Remember the last dinner you cooked in this kitchen?'

I give a reluctant smile. 'The lamb of doom, you mean.'

'The *chick peas*. I'll never forget those.' He takes a bite of fish, shaking his head incredulously. 'This is good, by the way.'

An image comes to me of those tiny blackened bullets; myself running around in frenzied chaos; the meringue dripping on the floor . . . and in spite of everything I want to giggle. I've already learned so much since then.

'Well, of course, I'd have been OK that night,' I say nonchalantly, 'if you hadn't insisted on *helping* me. I had it all under control till you got in my way.'

Nathaniel puts his fork down, still munching. For a few moments he just looks at me, his blue eyes crinkled up with something – amusement, maybe. I can feel the tell-tale heat rising in my cheeks, and as

I glance downwards I notice that my hands are resting on the table, palms up.

And I'm leaning forward, I realize in sudden horror. My pupils are probably half a mile wide, too. I could not be any clearer if I wrote 'I fancy you' in felt-tip on my forehead.

I hastily move my hands to my lap, sit up straight and adopt a stony expression. I haven't got over this morning's mortification. In fact, I might take the opportunity to say something.

'So—' I begin, just as Nathaniel starts speaking too.

'Go on.' He gestures towards me and takes another bite of fish. 'After you.'

'Well.' I clear my throat. 'After our . . . conversation this morning, I was just going to say that you're quite right about relationships. Obviously I'm not ready for anything new yet. Or even interested. At all.'

There. That told him. I'm not entirely sure how convincing I sounded, but at least I've salvaged my dignity a little.

'What were you going to say?' I ask, pouring more wine into his glass.

'I was going to ask you out,' says Nathaniel, and I nearly flood the table with wine.

He what?

The hands thing *worked*?

'But not to worry.' He takes a gulp of wine. 'I understand.'

Backtrack. I need to backtrack, very, very quickly. Yet subtly, so he doesn't actually *notice* I'm backtracking . . .

Oh bugger it, I'll just be inconsistent. I'm a woman, I'm allowed to be.

'Nathaniel,' I force myself to say calmly, 'I'd love to go out with you.'

'Good.' He looks unperturbed. 'How's Friday night?'

'Perfect.'

As I grin back I suddenly realize I feel hungry. I pull my plate of sea bream towards me, pick up my knife and fork and begin to eat.

FOURTEEN

I get to Friday morning without any major calamities. At least, none that the Geigers know about.

There was the vegetable-risotto disaster on Tuesday – but thank God I managed to get a last-minute substitute from the caterers. There was a peach camisole which, in hindsight, should have been ironed on a lower setting. There was the Dartington vase which I broke while trying to dust with the vacuum-cleaner attachment. But no one seems to have noticed it's gone yet. And the new one should arrive tomorrow.

So far, this week has only cost me two hundred pounds, which is a vast improvement on last week. I may even start making a profit before too long.

I'm hanging out Eddie's damp underwear in the utility room, averting my eyes as best I can, when I hear Trish calling me.

'Samantha! Where *are* you?' She doesn't sound pleased, and I feel a quailing inside. What's she discovered? 'I *can't* have you walking around like that any more.' Trish arrives at the door of the utility room, shaking her head vigorously.

'I'm sorry?' I peer at her.

'Your *hair*.' She makes a face.

'Oh, right.' I touch the bleached patch with a grimace. 'I meant to get it done at the weekend—'

'You're having it done now,' she cuts across me. 'My *super* hairdresser's here.'

'Now?' I stare at her. 'But . . . I've got vacuuming to do.'

'I'm not having you walk around like a fright any more. You can make up the hours later. And I'll take the money out of your wages. Come on. Annabel's waiting!'

I guess I have no choice. I dump the rest of Eddie's underpants on the rack and follow her up the stairs.

'Now, I've been meaning to mention my cashmere cardigan,' Trish adds sternly as we reach the top. 'The cream one?'

Shit. Shit. She's found out I replaced it. Of course she has. I should have known she couldn't be that stupid—

'I don't know what you've done to it.' Trish blows out a cloud of smoke and pushes open her bedroom door. 'But it looks *marvellous*. That little ink stain on the hem has completely disappeared! It's like new!'

'Right.' I give a smile of relief. 'Well . . . all part of the service!'

I follow Trish into the bedroom, where a thin woman with big blonde hair, white jeans and a gold chain belt is setting up a chair in the middle of the floor.

'Hello!' She looks up, cigarette in hand, and I realize that she's about sixty years old. 'Samantha! I've heard *all* about you.'

Her voice is gravelly, her mouth is pursed with lines from dragging on cigarettes, and her make-up looks like it's been welded to her skin. She's basically Trish, fifteen years on. She comes forward, surveys my hair and winces.

'What's all this? Thought you'd try the streaky look?' She gives a raucous laugh at her own joke.

'It was a . . . bleach accident.'

'Accident!' She runs her fingers through my hair, clicking. 'Well, it can't stay this colour. We'd better go a nice blonde. You don't mind going blonde, do you, dear?'

Blonde?

'I've never been blonde,' I say in alarm. 'I'm not really sure—'

'You've got the colouring for it.' She's brushing my hair out.

'Well, as long as it's not *too* blonde,' I say hurriedly. 'Not . . . you know, that fake, tarty, platinum blonde . . .'

I trail off as I realize both the other women in the room have fake, tarty, platinum-blonde hair.

'Or . . . um . . .' I swallow, unable to look up. 'Whatever you think. Really.'

I sit down on the chair, wrap a towel around my shoulders and try not to flinch as Annabel briskly pastes some chemical-smelling paste on my head and layers in what feels like a thousand bits of silver foil.

Blonde. Yellow hair. Barbie dolls.

Oh God. What am I *doing*?

'I think this was a mistake,' I say abruptly, trying to get out of my chair. 'I don't think I'm a natural blonde—'

'Relax!' Annabel clamps my shoulders, forcing me back down into my seat, and puts a magazine in my hand. Behind, Trish is opening a bottle of champagne. 'You'll look lovely. Pretty girl like you should *do* something with her hair. Now, read us our signs.'

'Signs?' I say in bewilderment.

'Horoscopes!' Annabel clicks her tongue. 'Not the brightest penny, is she?' she adds in an undertone to Trish.

'She is a little dim,' Trish murmurs back discreetly. 'But *marvellous* at laundry.'

So this is what being a lady of leisure is like. Sitting with foil in your hair, drinking Buck's Fizz and reading glossy magazines. I haven't read any magazines except *The Lawyer* since I was about thirteen. Normally I spend hairdressers' appointments typing emails or reading contracts.

But I can't relax and enjoy myself. I'm feeling more and more apprehensive as I read 'Ten Ways To Know Your Bikini Is Too Small'. By the time I've got to 'Real-Life Holiday Romances' and Annabel is blow-drying my hair, my entire body is seized up in fear.

I can't be blonde. It's just not who I am.

'There we are!' Annabel gives a final blast and switches the hair-dryer off. There's silence. I can't open my eyes.

'*Much* better!' Trish says approvingly.

I slowly open one eye. Then the other.

My hair isn't blonde.

It's caramel. It's warm caramel with streaks of honey and the tiniest threads of gold here and here. As I move my head it shimmers.

I swallow a few times, trying to keep control of myself. I almost think I might cry.

'You didn't believe me, did you?' Annabel raises her eyebrows at me in the mirror, a satisfied smile on her lips. 'Thought I didn't know what I was doing.'

She can so obviously read my mind, I feel abashed.

'It's wonderful,' I say, finding my voice. 'I'm ...
Thank you so much.'

I'm entranced by my reflection. I can't take my eyes
off my new, glowing, caramel, honey self. I look alive.
I look *colourful*.

I'm never going back to the way I looked before.
Never.

My pleasure doesn't fade. Even when I've gone downstairs again and am pushing the Hoover round the
drawing room. I'm totally preoccupied by my new
hair. As I pass any shiny surface I stop to admire
myself, and flick up my hair so it cascades back down
in a caramelly shower.

Vacuum under the rug. *Flick.* Vacuum under the
coffee table. *Flick. Flick.*

It never even occurred to me to dye my hair before.
What else have I been missing out on?

'Ah, Samantha.' I look up to see Eddie coming into
the room, wearing a jacket and tie. 'I'm having a meeting in the dining room. I'd like you to make some
coffee and bring it in to us.'

'Yes, Sir.' I curtsey. 'How many of you are there?'

'Four altogether. And some biscuits. Snacks.
Whatever.'

'Of course.'

He looks hyped up and red in the face. I wonder
what this meeting is. As I head to the kitchen I glance
curiously out of the front window, and see an unfamiliar Mercedes Series 5 parked in the drive, next to
a convertible BMW.

Hmm. Probably not the local vicar, then.

I make a pot of coffee, put it on a tray, add a plate of
biscuits and some muffins I bought for tea. Then I head
to the dining room and knock.

'Come in!'

I push the door open to see Eddie sitting with three men in suits around the dining-room table, with papers in front of them.

'Your coffee,' I murmur in deferential tones.

'Thank you, Samantha.' Eddie's cheeks are glowing. 'If you could serve it out?'

I put the tray down on the sideboard and distribute the cups. As I'm doing so I can't help glancing at the papers – and immediately recognize them as contracts.

'Er . . . white or black?' I say to the first man.

'White, please.' He doesn't even look up. As I pour the coffee, I have another casual look. It looks like some kind of property-investment deal. Is Eddie sinking his money into something?

'Biscuit?' I offer.

'I'm sweet enough.' The man bares his teeth in a grin, and I smile politely back. What an asshole.

'So, Eddie. You understand that point now?' A man in a purple tie is speaking, in a smooth, concerned voice. 'It's pretty clear when you hack through the jargon.'

I feel a blade of recognition as he speaks. Not that I know his face – but I know people like this. I worked with them for seven years. And I know instinctively that this man doesn't care two jots whether Eddie understands.

'Yes!' Eddie gives a jovial laugh. 'Yes, I'm sure it is. He peers at the contract uncertainly, then puts it down.

'We're as concerned about security as you,' says the man in the purple tie, with a smile.

'When it comes to money, who isn't?' quips the first guy.

OK. What exactly is going on here?

As I move round to the next guy and pour his coffee, the contract is clearly visible and I run my eyes down it with practised speed. It's a property-development partnership. Both sides putting up money . . . residential development . . . so far so standard . . .

Then I see something that makes me freeze in shock. It's very carefully worded, in an innocuous-looking little clause at the bottom of the page. In one line, it commits Eddie to funding any shortfall. With no reciprocity, as far as I can see.

If things go wrong Eddie has to foot the bill. Does he *realize*?

I'm totally aghast. My urge to reach for the contract and rip it up is almost overpowering. If this were at Carter Spink these guys would not last two minutes. Not only would I throw their contract out, but I would recommend to my client that—

'Samantha?' I jerk back to reality to see Eddie frowning slightly at me, and gesturing to the biscuit plate.

I'm not at Carter Spink. I'm in a housekeeper's uniform and I have refreshments to serve.

'Chocolate biscuit?' Somehow I force a polite tone as I offer the plate to the guy with dark hair. 'Or a muffin?'

He just grabs one without even acknowledging me, and I move round to Eddie, thinking quickly. I have to warn him somehow.

'So. Enough talk. The adventure begins.' The purple-tie guy is unscrewing the lid of a smart fountain pen. 'After you.' He hands it to Eddie.

He's about to *sign*? *Now*?

No. No. He cannot sign this contract.

'Take your time,' the man adds with a perfect-toothed smile. 'If you'd like to read it through again . . .'

I feel a surge of sudden fury at these guys, with their flash cars and purple ties and smooth voices. They are not going to rip off my boss. I'm not going to let it happen. As Eddie's pen touches the page I lean forward.

'Mr Geiger,' I say urgently. 'Could I see you for a minute please? In private?'

Eddie looks up in annoyance.

'Samantha,' he says with heavy humour. 'I'm in the middle of rather important business here. Important to me, at any rate!' He glances round the table, and the three men laugh sycophantically.

'It's very urgent,' I say. 'It won't take long.'

'Samantha—'

'Please, Mr Geiger. I *need* to speak to you.'

At last Eddie exhales in exasperation and puts down the pen.

'All right.' He gets up, ushers me out of the room and demands, 'What is it?'

I stare back at him dumbly. Now I've got him out here I have no idea how to bring up the subject. What can I say?

Mr Geiger, I would recommend reviewing clause 14.

Mr Geiger, your liabilities are not sufficiently protected.

It's impossible. I can't say anything. Who takes legal advice from their housekeeper?

His hand is on the door handle. This is my last chance.

'Do you take sugar?' I blurt out.

'*What?*' Eddie gapes at me.

'I couldn't remember,' I mumble. 'And I didn't want to draw attention to your sugar consumption in public.'

'Yes, I take one lump,' says Eddie testily. 'Is that all?'

'Well ... there was something else. It looks like you're signing some papers in there.'

'That's right.' He frowns. 'Private papers.'

'Of course!' I swallow. 'I was just wondering if you had a lawyer. It just ... um ... crossed my mind. I remember you telling me always to be very careful with documents.'

I look into his eyes, willing the message to get through. *Consult a lawyer, you stupid schmuck.*

Eddie gives a jovial laugh.

'Very thoughtful of you, Samantha. But you don't need to worry. I'm not a fool.' He opens the door and strides back in. 'Where were we, gentlemen?'

I watch in dismay as he picks up the pen again. I can't stop him. The idiot's going to get fleeced.

But not if I can help it.

'Your coffee, Mr Geiger ...' I murmur, hurrying into the room. I pick up the pot, start pouring, then accidentally-on-purpose drop it on the table.

'Aaargh!'

'Jesus!'

There's total mayhem as the coffee spreads in a dark-brown lake over the table, soaking into papers and dripping onto the floor.

'The contracts!' shouts the purple-tied man in annoyance. 'You stupid woman!'

'I'm really sorry,' I say in my most flustered voice. 'I'm really, really sorry. The coffee pot just ... slipped.' I start mopping the coffee with a tissue, making sure to spread it over all the remaining paperwork.

'Do we have any copies?' asks one of the men, and I freeze.

'They were all on the bloody table,' says the dark-haired guy in exasperation. 'We'll have to get them printed out again.'

'You know, if you *are* printing out more copies, I'd like you to print out an extra one if you don't mind.' Eddie clears his throat. 'I think I'll pass it to my lawyer for a look-see. Just in case.'

The men all exchange looks. I can sense consternation rising.

'Of course,' says the purple-tied man after a long pause. 'No problem.'

Ha. Something tells me this deal may not be happening after all.

'Your jacket, Sir?' I say with a smile, handing it to him. 'And again, I'm dreadfully, dreadfully sorry.'

The great thing about a legal training is it *really* teaches you to lie.

It also teaches you to put up with being yelled at by your boss. Which is handy, because as soon as Trish hears what I've done, I'm forced to stand in the kitchen for twenty minutes while she strides around, haranguing me.

'Mr Geiger is putting together a very important business deal!' She inhales furiously on her cigarette, her newly dyed hair bouncing around her shoulders. 'That meeting was crucial!'

'I'm very sorry, Madam,' I say, eyes downcast.

'I know you have no understanding of these things, Samantha.' Her eyes swivel towards me. 'But a lot of money is at stake! Money which you probably have no conception of.'

Stay calm. Stay humble.

'A lot of money,' Trish repeats, impressively.

She's *itching* to tell me more. I can see the urge to show off and the urge to remain discreet fighting it out on her face.

'*Seven figures*,' she says at last.

'Gosh.' I do my best to look awestruck.

'We've been very good to you, Samantha. We've made *every* effort.' Her voice throbs with resentment. 'And we expect you to make every effort in return.'

'I'm very sorry,' I say for the millionth time.

Trish shoots me a dissatisfied look. 'Well, I'll expect far more care tonight.'

'Tonight?' I echo in puzzlement.

'At dinner.' Trish raises her eyes skywards.

'But I've got tonight off,' I say in alarm. 'You said it would be OK, I could leave you a cold supper . . .'

Trish has clearly forgotten all about our conversation.

'Well,' she says querulously, 'that was before you *threw* coffee over our guests. That was before you spent all morning sitting about having your hair done.'

What? That is so unfair I can't even find a response.

'Frankly, Samantha, I expect a little better. You will stay in tonight and serve dinner.' She gives me a hard look, picks up a magazine and strides out of the kitchen.

I stare after her, a familiar, heavy resignation creeping over me. This has happened so many times, I'm used to it. I'll have to call off my date with Nathaniel. Another date . . . another cancellation . . .

And then my thoughts stop mid track. I'm not at Carter Spink any more. I don't have to put up with this.

I stalk out of the kitchen and find Trish in the living room.

'Mrs Geiger,' I say as forcefully as I can. 'I'm sorry about the coffee and I'll make every effort to do better. But I have to have tonight off. I've made arrangements – and I'm going to stick to them. I'll be going out at seven as planned.'

212

My heart is beating fast as I finish. I've never asserted myself like that before in my life. If I'd ever spoken like that at Carter Spink I'd have been dead meat.

For a moment Trish looks livid. Then, to my astonishment, she gives an irritated click with her tongue and turns a page.

'Oh, very well. If it's *that* important—'

'Yes.' I swallow. 'It's important. My personal life is important.'

As I say the words, I feel stirred up. I almost want to say something more to Trish. Something about priorities, about balance . . .

But Trish is already engrossed in an article on 'The Red Wine Diet – How It Can Work For You'. I'm not sure she'd appreciate being disturbed.

FIFTEEN

By seven o'clock that evening, Trish's mood has unaccountably transformed. Or maybe not so
unaccountably. I arrive downstairs in the hall to see
her wandering out of the living room with a cocktail
glass, bloodshot eyes and a high colour.

'So!' she says benevolently. 'You're going out with
Nathaniel tonight.'

'That's right.' I glance at myself in the mirror. I've
gone for a fairly informal outfit. Jeans, nice simple top,
sandals. New shiny hair. *Flick*.

'He's a very attractive young man.' She eyes
me inquisitively over the top of her glass. 'Very
muscular.'

'Er . . . yes. I suppose so.'

'Is that what you're wearing?' She runs her eyes over
my outfit. 'It's not very *jazzy*, is it? Let me lend you a
little something.'

'I don't mind not being jazzy,' I begin, feeling a few
qualms, but Trish has already disappeared up the
stairs. A few moments later she appears, holding a
jewel box.

'Here we are. You need a bit of *glitz*.' She produces

a diamanté clip in the shape of a sea-horse. 'I got this in Monte Carlo!'

'Er . . . lovely!' I say, eyeing it in horror. Before I can stop her, she sweeps my hair to one side and plonks it on. She looks at me appraisingly. 'No . . . I think you need something *larger*. Here.' She fishes out a large jewelled beetle and clips it to my hair. '*Now*. You see how the emerald brings out your eyes?'

I gaze at myself speechlessly. I cannot go out with a sparkly beetle on my head.

'And this is very glam!' Now she's garlanding a gilt chain around my waist. 'Let me just hang the charms on . . .'

Charms?

'Mrs Geiger . . .' I begin, flustered, as Eddie appears out of the study.

'Just got the quote in for the bathroom,' he says to Trish.

'Isn't this twinkly elephant *gorgeous*?' says Trish, hooking it on the gilt belt. 'And the frog!'

'Please,' I say desperately. 'I'm not sure I need any elephants—'

'Seven thousand,' Eddie cuts across me. 'Seems quite reasonable. Plus VAT.'

'Well, how much is it with VAT?' says Trish, rifling in her box. 'Where's that monkey gone?'

I feel like a Christmas tree. She's hanging more and more glittery baubles off the belt, not to mention the beetle. And Nathaniel will arrive any moment . . . and he'll *see* me . . .

'I don't know!' retorts Eddie impatiently. 'What's seventeen and a half per cent of seven thousand?'

'One thousand, two hundred and twenty-five,' I respond absently.

There's a stunned silence.

Shit. That was a mistake.

I look up to see Trish and Eddie goggling at me.

'Or . . . something.' I give a distracting laugh. 'Just a guess. So . . . have you got any more charms?'

Neither of them takes the slightest notice of me. Eddie's eyes are fixed on the paper he's holding. Very slowly he looks up, his mouth working strangely.

'She's right,' he says in a strangled voice. 'She's bloody right. That's the correct answer.' He jabs the paper. 'It's here!'

'She's *right*?' Trish breathes in sharply. 'But how . . .'

'You saw her.' Eddie's voice rises to an incredulous squeak. 'She did it in her head!'

They both swivel round to gaze at me again.

'Is she *autistic*?' Trish seems beside herself.

Oh, for God's sake. *Rain Man* has a lot to answer for, if you ask me.

'I'm not autistic!' I say. 'I'm just . . . I'm just quite good with numbers. It's no big deal . . .'

To my huge relief the doorbell rings, and I go to answer it. Nathaniel is standing on the doorstep, looking a little smarter than usual, in tan jeans and a green shirt.

'Hi,' I say hurriedly. 'Let's go.'

'Wait!' Eddie blocks my way. 'Young lady, you may be a lot brighter than you realize.'

Oh no.

'What's going on?' asks Nathaniel.

'She's a mathematical genius!' says Trish wildly. 'And we discovered it! It's just extraordinary!'

I shoot Nathaniel an agonized 'she's talking nonsense' look.

'What formal education have you had, Samantha?' Eddie demands. 'Other than cooking.'

Oh God. What did I say in my interview? I honestly can't remember.

'I . . . um . . . here and there.' I spread my hands vaguely. 'You know . . .'

'It's the schools today.' Trish inhales sharply on her cigarette. 'Tony Blair should be *shot*.'

'Samantha,' Eddie says, looking self-righteous, 'I will take on your education. And if you're prepared to work hard – hard, mind – I'm sure we can get you some qualifications.'

No. This gets worse.

'I don't really want any qualifications, Sir,' I mumble, looking at the floor. 'I'm happy as I am. Thanks anyway.'

'I won't take no for an answer!' insists Eddie.

'Aim higher, Samantha!' says Trish with sudden passion, gripping my arm. 'Give yourself a chance in life! Reach for the stars!'

As I look from face to face, I can't help feeling touched. They only want the best for me.

'Um . . . well . . . maybe.' I surreptitiously divest myself of all the jewelled creatures and slip them back into the jewellery box. Then I look at Nathaniel, who has been waiting patiently on the doorstep. 'Shall we go?'

'So, what was all that about?' asks Nathaniel as we start walking along the village road. The air is soft and warm and my new hair is bouncing lightly, and with every step I can see my toes, painted in Trish's pink nail polish. 'You're a mathematical genius?'

'No.' I can't help laughing. 'Of course not!'

'What *is* your background then?'

'Oh . . . you don't want to know.' I give him a brush-off smile. 'Very boring.'

'I don't believe that for a minute.' His tone is light but persistent. 'Did you have a career? Before you came here?'

I walk for a few paces without saying anything, my eyes on the ground, trying to think what to say. I can feel Nathaniel's eyes on me, but I twist my head away from his scrutiny.

'You don't want to talk about it,' he says at last.

'It's . . . it's hard.'

Nathaniel exhales sharply. 'You've had a bad time of it?'

Oh God, he still thinks I'm an abused wife.

'No! It's not that.' I push my hands through my hair. 'It's just . . . a long story.'

Nathaniel shrugs. 'We've got all evening.'

As I meet his steady gaze I feel a sudden pull, like a fishhook inside my chest. I want to tell him. I want to unburden everything. Who I am, what happened, how hard it's been. Of all people, I could trust him. He wouldn't tell anyone. He'd understand. He'd keep it secret.

'So.' He stops still in the street, his thumbs in his pockets. 'Are you going to tell me who you are?'

'Maybe,' I say at last, and find myself smiling. Nathaniel smiles back, his eyes crinkling with a slow, delicious ease.

'But not right now.' I look around the golden village street. 'It's too nice an evening to spoil with a story of disaster and woe. I'll tell you later.'

We walk on, passing an old stone wall covered with a profusion of climbing roses. And as I breathe in the delicious scent, I feel a sudden lightness; almost euphoria. The street is dappled with soft evening light and the last rays of sun are warm on my shoulders.

'Nice hair, by the way,' he says.

'Oh, thanks.' I give a nonchalant smile. 'It's nothing really.' *Flick.*

We walk over the bridge and pause to look at the river. Moorhens are diving for weed and the sunlight is like amber puddles on the water. A couple of tourists are taking pictures of each other, and I feel a glow of pride. I'm not visiting this beautiful place, I feel like informing them. I *live* here.

'So where are we heading?' I say as we start walking again.

'The pub,' he says. 'If that's OK?'

'Perfect!'

As we approach The Bell I see a small crowd of people outside: some standing by the door; others sitting at the wooden tables.

'What are they doing?' I say, puzzled.

'Waiting,' he says. 'Landlord's late.'

'Oh,' I say. I look around but all the tables are already taken. 'Well, never mind. We can sit here.'

I perch on an old barrel – but Nathaniel has already headed for the door of the pub.

And . . . that's weird. Everyone is standing back to let him through. I watch in astonishment as he reaches in his pocket and produces a big bunch of keys, then looks around to find me.

'Come on,' he beckons with a grin. 'Opening time.'

Nathaniel owns a *pub*?

'You own a *pub*?' I say, as the initial melee of the evening dies down.

I've watched in wonderment for fifteen minutes as Nathaniel has pulled pints, bantered with customers, given instructions to the bar staff and made sure everyone is happy. Now the initial rush is over, he's come round to where I'm perched on a bar stool with a glass of wine.

'Three pubs,' he corrects me. 'And it's not just me. It's our family business. The Bell, The Swan over in Bingley and The Two Foxes.'

'Wow. But . . . it's so busy!' I look around the pub. Every seat seems to be full, with people spilling outside into the tiny garden and onto the forecourt in front. The noise of chatter is tremendous. 'How do you do this and be a gardener?'

'OK, I'll come clean.' Nathaniel lifts his hands. 'I don't serve very often. We have a great bar staff. But I thought it might be fun tonight.'

'So you're not really a gardener!'

'I am really a gardener.' He looks down briefly, straightening a bar mat. 'This is . . . business.'

There's the same tone in his voice as before. As though I've trodden on something sensitive. I look away – and my attention is caught by a picture on the wall of a middle-aged man. He has Nathaniel's strong jaw and blue eyes, and the same crinkles around his eyes as he smiles.

'That's your dad?' I say cautiously. 'He looks wonderful.'

'He was the life and soul.' Nathaniel's eyes soften. 'Everyone here, they all loved him.' He takes a deep slug of beer, then puts his glass down. 'But listen. We don't have to stay here. If you'd rather go somewhere else, somewhere smarter . . .'

I look around the bustling pub. Music is playing above the noise of talk and laughter. A group of regulars are greeting each other by the bar with cheerful insults. A pair of elderly American tourists in Stratford T-shirts are being advised on local beers by a barman with red hair and twinkling eyes. Across the room a darts game has started. I can't remember the last time I was somewhere with such an easy, friendly atmosphere.

'Let's stay. And I'll help!' I slip off my bar stool and head behind the bar.

'Have you ever pulled a pint before?' Nathaniel follows me, looking amused.

'No,' I say, picking up a glass and putting it under one of the beer taps. 'But I can learn.'

'OK.' Nathaniel comes round the bar. 'You tilt the glass like this . . . now pull.'

I pull the tap, and a burst of foam splutters out. 'Damn!'

'Slowly . . .' He puts his arms around me, guiding my hands. 'That's better . . .'

Mmm, this is nice. He's saying something to me, but I'm not listening to a word. I'm in a blissful happy haze, enveloped in his strong arms. Maybe I'll pretend I'm very slow at learning how to pull pints. Maybe we can stand like this all evening.

'You know,' I begin, turning my head towards him. And then I stop as my eyes focus on something. There's an old wooden notice on the wall, stating 'No Muddy Boots Please' and 'No Working Clothes'. Underneath, another notice has been pinned. It's printed on yellowing paper in faded marker pen – and it reads: NO LAWYERS.

I stare at it, dumbfounded. No lawyers?

Am I reading that correctly?

'There we are.' Nathaniel holds up the glass, full of a gleaming amber liquid. 'Your first-ever pint.'

'Er . . . great!' I say. I force myself to leave a natural pause, then gesture casually at the sign. 'What's this?'

'I don't serve lawyers,' he replies without a flicker.

'Nathaniel! Get over here!' someone calls from

the other end of the bar and he clicks in annoyance.

'I'll only be a moment.' He touches my hand, then moves away. Immediately I take a deep gulp of wine. He doesn't serve lawyers. Why doesn't he serve lawyers?

OK . . . just calm down, I instruct myself firmly. It's a *joke*. Obviously it's a joke. Everyone hates lawyers, just like everyone hates estate agents and tax collectors. It's an accepted fact of life.

But they don't all put signs up in their pubs, do they?

As I'm sitting there, the barman with red hair comes up to where I'm standing, and scoops some ice out of the tank.

'Hi,' he says, holding out his hand. 'I'm Eamonn.'

'Samantha.' I shake it with a smile. 'I'm here with Nathaniel.'

'He said.' His eyes twinkle. 'Welcome to Lower Ebury.'

As I watch him serving, it suddenly strikes me that this guy might know something about the sign.

'So,' I say carelessly when he comes back over, 'that sign about lawyers. It's a joke, right?'

'Not really,' Eamonn replies cheerfully. 'Nathaniel can't stand lawyers.'

'Right!' Somehow I manage to keep on smiling. 'Um . . . why's that?'

'Ever since his dad died.' Eamonn hefts a crate of orange mixers onto the bar and I shift round on my stool so I can see him properly.

'Why? What happened?'

'There was some law suit between him and the council.' Eamonn pauses in his work. 'Nathaniel says it should never have been started in the first place, but Ben got talked into doing it by the lawyers. He wasn't well anyway, and he got more and more stressed by it, couldn't think about anything else. Then he had a heart attack.'

'God, how awful,' I say in horror. 'And Nathaniel blamed the lawyers?'

'He reckons the case should never have been brought.' Eamonn resumes hefting crates. 'Worst thing was, after Ben died they had to sell off one of the pubs. To pay the legal bills.'

I'm totally aghast. I glance at Nathaniel on the other side of the bar listening to some guy, a deep frown furrowing his brow.

'The last lawyer came in this pub . . .' Eamonn leans conspiratorially across the bar, 'Nathaniel punched him.'

'He *punched* him?' My voice comes out a petrified squeak.

'It was on the day of his dad's funeral.' Eamonn lowers his voice. 'One of his dad's lawyers came in here and Nathaniel socked him one. We tease him about it now.'

He turns away to serve someone and I take another gulp of wine, my heart hammering with nerves.

Let's not freak out here. So he doesn't like lawyers. That doesn't mean *me*. Of course it doesn't. I can still be honest with him. I can still tell him about my past. He won't take it against me. Surely.

But what if he does?

What if he punches me?

'Sorry about that.' All of a sudden Nathaniel is in front of me, his face warm and friendly. 'Are you OK?'

'I'm fine!' I say over-brightly. 'Having a lovely time!'

'Hey, Nathaniel,' says Eamonn, polishing a glass. He winks at me. 'What do you call five thousand lawyers at the bottom of the ocean?'

'A start!' The words jump out of my mouth before I can stop them. 'They should all . . . rot. Away. Into hell.'

There's a surprised silence. I can see Eamonn and Nathaniel exchanging raised eyebrows.

OK. Change the subject. Now.

'So! Er . . .' I quickly turn to a group standing by the bar. 'Can I serve anyone?'

By the end of the evening I've pulled about forty pints. I've had a plate of cod and chips and half a dish of sticky toffee pudding – and beaten Nathaniel at darts, to loud cheers and whoops from everyone watching around.

'You said you hadn't played before!' he says in disbelief after I nail my winning double eight.

'I haven't,' I say innocently. There's no need to mention that I did archery at school for five years.

At last Nathaniel rings Last Orders with a resounding clang of the bell, and a good hour later the last few stragglers make it to the door, each pausing to say goodbye as they leave.

'Bye.'

'Cheers, Nathaniel.'

I've been watching everyone leave the pub – and apart from the tourists, they've all made Nathaniel some kind of farewell. He must know every single person in this village.

'We'll clear up,' says Eamonn firmly, as Nathaniel starts picking up glasses, five at a time. 'Give those here. You'll want to be enjoying the rest of the evening.'

'Well . . . OK.' Nathaniel claps him on the back. 'Thanks, Eamonn.' He looks at me. 'Ready to go?'

Almost reluctantly I slide down off my bar stool.

'It's been an amazing evening,' I say to Eamonn. 'Brilliant to meet you.'

'Likewise.' He grins. 'Send us your invoice.'

I beam back, still buoyed up by the atmosphere; by my win at darts; by the satisfaction of having spent the evening actually *doing* something. I've never had an evening out like this in my life.

No one in London ever took me to a pub for a date – let alone to the other side of the bar. On my first evening out with Jacob he took me to *Les Sylphides* at Covent Garden, then left after twenty minutes to take a call from the States and never returned. He said the next day he was so bound up in a point of commercial contract law, he forgot I was there.

And the worst thing is, instead of saying 'You bastard!' and punching him, I asked what point of commercial contract law.

After the beery warmth of the pub, the summer night is fresh and cool. As we start walking along I can hear the faint laughter of pub-goers up ahead, and a car starting in the distance. There are no street lamps; the only light comes from a big full moon and curtained cottage windows.

'Did you enjoy yourself?' Nathaniel sounds a bit anxious. 'I didn't mean for us to stay there all night . . .'

'I really, really loved it,' I say with enthusiasm. 'It's a great pub. And I can't get over how friendly it is. The way everyone knows you! And the village spirit. Everyone cares about each other. You can tell.'

'How can you tell that?' Nathaniel sounds amused.

'From the way everyone claps each other on the back,' I explain. 'Like, if someone were in trouble, everyone would rally round in a heartwarming way. You can just see it.'

I hear Nathaniel stifle a laugh. 'We did get the Most Heartwarming Village award last year,' he says.

'You can laugh,' I retort. 'But in London, no one's heartwarming. If you fell over dead in the street they'd just push you into the gutter. After emptying your wallet and stealing your identity. That wouldn't happen here, would it?'

'Well, no,' says Nathaniel. He pauses thoughtfully. 'If you die here, the entire village gathers round your bed and sings the village lament.'

My mouth twists into a smile. 'I knew it. Strewing flower petals?'

'Naturally.' He nods. 'And making ceremonial corn dollies.'

We walk on in silence for a few moments. A small animal runs across the road, stops and regards us with two tiny yellow headlamps, then skitters into the hedgerow.

'How does the lament go, then?' I say.

'It goes something like this.' Nathaniel clears his throat, then sings, in a low, mournful monotone. 'Oh no. He's gone.'

I feel an explosive giggle inside, which somehow I conceal.

'What about if it's a woman?'

'Good point. Then we sing a different lament.' He draws a deep breath and sings again, on exactly the same tuneless note: 'Oh no. She's gone.'

My stomach is clenched from trying not to laugh.

'Well, we don't have laments in London,' I say. 'We move on. Big on moving, Londoners. Big on staying ahead.'

'I know about Londoners.' Nathaniel looks wry. 'I lived in London for a time.'

I gape at him in the moonlight. Nathaniel lived in

London? I try, and fail, to picture him strap-hanging on the Tube, reading *Metro*.

'Seriously?' I say at last and he nods.

'And I hated it. Seriously.'

'But what – why . . .'

'I was a waiter on my year off before uni. My flat was opposite a twenty-four-hour supermarket. It was lit up all night with these bright fluorescent strips. And the noise . . .' He winces. 'In ten months of living there, I never had a single moment of total darkness or total quiet. I never heard a bird. I never saw the stars.'

Instinctively I tilt my head back to look up at the clear night sky. Slowly, as my eyes adjust to the blackness, the tiny pinpricks begin to appear all over it, forming whorls and patterns which I can't begin to decipher. He's right. I never saw the stars in London either.

'How about you?' His voice brings me back to earth.

'What do you mean?'

'You were going to tell me your story,' he says. 'How you came to be here.'

'Oh.' I feel a spasm of nerves. 'Yes, right. So I was.' Even though he can barely see me in the dark I look away, my mind working as best it can after three glasses of wine.

I have to say something. Maybe I can keep it to a minimum. Tell the truth without mentioning the lawyer bit.

'Well,' I say at last. 'I was in London. In this . . . this . . .'

'Relationship,' he prompts.

'Er . . . yes.' I swallow. 'Well. Things went wrong. I got on a train . . . and I ended up here.'

There's an expectant silence. 'That's it,' I add.

'That's *it*?' Nathaniel sounds incredulous. 'That's the long story?'

Oh God.

'Look.' I turn to face him in the moonlight, my heart pumping. 'I know I was going to tell you more. But are the details really important? Does it matter, what I used to do . . . or be? The point is, I'm here. And I've just had the best evening of my life. Ever.'

I can see he wants to challenge me; he even opens his mouth to speak. Then his expression relents and he turns away without saying whatever it was.

I feel a plunge of despair. Maybe I've ruined everything. Maybe I should have told the truth anyway. Or made up some convoluted story about a nasty boyfriend.

We walk on again into the night without speaking. Nathaniel's shoulder brushes against mine. Then I feel his hand. His fingers graze against my own casually at first, as though by accident – then, slowly, entwine themselves round mine.

I feel an arching inside as my entire body responds, but somehow force myself not to catch my breath. Neither of us says a word. There's no sound except our footsteps on the road and a distant owl hooting. Nathaniel's hand is sure and firm round my own. I can feel the roughened callouses on his skin; his thumb rubbing over mine.

Still neither of us has spoken. I'm not sure I *can* speak.

We come to a stop at the entrance to the Geigers' drive. He looks down at me silently, his expression almost grave. I can feel my breath thickening; catching every second beat. I don't care if it's obvious I want him.

I was never any good at the rules, anyway.

He releases my hand and puts both hands round my waist. Now he's slowly pulling me towards him. I close my eyes, prepared to lose myself.

'For goodness' sake!' comes an unmistakable voice. 'Aren't you going to *kiss* her?'

I jump and open my eyes. Nathaniel looks equally shocked, and takes an automatic step away. I swivel round – and to my utter horror, Trish is leaning out of an upstairs window, holding a cigarette and looking straight down at us.

'I'm not a *prude*, you know,' she says. 'You are allowed to kiss!'

I shoot furious daggers at her. Has she never heard the word 'privacy'?

'Carry on!' Her cigarette end glows as she waves it. 'Don't mind me!'

Don't mind her? I'm sorry, but I am not doing this with Trish as a spectator. I glance uncertainly at Nathaniel, who looks as nonplussed as I feel.

'Should we—' I stop, not sure what I'm about to suggest.

'Isn't it a lovely summer's night?' adds Trish conversationally.

'Lovely,' calls back Nathaniel politely.

I meet his eye and suddenly feel uncontrollable laughter rising. This is disastrous. The mood is totally broken.

'Um . . . thanks for a great evening,' I say, trying to keep a straight face. 'I had a lovely time.'

'Me too.' His eyes are almost indigo in the shadows; his mouth twisted in amusement. 'So. Are we going to give Mrs Geiger her kicks? Or leave her in an unbearable frenzy of frustration?'

We both glance up at Trish, still leaning avidly out of the window. As if we're the floor show, and any minute I might give Nathaniel a lap dance.

'Oh . . . I think she probably deserves the unbearable frenzy of frustration,' I say with a tiny smile.

'So I'll see you tomorrow?'

'I'll be at your mum's at ten o'clock.'

'See you then.'

He holds out his hand and we barely brush fingertips before he turns and walks away. I watch him disappear into the darkness, then turn and head down the drive to the house; my whole body still pulsating.

It's all very well, getting one over on Trish. But what about *my* unbearable frenzy of frustration?

SIXTEEN

I'm woken the next day by Trish banging sharply on my door. 'Samantha! I need to speak to you! Now!'

It's not even eight o'clock on a Saturday morning. Where's the fire?

'OK!' I call blearily. 'Hang on a sec!'

I stumble out of bed, my head filled with delicious memories of last night. Nathaniel's hand in mine ... Nathaniel's arms around me ...

'Yes, Mrs Geiger?' I open my door to see Trish standing there in a dressing gown, her face flushed and her eyes bloodshot. She puts her hand over the cordless phone she's holding.

'Samantha.' Her eyes are narrower than ever and there's a strange note of triumph in her voice. 'You've fibbed to me, haven't you?'

I feel a white flash of shock and my stomach plunges to my feet. How did she ... How could she ...

'Haven't you?' She gives me a penetrating look. 'I'm sure you know what I'm talking about.'

My mind frantically runs over all the fibs I've ever told Trish, up to and including 'I'm a housekeeper'. It

231

could be anything. It could be something small and insignificant. Or she could have found out the whole lot.

'I don't know what you're referring to,' I say in a throaty voice. 'Madam.'

'Well.' Trish walks towards me, swishing her silk dressing gown crossly. 'As you can imagine, I'm *rather* upset that you never told me you'd cooked paella for the Spanish ambassador.'

My mouth hangs open. The Spanish what?

'I asked you only the other day if you had cooked for any notable persons.' Trish arches her eyebrows in reproof. 'You never even *mentioned* the banquet for three hundred at the Mansion House.'

The what? Has she lost it?

OK, has she been bipolar all this time? It would explain a lot.

'Mrs Geiger,' I say, a little nervously, 'would you like to sit down?'

'No, thank you!' she says crisply. 'I'm still on the phone with Lady Edgerly.'

The floor seems to wobble beneath me. *Freya's on the phone?*

'Lady Edgerly . . .' Trish lifts the phone to her ear. 'You're quite right, *far* too unassuming . . .' She looks up. 'Lady Edgerly would like to have a word with you.'

She hands me the phone and in a blur of disbelief I lift it to my ear. 'Hello?'

'Samantha?' Freya's familiar, raspy voice erupts into my ear through a sea of crackle. 'Are you OK? What the *fuck* is going on?'

'I'm . . . fine!' I glance at Trish, who is standing approximately two metres away. 'I'll just . . . go somewhere a bit more . . .'

Ignoring Trish's laser-like eyes, I retreat into my bedroom and close the door tight. Then I lift the phone to my ear again.

'I'm fine!' I feel a rush of joy to be talking to Freya again. 'It's so amazing to hear from you!'

'What on earth's going on?' she demands again. 'I got this message but it made no sense! You're a *housekeeper*? Is this some huge wind-up?'

'No.' I glance at the door, then move into the bathroom and turn the fan on. 'I'm a full-time housekeeper,' I say in a lower voice. 'I've left my job at Carter Spink.'

'You've *quit*?' says Freya incredulously. 'Just like that?'

'I didn't quit. I was . . . thrown out. I made a mistake and they fired me.'

It's still hard to say it. Or even to think about it.

'You were thrown out for a simple *mistake*?' Freya sounds outraged. 'Jesus H Christ, these people—'

'It wasn't a simple mistake,' I cut her off in mid flow. 'It was a really big, important mistake. Anyway, that's what happened. And I decided to do something different. Become a housekeeper for a bit.'

'You decided to become a housekeeper,' echoes Freya slowly. 'Samantha, did you totally lose your mind?'

'Why not?' I say defensively. 'You were the one who said I should have a break.'

'But a *housekeeper*? You can't cook!'

'Well, I know.'

'I mean, you *really* can't cook!' She's giggling now. 'I've seen your cooking. And your non-existent cleaning.'

'I know!' A wave of hysteria is coming over me. 'It was a bit of a nightmare to begin with. But I'm kind of

'. . . learning. You'd be surprised.'

'Do you have to wear an apron?'

'I've got this hideous nylon uniform . . .' I'm snuffling with laughter now. 'And I call them Madam . . . and Sir . . . and I curtsey . . .'

'Samantha, this is insane,' says Freya between gurgles. 'Absolutely insane. You cannot stay there. I'm going to rescue you. I'll fly back tomorrow . . .'

'No!' I say with more vehemence than I intended. 'No! I'm . . . having a good time. It's fine.'

There's a suspicious silence down the phone. Dammit. Freya knows me far too well.

'With a man?' her teasing voice comes at last.

'Maybe.' I feel an unwilling grin come to my face. 'Yes.'

'Details?'

'It's early days. But he's . . . you know. Nice.' I beam foolishly at my own reflection in the bathroom mirror.

'Well, even so. You know I'm only a phone call away. You can stay at our place . . .'

'Thanks, Freya.' I feel a tug of affection for her.

'No problem. Samantha?'

'Yes?' There's a long silence, until I think the line must have cut out.

'What about the law?' says Freya at last. 'What about partnership? I know I gave you a hard time about it. But it was your dream. Are you just going to abandon it?'

I feel a twinge of deep, buried grief.

'That dream's over,' I say shortly. 'Partners don't make fifty-million-quid mistakes.'

'*Fifty million quid?*'

'Uh huh.'

'Jesus,' she breathes, sounding shocked. 'I had no idea. I can't imagine how you've coped with all this—'

'It's fine,' I cut her off. 'I've got over it. Really.'

Freya sighs. 'You know, I had a feeling something was up. I tried to send you an email via the Carter Spink website. But your page was gone.'

'Really?' I feel an odd little tweak inside.

'And then I thought—' She breaks off, and I can hear some kind of mayhem in the background. 'Oh bugger. Our transport's here. Listen, I'll call again soon—'

'Wait!' I say urgently. 'Before you go, Freya, what on *earth* did you say to Trish about the Spanish ambassador? And the Mansion House?'

'Oh, that.' She giggles. 'Well, she kept asking questions, so I thought I'd better make some stuff up. I said you could fold napkins into a scene from Swan Lake . . . and make ice sculptures . . . and David Linley once asked for your cheese-straw recipe . . .'

'Freya . . .' I close my eyes.

'I made quite a lot up, actually. She lapped it up! I have to go, babe. Love you.'

'Love you too.'

The phone goes dead and I stand motionless for a moment, the bathroom suddenly very silent without Freya's husky voice amid the background clamour of India.

I look at my watch. Nine forty-five. I just have time to have a look.

Three minutes later I'm sitting at Eddie's desk, tapping my fingers as I wait for the Internet connection to work. I asked Trish if I could possibly send an email to Lady Edgerly, and she was only too eager to open up the study for me and loiter behind the chair, until I politely asked her to go away.

Eddie's home page opens and I immediately type in www.carterspink.com.

As the familiar purple logo appears and describes a 360-degree circle on the screen, I can feel all the old tensions rising, like leaves off the bottom of a pond. Taking a deep breath, I click swiftly past the Introduction, straight to Associates. The list comes up – and Freya's right. The names segue straight from Snell to Taylor. No Sweeting.

I exhale, telling myself to be rational. Of course they've taken me off. I've been fired, what else did I expect? That was my old life and I'm not concerned with it any more. I should just close down, go to Iris's house and forget about it. That's what I should do.

Instead, I find myself reaching for the mouse and tapping 'Samantha Sweeting' into the search box. 'No result' pings up a few moments later and I stare at it, taken aback.

No result? Nowhere on the whole *website*? But . . . what about in the Media section? Or News Archives?

I quickly click onto the Done Deals box, and search for 'Euro-Sal, merger, DanCo'. That was a big European deal last year and I handled the financing. The report appears on the screen, with the headline 'Carter Spink advises on £20bn merger'. My eyes run down the familiar text. 'The Carter Spink team was led from London by Arnold Saville, with associates Guy Ashby and Jane Smilington.'

I stop in disbelief, then go back and read the text more carefully, searching for the missing words – 'and Samantha Sweeting', it should read. But the words aren't there. I'm not there. Quickly I click on another deal, the Conlon acquisition. I *know* I'm in this report. I've read it, for Christ's sake. I was on the team, I've got a tombstone to prove it.

But I'm not mentioned here either.

My heart is thudding as I click from deal to deal,

tracking back a year. Two years. Five years. They've wiped me out. Someone has gone painstakingly through the entire website and removed my name. I've been erased from every deal I was involved with. It's as if I never even existed.

I take a breath, trying to stay calm. But anger is bubbling up, hot and strong. How dare they change history? How dare they wipe me out? I gave them seven years of my *life*. They can't just blot me out; pretend I was never even on the pay roll . . .

Then a new thought hits me. Why have they bothered doing this? Other people have left the firm and haven't been completely wiped out. Why am I such an embarrassment? I look at the screen silently for a moment. Then, slowly, I type in www.google.com and enter 'Samantha Sweeting' in the box. I add 'lawyer' to be on the safe side, and press enter.

A moment later the screen fills with text. As I scan the entries I feel as though I've been hit over the head.

. . . the **Samantha Sweeting** debacle . . .
. . . discovery, **Samantha Sweeting** went AWOL, leaving colleagues to . . .
. . . heard about **Samantha Sweeting** . . .
. . . **Samantha Sweeting** jokes. What do you call a lawyer who . . .
. . . **Samantha Sweeting** fired from Carter Spink . . .

One after another. From lawyers' websites, legal news services, law students' message boards. It's as if the whole legal world has been talking about me behind my back. In a daze, I click to the next page – and there are still more. And on the next page, and the next.

I feel as though I'm surveying a wrecked bridge. Looking at the damage; realizing for the first time quite how bad the devastation is.

I can never go back.

I knew that.

But I don't think I really *knew* it. Not deep down in the pit of my stomach. Not where it counts.

I feel a wetness on my cheek and jump to my feet, shutting all the web pages down; clearing History in case Eddie gets curious. I shut down the computer and look around the silent room. This is where I am. Not there. That part of my life is over.

Iris's cottage is looking as idyllic as ever as I dash up to the front door, out of breath. In fact, even more idyllic, as a goose is now wandering about with her hens.

'Hello.' She looks up with a smile from where she's sitting with a mug of tea. 'You seem in a hurry.'

'I just wanted to get here on time.' I look around the garden, but I can't see any sign of Nathaniel.

'Nathaniel had to go and sort out a leaking pipe at one of the pubs,' says Iris, as though reading my mind. 'But he'll be back later. Meanwhile, we're going to make bread.'

'Great!' I say. I follow her into the kitchen and put on the same stripy apron as last time.

'I've started us off already,' says Iris, going over to a large, old-fashioned mixing bowl on the table. 'Yeast, warm water, melted butter and flour. Mix together and you have your dough. Now, you're going to knead it.'

'Right,' I say again, looking blankly at the dough.

She shoots me a curious look. 'Are you all right, Samantha? You seem . . . out of sorts.'

'I'm fine.' I try to smile. 'Sorry.'

She's right. I'm not with it. Come on. Concentrate.

'I know people have machines to do this for them,' she says, hefting the dough onto the table. 'But this is how we make it the old-fashioned way. You'll never taste better.'

She kneads it briskly a couple of times. 'You see? Fold it over, make a quarter turn. You need to use a bit of energy.'

Cautiously I plunge my hands into the soft dough and try to imitate what she was doing.

'That's it,' says Iris, watching carefully. 'Get into a rhythm and really *work* it. Kneading's very good for releasing stress,' she adds wryly. 'Pretend you're bashing all your worst enemies.'

'I'll do that!' I manage a cheerful tone.

But there's a knot of tension in my chest, which doesn't dwindle away as I knead. In fact the more I fold and turn the dough, the worse it seems to get. I can't stop my mind flicking back to that website. I can't stop the burn of injustice inside my chest.

I did good things for that firm. I won clients. I negotiated deals. I was not nothing.

I was *not* nothing.

'The more you work the dough, the better the bread will be,' says Iris, coming over to the table with a smile. 'Can you feel it becoming warm and elastic in your hands?'

I look at the dough in my fingers, but I can't connect with it. I can't feel what she's talking about. My senses aren't plugged in. My mind is skittering about like a bird on ice.

I start kneading again, harder than before, trying to capture it. I want to find that contentment I had last time I was here; that feeling of simplicity and earthiness. But I keep losing my rhythm; cursing in frustration as my fingers catch on the dough. My upper arms are aching; my face is sweating. And the turmoil inside me is only getting worse.

How dare they wipe me out? I was a good lawyer.

I was a good fucking lawyer.

'Would you like a rest?' Iris comes over and touches my shoulder. 'It's hard work when you're not used to it.'

'What's the point?' My words shoot out before I can stop them. 'I mean, what's the point of all this? Making bread. You make it and you eat it. And then it's gone.'

I break off abruptly, not quite knowing what's come over me. My breaths are short and jerky. I don't feel totally on top of myself.

Iris gives me a careful look. 'You could say the same of all food,' she points out gently. 'Or life itself.'

'Exactly.' I rub my forehead with my apron. 'Exactly.'

I don't know what I'm saying. Why am I picking a fight with Iris? I have to calm down. But I can feel the agitation fermenting inside me.

'I think that's enough kneading,' she says, taking the dough from me and patting it into a round shape.

'Now what?' I say, trying to speak more normally. 'Shall I put it in the oven?'

'Not yet.' Iris places the dough back in the bowl and puts it on top of the stove. 'Now we wait.'

'Wait?' I stare at her. 'What do you mean, wait?'

'We wait.' She pops a tea towel over the bowl. 'Half an hour should do it. I'll make a cup of tea.'

'But . . . what are we waiting *for*?'

'For the yeast to rise and work its magic on the dough.' She smiles. 'Underneath that towel, a small miracle is happening.'

I look at the bowl, trying to think miracles. But it

isn't working. I can't feel calm or serene. My body is wound up too far; every nerve is hopping with tension. I used to be in control of my time to the minute. To the second. And now I'm supposed to wait for yeast? I'm supposed to stand here, in an apron, waiting for a . . . *fungus*?

'I'm sorry,' I hear myself say. 'I can't do it.' I head for the kitchen door and out into the garden.

'What?' Iris comes after me, wiping her hands on her apron. 'Sweetie, what's wrong?'

'I can't do this!' I wheel round. 'I can't just . . . just sit around patiently, waiting for *yeast* to get its act together.'

'Why not?'

'Because it's such a waste of time!' I clutch my head in frustration. 'It's such a waste of time. All of it!'

'What do you think we should be doing instead?' she asks with interest.

'Something . . . *important*. OK?' I walk to the apple tree and back again, unable to keep still. 'Something constructive.'

I glance at Iris, but she doesn't seem offended. Instead, she appears amused.

'What's more constructive than making bread?'

Oh *God*. I feel an urge to scream. It's OK for her, with her hens and her apron and no wrecked career on the Internet.

'You don't understand anything,' I say, close to tears. 'I'm sorry, but you don't. Look . . . I'll just leave.'

'Don't leave.' Iris's voice is surprisingly firm. The next moment she's in front of me, placing her two hands on my shoulders, looking at me with her searching blue eyes.

'Samantha, you've had a trauma,' she says in kind, even tones. 'And it's affected you very deeply—'

'I *haven't* had a trauma!' I wheel away, out of her grasp. 'I just . . . I can't do this, Iris. I can't pretend to be this. I'm not a bread-maker, OK? I'm *not* a domestic goddess.' I look around the garden desperately, as though searching for clues. 'I don't know who I am any more. I have no bloody idea.'

A single tear rolls down my cheek and I wipe it away roughly. I'm not going to cry in front of Iris.

'I don't know who I am.' I exhale, more calmly. 'Or what my goal is . . . or where I'm headed in life. Or anything.'

My energy's gone and I sink down on the dry grass. A few moments later Iris comes and squats down beside me.

'It doesn't matter,' she says, her voice soft. 'Don't beat yourself up for not knowing all the answers. You don't always have to know who you are. You don't have to have the big picture, or know where you're heading. Sometimes it's enough just to know what you're going to do next.'

For a while I don't say anything. I let her words run through my head, like cool water on a headache.

'And what am I going to do next?' I say at last, with a hopeless shrug.

'You're going to help me shell the beans for lunch.' She sounds so matter-of-fact I can't help half smiling.

I meekly follow Iris into the house, collect a big bowl of broad beans and start splitting the pods as she shows me. Pods into a basket on the floor. New broad beans into the basin. Over and over and over.

I become a little calmer as I get immersed in my task. I never even knew broad beans came from pods like this.

To be honest, my total experience of broad beans has

been picking them up in a plastic-covered packet from Waitrose, putting them in my fridge, taking them out a week after the sell-by date and throwing them away.

But this is the real thing. This is what they're like, dug straight out of the ground. Or . . . picked off the bush. Whatever it is.

Each time I split one open it's like finding a row of pale-green jewels. And when I put one in my mouth, it's like—

Oh, OK. It needs to be cooked.

Yuck.

When I've finished the beans we knead the dough again. We shape it into loaves, put them into loaf tins and then have to wait another half hour for them to rise again. But somehow this time I don't mind. I sit at the table with Iris, hulling strawberries and listening to the radio until it's time to put the tins into the oven. Then Iris loads a tray with cheese, bean salad, biscuits and strawberries and we take it outside to a table set under the shade of a tree.

'There,' she says, pouring some iced tea into a tumbler made of bubbled glass. 'Better?'

'Yes. Thanks,' I say awkwardly. 'I'm sorry about earlier. I just . . .'

'Samantha, it's all right.' She gives me a brief look, between slicing the cheese. 'You don't have to apologize.'

'But I do.' I take a deep breath. 'I'm really grateful, Iris. You've been so kind . . . and Nathaniel . . .'

'He took you to the pub, I heard.'

'It was amazing!' I say with enthusiasm. 'You must be so proud, to have that in your family.'

Iris nods. 'Those pubs have been run by Blewetts for generations.' She sits down and helps us both to bean salad, dressed with oil and speckled with herbs. I take a mouthful – and it's absolutely delicious.

'It must have been hard when your husband died,' I venture cautiously.

'Everything was in a mess.' Iris sounds matter-of-fact. A chicken wanders over to the table and she shoos it away. 'There were financial difficulties. I wasn't well. If it hadn't been for Nathaniel we might have lost the pubs. He made sure they got back on track. For his father's memory.' Her eyes cloud a little and she hesitates, fork halfway to mouth. 'You never know how things are going to turn out, however much you plan. But you already know that.'

'I always thought my life would be a certain way,' I say, gazing down at my plate. 'I had it all mapped out.'

'But it didn't happen like that?'

For a few seconds I can't answer. I'm remembering the moment I heard I was going to be partner. That instant of undiluted, dazzling joy. When I thought my life had finally fallen into place; when I thought everything was perfect.

'No,' I say, trying to keep my voice level. 'It didn't happen like that.'

Iris is watching me with such clear, empathetic eyes I almost think she must be able to read my mind.

'Don't be too hard on yourself, chicken,' she says. 'We all flounder.'

I can't imagine Iris ever floundering. She seems so calm and put-together.

'Oh, I floundered,' she says, reading my expression. 'After Benjamin went. It was so sudden. Everything I thought I had, gone overnight.'

'So . . . what did you . . .' I spread my hands helplessly.

'I found another way,' she says. 'But it took time.'

For a moment she holds my gaze, then looks at her watch. 'Speaking of which, I'll make some coffee. And see how that bread's getting on.'

I get up to follow her, but she bats me down again.

'Sit. Stay. Relax.'

I sit there in the dappled sunlight, sipping my iced tea, trying to relax. Trying to enjoy just sitting here in a beautiful garden. But emotions are still darting around me like unsettled fish.

Another way.

But I don't know any other way. I have no idea what I'm doing; I have no idea what the big picture is. I feel like the light's gone out and I'm feeling my way forward, one step at a time. And all I know is I can't go back to what I was.

I clench my eyes shut, trying to clear my mind. I should never have looked at that website. I should never have read those comments. That's a different world now.

'Hold out your arms, Samantha.' Iris's voice is suddenly behind me. 'Don't open your eyes. Go on.'

I have no idea what she's up to, but I close my eyes and hold out my arms. The next moment I feel something warm being put into them. A yeasty smell is rising up. I open my eyes to see a loaf of bread in my arms.

I stare at it in utter disbelief. It looks like proper bread. Real, proper bread like you'd see in a baker's window. Fat and plump and golden-brown, with faint striations and a crusty, almost flaky top. It smells so delicious I can feel my mouth watering.

'Tell me that's nothing,' says Iris, squeezing my arm. 'You made that, sweetie. And you should be proud of yourself.'

I can't reply. Something hot is wadding my throat as I clutch the warm loaf. I made this bread. I made it. I, Samantha Sweeting, who couldn't even microwave a packet of soup. Who gave up seven years of her life to end up with nothing, to be wiped out of existence. Who has no idea who she even is any more.

I made a loaf of bread. Right now I feel like this is the only thing I have to hold on to.

To my horror a tear suddenly rolls down my cheek, followed by another. This is ridiculous. I have to get a grip on myself.

'Looks good,' comes Nathaniel's easy voice behind me, and I wheel round in shock. He's standing next to Iris, his hair glowing in the sun.

'Hi,' I say, flustered. 'I thought you were . . . fixing a pipe or something.'

'Still am.' He nods. 'I just popped home.'

'I'll go and get the other loaves out,' says Iris, patting me on the shoulder, and disappears over the grass towards the house.

I stand up and look at Nathaniel over the bread. Just the sight of him is adding all sorts of emotions into the mix: more fish darting around my body.

Although now I think about it, they're mainly varieties of the same fish.

'Are you all right?' he says, glancing at my tears.

'I'm fine. It's just been a weird day,' I say, brushing them away in embarrassment. 'I don't usually get so emotional about . . . bread.'

'Mum said you got a bit frustrated.' He raises his eyebrows. 'All that kneading?'

'It was the rising.' I raise a rueful smile. 'Having to wait. I've never been good at waiting.'

'Uh huh.' Nathaniel's steady blue eyes meet mine.

'For anything.' Somehow I seem to be edging closer

and closer to him, I'm not entirely sure how. 'I have to have things *now*.'

'Uh huh.'

We're inches apart now. And as I gaze up at him, breathing hard, all the frustrations and shocks of the last couple of weeks seem to be distilling inside me. A huge block of pressure is growing, until I can't bear it. I need release. Unable to stop myself, I reach up and pull his face down towards mine.

I haven't kissed like this since I was a teenager. Arms wrapped around one another; oblivious of anything else in the world. Completely lost. Trish could be standing there with a video camera, issuing directions, and I wouldn't notice.

It seems hours later that I open my eyes and we draw apart. My lips feel swollen; my legs are staggery. Nathaniel looks equally shell-shocked. His eyes are opaque and he's breathing more swiftly.

The bread is totally squashed, I suddenly notice. I try to reshape it as best I can, putting it on the table like a deformed pottery exhibit while I gather my breath.

'I don't have long,' Nathaniel says. 'I have to get back to the pub.' His hand runs lightly down my back and I feel my body curving towards his.

'I don't take long,' I say, my voice husky with desire.

When did I become so brazen, exactly?

'I *really* don't have long.' He glances at his watch. 'About six minutes.'

'I only take six minutes,' I murmur with an enticing glance, and Nathaniel smiles back, as though I'm joking.

'Seriously,' I say, trying to sound modest yet sexy. 'I'm fast. Six minutes, give or take.'

There's silence for a few moments. An incredulous

expression is coming over Nathaniel's face. Somehow he doesn't look as impressed as I thought he would.

'Well . . . round here we take things a bit slower,' he says at last.

'Right,' I say, trying not to look at all disappointed. What's he trying to say? That he has some kind of *problem* or something? 'Er . . . well . . . I'm sure . . .' I trail off.

I should not have started that sentence.

He looks at his watch again. 'I have to be off. I have to drive over to Gloucester tonight.'

I feel an inward drop at his businesslike tone. He's barely looking at me any more. I should never have mentioned timings, I realize in dismay. Everyone knows, you never bring up any kind of numerical measurement during sex with a man. It's the most basic rule. That, and don't reach for the remote control halfway through unless you're sure it's on mute.

'So . . . I'll see you,' I say, trying to sound casual yet encouraging. 'What are you doing tomorrow?'

'I'm not sure yet.' He gives a noncommittal shrug. 'Are you around?'

'I guess so. Maybe.'

'Well . . . I may see you.'

And with that he's striding away again over the grass, and I'm left with nothing but a misshapen loaf of bread and total confusion.

SEVENTEEN

Like I said, there should be a different system. There should be some kind of universal arrangement which leaves no room for misunderstanding. It could involve hand signals, perhaps. Or small, discreet stickers placed on the lapel, colour coded for different messages:

Available/Not available.

Relationship on/Relationship off.

Sex imminent/Sex cancelled/Sex merely postponed.

How else are you supposed to know what's going on? How?

By the next morning I've thought long and hard and have got nowhere. Either a) Nathaniel was offended by my references to sex, and isn't interested any more, or b) he's fine, it's all still on, he was just being a man and not saying much, and I should stop obsessing.

Or somewhere in between.

Or some other option I haven't even considered. Or . . .

Actually, I think that might cover it. But still. I'm totally confused just thinking about it.

I stumble downstairs in my dressing gown at around

nine, to find Eddie and Trish in the hall, dressed up very smartly. Eddie is in a blazer with shiny gold buttons and Trish is in a white slub-silk suit, with the biggest corsage of fake red roses I've ever seen. She also seems to be having the teeniest problem doing up the buttons of her jacket. At last she edges the last one into its buttonhole and stands back to look at herself in the mirror, panting slightly.

Now she looks as though she can't move her arms.

'What do you think?' she says to Eddie.

'Yes, very nice,' he says, frowning at a copy of *Road Map of Britain 1994*. 'Is it the A347? Or the A367?'

'Um . . . I think it looks nice with the jacket un-buttoned,' I venture. 'More . . . relaxed.'

Trish darts me a narrow look, as though suspecting me of deliberately sabotaging her appearance.

'Yes,' she says at last. 'Maybe you're right.' She makes to undo her buttons – but she's so trussed up, she can't get her hands near enough. And now Eddie's wandered off into the study.

'Shall I . . .' I offer.

'Yes.' Her neck flames red. 'If you would be so kind.'

I move forward and undo the buttons as gently as I can, which is not very, given how stiff the fabric is. When I've finished she takes a step backwards and regards herself again, looking slightly dissatisfied, plucking at her silky shirt thing.

'Tell me, Samantha,' she says casually, 'if you saw me now for the first time, what *word* would you use to describe me?'

Oh, bloody hell. I'm sure this wasn't in my job description. I rack my brains hastily for the most flattering word I can come up with.

'Um . . . um . . . elegant,' I say at last, nodding as

though to add conviction to what I'm saying. 'I'd say you were elegant.'

'Elegant?' Her eyes snap round at me. Something tells me I got it wrong.

'I mean, thin!' I amend, in sudden realization.

How could I have overlooked thin?

'Thin.' She looks at herself for a few moments, turning from side to side. 'Thin.'

She doesn't sound entirely happy. What's wrong with being thin and elegant, for God's sake?

Not that she's either, let's be honest.

'What about . . .' She shakes back her hair, deliberately avoiding my eye. 'What about . . . "Young"?'

For a moment I'm too flummoxed to answer. Young? Young compared to what?

'Er . . . absolutely,' I say at last. 'That . . . goes without saying.'

Please don't say 'How old do you think I—'

'How old would you say I am, Samantha?'

She's moving her head from side to side, flicking dust off her jacket, as though she's not really interested in the answer. But I know her ears are ready and waiting, like two giant microphones ready to pick up the slightest sound.

My face is prickling. What am I going to say? I'll say . . . thirty-five. No. Don't be ridiculous. She can't be *that* self-deluded. Forty? No. I can't say forty. It's too near the truth.

'Are you about . . . thirty-seven?' I hazard at last. Trish turns round – and from her smug expression of pleasure I reckon I hit about the right note of flattery.

'I'm actually thirty-nine!' she says, two spots of colour appearing on her cheeks.

'No!' I exclaim, trying not to look at her crow's feet. 'That's amazing!'

She is such a liar. She was forty-six last February. And if she doesn't want people to know, she shouldn't leave her passport out on her dressing table.

'Now!' she says, clearly cheered up. 'We'll be out *all* day at my sister's party. Nathaniel will be coming over to work in the garden, but I expect you know that—'

'Nathaniel?' I feel an electric jolt. 'He's coming here?'

'He called this morning. The sweet peas need . . . stringing or looping or something?' She gets out a lip pencil and begins outlining her already-lined lips.

'Right. I didn't realize.' I'm trying to stay collected but tentacles of excitement are creeping through me. 'So . . . he's working on a Sunday?'

'Oh, he often does. He's *very* dedicated.' She stands back to look at her reflection, then starts shading in her lips with yet more lipstick. 'I heard he took you to his little pub?'

His *little* pub. What is she like?

'Er . . . yes. He did.'

'I was *so* glad about that, really.' She takes out a mascara wand and starts adding more layers to her already spiky lashes. 'We nearly had to look for another gardener, can you *imagine*. Although of course it was a great shame for him. After all his plans.'

I look at her, nonplussed. I feel like I've missed a beat or three. What's she talking about?

'What was a shame?' I say.

'Nathaniel. His nursery. Plant thing.' She frowns at her reflection and flicks at a speck of mascara beneath her eye. 'Organic something or other. He showed us the business proposition. In fact, we were even considering backing him. We are very *supportive* employers, Samantha.' She fixes me with a blue gaze as though daring me to disagree.

'Of course!'

'Ready?' Eddie comes out of the study wearing a Panama hat. 'It's going to be bloody sweltering, you know.'

'Eddie, don't start,' snaps Trish, shoving her mascara wand back in the tube. 'We are going to this party and that's final. Have you got the present?'

'And what happened?' I ask, trying to haul the conversation back on track. 'With Nathaniel's plans?'

Trish makes a small, regretful moue at herself in the mirror.

'Well, his father passed away very suddenly, and there was all that dreadful business with the pubs. And he changed his mind. Never bought the land.' She gives herself another, dissatisfied look. 'Should I wear my *pink* suit?'

'*No*,' Eddie and I say in unison. I glance at Eddie's exasperated face and stifle a giggle.

'You look lovely, Mrs Geiger,' I say. 'Really.'

Somehow, between us, Eddie and I manage to chivvy her away from the mirror, out of the front door and across the gravel to Eddie's Porsche. Eddie's right, it's going to be a boiling day. The sky is already a translucent blue, the sun a dazzling ball.

'What time will you be back?' I ask as they get in.

'Not until late this evening,' says Trish. 'Eddie, where's the *present*? Ah, Nathaniel, here you are.'

I look over the top of the car in slight apprehension. There he is, coming down the drive, in jeans and espadrilles and an old grey T-shirt, his rucksack over his shoulder. And here I am, in my dressing gown with my hair all over the place.

And still not sure how things have been left between us.

Although certain bits of my body are already

253

responding to the sight of him. They don't seem to be in any confusion at all.

'Hi,' I say as he gets near.

'Hi.' Nathaniel's eyes crinkle in a friendly way, but he doesn't make any attempt to kiss me or even smile. Instead, he just comes to a halt and looks at me. There's something about his intent, purposeful gaze that makes me feel a bit wobbly around the legs.

Either things have been left pretty much as they were mid kiss yesterday, or it's my fate to find him desperately sexy, whatever vibes he's giving off.

'So.' I wrench my eyes away and look at the gravel for a few moments. 'You're . . . working hard today.'

'I could do with some help,' he says casually. 'If you're at a loose end.'

I feel a dazzling leap of delight, which I attempt to hide with a cough.

'Right.' I shrug slightly, almost frowning. 'Well . . . maybe.'

'Great.' He nods to the Geigers and saunters off towards the garden.

Trish has been watching this exchange in increasing dissatisfaction.

'You're not very *affectionate* with each other, are you?' she says. 'You know, in *my* experience—'

'Leave them alone, for God's sake!' retorts Eddie, starting the engine. 'Let's get this bloody thing over with.'

'Eddie Geiger!' Trish shrills, swivelling round in her seat. 'This is my sister's party you're talking about! Do you realize—'

Eddie revs the engine, drowning out her voice, and with a spattering of gravel the Porsche disappears out of the drive, leaving me alone in the silent, baking sunshine.

Right.

So ... it's just Nathaniel and me. Alone together. Until eight o'clock this evening. That's the basic scenario.

A pulse is starting to thud somewhere deep inside me. Like a conductor setting the beat; like an introduction.

Deliberately nonchalant, I turn on the gravel and start to make my way back towards the house. As I pass a flower bed I even pause and study a random plant for a moment, holding the green leaves between my fingers.

I guess I could wander down and offer him a helping hand. It would be polite.

I force myself not to rush. I take a shower and get dressed and have breakfast, consisting of half a cup of tea and an apple. Then I go upstairs and put on a little make-up. Not a lot. But enough.

I've dressed low key. A T-shirt, a cotton skirt and flip flops. As I look in the mirror I feel almost shivery with anticipation. But other than that my mind is weirdly blank. I seem to have lost all my thought processes. Which is probably no bad thing.

After the cool house, the garden feels scorching; the air still and almost shimmery. I stay in the shade, heading down the side path, not knowing where he's working; where I'm heading. And then I see him, in the midst of a row of lavender and lilac-coloured flowers, his brow furrowed against the sun as he knots a length of twine.

'Hi,' I say.

'Hi.' He looks up and wipes his brow. I'm half expecting him to drop what he's doing, come forward and kiss me. But he doesn't. He just carries

255

on knotting, then cuts the twine off with a knife.

'I came to help,' I say after a pause. 'What are we doing?'

'Tying up the sweet peas.' He gestures at the plants, which are growing up what look like cane wigwams. 'They need support otherwise they just flop.' He throws a ball of twine over to me. 'Have a go. Just tie them gently.'

He's not joking. I really *am* helping with the gardening. Cautiously I unwind a length of twine and follow what he's doing. The soft leaves and petals tickle me as I work, and fill the air with an amazing sweet scent.

'How's that?'

'Let's see.' Nathaniel comes over to take a look. 'Yup. You could tie a little tighter.' His hand brushes briefly against mine as he turns away. 'Let's see you do the next one.'

My hand tingles at his touch. Did he mean to do that? Uncertain, I tie up the next plant, knotting harder than before.

'Yeah, that's good.' Suddenly Nathaniel's voice is behind me and I feel his fingers on the back of my neck, tracing around my earlobe. 'You need to do the whole row.'

He definitely meant to do that. No question. I turn round, wanting to reciprocate, but he's already on the other side of the row, intent on a sweet-pea plant, as though nothing happened.

He has a game plan, I suddenly realize.

OK, now I really am turned on.

The pulsating is growing stronger inside me as I move from plant to plant. There's silence except the rustling of leaves and faint snap of twine as I cut it off. I tie up three more plants and get to the end of the row.

'Done,' I say without turning round.

'Great, let's see.' He comes over to inspect my knotted twine. I can feel his other hand edging up my thigh, pushing up my skirt, his fingers feeling for my flesh. I can't move. I'm transfixed. Then suddenly he moves away, businesslike again, picking up a pair of trugs.

'What . . .' I can't even frame a sentence properly.

He kisses me briefly, hard on the mouth. 'Let's move on. Raspberries need picking.'

The raspberry cages are further down the garden, like rooms of green netting, with dry, earthy floors and rows of raspberry plants. As we enter there's no sound except that of buzzing insects and the flapping of a trapped bird, which Nathaniel shoos out.

We work the first row wordlessly, intently, picking the fruit off the plants. By the end of the row my mouth is tangy with the taste of them; my hands are scratched and aching from the constant plucking and I'm sweating all over. The heat seems more intense in this raspberry cage than anywhere else in the garden.

We meet at the end of the row and Nathaniel looks at me a still second, sweat running down the side of his face.

'Hot work,' he says. He puts his trug down and strips off his T-shirt.

'Yes.' There's a still beat between us. Then, almost defiantly, I do the same. I'm standing there in my bra, inches from him, my skin pale and milky compared to his.

'Have we done enough?' I gesture at the trug, but Nathaniel doesn't even glance down.

'Not yet.'

Something about his expression makes me damp

and prickly behind my knees. I meet his eyes and it's like we're playing truth or dare.

'I couldn't reach those ones.' I point at a high cluster of fruit just out of reach.

'I'll help.' He leans over me, skin against skin, and I feel his mouth on my earlobe as he picks the fruit. My entire body responds. I can't bear this; I need it to stop. And I need it not to stop.

But it goes on. We move up and down the rows like two performers in a courtly dance. Outwardly concentrating on our moves yet aware only of each other. At the end of every row, he brushes some part of me with his mouth or fingers. One time he feeds me raspberries and I graze his fingers with my teeth. I want to get at him, I want my hands all over him, but every time he turns away before anything can progress.

I'm starting to shiver all over with desire. He unhooked my bra two rows ago. I've discarded my knickers. He's unbuckled his belt. And still, *still* we're picking raspberries.

The trugs are full and heavy and my arms are aching, but I'm barely aware of them. All I'm aware of is that my whole body is throbbing; that the pulsing has become a pounding; that I can't stand it for much longer. As I reach the end of the last row I put the trug down and face him, unable to hide how desperate I am.

'Are we done?'

My breath is coming in short, hot bursts. I have to have him. He has to realize. I don't know what more I can do.

'We've done pretty well.' His gaze drifts towards the other fruit cages. 'There's still more to do . . .'

'No,' I hear myself saying. 'No more.'

I stand there in the heat and the dusty earth, panting and aching. And just as I think I might explode, he comes forward and bends his mouth down to my nipple, and I nearly swoon. And this time he doesn't move away. This time is for real. His hands are moving over my body, my skirt is falling to the ground, his jeans are sliding off. Then I'm shuddering, and clutching him, and crying out. And the raspberries are forgotten, scattered on the ground, squashed, crushed beneath us.

We seem to lie still for hours afterwards. I feel numb with euphoria. There's dust and stones embedded in my back and knees and hands and raspberry stains all over my skin. I don't mind. I can't even bring myself to lift a hand and remove the ant which is crawling up my stomach like a tickling dot.

My head is on Nathaniel's chest, his heartbeat like a deep, comforting clock tick. The sun is hot on my skin. I have no idea what time it is. I don't care what time it is. I've lost all sense of minutes and hours.

At last Nathaniel shifts his head slightly. He kisses my shoulder, then smiles. 'You taste of raspberry.'

'That was . . .' I break off, almost too stupefied to frame any sensible words. 'You know . . . normally I . . .' A huge yawn suddenly overcomes me and I clap my hand over my mouth. I want to go to sleep now, for several days.

Nathaniel lifts a hand and traces lazy circles around my back.

'Six minutes isn't sex,' I hear him saying as my eyes crash shut. 'Six minutes is a boiled egg.'

By the time I wake up, the raspberry cages are in partial shade. Nathaniel has removed himself from underneath me, given me a pillow constructed from my crumpled, raspberry-stained skirt, put on his jeans and brought down some beer from the Geigers' fridge. I sit up, my head still groggy, to see him leaning against a tree on the grass, swigging from the bottle.

'Slacker,' I say. 'The Geigers think you're tying up sweet peas.'

He turns towards me, a flicker of amusement passing over his face. 'Sleep well?'

'How long was I asleep?' I put my hand to my face and remove a small stone. I feel totally disoriented.

'Couple of hours. You want some of this?' He gestures to the bottle. 'It's cold.'

I get to my feet, brush myself down, put on my skirt and bra as a good compromise outfit and join him on the grass. He gives me a bottle and I take a cautious swig. I've never drunk beer before. But like this, cold and foamy from the bottle, it's the most refreshing drink I've ever tasted.

I sink back against the tree trunk, my bare feet in the cool grass.

'God, I feel so . . .' I lift a hand and let it drop down with a heavy thump.

'You're not as twitchy as you were,' says Nathaniel. 'You used to jump a mile whenever I spoke to you.'

'No I didn't!'

'Uh huh, you did.' He nods. 'Like a rabbit.'

'I thought I was a badger.'

'You're a rabbit-badger cross. Very rare breed.' He grins at me and takes a swig of beer. For a while neither of us speaks. I watch a tiny plane high above, leaving a white trail in the sky.

'Mum says you've changed, too.' Nathaniel shoots me a swift, querying look. 'She said she reckons whoever you've run away from . . . whatever happened . . . they're losing their grip on you.'

The question is there in his voice, but I don't respond. I'm thinking of Iris, yesterday. Letting me take all my frustrations out on her. It's not like she's had it easy herself.

'Your mum's amazing,' I say at last.

'Yup.'

I put the bottle down and roll onto the grass, staring up at the blue sky. I can smell the earth beneath my head and feel grass stems against my ears and hear a grasshopper chirruping near by.

I have changed. I can feel it in myself. I feel . . . stiller.

'Who would you be?' I say, twisting a grass stem round my finger. 'If you could just run away. Become a different person.'

Nathaniel's silent for a moment, looking over his bottle at the garden.

'I'd be me,' he says at last with a shrug. 'I'm happy as I am. I like living where I live. I like doing what I do.'

I roll over onto my front and look up at him, squinting in the sunlight. 'There must be something else you'd like to do. Some dream you've got.'

He shakes his head, smiling. 'I'm doing what I want to do.'

Suddenly I remember my conversation with Trish and sit upright on the grass.

'But what about the nursery you were going to set up?'

Nathaniel's face jolts in surprise. 'How did you—'

'Trish told me about it this morning. She said you had business plans and everything. What happened?'

For a moment he's silent, his eyes averted from mine. I can't tell what's going on inside.

261

'It was just an idea,' he says at last.

'You gave it up for your mum. To run the pubs.'

'Maybe.' He reaches for a low-growing branch and starts stripping it of leaves. 'Everything changed.'

'But do you really want to run the pubs?' I edge forward on the grass, trying to intercept his gaze. 'You said it yourself, you're not a landlord. You're a gardener.'

'It's not a question of *want*.' Nathaniel's voice has a sudden edge of frustration. 'It's a family business. Someone has to run it.'

'Why you?' I persist. 'Why not your brother?'

'He's . . . different. He does his own thing.'

'*You* could do your own thing!'

'I have responsibilities.' His frown grows heavier. 'My mum—'

'She'd want you to do whatever you want to do,' I insist. 'I know she would. She'd want you to be happy in your life, not give it up for her.'

'I am happy. It's ridiculous to say—'

'But couldn't you be *happier*?'

There's silence in the garden. Nathaniel is looking away, his shoulders bent round as if he wants to shut out what I'm saying.

'Don't you ever want to ditch your responsibilities?' I throw my arms out wide in sudden abandon. 'Just . . . walk out into the world and see what happens?'

'Is that what you did?' he demands, wheeling round, a sudden aggression in his voice.

I stare at him uncertainly.

'I . . . we're not talking about me,' I say at last. 'We're talking about you.'

'Samantha.' He exhales and rubs his brow. 'I know you don't want to talk about the past. But I want you to tell me one thing. And be truthful.'

I feel a deep tremor of alarm. What's he going to ask me?

'I'll try,' I say at last. 'What is it?'

Nathaniel looks me directly in the eye and takes a deep breath. 'Do you have kids?'

I'm so dumbfounded, I can't speak for a moment. He thinks I have *kids*? A gurgle of relieved laughter rises through me before I can stop it.

'No, I don't have kids! What, you think I've left five starving little mouths behind?'

'I don't know.' He frowns, looking sheepish but defensive. 'Why not?'

'Because . . . I mean . . . do I *look* like I've had five kids?' I can't help a note of indignation, and he starts to laugh too.

'Maybe not *five* . . .'

'What's that supposed to mean?' I'm about to hit him with his shirt when a voice pierces the air.

'Samanth*a*?'

It's Trish. Coming from the house. They're *home*?

I meet Nathaniel's eye in disbelief.

'Samanth*a*?' her voice trills again. 'Are you outside?'

Oh fuck. My eyes swivel madly over the two of us. I'm naked except for a skirt and a bra, and covered in dust and raspberry stains. Nathaniel is much the same, except in jeans.

'Quick! My clothes!' I hiss, scrabbling to my feet.

'Where are they?' says Nathaniel, looking around.

'I don't *know*!' I look at him and feel helpless laughter rising. 'We're going to get the sack.'

'Samanth*a*?' I can hear the clunk of the conservatory doors being opened.

'Shit!' I squeak. 'She's coming!'

'It's fine,' says Nathaniel, retrieving his T-shirt from

263

the raspberry cage. He pops it over his head and at once looks pretty normal. 'I'll create a diversion. You sneak up the side, behind the shrubs, go in the kitchen door, run upstairs and get changed. OK?'

'OK,' I say breathlessly. 'And what's our story?'

'Our story is . . .' He pauses as though thinking. 'We didn't shag in the garden or help ourselves to beers from the fridge.'

'Right.' I can't help giggling. 'Good plan.'

'Go swiftly, Brown Rabbit.' He kisses me, and I dart across the lawn to the cover of a huge rhododendron bush.

I sneak up the side of the garden, keeping behind the shrubs all the time, trying not to rustle too much. My bare feet are cool on the damp, shaded earth; I step on a sharp pebble and wince in total silence. I feel about ten years old, playing hide and seek, the same mixture of terror and delight pounding in my heart.

When I'm only ten yards or so from the house I crouch behind a shrub and wait. After a minute or two I see Nathaniel firmly leading the Geigers down the lawn towards the lily pond.

'I think we could have a case of powdery mildew,' he's saying. 'I thought you should see it for yourselves.'

I wait until they're well past, then sprint on light feet to the conservatory, in through the house and up the stairs. When I'm in my room and the door is safely closed I collapse on the bed, wanting to laugh at my own relief, at the hilarity, at the *stupidity* of it all. Then I get up and look out of the window. I can just see them all down by the pond. Nathaniel is pointing at something with a stick.

I hurry into the bathroom, turn on the shower full blast and stand under it for thirty seconds. Then I pull on clean underwear, a pair of fresh jeans and a demure long-sleeved top. I even add fresh lipstick. Then, slipping on a pair of espadrilles, I head downstairs and out into the garden.

Nathaniel and the Geigers are by now making their way back up to the house. Trish's heels are sinking into the lawn and both she and Eddie look hot and bothered.

'Hi,' I say casually as they approach.

'*There* you are,' says Nathaniel. 'I haven't seen you all afternoon.'

'I was studying cookery recipes,' I say innocently, and turn to Trish with a polite smile. 'Did you enjoy the party, Mrs Geiger?'

Too late I see Nathaniel making deathlike, finger-across-the-throat gestures behind their backs.

'Thank you for asking, Samantha.' Trish inhales sharply. 'But I'd rather not talk about the party, thank you.'

Eddie makes an incensed spluttering sound. 'You won't bloody give up, will you? All I said was—'

'It was the *way* you said it!' shrieks Trish. 'Sometimes I think your *sole* purpose in life is to embarrass me!'

Eddie huffs furiously and stalks off towards the house, his Panama hat lopsided on his head.

Uh-oh. I raise my eyebrows at Nathaniel, who grins back over Trish's quivering hair-do.

'Would you like a nice cup of tea, Mrs Geiger?' I say soothingly. 'Or . . . a Bloody Mary?'

'Thank you, Samantha,' she replies, lifting her chin in a dignified manner. 'A Bloody Mary would be very nice.'

As we walk up to the conservatory, Trish seems to calm down a little. She even mixes her own Bloody

Mary instead of bossing me around as I do it, and makes one each for me and Nathaniel, too.

'*Now*,' she says, after we've each taken a gulp and sat down amongst the frondy plants, 'there was something I needed to tell you, Samantha. We're having a visitor.'

'Oh, right,' I say, trying not to smile. Nathaniel is sitting next to me, and is edging off my espadrille with his foot under the coffee table.

'My niece is coming to stay tomorrow for a few weeks. She's coming to get some peace and quiet in the country. She has some work to do, and it's *very* important she isn't disturbed, so Mr Geiger and I offered her a place here. I'd like you to get the spare room ready for her.'

'Very good.' I nod dutifully.

'She'll need a bed made up and a desk . . . I believe she's bringing a laptop computer with her.'

'Yes, Mrs Geiger.'

'She's a very bright girl, Melissa.' Trish lights a cigarette with her Tiffany lighter. '*Extremely* high-powered. One of these City girls.'

'Oh, right,' I say, stifling a giggle as Nathaniel finally manages to push my espadrille off. 'What does she do?'

'She's a lawyer,' says Trish – and I look up, speechless. A lawyer?

A lawyer is coming to stay in this house?

Nathaniel is tickling the sole of my foot, but I can only respond with a weak smile. This could be bad. In fact, this could be a disaster.

What if I *know* this lawyer?

As Trish mixes herself another Bloody Mary, I'm racking my brains frantically. *Melissa*. It could be Melissa Davis from Freshwater. It could be Melissa

Christie from Clark Forrester. It could be Melissa Taylor who worked on the DeltaCo merger. We spent hours in the same room together. She'd recognize me straight away.

'So . . . is she a niece on your side, Mrs Geiger?' I ask casually as Trish sits down. 'Is she called Geiger too?'

'No, she's called Hurst.'

Melissa Hurst. It doesn't ring any bells.

'And where does she work?' *Please let it be abroad . . .*

'Oh, she's at some high-powered place in London.' Trish gestures vaguely with her glass.

OK, so I don't know her. But this is not looking good. A high-powered London lawyer. If she's at any of the big law firms she's bound to have heard about me. She's bound to know about the Carter Spink lawyer who lost fifty million and ran away. She'll know every humiliating detail of my disgrace.

I'm feeling cold all over at the thought of it. All it takes is for her to recognize my name, to put two and two together . . . and the whole story will come out. I'll be as humiliated here as I was in London. Everyone will know my background. Everyone will know my lies. I glance at Nathaniel and feel a twinge of dread.

I *can't* let things be spoiled. Not now.

He winks at me and I take a deep gulp of Bloody Mary. The answer is simple. I'll just have to do whatever it takes to keep my secret hidden.

EIGHTEEN

There's no reason why this lawyer should recognize my face. But just to be on the safe side, I opt for a simple disguise. After I've prepared the spare room the following afternoon, I hurry to my own room and pin my hair up on top of my head with artistic strands falling down and concealing my face. Then I add a pair of old sunglasses I found in the dressing-table drawer. They date from the 1980s and have big green frames which totally hide my face. They also make me look like Elton John, but I'll live with that. The point is, I look nothing like my old self.

As I come downstairs, Nathaniel is heading out of the kitchen, looking pissed off. He looks up at me and stops dead in surprise.

'Samantha . . . what have you done?'

'Oh, my hair?' I touch it casually. 'I just wanted it in a different style.'

'Are those *your* sunglasses?' He peers at me incredulously.

'I've got a bit of a headache. So, what's up?' I add, hastily changing the subject.

'Trish.' He scowls. 'She's been lecturing me on

noise. I can't mow the lawn between the hours of ten and two. I can't use the trimmer without giving warning. Could I please tiptoe on the gravel. *Tiptoe.*'

'Why?'

'Because of this blasted visitor. We all have to dance around her. A bloody *lawyer.*' He shakes his head in disbelief. '*Her* work's important. *My* work's important!'

'She's coming!' Trish's voice suddenly shrills from the kitchen and she comes hurrying out. 'Are we all ready?' She flings open the front door and I hear the sound of a car door opening in the drive.

My heart starts to bang in my chest. This is it. I pull a few more strands of hair over my face and clench my fists by my sides. If I recognize this woman I'll just keep my eyes down, mumble my words and play my part. I'm a housekeeper. I have never been anything but a housekeeper.

'Now, you should get *lots* of peace here, Melissa,' I can hear Trish saying. 'I've instructed the staff to look after you with *extra* special care . . .'

I exchange looks with Nathaniel, who rolls his eyes.

'Here we are! Let me hold the door open . . .'

I hold my breath. A moment later Trish enters the house, followed by a girl in jeans and a tight white top, dragging a suitcase.

This is the top, high-powered lawyer?

I stare at her in bewilderment. She has long dark hair and a pert, pretty face, and can't be much out of her teens.

'Melissa, this is our *wonderful* housekeeper, Samantha—' Trish breaks off in surprise. 'Samantha, what on earth are you wearing? You look like Elton John!'

Great. All I've done is attract attention to myself.

269

'Hello,' I say awkwardly, taking the sunglasses off, but keeping my head down. 'It's very nice to meet you.'

'It's *fab* to be here.' Melissa has a boarding-school drawl and matching toss of the hair. 'London was, like *sooo* getting me down.'

'Mrs Geiger said you're a lawyer at some . . . big place in London?'

'Yah.' She gives me a smug smile. 'I'm at Chelsea Law School.'

What?

She's not even a qualified lawyer. She's a law student. She's a *baby*. I cautiously raise my head and meet her eyes – but there's not a blink of recognition. Oh, for God's sake. I have nothing to worry about from this girl. I almost want to laugh.

'And who's this?' Melissa bats her mascaraed eyelashes alluringly at Nathaniel, whose scowl deepens.

'This is Nathaniel, our gardener,' says Trish. 'But don't worry, he's under *strict* instructions not to disturb you. I've told him, you need absolute quiet for your work.'

'I've got *loads* of revision to do.' Melissa gives a world-weary sigh and pushes a hand through her hair. 'You wouldn't believe the work load, Auntie Trish. I've been *soooo* stressed.'

'I don't know how you do it!' Trish puts an arm around her shoulders and squeezes tight. 'Now, what would you like to do first? We're *all* at your disposal.'

'Could you unpack my things?' Melissa turns to me. 'They'll be creased, so they'll all need ironing.'

I feel a slight jolt. She's not going to do her own unpacking? I've turned into this girl's personal *maid*?

'I might take my books out in the garden,' she adds

270

airily. 'Maybe the gardener could set up a table for me in the shade?'

Trish is watching in total admiration as Melissa rummages in a backpack full of text books.

'*Look* at all those books, Samantha!' she exclaims as Melissa retrieves *Beginner's Guide to Litigation*. 'Look at all those long words!'

'Er . . . wow,' I say politely.

'Why don't you make us all some coffee first?' Trish turns to me. 'We'll take it on the terrace. Bring some biscuits out, too.'

'Of course, Mrs Geiger,' I say, bobbing an automatic curtsey.

'Could you make mine half caffeinated, half decaf?' Melissa adds over her shoulder. 'I, like, don't want to get too wired.'

No I bloody couldn't, you pretentious little cow.

'Of course.' I smile through gritted teeth. 'My pleasure.'

Something tells me this girl and I are not going to get along.

As I carry the coffee out to the terrace five minutes later, Trish and Melissa are ensconced in chairs under a parasol along with Eddie.

'You've met Melissa, have you?' he says as I set down the tray on a wrought-iron table. 'Our little star? Our legal eagle?'

'Yes, I have. Your coffee,' I add, handing the cup to Melissa. 'Just as you asked for it.'

'Melissa's under a great deal of pressure,' says Eddie. 'It's up to us to make things easy for her.'

'You can't *imagine* what the strain's like,' says Melissa seriously. 'I've been working into the evenings and everything. My social life's, like, gone out of the window.' She takes a sip of coffee, then turns to me. 'By the way, I meant to say . . .' She frowns. 'What's your name again?'

'Samantha.'

'Yes, Samantha. Be really careful with my red beaded top, OK?' She tosses her hair back and takes another gulp of coffee.

'I'll do my best,' I reply in polite tones. 'Will that be all, Mrs Geiger?'

'Wait!' Eddie puts his cup down. 'I've got something for you. I haven't forgotten our conversation the other day!' He reaches under his chair and produces a brown paper bag. I can see a couple of shiny books poking out of the top. 'Now, you're not going to get out of this one, Samantha. This can be our little project!'

I feel a sudden shot of foreboding. Oh no. Please do not let this be what I think it is.

'Mr Geiger,' I begin quickly, 'it's really nice of you, but—'

'I won't hear another word!' he interrupts with a raised hand. 'You'll thank me one day!'

'What are you talking about?' Melissa wrinkles her button nose in curiosity.

'Samantha's going to take some qualifications!' With a flourish Eddie pulls two work books from the bag. Both are brightly coloured, with big jazzy letters and illustrations. I can see the words 'Maths' and 'English' and 'Adult Learning'.

He opens one up to show a jaunty cartoon cow. A bubble coming from its mouth is asking 'What is a pronoun?'

I stare at it, totally speechless.

'You see?' says Eddie proudly. 'You'll have fun with these! There are gold sticky stars for progress!'

'I'm sure Melissa will be delighted to help with

anything tricky,' chips in Trish. 'Won't you, love?'

'Of course,' says Melissa with a patronizing smile. 'Well done you, Samantha! It's never too late.' She pushes her full cup of coffee towards me. 'Make me another coffee, will you? This one's too weak.'

I head back into the house and toss the work books onto the kitchen table. I refill the kettle, then dump the coffee pot into the sink with a bang.

'All right?' Nathaniel is regarding me with amusement from the kitchen door. 'What's the girl like?'

'Awful!' I can't help bursting out. 'She has no manners. She's treating me like a skivvy. I've got to unpack her stuff . . . and make this stupid decaf mix . . .'

'Only one thing for it,' says Nathaniel. 'Spit in her coffee.'

'Eeww!' I pull a face. 'I'm not doing that.' I spoon coffee into the coffee pot, then add a spoonful of decaf. I cannot believe I'm actually pandering to her stupid whims.

'Don't let her wind you up.' Nathaniel comes over, puts his arms round me and kisses me. 'She's not worth it.'

'I know.' I put down the coffee and nestle into his hold with a little smile, feeling myself relax. 'Mmm. I've missed you.'

He runs his hands down my back and I feel a tingle of delight. Last night I stayed over with Nathaniel at the pub and crept back to the Geigers at six o'clock in the morning. Something tells me this could become a regular pattern.

'I've missed you.' He touches my nose with a quizzical look. 'And by the way, Samantha, don't think I don't know.'

273

I stiffen in his arms. 'Know what?' I say casually.

'I know you have your little secrets.' He studies my face. 'But one's slipped out. And there's nothing you can do about it.'

One's slipped out? What on earth is he talking about?

'Nathaniel, what do you mean?' I try to sound relaxed but I can feel all my alarm systems on full alert.

'Come on.' He seems amused. 'You must know what I mean. Samantha, you can play ignorant but it's out. We *know*.'

'Know *what*?' I say in bewilderment.

Nathaniel shakes his head as though he wants to laugh. 'I'll give you a clue. Tomorrow.' He kisses me again, then heads for the door.

I have no idea what he's talking about. Tomorrow? What's that got to do with anything?

By the middle of the following day I still haven't figured it out. Which could be because I haven't had a single moment to sit down and think. Which could be because I've been running after Melissa the whole bloody time.

I've made her about fifty cups of coffee, half of which she hasn't bothered to drink. I've brought her chilled water. I've rustled up sandwiches. I've washed all the dirty laundry which it turned out her suitcase contained. I've ironed her a white shirt to wear in the evening. Every time I try to start on one of my regular jobs I hear Melissa's high-pitched voice, summoning me.

Meanwhile, Trish is tiptoeing around as though we have T. S. Eliot himself in the garden, writing his last great epic work. As I dust the living room, she's staring out at where Melissa is sitting, at a table set up on the lawn.

'She's working so hard.' She inhales deeply on her cigarette. 'Such an *intelligent* girl, Melissa.'

'Mmm,' I grunt noncommittally.

'You know, it's not easy to get into law school, Samantha. Especially the best one!' She gives me a significant look. 'Melissa had to beat hundreds of people, just to get the place!'

'Fantastic.' I flick my cloth roughly over the TV. 'That's great.'

She's not at the best law school. Just for the record.

'How long is she staying?' I try to ask the question casually.

'It depends.' Trish blows out a cloud of smoke. 'Her exams are in a few weeks, and I've said she's welcome to stay as long as she likes!'

A few *weeks*? It's only been one day, and already she's driving me mad.

I spend the afternoon in the kitchen, pretending to have selective deafness. Whenever Melissa calls me, I turn the blender on, or the radio up, or clatter around with baking trays. If she wants me she can find me herself.

At last, she appears at the kitchen door, her cheeks flushed with annoyance.

'Samantha, I've been calling you!'

'Really?' I look up innocently from the butter I'm chopping to make pastry. 'I didn't hear.'

'We need a bell system or something.' She blows out in impatience. 'This is ridiculous, me having to stop what I'm doing.'

'What did you want?'

'My water jug is empty. And I need some kind of snack. To keep my energy levels up.'

'You could have brought your jug into the kitchen,' I suggest mildly. 'Or made your own snack.'

'Look, I don't have time to be making snacks, OK?' snaps Melissa. 'I'm under a great deal of time pressure right now. I have piles of work, I have exam deadlines . . . you have no *idea* what my life is like.'

I look back at her silently, breathing hard, trying to get my resentment under control.

'I'll bring you out a sandwich,' I say at last.

'*Thank* you,' she says sarcastically, then stands with her arms folded, as though she's waiting for something.

'What?' I say.

'Go on.' She gestures with her head. 'Curtsey.'

What? She can't be serious. 'I'm not curtseying to *you*!' I say, almost laughing.

'You curtsey to my aunt. And my uncle.'

'They're my employers,' I retort tightly. 'It's different.' *And believe me, if I could turn back the clock, curtseying would not be featuring in any of our lives.*

'I'm living in this house.' She tosses back her hair. 'So I'm your employer too. You should show me the same respect.'

I want to *slap* this girl. If she was my junior at Carter Spink I would . . . annihilate her.

'Right.' I put my knife down. 'I'll go and ask Mrs Geiger, shall I?' Before she can reply I stride out of the kitchen. I cannot tolerate this. If Trish takes her side, that's it. I'm leaving.

I can't see Trish anywhere so I head upstairs, heart racing. I arrive outside her room and knock. 'Mrs Geiger? I'd like a word.'

A few moments later, Trish opens the door a crack and pokes her head out, looking a little ruffled.

'Samantha! What do you want?'

'I'm not happy with the current situation,' I say, attempting a calm, civilized voice. 'I'd like to discuss it, please.'

'What situation?' She wrinkles her brow.

'With Melissa. And her . . . her constant needs. I'm being taken away from my regular duties. The house-keeping will suffer if I have to keep attending to her.'

Trish doesn't seem to have heard a word.

'Oh, Samantha . . . not now.' She waves a distracted, dismissive hand. 'We'll talk about this later.'

I can hear Eddie mumbling something from inside the room. Great. They were probably having sex. She probably wants to get back to Turkish Style.

'Right.' I try to control my frustration. 'So I'll just . . . get on, then, shall I?'

'Wait.' Trish suddenly seems to focus on me. 'Samantha, we'll be having champagne on the terrace in half an hour with some . . . ahm . . . friends. I'd like you to wear something other than your uniform.' Her eyes runs over it with slight distaste. 'It's not the most *flattering* garment you possess.'

You bloody chose it! I want to yell back at her. But instead, I curtsey, turn away and walk to my room, fuming.

Bloody Trish. Bloody Melissa. If she's expecting a sandwich, she can just wait.

I close the door, slump onto my bed and look down at my hands, red raw from handwashing Melissa's delicate garments.

What am I doing here?

I can feel disappointment and disillusionment spreading through me. Maybe I was being naive – but I honestly thought Trish and Eddie had come to respect me. Not just as their housekeeper but as a person. But the way Trish behaved just now . . . it's plain I'm just 'staff' to them. Like some sort of useful object, one notch above the Hoover. I almost feel like packing my bags and walking out.

I have a sudden vision of myself flouncing down the stairs, flinging open the door, shooting over my shoulder to Melissa, 'And by the way, I've got a law degree too, and mine is *better* than yours.'

But that would be petulant. No, worse. It would be pathetic.

I massage my temples, feeling my heart rate subside, gradually getting things in perspective.

I chose to do this. No one forced me. And maybe it wasn't the most rational move in the world, and maybe I won't stay here for ever. But it's up to me to make the most of it while I am here. It's up to me to be professional.

Or at least . . . as professional as I can be, bearing in mind I still haven't a clue what a savarin mould is.

At last I summon some energy and get up off the bed. I change out of my uniform into a dress, and brush out my hair. I even add some lipstick for good measure. Then I reach for my mobile and text Nathaniel:

hi! RU there? sam

I wait for a reply but none comes. He hasn't been around all afternoon, I suddenly realize. And I still have no idea what he was talking about yesterday. One of my secrets has 'slipped out'? What secret? As I meet my own eyes in the mirror I feel the tiniest bubbles of disquiet. He can't have—

I mean, he couldn't have—

No. How would he? It's impossible. There'll be some explanation. There always is.

As I descend the stairs into the hall, the house is still and silent. I don't know what time Trish's friends are coming, but there's no sign of them yet. Maybe I've got time to finish my pastry quickly. I might even get the vegetables peeled.

I'm hurrying towards the kitchen when Nathaniel appears.

'*There* you are.' He puts his arms round me and kisses me, pulling me under the stairs, which we've discovered is quite a convenient hiding place. 'Mmm. I've missed you.'

'Nathaniel—' I protest, but his grip around me only gets tighter. After a few moments I manage to wriggle free.

'Nathaniel, I've got pastry to make. I'm already behind schedule, and apparently I've got to serve drinks to some people—'

'Wait.' Nathaniel tugs me back, glancing at his watch. 'One more minute. Then we can go.'

I peer at him uncertainly, feeling a faint foreboding.

'Nathaniel . . . what are you talking about?'

'Still playing dumb.' He shakes his head in amusement. 'Did you really think you could fool us? Sweetheart, we're not stupid! I told you, we *know*.'

I feel a plunging dread. They know. What do they know? *What the hell have they found out?*

I swallow, my mouth suddenly dry. 'What exactly—'

'No, no, no.' Nathaniel puts a finger to my lips. 'Too late. You're going to get your surprise, whether you like it or not.'

'Surprise?' I falter.

'Now come out. They're waiting for you. Close your

eyes . . .' He puts one arm around my waist and the other hand over my eyes. 'Come this way . . . I'll lead you . . .'

As I walk forward in darkness, guided only by Nathaniel's arm, I feel almost sick with fear. My mind is ranging wildly about, trying to work out what might have been going on behind my back. Who's waiting for me out there?

Please, please, don't say they've tried to fix my life up. Please don't say they've arranged some kind of reunion. I have a sudden image of Ketterman standing on the lawn, his steel glasses glinting in the sunlight. Or Arnold. Or my mother.

'Here she is!' Nathaniel guides me out of the french windows and down the steps into the garden. I can feel sun on my face and hear some kind of flapping sound and . . . music? 'All right! Open your eyes!'

I can't open my eyes. Whatever it is, I don't want to know.

'It's OK!' Nathaniel's laughing. 'No one's going to eat you! Open them!'

My heart thudding, I open my eyes. I blink several times, wondering if I'm dreaming.

What . . . what's going on?

An enormous banner reading 'Happy Birthday Samantha!' is tied between two trees. That's what's making the flapping noise. The garden table is laid with a white tablecloth, a bouquet of flowers and several bottles of champagne. A bunch of shiny helium balloons reading 'Samantha' is tethered to a chair. A CD player is emitting jazz. Eddie and Trish are standing on the grass, together with Iris, Eamonn and Melissa – and they're all beaming at me, apart from Melissa, who's pouting.

I feel as though I've lurched into some parallel universe.

'Surprise!' they all cry out in unison. 'Happy birthday!'

I open my mouth, but no sound comes out. I'm too pole-axed to speak. Why do the Geigers think it's my birthday?

'Look at her,' says Trish. 'She's stunned! Aren't you, Samantha?'

'Um . . . yes,' I stutter.

'She had no idea,' confirms Nathaniel with a grin.

'Happy birthday, sweetie.' Iris comes over, clasps me tightly and gives me a kiss.

'Eddie, open the champagne!' I can hear Trish exclaiming impatiently behind me. 'Come on!'

I'm in a total daze. What do I do? What do I say? How do you break it to the people who have organized your surprise birthday party that actually . . . it's not your birthday?

Why would they think it's my birthday? Did I give them some made-up date of birth at the interview? But I don't remember doing that—

'Champagne for the birthday girl!' Eddie pops open a bottle and the champagne froths into a glass.

'Many happy returns!' Eamonn is coming towards me with a beam. 'Ah, you should have seen your face just now!'

'Priceless!' agrees Trish. 'Now, let's have a toast!'

I can't let this go on any longer.

'Um . . . Mr and Mrs Geiger . . . everyone . . . this is lovely, and I'm really touched.' I swallow hard, screwing myself up to say it. 'But . . . it's not my birthday.'

To my surprise, everyone bursts into laughter.

'I told you this would happen!' Trish says in delight. 'She *said* you'd deny it!'

'It's not *that* bad, getting a year older,' says Nathaniel with a teasing smile. 'Now, face it, we know. So have your champagne and enjoy yourself.'

I'm totally confused. 'Who said I'd deny it?'

'Lady Edgerly, of course!' Trish beams. 'She's the one who gave away your little secret!'

Freya? Freya is behind this?

'What . . . what exactly did she say?' I try to sound casual. 'Lady Edgerly.'

'She told me that your birthday was coming up,' says Trish, looking pleased. 'And she warned me you'd try to keep it secret. Naughty, naughty!'

I do not believe Freya. I do not *believe* her.

'She also told me . . .' Trish lowers her voice sympathetically, 'your last birthday was rather a *let down.* She said we simply had to make it up to you. In fact, she was the one who suggested we should do it as a big surprise!' Trish raises her glass. 'So here's to Samantha! Happy Birthday!'

'Happy Birthday!' the others echo, lifting their glasses.

I'm not sure if I want to laugh or cry. Or both. I look around at the banner and silvery balloons, bobbing in the breeze; at the champagne bottles; at everyone's smiling faces. There's nothing I can say. I'll have to go with it.

'Well . . . thank you. I really appreciate it.'

'I'm sorry I was a little *short* with you this afternoon,' says Trish cheerfully, taking another gulp. 'We were rather *struggling* with the helium balloons. We'd already lost one bunch this afternoon.' She darts a baleful glance at Eddie.

'Have you ever tried to get helium balloons into a car boot?' Eddie retorts hotly. 'I'd like to see you do it! I haven't got three bloody hands, you know.'

An image comes to me of Eddie battling with a load of shiny balloons, trying to stuff them into the Porsche, and I bite my lip hard.

'We didn't put your *age* on the balloons, Samantha,' Trish adds in a breathy undertone. 'As one woman to another, I thought you'd appreciate that gesture.' She lifts her glass and gives me the faintest of winks.

I look from her vivid, over-made-up face to Eddie's fleshy pink one and suddenly feel so moved I don't know what to say. All the time, they were planning this. They were doing a banner. They were ordering balloons.

'Mr Geiger, Mrs Geiger, I'm ... I'm so bowled over ...'

'It's not over yet!' says Trish, nodding over my shoulder.

'Happy birthday to you ...' A voice behind me is singing and after a moment the others join in. I swivel round in shock to see Iris coming forward over the lawn, holding the most enormous, two-tier birthday cake. It's iced all over in palest pink, with sugar roses and raspberries, one elegant white candle and, in silver writing, *Happy Birthday Dear Samantha From Us All.*

It's the most beautiful thing I've ever seen. I gaze at it, my throat tight, unable to speak. No one's ever made a cake for me in my life before.

'Blow out your candle!' calls Eamonn as the singing comes to an end.

Somehow I puff feebly at the flame, and everyone cheers.

'You like it?' Iris smiles.

'It's wonderful,' I gulp. 'I've never seen anything like it.'

283

'Happy birthday, chicken.' She pats my hand. 'You deserve it, if anyone does.'

As Iris sets the cake down and begins to slice it up, Eddie tinkles his glass with the end of a pen.

'If I could have your attention . . .' He takes a step up onto the terrace and clears his throat. 'Samantha, we're all very glad you've come into our family. You're doing a marvellous job and we all appreciate it.' Eddie raises his glass to me. 'Er . . . well done.'

'Thank you, Mr Geiger,' I falter. I look around all the friendly faces, framed by blue sky and cherry blossom. 'I'm . . . I'm glad I've come here too. You've all been really welcoming and kind to me.' Oh God, I'm starting to well up. 'I couldn't wish for better employers . . .'

'Oh, stop!' Trish flaps her hands and dabs her eye with a napkin.

'For she's a jolly good fellow,' Eddie begins gruffly. 'For she's a jolly good fellow—'

'*Eddie!* Samantha doesn't want to hear your stupid singing!' interrupts Trish shrilly, still dabbing her eyes. 'Open some more champagne, for goodness' sake!'

It's one of the warmest evenings of the year. As the sun slowly lowers in the sky, we all loll on the grass, drinking champagne and talking. Eamonn tells me about his girlfriend, Anna, who works in a hotel in Gloucester. Iris produces tiny feather-light tarts filled with chicken and herbs. Nathaniel rigs up a set of fairy lights in a tree. Melissa announces loudly several times that she can't sit around, she has to get back to work – then accepts just one more champagne refill.

The sky is an endless, evening blue and there's the smell of honeysuckle in the air. Music is burbling away gently in the background and Nathaniel's hand is resting casually on my thigh. I have never felt so content in my life.

'Presents!' says Trish suddenly. 'We haven't done presents!'

I'm pretty sure she's drunk more champagne than anyone else. She lurches unsteadily over to the table, searches in her bag and produces an envelope. 'This is a little *bonus*, Samantha,' she says, handing it to me. 'To spend on a treat for yourself.'

'Thank you!' I say, taken aback. 'That's incredibly kind of you!'

'We're not increasing your *pay*,' she adds, eyeing me with slight mistrust. 'You do understand this isn't a *raise* or anything. It's just a one-off.'

'I understand,' I say, trying not to smile. 'It's very generous of you, Mrs Geiger.'

'I've got something, too.' Iris reaches into her basket and produces a parcel wrapped in brown paper. Inside I find four shiny new bread tins and a rose-sprigged, goffered apron. I look up at Iris and can't help laughing out loud.

'Thank you,' I say. 'I'll put these to good use.'

Trish is peering at the bread tins in bemused dissatisfaction. 'But . . . surely Samantha has loads of bread tins already?' she says, picking one up in her manicured hand. 'And aprons?'

'I took a chance,' Iris says, her eyes twinkling at me.

'Here you are, Samantha.' Melissa hands me a Body Shop shampoo gift set which I know for a fact has been sitting in Trish's bathroom cupboard since I got here.

'Thanks,' I say politely. 'You shouldn't have.'

'And Melissa,' chimes in Trish, abruptly abandoning interest in the bread tin, 'stop making extra work for Samantha! She can't spend all her time running after you! We can't afford to lose her, you know.'

I can see the shock on Melissa's face. She looks as outraged as if Trish has slapped her.

'And this is from me,' says Nathaniel, stepping in quickly. He hands me a tiny present wrapped in white tissue paper, and everyone turns to see what it is.

I unwrap the little parcel, and a pretty silver charm bracelet falls into my hand. There's only one charm on it: a tiny wooden spoon. I give another snuffle of laughter. A frilly apron, and now a wooden spoon.

'It reminded me of the first time we met,' says Nathaniel, his mouth curving into a smile.

'It's . . . fantastic.' I put my arms round him and kiss him. 'Thank you so much,' I murmur into his ear.

Trish is watching with avid eyes as we draw apart.

'Well, it's obvious what drew *you* to Samantha,' she says to Nathaniel. 'It was her cooking, wasn't it?'

'It was her chick peas,' agrees Nathaniel gravely.

Eamonn has been up on the terrace. Now he bounds down the steps and hands me a bottle of wine. 'This is from me,' he says. 'It's not much, but—'

'Oh, that's lovely!' I say, touched. 'Thanks, Eamonn.'

'And I was going to say, would you be interested in waitressing ever?'

'At the pub?' I say in surprise, but he shakes his head.

'Private functions. We have a little concern going in the village. It's not really a business, more like passing on work to friends. Make a little extra money, that kind of thing.'   •

Passing on work to friends. I suddenly feel a little warm glow inside.

'I'd love to.' I smile at him. 'Thanks for thinking of me.'

Eamonn grins back. 'And there's a drink or two

waiting for you behind the bar if you want to come along?'

'Well . . . er . . .' I glance at Trish. 'Maybe later . . .'

'You go!' says Trish, waving a hand. 'Enjoy yourselves! Don't *think* about work! We'll put the dirty glasses in the kitchen,' she adds, 'and you can deal with them tomorrow.'

'Thanks, Mrs Geiger.' I force myself to stay straight-faced. 'That's very good of you.'

'I must go too,' says Iris, getting up. 'Good night, and thanks.'

'We can't tempt you to the pub, Iris?' says Eamonn.

'Not tonight.' She smiles, her face illuminated by the twinkling fairy lights. 'Good night, Samantha. Night, Nathaniel.'

'Good night, Mum.'

'Night, Eamonn.'

'Night, Iris.'

'Night, Grandpa,' I say.

It comes out before I can stop myself. I stand, frozen to the spot, hot with embarrassment, hoping no one picked it up. But Nathaniel is slowly swivelling towards me, his face creased in amusement. *Trust* him to have heard.

'Good night, Mary Ellen.' He lifts his eyebrows.

'Good night, Jim Bob,' I retort nonchalantly.

'I see myself as more of a John Boy.'

'Hmmm.' I look him up and down. 'OK, you can be John Boy.'

I had a total crush on John Boy when I was a child. Not that I'll mention this fact to Nathaniel.

'C'mon.' Nathaniel holds out his hand. 'Let's get to Ike's Tavern.'

'Ike had the *store*.' I roll my eyes. 'Do you know nothing?'

287

As we head up to the house we pass Melissa and Eddie on the terrace, sitting at the garden table, which is covered in papers and brochures.

'It's just *sooo* difficult,' Melissa is saying. 'I mean, this is a decision which will affect my whole life. It's, like, how are you supposed to know?'

'Mr Geiger?' I interrupt awkwardly. 'I just wanted to thank you very much for this evening. It's been absolutely incredible.'

'It was fun!' says Eddie.

'Have a nice evening,' says Melissa, heaving an enormous sigh. 'I've still got work to do.'

'It'll be worth it, love.' Eddie pats her hand reassuringly. 'When you're at . . .' He picks up a brochure from the table and peers at it through his reading glasses. 'Carter Spink.'

For a few moments I can't move.

Melissa is going for a job at Carter Spink?

'Is that . . .' I try to speak naturally. 'Is that the name of the law firm where you're applying?'

'Oh, I don't know,' says Melissa, looking sulky. 'It's the top one. But it's *incredibly* competitive. Hardly anyone gets a place.'

'Looks very swanky!' says Eddie, flipping over the glossy pages, each illustrated with a photograph. 'Look at these offices!'

As he flips through, I'm transfixed. There's a picture of the foyer. There's one of the floor I used to work on. I can't tear my eyes away – but at the same time I don't want to look. That's my old life. It doesn't belong here. And then suddenly, as Eddie flips another page over, I feel a jolt of disbelief.

It's a picture of me. Me.

I'm in my black suit, my hair pinned up, sitting at a meeting-room table along with Ketterman, David

Elldridge and a guy who was over from the States. I remember that picture being taken, now. Ketterman was absolutely livid at being disturbed.

I look so *pale*. I look so *serious*.

'And it's like . . . do I *want* to give up all my time?' Melissa is jabbing the page. 'These people work every night! What about a social life?'

My face is right there in full view. I'm just waiting for someone to frown in recognition, to say '*Hang* on a moment . . .'

But no one does. Melissa is still rabbiting on, gesturing to the brochure. Eddie is nodding. Nathaniel is staring upwards, obviously bored.

'Although, you know, the money *is* really good . . .' Melissa sighs, and flips the page.

The picture's gone. I'm gone.

'Shall we go?' Nathaniel's warm hand tugs mine and I clasp it tightly back.

'Yes.' I smile up at him. 'Let's.'

NINETEEN

I don't see the Carter Spink brochure again for two weeks, when I'm drifting into the kitchen to make lunch.

I don't know what happened to time. I barely recognize it any more. The minutes and hours don't tick past in rigid chunks, they ebb and flow and swirl around. I don't even wear a watch any more. Yesterday I lay in a hayfield all afternoon with Nathaniel, watching dandelion seeds floating by, and the only ticking sound came from the crickets.

I barely recognize myself any more, either. I'm tanned from lying in the sun at lunchtimes. There are golden streaks at the tips of my hair. My cheeks are full and flushed. My arms are gaining muscles from all the polishing and kneading and carting heavy saucepans around.

The summer is in full throttle and each day is hotter than the last. Every morning, before breakfast, Nathaniel walks me back through the village to the Geigers' house – and even at that hour the air is already warming up. Everything seems slow and lazy, these days. Nothing seems to matter. Everyone's in holiday mood – except Trish, who is in full-frenzy mood. She's holding a big charity lunch next week, having read in a magazine that this is what upper-class ladies do. From the fuss she's making, you'd think it was a Royal wedding.

I'm tidying away the papers which Melissa has left littered on the table when I spot the Carter Spink brochure, underneath a folder. I can't resist picking it up and leafing through the familiar pictures. There are the steps I went up every day of my life for seven years. There's Guy, looking as dazzlingly handsome as ever. There's that girl Sarah from the Litigation department, who was up for partnership too. I never even heard if she got it.

'What are you doing?' Melissa has come into the kitchen without me hearing. She eyes me suspiciously. 'That's mine.'

Honestly. Like I'm going to steal a brochure.

'Just tidying your things,' I say pointedly, putting the brochure down. 'I've got to use this table.'

'Oh. Thanks.' Melissa rubs her face. She looks haggard, these days. There are shadows under her eyes, and the sheen to her hair has gone.

'You're working hard,' I volunteer more kindly.

'Yah, well.' She lifts her chin. 'It'll be worth it in the end. They work you really hard to start, but after you qualify, it calms down.'

I look at her tired, pinched, arrogant little face. Even if I could tell her what I know, she wouldn't believe me.

'Yup,' I say after a pause. 'I'm sure you're right.' I glance down at the Carter Spink brochure again. It's open at a picture of Arnold. He's wearing a bright-blue spotted tie and matching handkerchief and is beaming out at the world. Just seeing him makes me want to smile.

'So are you applying to this law firm?' I ask casually.

'Yup. They're the best.' Melissa is getting a Diet Coke from the fridge. 'That's the guy who was supposed to be interviewing me.' She jerks her head at the picture of Arnold. 'But he's leaving.'

I feel a jerk of astonishment. Arnold's leaving Carter Spink?

'Are you sure?' I say before I can stop myself.

'Yes.' Melissa gives me an odd look. 'What's it to you?'

'Oh, nothing,' I say, hastily throwing down the brochure. 'I just meant . . . he doesn't look old enough to retire.'

'Well, he's going.' She shrugs and wanders out of the kitchen, leaving me staring down in puzzlement.

Arnold is leaving Carter Spink? But he's always boasted about never retiring. He's always boasted about lasting another twenty years. Why would he be leaving now?

I'm totally out of touch. For the last few weeks I've been living in a bubble. I haven't seen *The Lawyer*, I've barely even seen a normal paper. I don't know any of the gossip, and I haven't cared a bit. But now, as I look at Arnold's familiar face, I can feel prickles of curiosity.

I know I'm not in that world any more, but I still want to know. Why on earth is Arnold leaving Carter Spink? What else has happened that I don't know about?

So that afternoon, when I've cleared up lunch, I slip into Eddie's study, switch on the computer and click on Google. I search for 'Arnold Saville' – and sure enough on the second page I come across a little diary item about his early retirement. I read the fifty-word piece over and over, trying to glean clues. Why would Arnold retire early? Is he ill?

I search for further items, but that's the only one I can find. After a moment's hesitation, I go to the search box and – telling myself I shouldn't – type in 'Samantha Sweeting'. Immediately a zillion stories about me pop up again on the screen. I don't feel so freaked out this time, though. It almost doesn't feel like me any more.

I scan entry after entry, seeing the same details replayed. After clicking through about five pages I add 'Third Union Bank' to my search, and scan the resulting entries. Then I type in 'Third Union Bank, BLLC Holdings', then 'Third Union Bank, Glazerbrooks'. Then, with a weird frisson, I type in 'Samantha Sweeting, £50 million, career over' and wait for all the really nasty stories to appear. It's like watching my own car crash, on action replay.

God, Google is addictive. I sit there, totally absorbed, clicking and typing and reading, gorging on endless web pages, automatically using the Carter Spink password wherever I need to. After an hour I'm slumped in Eddie's chair, like a zombie. My back is aching and my neck is stiff, and the words are all running into each other. I'd forgotten what it was like, to sit at a computer. Did I really use to do this all day?

I rub my tired eyes and glance at the web page open in front of me, wondering what I'm even doing on it. It's some obscure list of guests at a lunch held earlier this year at the Painters Hall. About halfway down is the name BLLC Holdings, which must have been the link. On autopilot I move the cursor along the page – and into view comes the name 'Nicholas Hanford Jones, director'.

Something chimes inside my addled brain. *Nicholas*

Hanford Jones. Why do I know that name? Why am I somehow associating it with Ketterman?

Is BLLC Holdings a client of Ketterman? No. It can't be. I'd have heard of it before.

I screw my eyes up tight and concentrate as hard as I can. *Nicholas Hanford Jones*. I can almost see it in my mind's eye; I'm grasping at an association . . . an image . . . Come on, think . . .

This is the trouble with having a nearly photographic memory. People think it must be useful, when in fact all it does is drive you insane.

And then suddenly it comes to me. The swirly writing of a wedding invitation. It was stuck up on the pinboard in Ketterman's office, about three years ago. It was there for weeks. I used to see it every time I went in.

Mr and Mrs Arnold Saville
request the pleasure of your company
at the wedding of their daughter Fiona
to Mr Nicholas Hanford Jones.

Nicholas Hanford Jones is Arnold Saville's son-in-law? Arnold has a family connection with BLLC Holdings?

I sink back in my chair, totally disconcerted. How come he never mentioned that?

And then another thought strikes me. I was on the BLLC Holdings Companies House page a minute ago. Why wasn't Nicholas Hanford Jones listed as a director? That's illegal, for a start.

I rub my brow, then out of curiosity type in 'Nicholas Hanford Jones'. A moment later the screen is full of entries, and I lean forward expectantly.

Oh, for God's sake. The Internet is crap. I'm looking at other Nicholases and other Hanfords and other Joneses, mentioned in all sorts of different contexts. I peer at them in total frustration. Don't Google *realize* that's not what I'm interested in? Why would I want to read about some Canadian rowing team containing a Greg Hanford, a Dave Jones and a Chip Nicholas?

I'm never going to find anything here.

Even so, I start picking my way down, skimming each chunk of text, clicking onto the next page and the next. And then, just as I'm about to give up, my eye falls on an entry tucked away at the bottom of the page. *William **Hanford Jones**, Finance Director of Glazerbrooks, thanked **Nicholas** Jenkins for his speech . . .*

I stare at it for a few seconds in total disbelief. The finance director at Glazerbrooks is called Hanford Jones too? Are they from the same *family*? Feeling like some kind of private detective, I log on to Friends Reunited, and two minutes later I have my answer. They're brothers.

I feel a bit dazed. This is a pretty huge connection. The finance director of Glazerbrooks, which went bust owing Third Union Bank £50 million. A director of BLLC Holdings, which lent it £50 million three days before. And Arnold, representing Third Union Bank. All related; all in the same extended family. And the weirdest thing is I'm pretty sure nobody else knows.

Arnold's never mentioned it. No one at Carter Spink has ever mentioned it. Nor have I seen it brought up in any of the reports on the whole affair. Arnold's kept all of this very quiet.

I rub my eyes, trying to gather my jumbled thoughts. Isn't it a potential conflict of interest? Shouldn't he have disclosed the information straight away? Why on earth would Arnold keep such an important thing secret? Unless—

No.

No. It couldn't—

He couldn't possibly—

I open my eyes, feeling a bit light-headed, as though I've suddenly swum over the ledge into mile-deep water. My mind is flitting ahead, bouncing onto possibilities and shearing away again in disbelief.

Did Arnold discover something? Is he hiding something?

Is this why he's leaving?

I get up and thrust my hands through my hair. OK, let's just . . . stop all this, right now. This is Arnold I'm talking about. *Arnold*. I'm turning into some nutty conspiracy theorist. Next I'll be typing in 'aliens, Roswell, they live among us'.

With sudden resolution I get out my phone. I'll call Arnold. I'll wish him well in his retirement. Then maybe I can get rid of all these ridiculous ideas floating round my head.

It takes me about six failed attempts before I muster the courage to dial the entire number and wait for a reply. The idea of talking to anyone at Carter Spink – let alone Arnold – makes me feel slightly sick. I keep bottling out before being connected; thrusting the phone down as though I've had a narrow escape.

But at last I steel myself to press the digits and hold the line. I'm never going to know unless I do this. I can talk to Arnold. I can hold my head up.

After three rings the phone is picked up by Lara. 'Arnold Saville's office.'

I have a sudden vision of her sitting at her pale wooden desk, in the burgundy jacket she always wears, tapping away. It all seems a million miles away now.

'Hi, Lara,' I say. 'It's ... Samantha. Samantha Sweeting.'

'*Samantha?*' Lara sounds pole-axed. 'Bloody hell! How are you? What are you up to?'

'I'm fine, thanks. Really good.' I quell a spasm of nerves. 'I just rang because I've heard that Arnold's leaving. Is it true?'

'It's true!' says Lara with relish. 'I was gobsmacked! Apparently, Ketterman took him out to dinner and tried to get him to stay, but he'd made up his mind. Get this, he's moving to the Bahamas.'

'The *Bahamas*?' I say in astonishment.

'He's bought a house there! Looks lovely. His retirement party's next week,' Lara continues. 'I'll be transferring to Derek Green's office, you remember him? Taxation partner? Very nice guy, though apparently he can have a bit of a temper—'

'Er ... great!' I cut her off, suddenly remembering her ability to gossip for hours without taking a breath. 'Lara, I just wanted to give Arnold my best wishes. If you could possibly put me through?'

'Really?' Lara sounds surprised. 'That's incredibly generous of you, Samantha. After what happened.'

'Well, you know,' I say awkwardly, 'it wasn't Arnold's fault, was it? He did what he could.'

There's a strange silence.

'Yes,' says Lara after a pause. 'Well. I'll put you through.'

After a few moments Arnold's familiar voice is booming down the line.

'Samantha, dear girl! Is it really you?'

'It's really me.' I manage a smile. 'I haven't *quite* disappeared off the face of the earth.'

'I should hope not! Now, you're all right, are you?'

'I'm . . . fine,' I say awkwardly. 'Thanks. I was just surprised to hear you're retiring.'

'I was never a glutton for punishment!' He gives an easy laugh. 'Thirty-three years at the coal-face of law. That's enough for any human. Let alone any lawyer!'

Just his jovial voice is reassuring me. I must be crazy. Arnold couldn't be involved in anything untoward. He couldn't be hiding anything. He's *Arnold*.

I'll mention it to him, I decide. Just to prove it to myself.

'Well . . . I hope it all goes well,' I say. 'And I . . . I guess you'll be seeing more of your family?'

'I'll be lumbered with the blighters, yes!' He booms with laughter again.

'I never knew your son-in-law was a director of BLLC Holdings!' I attempt a casual tone. 'Quite a coincidence!'

There's a moment of silence.

'I'm sorry?' says Arnold. His voice is still as charming as ever, but the warmth has disappeared.

'BLLC Holdings.' I swallow. 'You know, the other company involved with the Third Union Bank loan? The one that registered a charge? I just happened to notice . . .'

'I have to go now, Samantha!' Arnold cuts me off smoothly. 'Delightful to chat, but I'm leaving the country on Friday, and there's a lot to do. It's exceedingly busy here, so I wouldn't ring again if I were you.'

The line goes dead before I can say any more. I slowly put down the phone and stare at a butterfly fluttering outside the window.

That wasn't right. That wasn't a natural reaction. He got rid of me as soon as I mentioned his son-in-law.

Something is going on. Something is definitely going on.

What could it be? I have totally abandoned the housework for the afternoon and am sitting on my bed with a pad of paper and pencil, trying to work out the possibilities.

Who stands to gain? I stare at my scribbled facts and arrows yet again. Two brothers. Millions of pounds being transferred between banks and companies. Think. *Think . . .*

With a small cry of frustration I rip out the page and crumple it. Let's start again. Let's get everything in logical order. Glazerbrooks went into receivership. Third Union Bank lost their money. BLLC Holdings jumped ahead in the queue . . .

I tap my pencil impatiently on the paper. But so what? They only get back the money they loaned. They don't get any advantage, they don't get any benefit, it's pointless.

Unless – what if they never paid over anything in the first place?

The thought hits my brain out of nowhere. I sit bolt upright, unable to breathe. What if that's it? *What if that's the scam?*

My mind starts to race. Suppose there are two brothers. They know that Glazerbrooks is in serious financial trouble. They know that the bank has just paid in fifty million but the bank's charge wasn't registered. That means there's a fifty million unsecured loan swilling around in the company, up for grabs by anyone else who registers a charge . . .

I can't sit down any more. I'm pacing back and forth, feverishly gnawing my pencil, my brain sparking like an electrical circuit. It works. It works. They fiddle the

299

figures. BLLC Holdings get the money that Third Union Bank paid over, Carter Spink's insurers foot the bill—

I pause in my striding. No. It doesn't work. I'm being stupid. The insurers are only covering the fifty million because I was negligent. That's the crucial element. The whole plan would have depended on me, Samantha Sweeting, making that particular mistake.

But I mean . . . how on earth could they have planned that? It makes no sense. It's impossible. You can't plan a mistake in advance. You can't *make* someone forget to do something, you can't *make* someone fuck up—

And then I stop dead. My skin suddenly feels clammy. The memo.

I never saw that memo on my desk until it was too late. I know I didn't.

What if—

Oh my God.

I sink onto the window seat, my legs like rubber. What if someone planted that memo on my desk? Slipped it into a pile of papers after the deadline had passed?

My heart begins to pound and I clutch the curtain for balance.

What if I didn't make a mistake?

I feel like everything is cracking and reshaping around me. What if Arnold deliberately didn't register the bank charge – and made it look like my fault?

Like a looped tape, my conversation with Arnold is playing over and over in my mind. When I said I couldn't remember seeing the memo on my desk. And he immediately changed the subject.

I assumed the memo was there all the time. I assumed it was my error. My inefficiency. But what if it wasn't? Everyone at Carter Spink knew I had the messiest desk in the firm. It would be easy to slip the memo into a pile of papers. Make it look as if it had been there for weeks.

I'm breathing harder and harder, till I'm almost hyperventilating. I have lived with that mistake for two months. It's been there every morning when I wake up and every day when I go to bed. Like a constant background ache; like a chorus in my head: Samantha Sweeting ruined her life. Samantha Sweeting fucked up.

But . . . what if I was used? What if it wasn't my fault? *What if I didn't make a mistake after all?*

I have to know. I have to know the truth. Right now. With a shaking hand I reach for my mobile phone and punch in the number again.

'Lara, I need to speak to Arnold again,' I say as soon as I'm connected.

'Samantha . . .' Lara sounds awkward. 'I'm afraid Arnold won't take any more calls from you. And he asked me to tell you that you're not to pester him about your job any more.'

I feel a flash of shock. What has he been saying about me?

'Lara, I'm not pestering him about my job,' I say, trying to keep my voice steady. 'I just need to talk to him about a . . . matter. If he won't talk to me, I'll come to the office. Can you make me an appointment, please?'

'Samantha . . .' She sounds even more embarrassed than before. 'Arnold told me to inform you . . . if you try to come here to the offices, Security will eject you.'

'*Eject* me?' I stare at the phone in disbelief.

'I'm sorry. I really am. And I don't blame you!' she adds fervently. 'I thought what Arnold did to you was really shocking! A lot of us do.'

301

I feel a fresh confusion. What he *did* to me? Does Lara know about the memo?

'What – what do you mean?' I stammer.

'The way he got you fired!' says Lara.

'What?' I feel like all the breath has been squeezed from my chest. 'What are you talking about?'

'I *did* wonder if you knew.' She lowers her voice. 'He's leaving now, so I can say it. I took the minutes at that meeting, after you ran off. And Arnold talked round all the other partners. He said you were a liability and they couldn't risk taking you back and all sorts. A lot of them wanted to give you another chance, you know.' She clicks her tongue. 'I was appalled. Of course, I couldn't *say* anything to Arnold . . .'

'Of course not,' I manage. 'Thanks for telling me, Lara. I . . . had no idea.'

I feel dizzy. Everything is turning out distorted. Arnold didn't fight my corner at all. He got me fired. I don't know this man at all. All that genial, affable charm – it's an act. It's a bloody act.

With a sickening thud I suddenly recall him the day after it happened, insisting I should stay where I was, not come back. That's why. He wanted me out of the way so I couldn't fight for myself. So he could stitch me up.

And I trusted him. Totally and utterly. Like a stupid, *stupid* gullible fool.

My chest is heaving painfully. All my doubts have disappeared. Arnold is in on something crooked. I know it. He set me up. He planted that memo, knowing it would destroy my career.

And in three days he'll have disappeared to the Bahamas. I feel a stab of panic. I need to take action now.

'Lara,' I say, trying to sound calm, 'could you put me through to Guy Ashby?'

I know Guy and I had a row. But he's the only person I can think of right now who'll be able to help me.

'Guy's in Hong Kong,' says Lara in surprise. 'Didn't you know?'

'Right,' I say, my heart plummeting. 'No. I . . . didn't know.'

'But he'll have his BlackBerry with him,' she adds helpfully. 'You could send him an email.'

'Yes.' I take a deep breath. 'Yes, maybe I'll do that.'

TWENTY

I can't do it. I just can't. There is no way of writing this email without sounding like a paranoid crazy.

I look in despair at my tenth attempt.

Dear Guy
I need you to help me. I think I have been stitched up by Arnold. I think he planted that memo on my desk. Something is going on. He has family links with both BLLC Holdings and Glazerbrooks, did you know that?? Why did he never tell anyone? And now he's banned me from the building, which in itself is suspicious—

I sound delusional. I sound like some bitter, twisted, ex-employee with a grudge.

Which of course is what I am.

As I run my eyes over my words, I'm reminded of nothing more than the wild-eyed old woman who used to stand at the corner of our street, muttering 'They're coming to GET me.'

I have total sympathy for that old woman now. They probably *were* coming to get her.

Guy will just laugh. I can see him now. Arnold Saville a crook? It sounds insane. Maybe I *am* insane. It's only a theory. I don't have evidence; I don't have anything solid. I lean forward and rest my head hopelessly on my hands. No one's ever going to believe me. Or even listen to me.

If I only had some proof. But where am I supposed to get that from?

A bleeping from my mobile phone makes me jump, and I look up blearily. I'd almost forgotten where I was. I pick it up and see that I've got a text.

I'm downstairs. have a surprise to show you. nat.

As I head downstairs, I'm really not with it. Flashes of anger keep overwhelming me as I think of Arnold's jocular smile, the way he encouraged my messy desk, the way he told me he'd do his very best for me, the way he listened as I blamed myself, as I apologized and grovelled . . .

The worst thing is I never even tried to defend myself. I never questioned the fact that I couldn't remember seeing the memo. I immediately assumed the worst of myself; assumed it was my fault for having such a messy desk.

Arnold knows me pretty well. Maybe that's what he was counting on.

Bastard. *Bastard.*

'Hi.' Nathaniel waves a hand in front of my face. 'Earth to Samantha.'

'Oh . . . Sorry. Hi!' Somehow I muster a smile. 'What's the surprise?'

'Come this way.' He grins and ushers me out to his car, which is an ancient Beetle convertible. As usual, rows of seed pots are crowding the back seat and an old wooden spade is sticking out of the back.

'Madam.' He opens the door gallantly.

'So what are you showing me?' I ask as I get in.

'Magical mystery tour.' He gives an enigmatic smile, and starts up the engine.

We drive out of Lower Ebury and take a route which I don't recognize, through a tiny neighbouring village and up into the hills. Nathaniel seems in a cheerful mood and tells me stories about each farm and pub that we pass. But I barely hear a word. My mind is still churning.

I don't know what I can do. I can't even get into the building. I have no credibility. I'm powerless. And I only have three days. Once Arnold disappears off to the Bahamas that'll be it.

'Here we are!' Nathaniel turns off the road onto a gravel drive. He manoeuvres the car into place by a low brick wall, then stops the engine. 'What do you think?'

With an effort I wrench my mind back to the present. 'Um . . .' I peer around blankly. 'Yes. Lovely.'

What am I supposed to be looking at?

'Samantha, are you OK?' Nathaniel shoots me a curious glance. 'You seem on edge.'

'I'm fine.' I try to smile. 'Just a bit tired.'

I open the car door to get out, away from his gaze. I shut the door behind me, take a few steps forward and look around.

We're in some kind of courtyard, baking in the evening sun. There's a ramshackle house to the right, with a FOR SALE post. Ahead are banks of green-houses, glinting in the low sunlight. There are plots, filled with rows of vegetables, there's a portacabin marked GARDEN CENTRE . . .

Hang on.

I swivel round in bewilderment to see that Nathaniel has got out of the car too. He's grinning at me, and holding a sheaf of papers in his hand.

'A horticultural business opportunity,' he reads aloud. 'Four acres of land, with ten more available, subject to negotiation. Ten thousand square feet of glasshouses. Four-bedroom farmhouse, needs work . . .'

'You're *buying* this?' I say, my attention fully grabbed.

'I'm thinking about it. I wanted to show you first.' He spreads an arm out. 'It's a pretty good concern. Needs building up, but the land's there. We can get some polytunnels going, extend the offices . . .'

I can't take all this in. Since when did Nathaniel become so entrepreneurial?

'But what about the pubs? How come you're suddenly—'

'It was you. What you said in the garden that day.' He pauses, the breeze ruffling his hair. 'You're right, Samantha. I'm not a landlord, I'm a gardener. I'd be happier doing what I really want to do. So . . . I had a long talk with Mum and she understood. We both reckon Eamonn can take over. Not that he knows yet.'

'Wow.' I look around again, taking in a pile of wooden crates; stacks of seed trays; a tattered poster advertising Christmas trees. 'So you're really going to do it?'

Nathaniel shrugs, but I can see the excitement in his face. 'You only get one chance at life.'

'Well, I think it's fantastic.' I beam with genuine enthusiasm.

'And there's a house.' He nods towards it. 'Or at least, there will be a house. It's a bit run down.'

'Right.' I regard the ramshackle building with a grin. 'It does look a bit of a mess.'

'I wanted you to see it first,' says Nathaniel. 'Get your approval. I mean, one day you might . . .' He stops.

There's silence in the courtyard. All of a sudden my relationship sensors are swivelling round madly, like the Hubble spotting an alien ship. What did they just pick up? What was he going to say?

'I might . . . stay over?' I supply at last, a little awkward.

'Exactly.' Nathaniel rubs his nose. 'Shall we have a look?'

The house is bigger than it looks from the outside, with bare boards and old fireplaces and a creaking wooden staircase. One room has practically no plaster, and the kitchen is totally old-fashioned, with 1930s cupboards.

'Great kitchen.' I shoot him a teasing look.

'I'm sure I could refit it to your cordon bleu standards,' he returns.

We make our way upstairs and into a huge bedroom overlooking the rear of the house. From above, the vegetable plots look like an orderly patchwork quilt, stretching away into the green meadow. I can see a little terrace down below and a tiny private garden belonging to the house, all clematis and tangled roses.

'It's a beautiful place,' I say, leaning on the window sill. 'I love it.'

Standing here, looking out at the view, I feel like London is on another planet. Carter Spink and Arnold and all of them suddenly seem part of another life. I'm not just out of the loop, I'm off the string altogether.

But even as I'm gazing out at the restful country scene, I can feel myself grasping for the end of it. I can't let it go; I can't relax. All it would take is one phone call to the right person . . .

If I had some proof . . .

Anything . . .

My mind starts turning over the facts again, like a bird turning over empty snail shells. I'm going to drive myself crazy like this.

'What I was wondering is . . .'

Suddenly I become aware that Nathaniel is speaking. In fact I think he could have been speaking for a while – and I haven't heard a word. I hastily turn round, to see him facing me. His cheeks are flushed and he has an unfamiliar awkwardness about him. It looks like whatever he's been saying has required some effort.

'. . . do you feel the same way, Samantha?'

He coughs, and breaks off into an expectant silence.

I stare back at him dumbly. Do I feel the same way about what?

Oh shit. *Bollocks*. Was he saying something really heartfelt and meaningful? Was he making some sort of speech of love? And I *missed* it?

This just teaches me to obsess. The man I'm secretly falling in love with just made a romantic speech to me – probably the only one I'll get in my whole life – and *I wasn't listening*?

I want to shoot myself for being so *rubbish*.

And now he's waiting for me to reply. What am I going to do? He's just spilled his heart to me. I can't say, 'Sorry, I didn't quite catch that.'

'Um . . .' I push my hair back, playing for time. 'Well . . . you've given me quite a lot to think about.'

'But do you agree?'

Do I agree with what? Capital punishment for burglars? Threesomes?

OK, this is Nathaniel. I'm sure I agree with it, whatever it is.

'Yes.' I give him the most sincere look I can muster. 'Yes, I agree. Wholeheartedly. In fact . . . I've often thought so myself.'

A strange flicker passes over Nathaniel's face as he surveys me. 'You agree,' he says, as though to make sure. 'With everything?'

'Er . . . yes!' I'm starting to feel a bit nervous now. What have I agreed to?

'Even about the chimpanzees?'

'The *chimpanzees*?' I suddenly see Nathaniel's mouth twitching. He's twigged.

'You didn't listen to a word I was saying, did you?' he says matter-of-factly.

'I didn't realize you were saying something important!' I wail, hanging my head. 'You should have warned me!'

Nathaniel looks at me incredulously. 'That took some nerve, you know, saying all that.'

'Say it again,' I beg. 'Say it all again! I'll listen!'

'Uh huh.' He laughs, shaking his head. 'Maybe one day.'

'I'm sorry, Nathaniel. Really I am.' I turn away to stare out of the window again, pressing my head against the glass. 'I was just . . . distracted.'

'I know.' He comes over and puts his arms around me, over my own. I can feel his steady heartbeat against me, calming me down. 'Samantha, what's up? It's your old relationship, isn't it?'

'Yup,' I mutter after a pause.

'Why won't you tell me about it? I could help.'

I swivel round to face him. The sun is glowing in his eyes and on his burnished face. He's never looked more handsome. I have a sudden vision of him punching Arnold right in the face.

But I can't dump all this on him. It's too much. It's too big. It's too . . . sordid.

'I don't want to bring that world into this one,' I say at last. 'I just don't.'

Nathaniel opens his mouth again but I turn away before he can speak. I stare out at the idyllic view again, blinking against the rays of the sun, my mind in turmoil.

Maybe I should just give up on the whole nightmare. Forget about it. Let it go. The chances are I'll never be able to prove anything. Arnold has all the power; I have none. The chances are if I try to stir things up again all I'll get is more humiliation and disgrace.

I could so easily do nothing. I could just put it from my mind. Close the door on my old life and leave it behind for ever. I have a job. I have Nathaniel. I have a possible future here.

But even as I'm thinking it – I know that's not what I'm going to do. I can't forget about it. I can't let go.

TWENTY-ONE

OK. The one possible hitch is Arnold's password. If I can't guess that, I won't be able to access his computer files and I won't be able to find out anything. Also, if his office door is locked. That could be a bit of a problem.

So that's two possible hitches, in fact.

Plus I have to get into the building, of course. And not be recognized by anyone . . .

And not be discovered tapping at Arnold's computer by one of the cleaners . . .

Oh fuck. *What the hell am I doing?*

I take a deep gulp of skinny latte, trying to stay calm. But it's not easy.

Even being back in London has thrown me. The city isn't the way I remember it. I can't believe how dirty it is. How *rushed* it is. As I arrived at Paddington station this afternoon I felt almost bewildered by the commuter crowds, moving like a swarm of ants over the concourse. I could smell the fumes. I saw the litter. Things I never even noticed before. Did I just filter them out? Was I so used to them, they faded into the background?

But at the same time, the minute my feet hit the ground I felt the buzz. By the time I reached the Underground station I'd already picked up my pace: matching the stride of everyone else; feeding my travel card into the machine at exactly the right angle; whipping it out with not a second to spare.

And now I'm in the Starbucks around the corner from Carter Spink, sitting at the counter in the window, watching City-suited business people walking past, talking and gesticulating and making phone calls. The adrenaline is catching. My heart's already beating more quickly – and I haven't even got inside the building yet.

At the thought, my stomach turns inside out. Now I know why criminals operate in gangs when they pull off heists. Right now, I could really do with Ocean's Eleven to give me a bit of moral support.

I glance at my watch yet again. Nearly time. The last thing I want to do is arrive early. The less time I spend in there, the better.

As I drain my latte, my phone bleeps, but I ignore it. It'll be yet another message from Trish. She was livid when I told her I had to go away for a couple of days; in fact she tried to stop me. So I told her I had a foot complaint which needed urgent attention from my specialist in London.

In hindsight this was a huge mistake, as she wanted to know every single gory detail. She even demanded I take off my shoe and show her. I had to spend ten minutes improvising about 'bone misalignment' while she peered at my foot and said 'it looks perfectly normal to me' in tones of great suspicion.

She looked at me mistrustfully for the rest of the day. Then she left a copy of *Marie Claire* casually open at the 'Pregnant? Need Confidential Advice?'

advertisement. Honestly. I have to knock that one on the head or it'll be all over the village and Iris will be knitting bootees.

I look at my watch again and feel a swoop of nerves. Time to go. I head for the Ladies, face the mirror and check my appearance. Unfamiliar blonde hair: check. Tinted glasses: check. Magenta lipstick: check. I look nothing like my former self.

Apart from the face, obviously. If you look really closely.

But the point is, no one's going to look closely at me. This is what I'm counting on, anyway.

'Hi,' I say in a low, guttural voice. 'Pleased to meet you.'

I sound like a drag queen. But never mind. At least I don't sound like a lawyer.

Keeping my head down, I leave Starbucks and walk along the street, until I round the corner and see the distinctive granite steps and glass doors of Carter Spink. I gaze at the familiar facade and something seems to clutch at my chest. I feel unreal, being back here. The last time I saw those doors I was pushing my way out of them, gibbering with panic; convinced I'd wrecked my own career; convinced my life was over.

Anger starts boiling up again and I close my eyes briefly, trying to keep my emotions in line. I don't have any proof yet. I have to stay focused on what I'm doing. Come on. I can do this.

I cross the road and resolutely head up the steps. I can almost see myself that day, a ghost-like figure, running down them in a state of bewildered shock. It all seems like a lifetime ago now. I don't just look like a different person, I *feel* like a different person. I feel like I've been rebuilt.

With a deep breath, I pull my mac around me and

push open the glass doors. As I step into the foyer I feel a sudden giddy wave of disbelief. Am I actually doing this? Am I actually trying to blag my way, *incognito*, into the Carter Spink offices?

Yep. I am. My legs are wobbling and my hands feel damp, but I'm walking steadily forward over the shiny marble floor, my eyes fixed downwards. I head towards the new receptionist, Melanie, who only started a couple of weeks before I left.

'Hi,' I say in my drag-queen voice.

'Can I help you?' Melanie smiles at me. There's not a glimmer of recognition in her face. I can't believe this is so easy.

In fact, I feel a tad insulted. Was I *so* nondescript before?

'I'm here for the party?' I mumble, my head down. 'I'm waitressing. Bertram's Caterers,' I add for good measure.

'Oh yes. That's all happening up on the fourteenth floor.' She taps on her computer. 'What's your name?'

'It's . . . Trish,' I say. 'Trish Geiger.' Melanie peers at the computer screen, frowning and tapping her pen on her teeth.

'You're not on my list,' she says at last.

'Well, I should be there.' I keep my head well down. 'There must be a mistake.'

'Let me call up . . .' Melanie taps on her phone and has a brief conversation with someone called Jan, then looks up.

'She'll be down to see you.' She gestures to the leather sofas with a smile. 'Please take a seat.'

I head towards the seating area – then veer in a sharp U-turn as I see David Spellman from Corporate sitting on one of the sofas with a client. Not that he seems to have recognized me. I walk towards a rack of glossy leaflets on Carter Spink's philosophy and bury my head in one on Dispute Resolution.

I've never actually read any of the Carter Spink brochures before. God, they really are a load of meaningless crap.

'Trish?'

'Er . . . yes?' I swivel round to see a woman in a tuxedo with a raddled face. She's holding some typed sheets and regarding me with a frown.

'Jan Martin, head of waiting staff. You're not on my list. Have you worked for us before?'

'I'm new,' I say, keeping my voice low. 'But I've worked for Ebury Catering. Down in Gloucestershire.'

'Don't know it.' She consults her paper again and flicks to the second page, her brow creased in impatience. 'Love, you're not on the list. I don't know what you're doing here.'

'I spoke to a guy,' I say without flickering. 'He said you could do with extra.'

'A guy?' She looks perplexed. 'Who? Tony?'

'I don't remember his name. But he said to come here.'

'He couldn't have said—'

'This is Carter Spink, isn't it?' I look around. '95 Cheapside? A big retirement party?'

'Yes.' I see the beginnings of doubt on the woman's face.

'Well, I was told to come here.' I allow just the faintest belligerence into my voice. Just to get the message across: I'm not going to give up in a hurry.

I can see the calculation going on in this woman's head: if she turns me away I might cause a scene, she's got other pressing stuff to think about, what's one extra waitress . . .

'All right!' she says at last, with an irritated noise.

'But you'll have to change. What's your name, again?'

'Trish Geiger.'

'That's right.' She scribbles it down. 'Well you'd better come up, Trish.'

Oh my God. I'm in. I was obviously suited to a life of crime all along! Next time I'll up the stakes a bit. Fleece a Vegas casino or something.

I feel almost elated as I travel up in the service elevator with Jan, a plastic label reading TRISH GEIGER attached to my lapel. Now all I need is to keep my head down, bide my time and, when the time is right, get onto the eleventh floor. Which I can do by finding a loose ceiling panel, climbing up and crawling through the heating-duct system.

Or I could always go in the lift.

We come out in the kitchens attached to the executive function rooms, and I look around in surprise. I had no idea there was all this here. It's like going backstage at a theatre. Chefs are working busily at the cooking stations, and waiting staff are milling around in distinctive green and white striped uniforms.

'The outfits are in there.' Jan points to a huge wicker basket full of folded uniforms. 'You'll need to get changed.'

'OK.' I rummage around for an outfit in my size and take it off to the Ladies to change. I touch up my magenta lipstick and pull my hair further round my face, then look at my watch.

It's five forty now. The party's at six. By about ten past the eleventh floor should be clearing. Arnold is a very popular partner; no one's going to miss his farewell speech if they can help it. Plus at Carter Spink parties the speeches always happen early on, so people can get back to work if they need to.

And while everyone's listening I'll slip down to Arnold's office. It should work. It *has* to work. As I stare at my own bizarre reflection, I feel a grim resolve hardening inside me. He's not going to get away with everyone thinking he's a cheery, harmless old teddy bear. He's not going to get away with it.

At ten to six we all gather in one of the kitchens and receive our orders. Hot canapés . . . cold canapés . . . I barely listen to any of it. It's not like I'm intending to do any actual waiting. After Jan's lecture is over, I follow the herd of waiting staff out of the kitchen. I'm given a tray of champagne glasses to carry, which I put down as soon as I can. I head back to the kitchen and grab an open bottle of champagne and a napkin. Then, as soon as I'm sure no one's looking, I escape to the Ladies.

OK. This is the difficult bit. I lock myself in a cubicle and wait for fifteen minutes in utter silence. I don't clatter anything and I don't sneeze and I don't giggle when I hear a girl rehearsing her break-up speech to someone called Mike. It's the longest fifteen minutes of my life.

At last I cautiously unbolt the door, make my way out and peer round the corner. From where I'm standing I can see the corridor and the doors to the big function room. A crowd has already gathered and I can hear laughter and lots of loud talking. Waiters and waitresses are circulating and people are still coming down the corridor in a steady stream. I recognize the girls from PR . . . a couple of trainees . . . Oliver Swan, a senior partner . . . they all head into the party, taking a glass as they do so.

The corridor's clear. Go.

With trembling legs I walk straight past the entrance

to the function room, towards the lifts and the door to the stairwell. Within thirty seconds I'm safely through the door and walking as quietly as I can down the stairs. No one ever uses the stairs at Carter Spink, but still.

I reach the eleventh floor and peer out of the glass panel in the door. I can't see anyone. But that doesn't mean there's no one there. There could be a whole crowd of them, just out of my line of vision.

Well that's a risk I'll have to take. I take a few deep breaths, trying to psyche myself up. No one will ever recognize me in my green and white waitress gear. And I even have a story if anyone challenges me: I'm on this floor to place this bottle of champagne in Mr Saville's room as a surprise.

Come on. I can't waste any more time.

Slowly I push the door open, step out onto the blue-carpeted corridor, and breathe out in relief. It's empty. The whole floor is pretty much dead. Everyone must have gone up to the party. I can hear someone on the phone a few yards away – but as I start nervously walking towards Arnold's office, all the surrounding work stations are empty. All my senses are on red alert. I have never felt more self-conscious in my life.

The crucial thing is to use my time efficiently. I'll start with the computer and take it from there. Or maybe I should start with the filing cabinet. Have a quick look while the computer is warming up. Or I'll search his desk drawers. His BlackBerry could be in there. I hadn't thought of that.

To be honest, I haven't actually thought through the searching-through-the-office bit very well. Half of me never expected to get into the building, let alone actually get access to Arnold's office. Plus I'm not entirely sure what I'm looking for. Correspondence, maybe. Or figures. Or a disc marked 'Incriminating Information' would be good—

Abruptly I stop still. I can hear voices behind me, coming out of the lifts. Fuck. I need to get into Arnold's office before I'm seen.

In panic, I pick up my pace. I reach Arnold's office, wrench the door open, slam it behind me, and duck down underneath the glass panel. I can hear the voices getting closer. David Elldridge and Keith Thompson and someone I don't recognize. They pass by the door, and I don't move a muscle. Then they're receding into the distance. Thank God.

I breathe out, slowly rise to my feet and peep through the glass panel. I can't see anyone. I'm safe. Only then do I turn around and survey the office.

It's empty.

It's been cleared out.

I take a few steps into the room in bewilderment. The desk is empty. The shelves are empty. There are faint squares on the walls where framed photos have been taken down. There's nothing in this office apart from one piece of industrial tape on the floor and some drawing pins still stuck into the pinboard.

I can't believe it. After all this effort. After making it this far. There's nothing to bloody *search*?

There must be boxes, I think in sudden inspiration. Yes. It's all been put into boxes to be moved, and they'll all be stacked outside . . . I hurry out of the office and look around wildly. But I can't see any boxes. No crates. Nothing. Let's face it, I'm too late. I'm too fucking late. I feel like punching something in frustration.

Breathing hard, I walk back into the room and look around again. I might as well check the place out any-way. Just in case.

I head to the desk and start methodically checking every drawer, opening each wide open, peering inside and even feeling for stray papers. I turn the waste-paper bin upside down and shake it. I run my hand behind the pinboard. But there's nothing. Nor is there anything in the filing cabinet . . . nor in the built-in cupboards . . .

'Excuse me?'

I freeze, my hand still in Arnold's cupboard. Shit. *Shit.*

'Yes?' I turn round, pulling my hair over my face and gazing firmly downwards.

'What on earth are you doing here?'

It's a trainee. Bill . . . what's his name? He used to do occasional bits of work for me.

Stay calm. He hasn't recognized me.

'I was delivering a bottle of champagne, Sir,' I mumble in my best drag-queen voice, nodding to the bottle where I left it on the floor. 'Surprise for the gentleman. I was just wondering where to put it.'

'Well, not in a *cupboard*,' says Bill scathingly. 'I'd just leave it on the desk. And you shouldn't be up here.'

'I was just going back. Sir.' I bow my head and scuttle out. Bloody hell. That was close.

I head to the stairwell and hurry up the stairs, flustered. It's time to exit this building, before anyone else sees me. I'm not going to find out anything else now, anyway. God knows what I'll do about Arnold, but I'll think about that later. Right now, the priority is to get out.

The party's still in full swing as I creep out of the stair-well door and hurry towards the room where I left my clothes. I won't bother to change. I can always mail the waitress gear back—

'Trish?' Jan's voice hits the back of my head. 'Is that you?'

Fuck. Reluctantly I turn round to face her. She looks hopping mad. 'Where the hell have you *been*?'

'Um . . . serving?'

'No you haven't. I haven't seen you in there once!' she snaps. 'You're not working for me again, I can tell you. Now take these, and pull your weight.' She thrusts a plate of tiny little eclairs into my arms and pushes me roughly towards the doors of the party.

I feel a lurch of panic.

No. I can't go in there. No way.

'Absolutely! I just have to . . . get some cocktail napkins . . .' I try to back away, but she grabs me.

'No you don't! You wanted this job! Now work!'

She shoves me hard, and I stagger into the crowded room. I feel like a gladiator being pushed into the arena. Jan's standing at the door, her arms folded. There's no way out. I'm going to have to do this. I grip the tray more tightly, lower my head – and advance slowly into the crowded room.

I can't walk naturally. My legs feel like boards. The hairs on the nape of my neck are standing on end; I can feel the blood pulsating through my ears. I edge past expensive suits, not daring to look up; not daring to pause in case I attract attention. I can't believe this is happening. I'm dressed up in a green and white uniform, serving mini eclairs to my former colleagues.

And the bizarre thing is, no one seems to have noticed.

Several hands have plucked eclairs from the tray, without even glancing at me. Everyone's too busy laughing and chatting. The din is tremendous.

I can't see Arnold anywhere. But he has to be here somewhere. My stomach clenches with painful tension at the thought. I'm desperate to look for him; to raise my head and search him out. But I can't risk it. Instead I keep on moving steadily around the room. Familiar faces are everywhere. Snatches of conversation are making my ears prick up.

'Where's Ketterman?' someone is asking as I pass by.

'In Dublin for the day,' replies Oliver Swan, and I breathe out in relief. If Ketterman were here I'm sure his laser eyes would pick me up at once.

'Eclairs. Fab!'

About eight hands dive into my tray at once and I come to a standstill. It's a group of trainees. Hoovering food, as trainees always do at parties.

'Ooh. I'll have another.'

'Me too.'

I'm starting to feel edgy. The longer I stand here without moving, the more exposed I feel. But I can't get away. Their hands keep plunging in for more.

'Are there any more of the strawberry tarts, do you know?' a guy with rimless glasses asks me.

'Um . . . I don't know,' I mutter, staring down.

Shit. Now he's peering at me more closely. He's bending down to get a good look. And I can't pull my hair over my face because both hands are holding the tray . . .

'Is that . . . Samantha Sweeting?' He looks agog. 'Is that *you*?'

'Samantha Sweeting?' One of the girls drops her eclair. Another gasps and claps her hand over her mouth.

'Um . . . yes,' I whisper at last, my face boiling. 'It's me. But please, don't tell anyone. I want to keep a low profile.'

'So this is what you do now?' The rimless-glasses guy looks aghast. 'You're a *waitress*?'

The trainees are all staring at me as though I'm the Ghost of Failed Lawyers Future.

'It's not so bad.' I attempt an upbeat smile. 'You get free canapés!'

'So you make one mistake – and that's it?' gulps the girl who dropped her eclair. 'Your legal career is ruined for ever?'

'Er . . . pretty much.' I nod. 'Eclair?'

But no one seems hungry any more. In fact, they all look rather green about the gills.

'I might just . . . pop back to my desk,' stammers the guy with rimless glasses. 'Just check I haven't got anything outstanding . . .'

'Me too,' says the girl, thrusting down her glass.

'Samantha Sweeting is here!' I suddenly hear another of the trainees hissing to a group of junior associates. 'Look! She's a waitress!'

'No!' I gasp. 'Don't tell anyone else—'

It's too late. I can see all the people in the group turning to look at me with identical expressions of embarrassed horror.

For an instant I'm so mortified I want to curl up on the spot. These are people I used to work with. These are people who respected me. And now I'm dressed up in stripes, serving them.

But then, slowly, a feeling of defiance hardens within me.

Fuck you, I find myself thinking. Why shouldn't I work as a waitress?

'Hi,' I say, shaking back my hair. 'Care for a dessert?'

More and more people are turning to gasp at me. I can hear the whispering travelling round the room. The other waiting staff are all clustered together, goggling at me. Heads are swivelling everywhere now, like iron filings in a magnetic field. There isn't one friendly face among them.

'Jesus Christ!' I hear someone murmur. '*Look* at her.'

'Should she *be* here?' exclaims someone else.

'No,' I say, trying to sound composed. 'You're right. I shouldn't.'

I make to leave, but the melee is all around me now. I can't find a way out. And then my stomach plunges. Through a gap in the throng, I spot a familiar shock of woolly hair. Familiar ruddy cheeks. A familiar jovial smile.

Arnold Saville.

Our eyes meet across the room, and although he keeps smiling, there's a hardness to his gaze which I've never seen before. A special anger, just for me.

I feel sick as I stare back. Almost scared. Not of his anger – but of his duplicity. He's fooled everybody. To everyone else in this room, Arnold Saville is on a par with Father Christmas. A way has parted in the crowd, and he's coming towards me, a glass of champagne in his hand.

'Samantha,' he says pleasantly. 'Is this appropriate?'

'You had me banned from the building,' I hear myself bite back. 'I didn't have much choice.'

Oh God. Wrong answer. Too chippy.

I have to get control of myself, or I'm going to lose this conversation. I'm already at enough of a disadvantage, standing here in waitress gear, being peered at by the entire room as if I'm something the dog dragged in. I need to be calm and steely and inspired.

But seeing Arnold in the flesh after all this time has thrown me off balance. As hard as I try to stay calm, I can't. My face is burning, my chest is painfully heaving. All the emotions and traumas of the last few weeks are suddenly erupting inside me in a whoosh of hatred.

'You had me fired.' The words burst out before I can stop them. 'You *lied*.'

'Samantha, I know this must have been a very difficult time for you.' Arnold has the air of a headmaster dealing with a wayward pupil. 'But really . . .' He turns to a man I don't recognize and rolls his eyes. 'Former employee,' he says in an undertone. 'Mentally unstable.'

What? *What?*

'I'm not mentally unstable!' I cry in horror. 'I just want to know the answer to one little question. It's very simple. When exactly did you put that memo on my desk?'

Arnold gives an incredulous laugh.

'Samantha, I'm retiring. Is this really the time? Could someone get rid of her?' he adds as an aside.

'That's why you didn't want me to come back to the office, isn't it?' My voice is trembling with indignation. 'Because I might start asking tricky questions. Because I might work it out.'

A little frisson travels around the room. But not in a good way. I can hear people murmuring 'for God's sake' and 'how did she get *in* here?' If I want to retain any credibility or dignity at all I have to stop talking right now. But I can't stop.

'I didn't make that mistake, did I?' I walk towards him. 'You *used* me. You wrecked my career, you watched my whole life go into freefall . . .'

'Really,' snaps Arnold, turning away. 'This is getting beyond a joke.'

'Just answer the question!' I yell at his back. 'When did you put that memo on my desk, Arnold? Because I don't believe it was ever there before the deadline.'

'Of course it was there.' Arnold turns briefly, bored and dismissive. 'I came into your office on 28th May.'

28th May?

Where did 28th May come from? Why does that feel wrong?

'I don't believe you,' I say in helpless anger. 'I just don't believe you. I think you set me up. I think—'

'Samantha?' Someone pokes me on the shoulder and I wheel round to see Ernest the security guard. His familiar, gnarled face is screwed up in awkwardness. 'I'm going to have to ask you to leave the premises.'

I feel a jolt of humiliation. They're seriously throwing me out of the offices? After practically *living* here for seven years of my life? I can feel my last shreds of composure disappearing. Hot tears of rage are pressing against my eyes.

'Just leave, Samantha,' says Oliver Swan pityingly. 'Don't embarrass yourself any further.'

I stare at him for a few seconds, then transfer my gaze to each of the senior partners in turn.

'I was a good lawyer,' I say, my voice shaking. 'I did a good job. You all know it. But you just wiped me out, like I never existed.' I swallow down the lump in my throat. 'Well, your loss.'

The room is totally silent as I put the tray of eclairs down on a nearby table and stalk out of the room. The moment I'm out of the door I can hear an animated conversation breaking out behind me.

I travel down in the lift with Ernest in total silence. If I said anything, I might burst into tears. I can't believe I fucked up my plan so badly. I failed to find out anything new. I was recognized. I lost it in front of the whole staff. I'm even more of a joke than I was before.

* * *

When I get out of the building I check my mobile. There's a text from Nat, asking how things went. I read it several times, but I can't bring myself to reply. Nor can I bring myself to go back to the Geigers' house. Even though I could probably still catch a train, I can't face them tonight.

On automatic pilot I head down to the Underground and onto a Tube. I can see my face in the window opposite, pale and expressionless. And all the way, my mind is buzzing. *28th May. 28th May.*

I don't hit on the answer until I'm arriving at my building. 28th May. Chelsea Flower Show. Of course. We were at Chelsea all day on 28th May, Arnold, Ketterman, Guy and I, doing some corporate entertaining. Arnold arrived straight from Paris and afterwards he was driven home. He wasn't even in the office.

He lied. Of course he did. I feel a weary anger rising inside me. But there's nothing I can do now. No one will ever believe me. I'll live the rest of my life with everyone believing it was my mistake.

I get out at my floor, already fumbling for the key, hoping against hope that Mrs Farley won't hear me, already planning a long, hot bath. And then, as I'm almost at my door, I stop dead. I'm motionless for a few seconds, thinking hard.

Slowly I turn and head back to the lift. There's one more chance. I have nothing to lose.

I rise up two floors and come out of the lift. It's almost identical to my floor – same carpet, same wallpaper, same lamps. Just different numbers on the apartment doors. 31 and 32. I can't remember which one I want so in the end I plump for 31. It has a softer doormat. I sink down on the floor, put my bag down, lean against the door and begin to wait.

* * *

By the time Ketterman emerges from the lift I'm drained. I've been sitting here for three solid hours, without anything to eat or drink. I feel wan and exhausted. But at the sight of him I scramble to my feet, clutching the wall as I feel a wash of fatigue.

For a moment Ketterman looks shocked. Then he resumes his usual stony expression.

'Samantha. What are you doing here?'

As I stand there I wonder if he's heard about me going to the offices. He must have done. He'll have heard the whole gory tale. Not that he's giving anything away.

'What are you doing here?' he repeats. He's holding an enormous metal briefcase in one hand and his face is shadowed under the artificial lights.

I take a step forward. 'I know I'm the last person you want to see.' I rub my aching brow. 'Believe me, I don't want to be here either. Out of all the people in the world I could turn to for help . . . you would be the last. You *are* the last.'

I break off for a moment. Ketterman hasn't even flickered.

'So the fact that I'm here, coming to you . . . should prove it to you.' I look at him desperately. 'I'm serious. I have something to tell you, and you have to listen. You have to.'

There's a long silence between us. I can hear a car braking in the street outside and someone laughing raucously. Ketterman's face is still rigid. I can't tell what he's thinking. Then at last, he reaches into his pocket for a key. He walks past me, unlocks the door to flat 32 – and then finally turns.

'Come in.'

TWENTY-TWO

I wake up to the view of a cracked, grubby ceiling. My eyes run along to a huge cobweb in the corner of the room, then down the wall to a rickety bookshelf stuffed with books, tapes, letters, old Christmas decorations and the odd bit of discarded underwear.

How did I live in this mess for seven years?

How did I not *notice* it?

I push back the cover, get out of bed and look around blearily. The carpet feels gritty under my feet and I wince. It needs a good hoover. I guess the cleaner stopped coming after the money stopped appearing.

There are clothes lying all over the floor, and I search around until I find a dressing gown. I pull it on and head out to the kitchen. I'd forgotten how bare and cold and spartan it was in here. There's nothing in the fridge, of course. But I find a camomile teabag and fill the kettle, and perch on a bar stool, looking out at the brick wall opposite.

It's already nine fifteen. Ketterman will be at the office. He'll be taking whatever action he's going to take. I wait to feel the nerves rise . . . but they don't. I feel weirdly calm. Everything's out of my hands now; there's nothing I can do.

He listened to me. He actually listened, and asked questions, and even made me a cup of tea. I was there for over an hour. He didn't tell me what he thought or what he was going to do. He didn't even say whether he believed me or not. But something tells me he did.

The kettle's coming to the boil when the doorbell rings. I hesitate – then wrap my dressing gown around me and pad out to the hall. Through the spy-hole I can see Mrs Farley peering back at me, her arms laden with packages.

Of course. Who else?

I open the door. 'Hello, Mrs Farley.'

'Samantha, I *thought* it was you!' she exclaims. 'After all this time! I had no idea . . . I didn't know what to think . . .'

'I've been away.' I smile. 'I'm sorry I didn't let you know I was going away. But I didn't really have any warning myself.'

'I see.' Mrs Farley's eyes are darting all around, at my blonde hair, at my face, and past me into the flat, as though searching for clues.

'Thanks for taking in my parcels.' I hold out my hands. 'Shall I . . .'

'Oh! Of course.' She hands over a couple of jiffy bags and a cardboard box, still obviously avid with curiosity. 'I suppose these high-powered jobs *do* send you girls abroad with no notice . . .'

'I haven't been abroad.' I put the boxes down. 'Thanks again.'

'Oh, it's no trouble! I know what it's like when you've had a . . . a difficult family time?' she hazards.

'I haven't had a difficult family time,' I say politely.

'Of course not!' She clears her throat. 'Well, anyway.

You're back now. From ... whatever you've been doing.'

'Mrs Farley,' I try to keep a straight face, 'would you like to know where I've been?'

Mrs Farley reacts with horror. 'Dear me! No! It's absolutely none of my business! Really, I wouldn't *dream* of ... I must be getting on ...' She starts backing away.

'Thanks again!' I call as she disappears back into her flat.

I'm just closing the door as the phone rings. I pick up the receiver, suddenly wondering how many people must have rung this number over the last few weeks. The machine is crammed with messages, but after listening to the first three, all from Mum and each more furious than the last, I gave up.

'Hello?'

'Samantha,' comes a businesslike voice. 'John Ketterman here.'

'Oh.' In spite of myself I feel a nervous swoop. 'Hi.'

'I'd like to ask that you keep yourself available today. It may be necessary for you to speak to some people.'

'People?'

There's a slight pause, then Ketterman says, 'Investigators.'

Oh my God. Oh my *God*. I feel like punching the air or bursting into tears or something. But somehow I keep my composure.

'So have you found something out?'

'I can't say anything at the moment.' Ketterman sounds as distant and formal as ever. 'I just need to know if you'll be available.'

'Of course. Where will I have to go?'

'We'd like you to come here, to the Carter Spink

332

offices,' he says, without any trace of irony.

I look at the phone, almost wanting to laugh. Would that be the same Carter Spink offices I was thrown out of yesterday? I feel like saying. The same Carter Spink offices I've been banned from?

'I'll call you,' adds Ketterman. 'Keep your mobile with you. It could be a few hours.'

'OK. I will.' I take a deep breath. 'And please, just tell me. You don't have to go into specifics, but . . . was my theory right?'

There's a crackling silence down the phone. I can't breathe.

'Not in every detail,' says Ketterman at last, and I feel a painful thrill of triumph. That means I was right in some details.

The phone goes dead. I put the receiver down and look at my reflection in the hall mirror. My cheeks are flushed and my eyes are bright.

I was right. And they know it.

They'll offer me my job back, it suddenly hits me. They'll offer me partnership. At the thought I'm seized with excitement – and at the same time, a kind of weird fear.

I'll cross that bridge when I come to it.

I walk into the kitchen, keyed up, unable to stand still. What the hell am I going to do for the next few hours? I pour hot water onto my camomile teabag and watch it for a few moments, stirring it round with a spoon. And then I have an idea.

It only takes twenty minutes to pop out and get what I need. Butter, eggs, flour, vanilla, icing sugar. Baking tins. Mixers. A set of scales. Everything, in fact. I cannot *believe* how badly equipped my kitchen is. How did I ever do any cooking in here?

Well, I didn't.

I don't have an apron so I improvise with an old shirt. I don't have a mixing bowl and I forgot to buy one, so I use the plastic basin given to me as part of an aromatherapy kit.

An hour of whisking and baking later, I've produced a cake. Three tiers of vanilla sponge, sandwiched with butter cream, iced with lemon glacé and decorated with sugar flowers.

I look at it for a few moments, feeling a glow of satisfaction. This is my fifth cake ever, and the first time I've done more than two tiers. I take off my old shirt, check my mobile is in my pocket, pick up the cake and head out of the flat.

As Mrs Farley answers the doorbell she looks startled to see me.

'Hi!' I say. 'I've brought you something. To say thank you for looking after my post.'

'Oh!' She looks at the cake in astonishment. 'Samantha! That must have been expensive!'

'I didn't buy it,' I say proudly. 'I made it.'

Mrs Farley looks staggered.

'You *made* it?'

'Uh huh.' I beam. 'Shall I bring it in and make you some coffee?'

Mrs Farley looks too thunderstruck to answer, so I head past her into the flat. To my shame I realize I haven't been in here before. In three years of knowing her, I never once set foot over the threshold. The place is immaculately kept, full of little side tables and antiques and a bowl of rose petals on the coffee table.

'You sit down,' I say. 'I'll find what I need in the kitchen.' Still looking dazed, Mrs Farley sinks into an upholstered wing chair.

'Please,' she says faintly. 'Don't break anything.'

'I'm not going to *break* anything! Would you like frothy milk? And nutmeg?'

Ten minutes later I emerge from the kitchen, bearing two coffees and the cake.

'Here.' I cut Mrs Farley a slice. 'See what you think.'

Mrs Farley takes the plate and looks at it for a few moments.

'You made this,' she says at last.

'Yes!'

Mrs Farley takes the slice to her mouth. Then she stops. She looks increasingly nervous.

'It's *safe*!' I say, and take a bite of my own slice. 'See? I know how to cook! Honestly!'

Very gingerly, Mrs Farley takes a tiny bite. As she's chewing her eyes meet mine in astonishment. 'It's . . . delicious! So *light*! You really made this?'

'I whisked the egg whites separately,' I explain. 'It keeps cakes really light. I can give you the recipe if you like. Have some coffee.' I hand her a cup. 'I used your electric beater for the milk, if that's OK. It works fine, if you get it to just the right temperature.'

Mrs Farley is gazing at me as though I'm talking gobbledegook.

'Samantha,' she says at last. 'Where have you been these last few weeks?'

'I've been . . . away somewhere.' My eye falls on a duster and can of Pledge sitting on a side table. She must have been in the middle of cleaning when I rang. 'I wouldn't use those dusters if I were you,' I add politely. 'I can recommend some better ones.'

Mrs Farley puts down her cup and leans forward in her chair. Her brow is wrinkled in concern. 'Samantha, you haven't joined some sort of religion?'

'No!' I can't help laughing at her face. 'I've just

been . . . doing something different. More coffee?'

I head into the kitchen and froth up some more milk. When I return to the sitting room, Mrs Farley is on her second slice of cake.

'This is very good,' she says, her voice muffled. 'Thank you.'

'Well . . . you know.' I shrug, a little awkward. 'Thanks for looking out for me all that time.'

Mrs Farley finishes her cake, puts her plate down and regards me for a few moments, her head cocked to one side like a bird.

'Dear,' she says finally, 'I don't know where you've been, or what you're doing. But whatever it is, you're transformed.'

'I know my hair's different . . .' I begin, but Mrs Farley shakes her head.

'I used to see you, rushing in and out, arriving home late at night, always looking so *weary*. So troubled. And I used to think you used to look like . . . like the empty shell of a person. Like a dried-up leaf. A husk.'

A *dried-up leaf*? I think in indignation. A *husk*?

'But now you've blossomed! You look fitter, you look healthier . . . you look happy . . .' She puts her cup down and leans forward again. 'Whatever you've been doing, dear, you look wonderful on it.'

'Oh. Well, thanks.' I give a bashful smile. 'I suppose I do feel different. I suppose I'm more relaxed these days.' I take a sip of coffee and lean back in my chair, mulling it over. 'I enjoy life a bit more than I used to . . . I *notice* more than I used to . . .'

'You haven't noticed your phone's ringing,' Mrs Farley interrupts mildly, nodding at my pocket.

'Oh!' I say in surprise, and grab my phone. 'I should get this. Excuse me.'

I flip it open and immediately hear Ketterman's voice in my ear.

'Samantha.'

I spend three hours at the Carter Spink offices, talking in turn to a man from the Law Society, two of the senior partners and some guy from Third Union Bank. By lunchtime I feel drained from repeating the same things over and over to the same carefully blank faces. The office lights are making my head ache. I'd forgotten how airless and dry the atmosphere is here.

I still haven't worked out exactly what's going on. Lawyers are so bloody discreet. I know someone's been to see Arnold at his home and that's about it. But even if no one's going to admit it, I know I was right. I've been vindicated.

After the last interview, a plate of sandwiches is brought to the room I'm in, together with a bottle of mineral water and a muffin. I get to my feet, stretch out my arms and wander over to the window. I feel like a prisoner in here. There's a tapping at the door and Ketterman comes into the room.

'Haven't I finished yet?' I say. 'I've been here hours.'

'We may need to speak to you again.' He gestures to the sandwiches. 'Have some lunch.'

I cannot stay in this room a moment longer. I have to stretch my legs, at least.

'I'll just go and freshen up first,' I say, and hurry out of the room before he can object.

As I enter the Ladies, all the women in there stop talking immediately. I disappear into a cubicle and hear the sound of excited whisperings and murmurings outside. As I come out again, not one person has left the room. I can feel all the eyes on me, like sun lamps.

'So are you back now, Samantha?' says an associate called Lucy.

'Not exactly.' I turn away to the sink, feeling self-conscious.

'You look so *different*,' says another girl.

'Your arms!' says Lucy as I wash my hands. 'They're so brown. And *toned*. Have you been to a spa?'

'Er . . . no.' I give a mysterious smile. 'But thanks. So, how's life been here?'

'Good.' Lucy nods a few times. 'Really busy. Clocked up sixty-six billable hours last week. Two all-nighters.'

'I had three,' puts in another girl. She speaks casually, but I can see the pride in her face. And the dark-grey shadows under her eyes. Is that what I used to look like? All pale and strained and tense?

'Great!' I say politely, drying my hands. 'Well, I'd better get back now. See you.'

I exit the Ladies and am walking back to the inter-view room, lost in my own thoughts, when I hear a voice.

'Oh my God, *Samantha*?'

'*Guy?*' I look up in shock to see him hurrying down the corridor towards me. He looks fit and tanned and his smile is even more dazzling than ever.

I wasn't expecting to see Guy here. In fact, I feel a bit thrown by this.

'Look at you!' He grips my shoulders tightly and scans my face. 'You look fantastic.'

'I thought you were in Hong Kong.'

'Got back this morning. I've just been briefed on the situation. Bloody hell, Samantha, it's incredible.' He lowers his voice. 'Only you could work all that out. *Arnold*, of all people. I was *shell-shocked*. Everyone is. Those who know,' he adds, lowering his voice still further. 'Obviously it's not out yet.'

'I don't even know what the "situation" is,' I reply, with a touch of resentment. 'No one's telling me anything.'

'Well, they will.' Guy reaches into his pocket, gets out his BlackBerry and squints at it. 'You are flavour of the month right now. I knew it all along.' He looks up. 'I knew you never made a mistake.'

I gape at him. How can he say that?

'No you didn't,' I reply at last, finding my words. 'No you didn't. If you remember, you said I'd made errors. You said I was "unreliable".'

I can feel all the old hurt and humiliation starting to rise again, and look away.

'I said *other* people had said you made errors.' Guy pauses in tapping at his BlackBerry and looks up, frowning. 'Shit, Samantha. I did stand up for you. I was on your side. Ask anyone!'

Yup. Sure. That's why you wouldn't have me to stay.

But I don't say anything out loud. I really don't want to get into it. It's history.

'Fine,' I say at last. 'Whatever.'

We start walking along the corridor together, Guy still engrossed in the BlackBerry. God, he's addicted to that thing, I think, with slight irritation.

'So where the hell did you disappear to?' At last he stops tapping. 'What have you been doing all this time? You're not really a *waitress*?'

'No.' I can't help smiling at his expression. 'I'm not. I've got a job.'

'I knew you'd get snapped up.' He nods with satis-faction. 'Who's employed you?'

'Oh . . . no one you'd know,' I say after a pause.

'You're in the same area, though?' He puts his BlackBerry away. 'Doing the same kind of work?'

I have a sudden vision of me in my blue nylon overall, mopping Trish's bathroom floor.

'Er . . . as it happens, not really.' Somehow I keep a straight face.

Guy seems surprised. 'But you're still in banking law, right? Don't tell me you've made a complete change?' He suddenly looks galvanized. 'You haven't gone into commercial law, have you?'

'Um, no . . . not commercial law. I'd better go.' I cut him off and open the door to the interview room. 'See you later.'

I eat my sandwiches, I drink my mineral water. For half an hour no one disturbs me. I feel a bit like I'm in quarantine for some deadly illness. They could have given me some magazines, at least. I've developed quite a habit for gossip, after being surrounded by Trish's endless supply of *Heat* and *Hello*.

At last I hear a knock at the door and Ketterman comes in.

'Samantha, we would like to see you in the boardroom.'

The *boardroom*? Blimey.

I follow Ketterman down the corridors, aware of the nudges and whisperings from everyone we pass. He opens the huge double doors to the boardroom and I walk in, to see about half the partners standing there, waiting for me. There's silence as Ketterman closes the doors. I glance at Guy, who grins back encouragingly, but says nothing.

Am I supposed to speak? Did I miss the instructions? Ketterman has joined the group of partners. Now he turns to face me.

'Samantha, as you know, an investigation of . . . recent events is under way. The results have not yet

340

been fully determined.' He breaks off, looking tense, and I can see some of the others exchanging sober looks. 'However, we have come to one conclusion. You were wronged.'

I gape at him in stupefaction. He's *admitting* it? Getting a lawyer to admit they've made a mistake is like getting a movie star to admit they've had liposuction.

'I'm sorry?' I say, just to force him to repeat it.

'You were wronged.' Ketterman frowns, clearly not enjoying this part of the conversation at all.

I almost want to giggle. 'I was . . . wrong?' I hazard, looking puzzled.

'Wronged!' he snaps. 'Wronged!'

'Oh, *wronged*. Well, thank you.' I smile politely. 'I appreciate that.'

They'll probably offer me some kind of bonus, it crosses my mind. A luxury hamper. Or even a holiday.

'And therefore.' Ketterman pauses. 'We would like to offer you full equity partnership in the firm. Effective immediately.'

I'm so shocked I nearly sit down on the floor. *Full equity partnership?*

I open my mouth – but I can't speak. I feel winded. I look around helplessly, like a fish on the end of a line. Full equity partnership is the highest pinnacle. It's the most prestigious job in law. I never, ever, *ever* expected that.

'Welcome back, Samantha,' says Greg Parker.

'Welcome back,' chime in a few others. David Elldridge gives me a warm smile. Guy gives me the thumbs up.

'We have some champagne.' Ketterman nods to Guy, who opens the double doors. The next moment two waitresses from the Partners' Dining Room are coming in with trays of champagne glasses. Someone puts one in my hand.

This is all going too fast. I have to say something.

'Er . . . excuse me?' I call out. 'I haven't actually said if I'll accept it yet.'

The whole room seems to freeze, like a video-tape on pause.

'I'm sorry?' Ketterman turns to me, his face contorted with incredulity.

Oh God. I'm not sure they're going to take this very well.

'The thing is . . .' I break off and take a sip of champagne for Dutch courage, trying to work out how to put this tactfully.

I've been thinking about it all day, over and over. Being a partner at Carter Spink is the dream I've had all my adult life. The glittering prize. It's everything I ever wanted.

Except . . . all the things I never knew I wanted. Things I had no idea about until a few weeks ago. Like fresh air. Like evenings off. Unburdened weekends. Making plans with friends. Sitting in the pub after my work is done, drinking cider, with nothing to do, nothing to think about, nothing hanging over me.

Even if they're offering me full equity partnership, it doesn't change things. It doesn't change me. Mrs Farley was right: I've blossomed. I'm not a husk any more.

Why would I go back to being a husk?

I clear my throat and look around the room.

'It's a tremendous honour to be offered such an amazing opportunity,' I say earnestly. 'And I'm very grateful. Truly. However . . . the reason I came back wasn't to get my job back. It was to clear my name. To prove that I didn't make a mistake.' I can't help shooting a look at Guy. 'The truth is, since leaving Carter Spink I've . . . well . . . moved on. I have a job. Which I very much enjoy. So I won't be taking up your offer.'

There's a stunned silence.

'Thank you,' I add again, politely. 'And . . . er . . . thanks for the champagne.'

'Is she *serious*?' says someone at the back. Ketterman and Elldridge are exchanging frowns.

'Samantha,' says Ketterman, coming forward, 'you may have found opportunities elsewhere. But you are a Carter Spink lawyer. This is where you trained, this is where you belong.'

'If it's a question of salary,' adds Elldridge, 'I'm sure we can match whatever you're currently . . .' he glances at Guy. 'Which law firm has she gone to?'

'Wherever you are, I'll speak to the senior partner,' says Ketterman in a businesslike way. 'The personnel director . . . whoever would be appropriate. We'll sort this out. If you give me a number.' He's taking out his BlackBerry.

My mouth twists. I desperately want to giggle.

'There isn't a personnel director,' I explain. 'Or a senior partner.'

'There isn't a senior partner?' Ketterman looks impatient. 'How can there not be a senior partner?'

'I never said I was working as a lawyer.'

It's as if I've said I think the world is flat. I have never seen so many flummoxed faces in my life.

'You're . . . not working as a lawyer?' says Elldridge at last. 'What are you working as, then?'

I was hoping it wouldn't come to this. But on the other hand, why shouldn't they know?

'I'm working as a housekeeper.' I smile.

' "Housekeeper"?' Elldridge peers at me. 'Is that the

new jargon for troubleshooter? I can't keep up with these ridiculous job titles.'

'You're on the compliance side?' says Ketterman. 'Is that what you mean?'

'No, it's not what I mean,' I say patiently. 'I'm a housekeeper. I make beds. I cook meals. I'm a domestic.'

For about sixty seconds nobody moves. God, I wish I had a camera. Their *faces*.

'You're literally . . . a *housekeeper*?' stutters Elldridge at last.

'Uh huh.' I look at my watch. 'And I'm fulfilled and I'm relaxed and I'm happy. In fact, I should be getting back. Thank you,' I add to Ketterman, 'for listening to me. You're the only one who did.'

'You're turning down our offer?' says Oliver Swan incredulously.

'I'm turning down your offer.' I give an apologetic shrug. 'Sorry. Bye, everyone.'

As I head out of the room I feel slightly wobbly about the legs. And slightly manic inside. *I turned it down.* I turned down senior partnership of Carter Spink.

What the hell is my mother going to say?

The thought makes me want to burst into hysterical laughter.

I feel too keyed up to wait for the lift so I head down the stairwell, clattering on the cold stone steps.

'Samantha!' Guy's voice suddenly echoes above me. Oh, honestly. What does he want?

'I'm going!' I yell back. 'Leave me alone!'

'You can't go!'

I can hear him accelerating down the steps, so I pick up speed myself. I've said my piece – what more is there to talk about? My shoes are clacking as I tear down the steps, gripping the handrail for balance. But even so, Guy's gaining on me.

'Samantha, this is crazy!'

'No it's not!'

'I can't let you ruin your career out of . . . out of pique!' he calls.

I wheel round indignantly, nearly falling down the stairs. 'I'm not doing this out of pique!'

'I know you're angry with us all!' Guy joins me on the staircase, breathing hard. 'I'm sure it makes you feel really good to turn us down, to say you're working as a housekeeper . . .'

'I *am* working as a housekeeper!' I retort. 'And I'm not turning you down because I'm angry. I'm turning you down because I don't want the job.'

'Samantha, you wanted partnership more than anything else in the world!' Guy grabs my arm. 'I know you did! You've worked for it for all these years. You can't throw it away! It's too valuable.'

'What if I don't value it any more?'

'It's only been a few weeks! Everything can't have changed!'

'It has. *I* have.'

Guy shakes his head in disbelief. 'You're really serious about the housekeeper thing?'

'I'm really serious,' I snap. 'What's wrong with being a housekeeper?'

'Oh for God's—' He stops himself. 'Look, Samantha, come upstairs. We'll talk about it. The Human Resources department have come on board. You lost your job . . . you were badly treated . . . it's no wonder you can't think straight. They're suggesting counselling.'

'I don't need counselling!' I swivel on my heel and start down the stairs again. 'Just because I don't want to be a lawyer, what, I'm *crazy*?'

I reach the bottom of the stairwell and burst into the foyer with Guy in hot pursuit. Hilary Grant, Head of PR, is sitting on a leather sofa with some red-suited woman I don't recognize, and they both look up in surprise.

'Samantha, you cannot do this!' Guy is shouting after me as he emerges into the foyer. 'You are one of the most talented lawyers I know. I cannot let you turn down senior partnership to be a fucking ... *housekeeper*.'

'Why not, if it's what I want to do?' I come to a halt on the marble and turn round to face him. 'Guy, I've found out what it's like to have a life! I've found out what it's like, *not* working every weekend. *Not* feeling pressure all the time. And I like it!'

Guy isn't listening to a word I say. He doesn't even want to understand.

'You're going to stand there and tell me you prefer cleaning loos to being a partner of Carter Spink?' His face is flushed with outrage.

'Yes!' I say defiantly. 'Yes, I do!'

'Who's that?' says the woman in the red suit with interest.

'Samantha, you're making the biggest mistake of your entire existence!' Guy's voice follows me as I reach the glass doors. 'If you walk out now—'

I don't wait to hear any more. I'm out of the door. Down the steps. Gone.

I might have just made the biggest mistake of my entire existence. As I sit on the train back to Gloucestershire, sipping wine to steady my nerves, Guy's words keep ringing in my ears.

Once upon a time, just that thought would have sent me into a tailspin. But not any more. I almost want to laugh. He has no idea.

346

If I've learned one thing from everything that's happened to me, it's that there *is* no such thing as the biggest mistake of your existence. There's no such thing as ruining your life. Life's a pretty resilient thing, it turns out.

When I arrive at Lower Ebury I head straight to the pub. Nathaniel is behind the bar, wearing a chambray shirt I've never seen before, talking to Eamonn. For a few moments I just watch him from the doorway. His strong hands; the slant of his neck; the way his brow furrows as he nods. I can tell at once he disagrees with whatever Eamonn is saying. But he's waiting, wanting to be tactful about making his point.

Maybe I'm better at telepathy than I thought.

As if he's telepathic too, he looks up and his face jolts. He smiles a welcome – but I can see the tension underneath. These last couple of days can't have been easy for him. Maybe he thought I wasn't coming back.

A roar goes up from the dartboard, and one of the guys turns and spots me walking towards the bar.

'Samantha!' he shouts. 'At last! We need you on our team!'

'In a sec!' I call over my shoulder. 'Hi,' I say as I reach Nathaniel. 'Nice shirt.'

'Hi,' he says casually. 'Good trip?'

'Not bad.' I nod. Nathaniel lifts up the bar for me to come through, his eyes searching my face as though for clues.

'So . . . is it over?'

'Yup.' I put my arms around him and hug him tight. 'It's over.'

And at that moment, I truly believe it is.

TWENTY-THREE

Nothing happens until lunchtime.

I make the breakfast for Trish and Eddie as usual. I hoover and dust as usual. Then I put on Iris's apron, get out the chopping board and start squeezing oranges. I'm going to make bitter chocolate and orange mousse for the charity lunch tomorrow. We're going to serve it on a bed of crystallized orange slices, and each plate is going to be garnished with a real silver-leaf angel from a Christmas decoration catalogue.

This was Trish's idea. As are the angels hanging from the ceiling.

'How are we doing?' Trish comes tapping into the kitchen, looking flustered. 'Have you made the mousses yet?'

'Not yet,' I say, briskly squeezing an orange. 'Mrs Geiger, don't worry. It's all under control.'

'Do you know what I've *been* through, the last few days?' She clutches her head. 'More and more people keep accepting . . . I've had to change the seating plan . . .'

'It'll be fine,' I say soothingly. 'Try to relax.'

'Yes.' She breathes out, holding her head between

two lacquered fingernails. 'You're right. I'll just go and check the goody bags . . .'

I cannot believe how much Trish is spending on this lunch. Every time I question whether we really need to canopy the dining room in white silk, or give every guest an orchid buttonhole, she shrills 'It's all in a good cause!'

Which reminds me of something I've been meaning to ask her for quite a while now.

'Er . . . Mrs Geiger,' I say casually, 'are you charging your guests for entrance to the lunch?'

'Oh no!' she says. 'I think that's rather *tacky*, don't you?'

'Are you holding a raffle?'

'I don't think so.' She wrinkles her nose. 'People *loathe* raffles.'

I hardly dare ask this next question.

'So . . . um . . . how exactly are you planning on making money for the charity?'

There's silence in the kitchen. Trish has frozen, her eyes wide.

'*Bugger*,' she says at last.

I knew it. She hadn't given it a thought. Somehow I manage to keep my respectful, housekeeper's expression. 'Perhaps we could ask for voluntary donations?' I suggest. 'We could hand round a little bag with the coffee and mints?'

'Yes. Yes.' Trish peers at me as though I'm a genius. '*That's* the answer.' She exhales sharply. 'This is really very stressful, Samantha. I don't know how you stay so calm.'

'Oh . . . I don't know.' I smile, feeling a sudden wave of fondness for her. When I arrived back at the house last night it was like coming home. Even though Trish had left a mountain of crockery on the counter for my return, and a note saying 'Samantha, please polish all silver tomorrow.'

Trish heads out of the kitchen and I start whisking up egg whites for the mousse. Then I notice a man sidling down the drive. He's wearing jeans and an old polo shirt and has a camera slung round his neck. He disappears from view and I frown in puzzlement. Maybe he's a delivery man. I measure out the caster sugar, with half an ear out for the doorbell, and start folding it into the egg whites, just the way Iris taught me. Then suddenly the man is standing at the kitchen door, peering in through the window.

I'm not ruining my mixture for some door-to-door salesman. He can wait a few moments. I finish folding in the sugar – then head to the door and open it.

'Can I help?' I say politely.

The man gazes silently at me for a few seconds, glancing down every so often at a folded-up tabloid newspaper in his hand. 'Are you Samantha Sweeting?' he says at last.

I look back at him warily. 'Why?'

'I'm from the *Cheltenham Gazette*.' He flashes an ID card at me. 'I'm after an exclusive interview with you. "Why I chose the Cotswolds as my secret hideaway" – that kind of thing.'

I look at him blankly for a few seconds.

'Er . . . what are you talking about?'

'You haven't seen it?' He looks surprised. 'I take it this is you? He turns the newspaper round and as I see it, my stomach seizes up in shock.

It's a picture of me. In the newspaper. *Me*.

It's my official Carter Spink portrait. I'm wearing a black suit and my hair is screwed up. Above the picture, in bold black letters, is the headline: I'D

350

RATHER CLEAN LOOS THAN BE A PARTNER AT CARTER SPINK.

What the hell is going on?

With trembling hands I grab the paper from the guy and scan the text.

They are the Masters of the Universe; the envy of their peers. Top law firm Carter Spink is the most prestigious in the country. But yesterday one young woman turned down a high-ranking post as partner in order to work as a humble housekeeper.

GET A LIFE

Partners were left with egg on their faces as star £500-an-hour lawyer Samantha Sweeting rejected their offer, which carried a substantial six-figure salary. Having previously been fired, the high-flyer apparently uncovered a financial scandal at the firm. However, when offered full equity partnership, Sweeting cited the pressure and lack of free time as reason for her decision.

'I've got used to having a life,' she said, as partners begged her to stay.

A former Carter Spink employee who declined to be named confirmed the brutal working conditions of the legal firm. 'They expect you to sell your soul,' he said. 'I had to resign from stress. No wonder she prefers manual labour.'

A spokeswoman for Carter Spink defended the firm's practices. 'We are a flexible, modern firm with a sympathetic working ethos. We would like to talk to Samantha about her views and would certainly not expect employees to "sell their soul".'

VANISHED

She confirmed that Ms Sweeting's job offer is still open and Carter Spink partners are anxious to talk to her. However, in a further extraordinary twist, this modern-day Cinderella has not been seen since running away from the offices.

WHERE IS SHE?
See comment, page 34.

I peer at it in a daze. See comment? There's *more*? With fumbling hands I turn to page 34.

THE PRICE OF SUCCESS – TOO HIGH?

A high-flying lawyer with everything ahead of her gives up a six-figure salary and turns to domestic drudgery instead. What does this story say about today's high-pressure society? Are our career women being pushed too hard? Are they burning out? Does this extraordinary story herald the start of a new trend?

One thing is for certain. Only Samantha Sweeting can answer.

I stare at the page, numb with disbelief. How did— What did—? *How?*

A flash interrupts me and I look up in shock to see the guy pointing his camera at me.

'Stop!' I say in horror, putting my hands up in front of my face.

'Can I have a picture of you holding a toilet brush, love?' he says, zooming his lens in. 'They tipped me off at the pub it was you. Quite a scoop.' The camera flashes again and I flinch.

'No! You . . . you have made mistake.' I shove the paper back at him in a mess of pages. 'This . . . Zees ees not me. My name is Martine. I no lawyer.'

The journalist looks at me suspiciously, and down at the photo again. I can see a flicker of doubt cross his face. I do look fairly different now from the way I did then, with my blonde hair and everything.

'That's not a French accent,' he says.

He has a point. Accents aren't exactly my strong point.

'Am . . . half Belgian.' I keep my eyes fixed on the floor. 'Please leave 'ouse now. Or I call police.'

'Come on, love. You're not Belgian!'

'You go! Is trespass! Is prosecute!'

I shove him off the doorstep, slam the door shut and turn the key. Then I pull the curtain across the window and lean back against the door, my heart thudding. Fuck. Fuck. What am I going to do?

OK. The important thing is not to panic. The important thing is to stay rational and take a balanced view of the situation.

On the one hand, my entire past has been exposed in a national tabloid. On the other hand, Trish and Eddie don't read that particular tabloid. Or the *Cheltenham Gazette*. It's one silly story in one silly paper and it will die away by tomorrow. There's no reason to tell them anything. There's no need to rock the boat. I'll just carry on making my chocolate orange mousses as though nothing has happened. Yes. Total denial is the way forward.

Feeling slightly better I reach for the chocolate and start breaking chunks into a glass bowl.

'Samantha! Who was that?' Trish pokes her head round the door.

'No one.' I look up with a fixed smile. 'Nothing. Why don't I make you a cup of coffee and bring it out to the garden?'

Keep calm. Denial. It'll all be fine.

OK. Denial's not going to work, because there are three more journalists in the drive.

It's twenty minutes later. I've abandoned my chocolate mousses and am peering out of the hall window in rising horror. Two blokes and a girl have appeared out of nowhere. They all have cameras, and are chatting to the guy in the polo shirt, who's gesticulating towards the kitchen. Occasionally one of them breaks off and takes a shot of the house. Any minute one of them is going to ring the doorbell.

I cannot let this develop. I need a new plan. I need . . .

Diversion. Yes. At least it might buy me some time.

I head to the front door, grabbing one of Trish's floppy straw hats on the way. Then I cautiously step outside and make my way down the gravel drive to the entrance, where the four journalists crowd around me.

'Are you Samantha Sweeting?' says one, thrusting a tape recorder in my face.

'Do you regret turning down partnership?' demands another.

'My name is Martine,' I say, keeping my head down. 'You 'ave come to ze wrong house. I know Samantha Sweeting, and she leeves . . . over there.' I wave my hand towards the other end of the village.

I wait for the stampede, but no one moves.

'You 'ave ze wrong 'ouse!' I say again. 'Please leave ze premises!'

'What accent is that supposed to be?' says a guy in black glasses.

'Belgian,' I say after a pause.

'*Belgian?*' He peers under the brim of Trish's hat. 'It's her,' he says scornfully. 'Ned, it's her! Come over here!'

'She's there! She's come out!'

'It's her!'

I hear voices from across the street – and to my utter

horror, another load of journalists suddenly appears, hurrying down the road towards the gates, bearing cameras and Dictaphones.

Where did they come from?

'Ms Sweeting, Angus Watts, *Daily Express*.' Black-glasses guy lifts up his microphone. 'Do you have a message for young women of today?'

'Do you really enjoy cleaning toilets?' chimes in someone else, snapping a camera in my face. 'What brand of toilet cleaner do you use?'

'Stop it!' I say, flustered. 'Leave me alone!' I haul at the iron gates until they're closed, then turn and run up the drive, into the house and into the kitchen.

What am I going to do?

I catch a glimpse of my reflection in the fridge door. My face is flushed and my expression wild. I'm also still wearing Trish's floppy straw hat.

I grab it off my head and dump it on the table, just as Trish comes into the kitchen. She's holding a book called *Your Elegant Luncheon Party* and an empty coffee cup.

'Do you know what's going on, Samantha?' she says. 'There seems a bit of a *commotion* outside in the road.'

'Is there?' I say. 'I . . . I hadn't noticed.'

'It looks like a protest.' She wrinkles her brow. 'I do hope they're not still there tomorrow. Protesters are so *selfish* . . .' Her eye falls on the counter. 'Haven't you finished the mousses yet? Samantha, really! What have you been *doing*?'

'Um . . . nothing!' I swallow. 'I'm just getting on with them, Mrs Geiger.' I reach for the bowl and start doling out chocolate mixture into glasses.

I feel like I'm in some kind of parallel reality. Everything's going to come out. It's just a matter of time. What do I do?

'Have *you* seen this protest?' Trish demands as Eddie saunters into the kitchen. 'Outside our gates! I think we should tell them to move on.'

'It's not a protest,' he says, opening the fridge and peering inside. 'It's journalists.'

'*Journalists?*' Trish peers at him. 'What on earth would journalists be doing here?'

'Maybe we have a new celebrity neighbour?' suggests Eddie, pouring his beer into a glass.

At once Trish claps her hand over her mouth. 'Joanna Lumley! I *heard* a rumour she was buying in the village! Samantha, have you heard anything about this?'

'I . . . er . . . no,' I mumble, my face burning.

I have to say something. Come on. Say something. But what? Where do I start?

'Samantha, I need this shirt ironed by tonight.' Melissa comes wandering into the kitchen, holding out a sleeveless print shirt. 'And be really careful with the collar, OK?' she adds with a bad-tempered frown. 'The last one you did, the creases weren't straight.'

'Oh. Right. Um, sorry about that,' I say. 'If you put it in the laundry room . . .'

'And my room needs hoovering,' she adds. 'I spilt some loose powder on the floor.'

'I'm not sure I'll have time—' I begin.

'*Make* time,' she snaps, and picks up an apple. 'What's going on outside?'

'Nobody knows,' says Trish excitedly. 'But we think it's Joanna Lumley!'

Suddenly the doorbell rings.

My stomach seems to double over. For a moment I consider bolting out of the back door.

'I wonder if that's them!' exclaims Trish. 'Eddie, go and answer it. Samantha, put on some coffee.' She looks at me in impatience. 'Come on!'

I'm totally paralysed. I need to speak. I need to explain. But my mouth won't move. Nothing will move.

'Samantha?' She peers at me. 'Are you all right?'

With an almighty effort I look up. 'Um . . . Mrs Geiger . . .' My voice comes out a nervous husk. 'There's . . . there's something . . . I ought to . . .'

'Melissa!' Eddie's voice interrupts me. He's hurrying into the kitchen, a huge beam spread across his face. 'Melissa, love! They want you!'

'*Me?*' Melissa looks up in surprise. 'What do you mean, Uncle Eddie?'

'It's the *Daily Mail*. They want to interview you!' Eddie turns to Trish, glowing with pride. 'Did you know that our Melissa has one of the finest legal brains in the country?'

Oh no. Oh no.

'What?' Trish nearly drops her copy of *Your Elegant Luncheon Party*.

'That's what they said!' Eddie nods. 'They said it might come as quite a surprise to me to learn we had such a high-flying lawyer in the house. I said Nonsense!' He puts an arm around Melissa. 'We've always known you were a star!'

'Mrs Geiger,' I say urgently. No one takes any notice of me.

'It must be that prize I won at law school! They must have heard about it somehow!' Melissa is gasping. 'Oh my God! The *Daily Mail*!'

'They want to take photos, too!' puts in Eddie. 'They want an exclusive!'

'I need to put on some make-up!' Melissa looks totally flustered. 'How do I look?'

'Here we are!' Trish wrenches open her handbag. 'Here's some mascara . . . and lipstick . . .'

I have to stop this. I have to break it to them.

'Mr Geiger . . .' I clear my throat. 'Are you sure . . . I mean, did they ask for Melissa by . . . by name?'

'They didn't need to!' He twinkles at me. 'Only one lawyer in this house!'

'Make some coffee, Samantha,' instructs Trish sharply. 'And use the pink cups. Quickly! Wash them up.'

'The thing is . . . I have . . . I have something to tell you.'

'Not *now*, Samantha! Wash up those cups!' Trish thrusts the rubber gloves at me. 'I don't know *what's* wrong with you today—'

'But I don't think they've come to see Melissa,' I say desperately. 'There's something I . . . I should have told you . . .'

No one pays any attention. They're all focused on Melissa.

'How do I look?' Melissa smooths her hair back self-consciously.

'Lovely, darling!' Trish leans forward. 'Just a touch more lipstick . . . make you look really glamorous . . .'

'Is she ready for the interview?' An unfamiliar woman's voice comes from the kitchen door and everyone freezes in excitement.

'In here!' Eddie pulls open the door to reveal a dark-haired, middle-aged woman in a trouser suit, whose eyes immediately run appraisingly over the kitchen.

'Here's our legal star!' Eddie gestures to Melissa with a beam of pride.

'Hello.' Melissa tosses back her hair, then steps forward with an outstretched hand. 'I'm Melissa Hurst.'

The woman looks at Melissa blankly for a few moments. 'Not her,' she says. '*Her*.' And she points at me.

358

In puzzled silence, everyone swivels to stare at me. Melissa's eyes have narrowed to deepest suspicion. I can see the Geigers exchanging glances.

'That's Samantha,' says Trish, looking perplexed. 'The housekeeper.'

'You're Samantha Sweeting, I take it?' The woman brings out her reporter's pad. 'Can I ask you a few questions?'

'You want to interview the *housekeeper*?' says Melissa, with a sarcastic laugh.

The journalist ignores her. 'You *are* Samantha Sweeting, aren't you?' she persists.

'I . . . yes,' I admit at last, my face burning. 'But I don't want to do an interview. I don't have any comment.'

'*Comment?*' Trish's eyes dart around uncertainly. 'Comment on what?'

'What's going on, Samantha, love?' Eddie looks anxious. 'Are you in some kind of trouble?'

'You haven't *told* them?' The *Daily Mail* journalist looks up from her notepad. 'They have no idea?'

'Told us what?' says Trish, agitated. 'What?'

'She's an illegal immigrant!' says Melissa triumphantly. 'I knew it! I knew there was some-thing—'

'Your "housekeeper" is a top City lawyer.' The woman throws down a copy of the tabloid onto the kitchen table. 'And she's just turned down a six-figure partnership to work for you.'

It's as though someone's thrown a grenade into the kitchen. Eddie visibly reels. Trish totters on her high-heeled clogs and grabs a chair for balance. Melissa's face looks like a popped balloon.

'I meant to tell you . . .' I bite my lip awkwardly as I look at their faces. 'I was . . . getting round to it . . .'

Trish's eyes are bulging as she reads the headline. Her mouth is opening and closing, but no sound is coming out.

'You're a . . . a *lawyer*?' she stutters at last.

'There's been a mistake!' Melissa's cheeks are bright pink. '*I'm* the lawyer. *I'm* the one who got a prize at law school! She's the *cleaner*.'

'She's the one who got three prizes at law school.' The journalist jerks her head towards me. 'And the highest law degree of her year.'

'But . . .' Melissa's face is deepening to an ugly purple. 'It's impossible.'

'Youngest ever partner of Carter Spink . . .' The journalist consults her notes. 'Is that right, Ms Sweeting?'

'No!' I say. 'I mean . . . well . . . kind of. Can I make anyone a cup of tea?' I add desperately.

No one seems interested in tea. In fact, Melissa looks as though she's about to vomit.

'Did you have any idea your housekeeper has an IQ of 158?' The journalist is clearly loving this. 'She's borderline genius.'

'We knew she was bright!' says Eddie, defensive. 'We spotted that! We were helping her with her—' He breaks off, looking foolish. 'With her English GCSE.'

'And I'm really grateful!' I put in hurriedly. 'Really.'

Eddie mops his brow with a tea towel. Trish is still clutching the chair as though she might keel over any minute.

'I don't understand.' Eddie suddenly puts the tea towel down and turns to me. 'How did you combine being a lawyer with the housekeeping?'

'Yes!' exclaims Trish, coming to life. 'Exactly. How on earth could you be a City lawyer and *still* have time to train with Michel de la Roux de la Blanc?'

Oh God. They *still* don't get it?

'I'm not really a housekeeper,' I say desperately. 'I'm not really a cordon bleu cook. Michel de la Roux de la Blanc doesn't exist. I have no idea what this thing is really called.' I pick up the truffle beater, which is lying on the side. 'I'm a . . . a fake.'

I can't look at either of them. Suddenly I feel terrible. 'I'll understand if you want me to leave,' I mumble. 'I took the job under false pretences.'

'Leave?' Trish looks horrified. 'We don't want you to leave, do we, Eddie?'

'Absolutely not.' His face becomes even more ruddy. 'You've done a fine job, Samantha. You can't help it if you're a lawyer.'

'"I'm a fake",' says the journalist, writing it carefully down on her notepad. 'Do you feel guilty about that, Ms Sweeting?'

'Stop it!' I say. 'I'm not doing an interview!'

'Ms Sweeting says she'd rather clean loos than be a partner of Carter Spink,' says the journalist, turning to Trish. 'Could I see the loos in question?'

'*Our* loos?' Spots of pink appear on Trish's cheeks and she gives me an uncertain glance. 'Well, we did have the bathrooms refitted recently, they're all Royal Doulton . . .'

'How many are there?' The journalist looks up from her notepad.

'Stop this!' I clutch my hair. 'Look, I'll . . . I'll make a statement to the press. And then I want you all to leave me and my employers alone.'

I hurry out of the kitchen, the *Daily Mail* woman following behind, and fling open the front door. The crowd of journalists is still there, behind the gate. Is it my imagination or are there more than before?

'It's Martine,' says the guy in black glasses sardonically as I approach the gates.

I ignore him. 'Ladies and gentlemen of the press,' I begin. 'I would be grateful if you would leave me alone. There isn't any story here.'

'Are you going to stay a housekeeper?' calls a fat guy in jeans.

'Yes, I am.' I lift my chin. 'I've made a personal choice, for personal reasons, and I'm very happy here.'

'What about feminism?' demands a young girl. 'Women have fought for years to gain an equal foothold. Now you're telling them they should go back to the kitchen?'

'I'm not telling women anything!' I say, taken aback. 'I'm just leading my own life.'

'But you think there's nothing wrong with women being chained to the kitchen sink?' A grey-haired woman glares at me.

'No!' I say in alarm. 'I mean, yes! I think—' My answer is drowned out by a barrage of questions and flashing cameras.

'Was Carter Spink a sexist hell-hole?'

'Is this a bargaining ploy?'

'Do you think women should have careers?'

'We'd like to offer you a regular column on household hints!' says a chirpy blonde girl in a blue mac. 'We want to call it "Samantha Says".'

'*What?*' I gape at her. 'I don't have any household hints!'

'A recipe, then?' She beams. 'Your favourite dish?'

'Could you pose for us in your pinny?' calls out the fat guy with a lascivious wink.

'No!' I say in horror. 'I have nothing else to say! No comment! Go away!'

Ignoring the cries and shouts of 'Samantha!' I turn

and run with trembling legs back up the drive to the house.

The world is mad.

I burst into the kitchen, to find Trish, Eddie and Melissa transfixed in front of the newspaper.

'Oh no,' I say, my heart plunging. 'Don't read it. Honestly. It's just . . . stupid . . . tabloid . . .'

All three of them raise their heads and regard me as though I'm some kind of alien.

'You charge . . . £500 an hour?' Trish doesn't seem quite in control of her voice.

'They offered you full equity partnership?' Melissa looks green. 'And you said *no*? Are you *crazy*?'

'Don't read this stuff!' I try to grab the paper. 'Mrs Geiger, I just want to carry on as usual. I'm still your housekeeper—'

'You're one of the country's top legal talents!' Trish jabs the paper hysterically. 'It says so here!'

'Samantha?' There's a rapping at the door and Nathaniel comes into the kitchen, holding an armful of newly picked potatoes. 'Will this be enough for the lunch?'

I stare at him dumbly, feeling a clutch at my heart. He has no idea. He knows nothing. Oh God.

I should have told him. Why didn't I tell him? *Why didn't I tell him?*

'What are *you*?' says Trish, turning to him wildly. 'A top rocket scientist? A secret government agent?'

'I'm sorry?' Nathaniel shoots me a quizzical look but I can't raise a smile.

'Nathaniel . . .'

I trail off, unable to continue. Nathaniel looks from face to face, a crease of uncertainty deepening in his brow.

'What's going on?' he says at last.

*   *   *

I have never made such a hash of anything as I make of telling Nathaniel. I stammer, I stutter, I repeat myself and go round in circles.

Nathaniel listens in silence. He's leaning against an old stone pillar in front of the secluded bench where I'm sitting. His face is in profile, shadowed in the afternoon sun, and I can't tell what he's thinking.

At last I come to a finish and he slowly lifts his head. If I was hoping for a smile, I don't get it. I've never seen him look so shell-shocked.

'You're a lawyer,' he says at last.

'Yes.' I nod shamefacedly.

'I thought you were in an abusive relationship.' He thrusts his hands through his hair. 'I thought that's why you didn't want to talk about your past. And you let me believe it. When you went up to London, I was *worried* about you. Jesus.'

'I'm sorry.' I wince with guilt. 'I'm so sorry. I just . . . didn't want you to know the truth.'

'Why not?' he retorts, and I can hear the hurt in his voice. 'What, you didn't trust me?'

'No!' I say in dismay. 'Of course I trust you! If it had been anything else . . .' I break off. 'Nathaniel, you have to understand. When we first met, how could I tell you? Everyone knows you hate lawyers. You even have a sign in your pub – No Lawyers!'

'That sign's a *joke*.' He makes an impatient gesture.

'It's not. Not completely.' I meet his gaze. 'Come on, Nathaniel. If I'd told you I was a City lawyer when we first met, would you have treated me in the same way?'

Nathaniel doesn't reply. I know he's too honest to give me the easy response. He knows as well as I do, the true answer is no.

'I'm the same person.' I lean forward and take his hand. 'Even if I used to be a lawyer . . . I'm still me!'

For a while Nathaniel says nothing, just stares down at the dirt. I'm holding my breath, desperate with hope. Then he looks up with a reluctant half-smile.

'So, how much are you charging me for this conversation, then?'

I exhale in a gust of relief. He's OK. He's OK about it.

'Oh, about a thousand pounds,' I say carelessly. 'I'll send you a bill.'

'Samantha Sweeting, corporate lawyer.' He surveys me for a few moments. 'Nope. I can't see it.'

'Me neither! That part of my life is over.' I squeeze his hand tightly. 'Nathaniel, I'm really sorry. I never meant any of this to happen.'

'I know.' He squeezes my hand back and I feel myself relax. A bay leaf falls into my lap from the tree behind and I pick it up, automatically rubbing it to release the sweet scent.

'So what happens now?' says Nathaniel.

'Nothing. The media interest will die down. They'll get bored.' I lean forward and rest my head on his shoulder, and feel his arms close around me. 'I'm happy in my job. I'm happy in this village. I'm happy with you. I just want everything to stay the same.'

TWENTY-FOUR

I'm wrong. The media interest doesn't die down. I wake up the next morning to find twice as many journalists as yesterday camped outside, plus two TV vans. As I come downstairs, carrying a tray of used coffee cups, I see Melissa leaning on the window sill, gazing out at the scene.

'Hi,' she says. 'Have you seen all the journalists?'

'Yes.' I can't help stopping next to her for another look. 'It's totally crazy.'

'It must be really overwhelming.' She flicks her hair back and examines her nails for a moment. 'But you know . . . I'm here for you.'

For a moment I think I must have misheard.

'Er . . . I'm sorry?'

'I'm here for you.' Melissa looks up. 'I'm your friend. I'll help you through all this.'

For a moment I'm too flabbergasted even to laugh. 'Melissa, you're not my friend,' I say as politely as I can.

'Yes I am!' She looks totally unabashed. 'I've always admired you, Samantha. In fact, I knew all along you weren't really a housekeeper. I knew there was more to you.'

I do not believe this. How can she stand there and be so *brazen*?

'You're my friend all of a sudden.' I don't try to hide my scepticism. 'And this doesn't have anything at all to do with finding out I'm a lawyer? Or wanting a career in law?'

'I've always liked you,' she says stubbornly.

'Melissa, come *on*.' I give her the hardest look I can muster, and to my own satisfaction I see just a tiniest tinge of pink appearing around her ears. But her expression remains impassive.

I hate to say it – but this girl is going to make a great lawyer.

'So . . . you really want to help me?' I say with a thoughtful frown.

'Yup!' She nods, a spark of excitement in her face. 'I could liaise with Carter Spink . . . or you could hire me as your spokeswoman . . .'

'Maybe you could take this?' I hand her the tray I was carrying, with a sweet smile. 'And I've got a shirt which needs ironing. Only be really careful with the collar, won't you?'

Her scowl is *priceless*. Trying not to giggle I continue downstairs and into the kitchen. Eddie is sitting at the table, which is covered in newspapers, and looks up as I come in.

'You're in every single paper,' he informs me. 'Look.' He shows me a double-page spread in the *Sun*. There's a picture of me superimposed on the background of a loo, and someone's drawn a toilet brush in one of my hands. 'I'd rather clean loos!' is in huge letters next to my face.

'Oh my God.' I sink into a chair and stare at the picture. '*Why?*'

'It's August,' says Eddie, flicking through the

Telegraph. 'Nothing else in the news. Says here you're a "casualty of today's work-obsessed society".' He turns the paper around to show me a small item topped with the headline CARTER SPINK HIGH-FLYER CHOOSES DRUDGERY AFTER RUMOURS OF SCANDAL.

'It says here you're a "Judas to career women everywhere".' Behind me Melissa has dumped the tray on the counter with a crash and picked up the *Herald.* 'Look, this columnist Mindy Malone is really angry with you.'

'Angry?' I echo, bewildered. 'Why would anyone be angry with me?'

'But in the *Daily Mail* you're a saviour of traditional values.' Eddie reaches for the paper and opens it. ' "Samantha Sweeting believes women should return to the hearthside for the sake of their own health and that of society".'

'What? I never said that!' I grab the paper and scan the text in disbelief. 'Why are they all so *obsessed*?'

'Silly season,' says Eddie, reaching for the *Express.* 'Is it true you single-handedly uncovered Mafia connections at your law firm?'

'No!' I look up in horror. 'Who said that?'

'Can't remember where I saw it now,' he says, riffling through the pages. 'There's a picture of your mother in this one. Nice-looking lady.'

'My *mother*?' I stare in dismay.

'High-flying daughter of a high-flying mother,' Eddie reads aloud. 'Was the pressure to succeed too much?'

Oh God. Mum is going to *kill* me.

'This one has a poll, look.' Eddie has opened another paper. ' "Samantha Sweeting: Heroine or Fool? Phone or text your vote." Then they give a number to call.' He reaches for the phone and frowns. 'Which shall I vote for?'

'Fool,' says Melissa, grabbing the phone. 'I'll do it.'

'Samantha! You're up!'

I raise my head to see Trish coming into the kitchen, holding a bundle of newspapers under her arm. As she looks at me she has the same shell-shocked expression of awe that she had yesterday, as though I'm a priceless work of art which has suddenly pitched up in her kitchen. 'I've just been reading about you!'

'Good morning, Mrs Geiger.' I put down the *Daily Mail* and hastily get to my feet. 'What can I get you for breakfast? Some coffee to begin with?'

'Don't you make the coffee, Samantha!' she replies, looking flustered. 'Eddie, *you* can make the coffee!'

'I'm not making the coffee!' objects Eddie.

'Then ... Melissa!' says Trish. 'Make us all some nice coffee. Samantha, you sit down for once! You're our guest!' She gives an unnatural laugh.

'I'm not your guest!' I protest. 'I'm your housekeeper!'

I can see Eddie and Trish exchanging doubtful looks. What do they think? That I'm going to leave?

'Nothing's different!' I insist. 'I'm still your housekeeper! I just want to carry on my job as usual.'

'You're crazy.' Melissa rolls her eyes contemptuously. 'Have you *seen* how much Carter Spink want to pay you?'

'You wouldn't understand,' I retort. 'Mr and Mrs Geiger, *you'll* understand. I've learned a lot, living here. I've changed as a person. And I've found a fulfilling way of life. Yes, I could make a lot more money being a lawyer in London. Yes, I could have some high-powered, pressurized career. But it's not what I want.' I spread my arms around the kitchen.

'This is what I want to do. This is where I want to be.'

I'm half expecting Trish and Eddie to look moved by my little speech. Instead, they both peer at me in total incomprehension, then glance at each other again.

'I think you should consider the offer,' says Eddie. 'It says in the paper they're desperate to woo you back.'

'We won't be at *all* offended if you leave,' adds Trish, nodding emphatically. 'We'll *completely* understand.'

Is that all they can say? Aren't they *glad* I want to stay? Don't they *want* me as their housekeeper?

'I don't want to leave!' I say crossly. 'I want to stay here and enjoy a fulfilling life at a different pace.'

'Right,' says Eddie after a pause, then surreptitiously pulls a 'What?' face at Trish.

The telephone rings and Trish picks it up.

'Hello?' She listens for a moment. 'Yes, of *course*, Mavis. *And* Trudy. See you later!' She puts the receiver down. 'Two more guests for the charity lunch!'

'Right.' I glance at my watch. 'I'd better get going on the starters.'

As I'm getting out my pastry the phone rings again and Trish sighs. 'If this is more late guests . . . Hello?' As she listens, her expression changes and she puts her hand over the receiver.

'Samantha,' she hisses. 'It's an ad company. Are you willing to appear in a TV commercial for Toilet Duck? You'd wear a barrister's wig and gown, and you'd have to say—'

'No!' I say, recoiling. 'Of course not!'

'You should never turn down television,' says Eddie reprovingly. 'Could be a big opportunity.'

'No it couldn't! I don't want to be in any

370

commercials!' I can see Eddie opening his mouth to argue. 'I don't want to do any interviews,' I add quickly. 'I don't want to be a role model. I just want everything to go back to normal.'

By lunchtime everything is not back to normal. In fact everything is even more surreal than before.

I've had three more requests to appear on TV and one to do a 'tasteful' photoshoot for the *Sun* in a French maid's uniform. Trish has given an exclusive interview to the *Mail*. Callers to a radio phone-in which Melissa insisted on listening to have described me as an 'antifeminist moron', a 'Martha Stewart wannabe' and a 'parasite on the taxpayers who paid for my education'. I was so furious I almost phoned up myself.

But instead I switched the radio off and took three deep breaths. I'm not going to let myself get hassled. I have other things to think about. Fourteen guests have arrived for the charity lunch and are milling around on the lawn. I have wild-mushroom tartlets to bake, asparagus sauce to finish, and salmon fillets to roast.

I desperately wish Nathaniel was here to keep me calm. But he's gone off to Buckingham to pick up some koi carp for the pond, which Trish has suddenly decided she must have. Apparently they cost hundreds of pounds and all the celebrities have them. It's ridiculous. No one ever even *looks* in the pond.

The doorbell rings just as I'm opening the oven, and I sigh. Not another guest. We've had four late acceptances this morning, which has totally thrown my schedule. Not to mention the journalist from the *Mirror* who dressed up in a pink floral suit and tried to tell Eddie she was new to the village.

I put the tray of tarts in the oven, gather up the

remaining scraps of pastry, and start to wipe down my rolling pin.

'Samantha?' Trish taps at the door. 'We have another guest!'

'*Another* one?' I turn round, wiping flour off my cheek. 'But I've just put the starters in the oven . . .'

'It's a friend of yours. He says he needs to speak to you urgently. About business?' Trish raises her eyebrow at me significantly – then steps aside. And I freeze in astonishment.

It's Guy. Standing in Trish's kitchen. In his immaculate Jermyn Street suit and starched cuffs.

I stare at him, unable to speak, utterly flabbergasted.

Judging by his expression, he's pretty gobsmacked, too.

'Oh my God,' he says slowly, his eyes running over my uniform, my rolling pin, my floury hands. 'You really are a housekeeper.'

'Yes.' I lift my chin. 'I really am.'

'Samantha . . .' says Trish from the door. '*Not* that I want to interrupt, but . . . Starters in ten minutes?'

'Of course, Mrs Geiger.' I automatically bob a curtsey as Trish leaves and Guy's eyes nearly fall out of his head.

'You *curtsey*?'

'The curtseying was a bit of a mistake,' I admit. I catch his appalled eye and feel a giggle rising. 'Guy, what are you *doing* here?'

'I'm here to persuade you to come back.'

Of course he is. I should have guessed.

'I'm not coming back. Excuse me.' I reach for the broom and dust-pan and start sweeping up the flour and pastry scraps off the floor. 'Mind your feet!'

'Oh. Right.' Guy awkwardly moves out of the way.

I dump the pastry bits in the bin, then get my

asparagus sauce out of the fridge, pour it into a pan and set it on a gentle heat.

Guy is watching me in bemusement. 'Samantha,' he says as I turn round. 'We need to talk.'

'I'm busy.' The kitchen timer goes off with a shrill ring and I open the bottom oven to take out my rosemary garlic rolls. I feel a surge of pride as I see them, all golden brown and wafting a delicious, herby scent. I can't resist taking a nibble out of one, then offering it to Guy.

'You *made* these?' He looks astounded. 'I didn't know you could cook.'

'I couldn't. I learned.' I reach into the fridge again for some unsalted butter and break a knob into the foaming asparagus sauce. Then I glance at Guy, who's standing by the utensil rack. 'Could you pass me a whisk?'

Guy looks helplessly at the utensils. 'Er . . . which one is the . . .'

'Don't worry,' I say, clicking my tongue. 'I'll get it.'

'I have a job offer for you,' says Guy as I grab the whisk and start beating in the butter. 'I think you should look at it.'

'I'm not interested.' I don't even raise my head.

'You haven't even seen it yet.' He reaches into his inside pocket and produces a white letter. 'Here. Take a look.'

'I'm not interested!' I repeat in exasperation. 'Don't you understand? I don't want to go back. I don't want to be a lawyer.'

'You want to be a housekeeper instead.' His tone is so dismissive, I feel stung.

'Yes!' I thrust my whisk down. 'I do! I'm happy here. I'm relaxed. You have no idea. It's a different life!'

'Yup, I got that,' says Guy, glancing at my broom.

'Samantha, you have to see sense.' He takes a phone out of his inside pocket. 'There's someone you really should speak to.' He dials a number then looks up. 'I've been in contact with your mother over the situation.'

'You *what*?' I stare at him in horror. 'How *dare* you—'

'Samantha, I only want the best for you. So does she. Hi, Jane,' he says into the phone. 'I'm with her now. I'll pass you over.'

I cannot believe this. For an instant I feel like throwing the phone out of the window. But no. I can deal with this.

'Hi Mum,' I say, taking the phone from Guy. 'Long time.'

'Samantha.' Her voice is as icy as it was the last time we spoke. But somehow this time it doesn't make me feel tense or anxious. She can't tell me what to do. She has no idea about my life any more. 'What exactly do you think you're doing? Working as some kind of *domestic*?'

'That's right. I'm a housekeeper. And I suppose you want me to go back to being a lawyer? Well, I'm happy here and I'm not going to.' I taste the asparagus sauce and add some salt.

'You may think it's funny to be flippant,' she says curtly. 'This is your life, Samantha. Your career. I think you fail to understand—'

'*You* don't understand! None of you do!' I glare at Guy, then turn the hob down to a simmer and lean against the counter. 'Mum, I've learned a different way to live. I do my day's work, and I finish . . . and that's it. I'm *free*. I don't need to take paperwork home. I don't need to have my BlackBerry switched on 24/7. I can go to the pub, I can make weekend plans, I can go and sit in the garden for half an hour with my feet up . . . and it *doesn't matter*. I don't have that constant pressure any more. I'm not stressed out. And it suits me.' I reach for a glass, fill it with water and take a deep gulp, then wipe my mouth. 'I'm sorry, but I've changed. I've made friends. I've got to know the community here. It's like . . . the Waltons.'

'The *Waltons*?' She sounds startled. 'Are there children there?'

'No!' I say in frustration. 'You don't understand! They just . . . *care*. Like, a couple of weeks ago they threw me the most amazing birthday party.'

There's silence. I wonder if I've touched a sensitive spot. Maybe she'll feel guilty . . . maybe she'll understand . . .

'How very bizarre,' she says crisply. 'Your birthday was two months ago.'

'I know.' I sigh. 'Look, Mum, I've made up my mind.' The oven suddenly pings, and I reach for an oven glove. 'I've got to go.'

'Samantha, this conversation is not over!' she snaps furiously. 'We have not finished.'

'We have, OK? We *have*!' I switch off the phone, dump it on the table and exhale, feeling a bit shaky despite myself. 'Thanks a lot, Guy,' I say shortly. 'Any other nice little surprises for me?'

'Samantha . . .' He spreads his hands apologetically. 'I was trying to get through to you . . .'

'I don't need "getting through to".' I turn away. 'And now I have to work. This is my job.'

I open the bottom oven, take out my trays of tartlets and start decanting them onto small warmed plates.

'I'll help,' says Guy, coming over.

'You can't *help*.' I roll my eyes.

'Of course I can.' To my astonishment he takes off

his jacket, rolls up his sleeves and puts on a cherry-sprigged apron. 'What do I do?'

I can't help a tiny giggle. He looks so incongruous.

'Fine.' I hand him a tray. 'You can take in the starters with me.'

We head to the dining room, carrying the mushroom tartlets and the bread rolls. As we enter the white-canopied room, the babble of chatter breaks off and fourteen dyed, lacquered heads turn. Trish's guests are seated around the table, sipping champagne, each wearing a suit of a different pastel colour. It's like walking into a Dulux paint chart.

'And this is Samantha!' says Trish, whose cheeks are a bright shade of pink. 'You all know Samantha, our housekeeper . . . and also top lawyer!'

To my embarrassment a spattering of applause breaks out.

'We saw you in the papers!' says a woman in cream.

'I need to talk to you.' A woman in blue leans forward with an intense expression. 'About my *divorce settlement*.'

I think I'll pretend I didn't hear that.

'This is Guy, who's helping me out today,' I say, beginning to serve the mushroom tarts.

'He's *also* a partner at Carter Spink,' adds Trish proudly.

I can see impressed glances being exchanged across the table. An elderly woman at the end turns to Trish, looking bewildered. 'Is *all* your help lawyers?'

'Not all,' says Trish airily, taking a deep gulp of champagne. 'But you know, having *had* a Cambridge-educated housekeeper, I could never go back.'

'Where do you get them from?' a red-haired woman asks avidly. 'Is there a special agency?'

'It's called Oxbridge Housekeepers,' says Guy,

placing a mushroom tart in front of her. 'Very choosy. Only those with first-class honours can apply.'

'Goodness!' The red-haired woman gazes up, agog.

'I, on the other hand, went to Harvard,' he continues. 'So I'm with Harvard Help. Our motto is: "Because that's what an Ivy League education is for." Isn't that right, Samantha?'

'Shut *up*,' I mutter. 'Just serve the food.'

At last all the ladies are served and we retreat to the empty kitchen.

'Very funny,' I say, plonking the tray down with a crash. 'You're so witty.'

'Well, for God's sake, Samantha. Do you expect me to take all this *seriously*? Jesus.' He takes off the apron and throws it down on the table. 'Serving food to a bunch of airheads. Letting them patronize you.'

'I have a job to do,' I say tightly, opening the oven to check on the salmon. 'So if you're not going to help me—'

'This is not the job you should be doing!' he suddenly explodes. 'Samantha, this is a fucking *travesty*. You have more brains than anyone in that room, and you're serving them? You're *curtseying* to them? You're cleaning their *bathrooms*?'

He sounds so passionate, I turn round, shocked. His face is flushed and all traces of teasing have gone.

'Samantha, you're one of the most brilliant people I know.' His voice is jerky with anger. 'You have the best legal mind any of us has ever seen. I cannot let you throw away your life on this ... deluded crap.'

I stare at him, incensed. 'It's not deluded crap! Just because I'm not "using my degree", just because I'm not in some office, I'm wasting my life? Guy, I'm *happy*. I'm enjoying life in a way I've never done

377

before. I *like* cooking. I *like* running a house. I *like* picking strawberries from the garden—'

'You're living in fantasyland!' he shouts. 'Samantha, this is all a novelty! It's fun because you've never done it before! But it'll wear off! Can't you *see* that?'

I feel a pricking of uncertainty inside, which I ignore. 'No it won't.' I give my asparagus sauce a determined stir. 'I love this life.'

'Will you still love it when you've been cleaning bathrooms for ten years? Get real.' He comes over to the cooker and I turn away. 'So you needed a holiday. You needed a break. Fine. But now you need to come back to real life.'

'This *is* real life for me,' I shoot back. 'It's more real than my life used to be.'

Guy shakes his head. 'Charlotte and I went to Tuscany last year, and learned watercolour painting. I loved it. The olive oil . . . the sunsets . . . the whole bit.' He meets my eyes intently for a moment, then leans forward. 'It doesn't mean I'm going to become a fucking Tuscan watercolour painter.'

'It's different!' I wrench my gaze away from his. 'Guy, I'm not going back to that workload. I'm not going back to that pressure. I worked seven days a week, for seven bloody years—'

'Exactly. Exactly! And just as you get the reward, you *bail out*?' He clutches his head. 'Samantha, I'm not sure you understand the position you're in. You've been offered full equity partnership. You can basically demand any income you like. You're in control!'

'What?' I look at him, puzzled. 'What do you mean?'

Guy blows out and raises his eyes upwards, as though summoning the help of the Lawyer Gods. 'Do you realize,' he says carefully, 'the storm you've created? Do you realize how bad this all looks for

378

Carter Spink? This is the worst week of press since the Storesons scandal in the eighties.'

'I didn't *plan* any of it,' I say, defensive. 'I didn't ask the media to turn up on the doorstep—'

'I know. But they did. And Carter Spink's reputation has plummeted. The Human Resources department are *beside* themselves. After all their touchy-feely well-being programmes, all their graduate-recruitment workshops, you tell the world you'd rather clean loos.' He gives a sudden snort of laughter. 'Talk about bad PR.'

'Well, it's true,' I say, lifting my chin. 'I would.'

'Don't be so perverse!' Guy bangs the table in exasperation. 'You have Carter Spink over a barrel! They want the world to see you walking back into that office. They'll pay you whatever you want! You'd be crazy not to take up their offer!'

'I'm not interested in money,' I retort. 'I've got enough money—'

'You don't understand! Samantha, if you come back, you can earn enough to retire after ten years. You'll be set up for life! *Then* you can go and pick strawberries or sweep floors or whatever crap it is you want to do.'

I open my mouth automatically to respond . . . but all of a sudden my words have dried up. I can't quite track my thoughts. They're jumping about all over the place in confusion.

'You earned your partnership,' says Guy, his tone quieter. 'You earned it, Samantha. Use it.'

Guy doesn't say any more on the subject. He's always known exactly when to close an argument; he should have been a barrister. He helps me serve the salmon, then gives me a hug and tells me to call him as soon as I've had time to think. And then he's gone, and

I'm left alone in the kitchen, my thoughts churning.

I was so certain. I was so sure of myself. But now . . .

His arguments keep playing out in my mind. They keep hitting true notes. Maybe I am deluded. Maybe this is all a novelty. Maybe after a few years of a simpler life I won't be content, I'll be frustrated and bitter. I have a sudden vision of myself mopping floors with a nylon scarf round my head, assailing people: 'I used to be a corporate lawyer, you know.'

I have a brain. I have years ahead of me.

And he's right. I worked for my partnership. I earned it.

I bury my head in my hands, resting my elbows on the table, listening to my own heartbeat in my chest, thumping away like a question. *What am I going to do? What am I going to do?*

And yet all the time I'm being pushed towards one answer. The rational answer. The answer which makes most sense.

I know what it is. I'm just not sure I'm ready to face up to it yet.

It takes me until six o'clock. The lunch is over and I've cleared it away. Trish's guests have wandered round the garden and had cups of tea and melted away. As I walk out into the soft, balmy evening, Nathaniel and Trish are standing by the pond, with a plastic tank by Nathaniel's feet.

I feel like something's gripping my stomach as I approach him.

'This is a Kumonryu,' Nathaniel is saying as he scoops something out of the tank with a big green net. 'Want to have a look?' As I get nearer I see an enormous patterned fish flapping noisily in the net. He offers it to Trish and she reels back with a little shriek.

'Get it away! Put it in the pond!'

'It cost you two hundred quid,' says Nathaniel with a shrug. 'I thought you might want to say hello.' He shoots me an amused grin over Trish's shoulder and somehow I manage to smile back.

'Put them all in.' Trish shudders. 'I'll come and see them when they're swimming about.'

She turns on her heel and heads back towards the house.

'All right?' Nathaniel looks up at me. 'How was the great charity lunch?'

'It was fine.'

'Did you hear the news?' He scoops another fish into the pond. 'Eamonn's just got engaged! He's having a party next weekend at the pub.'

'That's . . . that's great.'

My mouth is dry. Come on. Just tell him.

'You know, we should have a koi pond at the nursery,' says Nathaniel, sloshing the rest of the fish into the pond. 'Do you know the profit margin on these—'

'Nathaniel, I'm going back.' I close my eyes, trying to ignore the stab of pain inside. 'I'm going back to London.'

For a moment he doesn't move. Then very slowly he turns round, the net still in his hand, his face expressionless.

'Right,' he says.

'I'm going back to my old job as a lawyer.' My voice shakes a little. 'Guy from my old firm came down today, and he convinced me – he showed me. He made me realize . . .' I break off and gesture helplessly.

'Realize what?' Nathaniel says, his brow furrowing a little.

He hasn't smiled. He hasn't said 'Good idea, that's

just what I was going to suggest.' Why can't he make this *easy* for me?

'I can't be a housekeeper all my life!' I sound more defensive than I'd like. 'I'm a trained lawyer! I have a brain!'

'I know you have a brain.' Now *he* sounds defensive. Oh God. I'm not managing this well.

'I've earned partnership. Full equity partnership at Carter Spink.' I gaze up at him, trying to convey the significance of this. 'It's the most prestigious ... lucrative ... amazing ... I can make enough money in a few years to retire!'

Nathaniel doesn't seem too impressed. He just looks at me steadily. 'At what cost?'

'What do you mean?' I avoid his gaze.

'I mean that when you turned up here, you were a nervous wreck. You were like some freaked-out rabbit. White as a sheet. Stiff as a board. You looked like you hadn't ever seen the sun, you looked like you hadn't ever *enjoyed* yourself—'

'You're exaggerating.'

'I'm not. Can't you *see* how much you've changed? You're not edgy any more. You're not a bundle of nerves.' He picks up my arm and lets it fall down. 'That arm would have stayed there!'

'OK, so I've relaxed a bit!' I throw up my hands. 'I know I've changed. I've calmed down and I've learned to cook and iron and pull pints ... and I've had a wonderful time. But it's like a holiday. It can't last for ever.'

Nathaniel shakes his head in despair. 'So after all this you're just going to go back, pick up the reins and carry on as though nothing happened?'

'It'll be different this time! I'll make it different. I'll keep a balance.'

'Who are you kidding?' Nathaniel grips my shoulders. 'Samantha, it'll be the same stress, the same lifestyle—'

I feel a sudden surge of anger towards him for not understanding; for not supporting me.

'Well at least I *tried* something new!' My words pour out in a torrent. 'At least I went out and tried a different life for a bit!'

'What's that supposed to mean?' His grasp loosens in shock.

'It means, what have *you* ever tried, Nathaniel?' I know I sound shrill and aggressive but I can't help myself. 'You're so narrow-minded! You live in the same village you grew up in, you run the family business, you're buying a nursery down the road . . . you're practically still in the *womb*. So before you lecture me on the way to live my life, try living one of your own, OK?'

I break off, panting, to see Nathaniel looking as though I've slapped him.

Immediately I want to bite my tongue. 'I . . . didn't mean it,' I mumble.

I take a few steps away, feeling near to tears. This isn't the way things were supposed to go. Nathaniel was supposed to support me and give me a hug and tell me I was making the right decision. Instead here we are, standing yards apart, not even looking at each other.

'I thought about spreading my wings.' Nathaniel suddenly speaks, his voice stiff. 'There's a nursery in Cornwall I'd die to own. Fantastic piece of land, fantastic business . . . but I didn't look at it. I preferred not to be six hours' drive away from you.' He shrugs. 'I guess you're right. That was pretty narrow-minded of me.'

I don't know how to reply. For a while there's silence, except for the cooing of pigeons down at the end of the garden. It is the most spectacular evening, I suddenly realize. Evening sun is slanting through the willow tree and the grass smells sweet underneath my feet.

'Nathaniel ... I have to go back.' My voice isn't quite steady. 'I don't have any choice. But we can still be together. The two of us. We can still make it work. We'll have holidays ... weekends ... I'll come back for Eamonn's party ... You won't know I've gone!'

He's silent for a moment, fiddling with the handle of the bucket. When at last he looks up, his expression makes my heart constrict.

'Yeah,' he says in a quiet voice. 'I will.'

TWENTY-FIVE

The news makes the front page of the *Daily Mail*. I am a genuine celebrity. SAMANTHA CHOOSES LAW OVER LOOS. As I come into the kitchen the next morning, Trish is poring over it, with Eddie reading another copy.

'Trish's interview has been printed!' he announces. 'Look!'

' " 'I always knew Samantha was a cut above the average housekeeper,' says Trish Geiger, thirty-seven," ' reads out Trish proudly. ' "We often discussed philosophy and ethics together over the Hoover." '

She looks up and her face changes. 'Samantha, are you all right? You look absolutely washed out.'

'I didn't sleep that well,' I admit, and flick on the kettle.

I spent the night at Nathaniel's. We didn't talk any more about my going. But at three o'clock, when I looked over at him, he was awake too, staring up at the ceiling.

'You need energy!' says Trish, perturbed. 'It's your big day! You need to look your best!'

'I will.' I try to smile. 'I just need a cup of coffee.'

It's going to be a huge day. The Carter Spink PR department swung into action as soon as I made my decision, and have turned my return into a full media event. There's going to be a big press conference at lunchtime in front of the Geigers' house, where I'll say how delighted I am to be going back to Carter Spink. Several of the partners are going to shake my hand for the photographers and I'll give a few short interviews. And then we're all going back to London on the train.

'So,' says Eddie as I spoon coffee into the pot. 'All packed up?'

'Pretty much. And Mrs Geiger . . . here.' I hand Trish the folded blue uniform which I've been carrying under my arm. 'It's clean and pressed. Ready for your next housekeeper.'

As Trish takes the uniform she looks suddenly stricken. 'Of course,' she says, her voice jumpy. 'Thank you, Samantha.' She clasps a napkin to her eyes.

'There, there,' says Eddie, patting her on the back. He looks rather moist around the eyes himself. Oh God, now I feel like crying myself.

'I'm really grateful for everything,' I gulp. 'And I'm sorry for leaving you in the lurch.'

'We know you've made the right decision. It's not *that*.' Trish dabs her eyes.

'We're very proud of you,' chips in Eddie gruffly.

'Anyway!' Trish pulls herself together and takes a sip of coffee. 'I've decided to make a *speech* at the press conference. I'm sure the press will be expecting me to speak.'

'Absolutely,' I say, a little nonplussed. 'Good idea.'

'After all, now we're becoming media personalities—'

'Media personalities?' interrupts Eddie incredulously. 'We're not media personalities!'

'Of course we are! I'm in the *Daily Mail*!' A faint flush comes to Trish's face. 'This could be just the beginning for us, Eddie. If we hired the right publicist we could be on reality TV! Or . . . advertise Campari!'

'Campari?' expostulates Eddie. 'Trish, you don't *drink* Campari!'

'I could!' Trish is saying defensively as the doorbell rings. 'Or they could use coloured water . . .'

Smiling, I head into the hall, pulling my dressing gown around myself. Maybe it's Nathaniel, come to wish me luck.

But as I open the door, I see the entire PR team from Carter Spink standing on the doorstep, all in identical trouser suits.

'Samantha.' Hilary Grant, Head of PR, runs her eyes over me. 'Ready?'

By twelve o'clock I'm wearing a black suit, black tights, black high heels, and the crispest white shirt I've ever seen. I've been professionally made up and my hair has been scraped back into a bun.

Hilary brought the clothes and the hairdresser and make-up artist. Now we're in the drawing room while she preps me on what to say to the press. For the thousand millionth time.

'What's the most important thing to remember?' she's demanding. 'Above anything?'

'Not to mention loos,' I say wearily. 'I promise, I won't.'

'And if they ask about recipes?' She wheels round from where she's been striding up and down.

'I answer, "I'm a lawyer. My only recipe is the recipe for success."' Somehow I manage to utter the words straight-faced.

I'd forgotten how seriously the PR department take

all of this. But I suppose it's their job. And I suppose this whole business has been a bit of a nightmare for them. Hilary has been outwardly pleasant ever since she got here, but I get the feeling there's a little wax doll of me on her desk, impaled by drawing pins.

'We just want to make sure you don't say anything else *unfortunate*.' She gives me a slightly savage smile.

'I won't! I'll stick to the script.'

'And then the *News Today* team will follow you back to London.' She consults her BlackBerry. 'We've given them access for the rest of the day. You're OK about that?'

'Well . . . yes. I suppose.'

I cannot believe how big this whole thing has become. A news programme actually wants to do a fly-on-the-wall TV documentary section about my return to Carter Spink. Is there nothing else happening in the world?

'Don't look at the camera.' Hilary is still briskly issuing instructions. 'You should be good-humoured and positive. You can talk about the career opportunities Carter Spink has given you and how much you're looking forward to getting back. *Don't* mention your salary—'

The door opens and I hear Melissa's voice coming from the hall.

'So I can call you at the office to talk about my career plan? Or we could have a drink?'

'Absolutely. Er . . . good idea.' Guy appears in the room and quickly shuts the door before Melissa can follow him in. 'Who the hell's *that*?'

'Melissa.' I roll my eyes heavenwards. 'Don't ask.'

'She says she's your protégée. You taught her everything she knows, apparently.' Guy gives an amused

388

grin. 'Would that be in corporate law – or scone-baking?'

'Ha ha,' I say politely.

'Hilary, there's some trouble outside.' Guy turns to her. 'Some TV guy kicking up a fuss.'

'Damn.' Hilary looks at me. 'Can I leave you for a moment, Samantha?'

'Absolutely!' I try not to sound too eager. 'I'll be fine!'

As she leaves I breathe a sigh of relief.

'So,' Guy raises his eyebrows. 'How are you? Excited?'

'Yes!' I smile.

Actually I feel a little surreal, being back in a black suit, surrounded by Carter Spink people. I haven't seen Trish or Eddie for hours. Carter Spink have totally commandeered the house.

'You made the right decision, you know,' says Guy.

'I know.' I brush a fleck of cotton off my skirt.

'You look sensational. You're going to blow them away.' He perches on a sofa arm opposite me and sighs. 'Jesus, I missed you, Samantha. It hasn't been the same.'

I peer at him for a few moments. Does he have any sense of irony? Or did they fix that at Harvard too?

'So now you're my best friend again.' I can't help a slight edge. 'Funny, that.'

Guy stares at me. 'What's that supposed to mean?'

'Come on, Guy.' I almost want to laugh. 'You didn't want to know me when I was in trouble. Now suddenly we're chums again?'

'That's unfair,' retorts Guy hotly. 'I did everything I could for you, Samantha. I fought for you in that meeting. It was Arnold who refused to have you back. At the time we had no idea why—'

'You wouldn't let me in your house though, would you?' I give him a half-smile. 'Friendship wouldn't quite extend that far.'

Guy looks genuinely thrown. He pushes his hair back with both hands.

'I felt terrible about that,' he says. 'It wasn't me. It was Charlotte. I was furious with her—'

'Of course you were.'

'I was!'

'Yeah, right,' I say sarcastically. 'So I suppose you had a huge row about it and broke up.'

'Yes,' says Guy.

The wind is totally taken out of my sails.

'*Yes?*' I gulp at last.

'We've split up.' He shrugs. 'Didn't you know?'

'No! I had no idea! I'm sorry. I really didn't . . .' I break off in confusion. 'It wasn't . . . it wasn't really over me?'

Guy doesn't answer. His brown eyes are becoming more intense. Deep inside I feel a thud of apprehension.

'Samantha,' he says, not moving his gaze from mine. 'I've always felt . . .' He thrusts his hands in his pockets. 'I've always felt we somehow . . . missed our chance.'

No. No. This can't be happening.

We missed our chance?

Now he says this?

'I've always really admired you. I always felt there was a spark between us.' He hesitates. 'I wondered whether you felt . . . the same.'

This is unreal. How many millions of times have I imagined Guy saying these words to me? How many times have I fantasized about him gazing at me with those dark, liquid eyes? But now he's actually *doing* it, it's too late. It's all wrong.

'Samantha?'

Suddenly I realize I'm staring at him like a zombie.

'Oh. Right.' I try to pull myself together. 'Well . . . yes. Maybe I used to feel like that too.' I fiddle with my skirt. 'But the thing is . . . I've met someone. Since I've been here.'

'The gardener,' says Guy without missing a beat.

'Yes!' I look up in surprise. 'How did you—'

'Some of the journalists were talking about it outside.'

'Oh. Well, it's true. His name's Nathaniel.' I feel myself blush. 'He's . . . he's really nice.'

Guy frowns as though he's not sure what point I'm trying to make. 'But that's just a holiday romance.'

'It's not a holiday romance!' I say, taken aback. 'It's a *relationship*. We're serious about each other.'

'Is he moving to London?'

'Well . . . no. He hates London. But we're going to make it work.'

Guy looks incredulous for a moment, then throws back his head and roars with laughter. 'You really are deluded. Living in fantasyland.'

'What's that supposed to mean?' I say, incensed. 'We'll make it work somehow. If we both want it enough—'

'I'm not sure you've quite got the situation yet.' Guy shakes his head. 'Samantha, you're *leaving* this place. You're coming back to London, back to reality, back to work. Believe me, you're never going to keep up some holiday fling.'

'It was *not* a holiday fling!' I yell furiously, as the door opens. Hilary looks from Guy to me with alert, suspicious eyes.

'Everything all right?'

'Fine,' I say, turning away from Guy. 'I'm fine.'

'Good!' She taps her watch. 'Because it's nearly time!'

The entire world seems to have descended on the Geigers' house. As I venture out of the front door with Hilary and two PR managers, there are what looks like hundreds of people in the drive. A row of TV cameras is trained on me, photographers and journalists are in a crowd behind, and Carter Spink PR assistants are milling around, keeping everyone in line and handing out coffee from a refreshments stand which seems to have sprung up from nowhere. At the gate I can see a group of regulars from the pub peering in curiously, and I shoot them a mortified grin.

'It'll be a few more minutes,' says Hilary, listening to her mobile. 'We're just waiting for the *Daily Telegraph*.'

I can see David Elldridge and Greg Parker standing by the cappuccino machine, both typing on their BlackBerries. The PR department wanted as many partners as possible for the photo-call, but none of the others could make it. Frankly, they were lucky to get this many. As I'm watching, to my disbelief I see Melissa approaching them, dressed up smartly in a beige suit and holding . . . is that a *CV*?

'Hi!' I hear her begin. 'I'm a very good friend of Samantha Sweeting and Guy Ashby. And they've both recommended I apply to Carter Spink.'

I can't help smiling. The girl has some nerve.

'Samantha.' I look up to see Nathaniel coming across the gravel. His face is shadowed and his blue eyes are tense. 'How are you doing?'

'I'm . . . fine.' I look at him for a couple of seconds. 'You know. It's all a bit crazy.'

I feel his hand clasping mine and intertwine my fingers between his as tightly as I can.

Guy's wrong. It's going to work. It's going to last. Of course it is.

I can feel his thumb rubbing mine, just like he did that first evening we had together. Like some private language; like his skin is talking to mine.

'Are you going to introduce me, Samantha?' Guy comes sauntering over.

'This is Guy,' I say reluctantly. 'I work with him at Carter Spink. Guy . . . Nathaniel.'

'Delighted to meet you!' Guy holds out his hand and Nathaniel is forced to let go of mine to shake it. 'Thanks for looking after our Samantha so well.'

Does he have to sound so *patronizing*? And what's this 'our' Samantha?

'It was my pleasure.' Nathaniel glowers back.

'So you look after the garden.' Guy looks around the drive. 'Very nice. Well done!'

I can see Nathaniel's fist forming at his side.

Please don't punch him, I pray urgently. *Don't* punch him—

To my relief I notice Iris coming through the gate, peering around at all the journalists with interest.

'Look!' I say quickly to Nathaniel. 'Your mum.'

I greet Iris with a wave. She's wearing cropped cotton trousers and espadrilles, her plaits wound round her head. As she reaches me she just looks at me for a few moments: at my bun, my black suit, my high-heeled shoes.

'Goodness,' she says at last.

'I know.' I give an awkward laugh 'A bit different.'

'So, Samantha.' Her eyes rest softly on mine. 'You found your way.'

'Yes.' I swallow. 'Yes I did. This is the right way for me, Iris. I'm a lawyer. I always was. It's a great opportunity. I'd be . . . I'd be crazy not to take it up.'

Iris nods, her expression guarded.

'Nathaniel told me all about it. I'm sure you've made the right decision.' She pauses. 'Well . . . goodbye, chicken. And good luck. We'll miss you.'

As I lean forward to hug her I suddenly feel tears pricking my eyes. 'Iris . . . I don't know how to thank you,' I whisper. 'For everything you did.'

'You did it all yourself.' She squeezes me tight. 'I'm very proud of you.'

'And it's not really goodbye.' I wipe my eyes with a tissue, praying my make-up hasn't run. 'I'll be back before you know it. I'm going to visit as many weekends as I can . . .'

'Here, let me.' She takes my tissue from me and dabs my eyes.

'Thanks.' I give her a shaky smile. 'This make-up has got to last all day.'

'Samantha?' Hilary calls me from the refreshments stand, where she's talking to David Elldridge and Greg Parker. 'Can you come over here?'

'I'll be right there!' I call back.

'Samantha, before you go . . .' Iris takes hold of both my hands, her face twisted a little in anxiety. 'Sweetie, I'm sure you're doing what's best for you. But just remember, you only get your youth once.' She looks at my hand, smooth against hers. 'You only get these precious years once.'

'I'll remember.' I bite my lip. 'I promise.'

'Good.' She pats my hand. 'Off you go.'

As I walk over to the refreshments stand, Nathaniel's hand is tightly in mine, our fingers twisted together. We're going to have to say goodbye in a couple of hours.

No. I can't think about that.

Hilary is looking a little stressed as I approach.

'Got your statement?' she says. 'Feeling prepared?'

'All set.' I take out the folded sheet of paper. 'Hilary, this is Nathaniel.'

Hilary's eyes run over him without interest. 'Hello,' she says. 'Now, Samantha, let's just go through the order again. You read your statement, then questions, then photos. We'll start in about three minutes. The team are just distributing press packs . . .' Suddenly she peers more closely at me. 'What happened to your *make-up*?'

'Um . . . I was just saying goodbye to someone,' I say apologetically. 'It's not too bad, is it?'

'We'll have to redo it.' Her voice is jerky with annoyance. 'This really is *all* I need.' She strides away, calling to one of her assistants.

Three more minutes. Three minutes before my old life begins again.

'So . . . I'll be back for Eamonn's party,' I say, still clutching Nathaniel's hand. 'It's only a few days away. I'll catch the train down on Friday night, spend the weekend . . .'

'Not next weekend,' chips in Guy, shaking chocolate onto a cappuccino. He looks up. 'You'll be in Hong Kong.'

'What?' I say stupidly.

'Samatron are delighted you're back and they've asked for you on this merger. We're flying to Hong Kong tomorrow. Has no one told you?'

'No,' I say, staring at him in shock. 'No one's even mentioned it.'

Guy shrugs. 'I thought you knew. Five days in Hong Kong and then on to Singapore. You and I are going to be wooing some new clients.' He takes a sip of coffee. 'You need to start pulling in business, Samantha

Sweeting, equity partner. Can't rest on your laurels.'

I haven't even *started* the job yet and they're already talking about resting on my laurels?

'So when will we be back?'

Guy shrugs. 'Couple of weeks?'

'Samantha!' says Elldridge, coming up. 'Has Guy mentioned, we want you on a corporate shooting weekend at the end of September? Up in Scotland, should be fun.'

'Right. Um, yes, that sounds great.' I rub my nose. 'The only thing is, I'm trying to keep some weekends free . . . keep a bit of balance in my life . . .'

Elldridge looks puzzled. 'You've *had* your break, Samantha,' he says jovially. 'Now it's back to work. And I must talk to you about New York.' He pats me on the shoulder and turns to the barista. 'Another espresso, please.'

'Realistically, I'd say you're not going to have a free weekend till Christmas,' puts in Guy. 'I did warn you.' He raises his eyebrows meaningfully and moves away to talk to Hilary.

There's silence. I don't know what to say. Everything's moving too fast. I thought it would be different this time. I thought I'd have more control.

'Christmas,' echoes Nathaniel at last, looking thunderstruck.

'No,' I say at once. 'He's exaggerating. It won't be that bad. I'll rearrange things.' I rub my brow. 'Look, Nathaniel . . . I'll be back before Christmas. I promise. Whatever it takes.'

A strange flicker passes over his face. 'Don't turn it into a duty.'

'*Duty?*' I stare at him. 'That's not what I meant. You know that's not what I meant.'

'Two minutes!' Hilary comes bustling up with the make-up artist, but I ignore her.

'Nathaniel—'

'Samantha!' snaps Hilary, trying to pull me away. 'You *really* don't have time for this!'

'You should go.' Nathaniel gestures with his head. 'You're busy.'

This is awful. It feels like everything is disintegrating between us. I have to do something. Reach out to him.

'Nathaniel, just tell me.' My voice trembles. 'Tell me before I go. That day in the farmhouse . . . what did you say to me?'

Nathaniel looks at me for a long moment, then something in his eyes seems to close up. 'It was long and boring and badly put.' He turns away with a half-shrug.

'*Please* do something with those smudges!' Hilary is saying. 'Could you please move?' she adds sharply to Nathaniel.

'I'll get out of your way.' Nathaniel lets go of my hand and retreats before I can say anything.

'You're not in my way!' I call after him, but I'm not sure he hears.

As the make-up artist begins her work my mind is spinning so fast I feel faint. Suddenly all my certainty has vanished.

Am I doing the right thing?

Oh God. *Am I doing the right thing?*

'Close, please.' The make-up artist is brushing at my eyelids. 'Now open . . .'

I open my eyes to see Nathaniel and Guy standing together, some way away. Guy's talking and Nathaniel is listening, his face taut. I feel a sudden stab of unease. What's Guy saying?

'Close again,' says the make-up artist. Reluctantly I close my eyes and feel her brushing yet more shadow on. For God's sake. Hasn't she finished? Does it *matter* what I look like?

At last she withdraws her brush. 'Open.'

I open my eyes to see Guy standing in the same spot, a few yards away. But Nathaniel's vanished. Where's he gone?

'Put your lips together . . .' the make-up artist instructs, producing a lipstick brush.

I can't speak. I can't move. My eyes are darting in panic around the crowded drive, looking for Nathaniel. I *need* him. I need to talk to him before this press conference goes ahead.

I get one life. Is this really what I want to do with it? Have I thought about it carefully enough?

'Ready for your big moment? Got your statement?' Hilary is upon me again, smelling of freshly applied scent. 'That looks a lot better! Chin up!' She taps my chin so sharply I wince. 'Any last-minute questions?'

'Um . . . yes,' I say desperately. 'I was just wondering . . . could we possibly put it off for a little bit? Just a few minutes.'

Hilary's face freezes.

'What?' she says at last. I have a dreadful feeling she's going to explode.

'I feel a bit . . . confused.' I swallow. 'I don't know if I've made the right decision. I need more time to think about it . . .' I trail off at Hilary's expression.

She comes towards me and brings her face very close to mine. She's still smiling but her eyes are snapping and her nostrils flared and white. I take a step back, quailing, but she grabs my shoulders so hard I can feel her nails digging into my flesh.

'Samantha,' she hisses, 'you will go out there, you

will read your statement and you will say Carter Spink is the best law firm in the world. And if you don't . . . I will kill you.'

I think she's serious.

'We're all confused, Samantha. We all need more time to think. That's life.' She gives me a little shake. 'Get over it.' She breathes out sharply and smooths down her suit. 'Right! I'm going to announce you.'

She marches onto the lawn. I just stand there, shaking.

I have thirty seconds. Thirty seconds to decide what to do with my life.

'Ladies and gentlemen of the press!' Hilary's voice is blaring through the microphone. 'I'm delighted to welcome you all here this morning.'

Suddenly I spot Guy, helping himself to a mineral water. 'Guy!' I call urgently. 'Guy! Where's Nathaniel?'

'I have no idea.' Guy gives an insouciant shrug.

'What did you say to him? When you were talking just now?'

'I didn't have to say much,' Guy replies. 'He could tell the way the wind was blowing.'

'What do you mean?' I stare at him. 'The wind wasn't blowing any way.'

'Samantha, don't be naive.' Guy takes a swig of water. 'He's a grown man. He understands.'

'. . . our newest partner at Carter Spink, Samantha Sweeting!' Hilary's voice and the applause breaking out barely touch my consciousness.

'Understands what?' I say in horror. 'What did you say?'

'Samantha!' Hilary interrupts with a sweetly savage smile. 'We're all waiting! Lots of busy people!' She grabs my hand with an iron grip and drags me with surprising force onto the grass. 'Off you go! Enjoy!'

She gives me a sharp dig in the back and walks away.

OK. Thirty seconds wasn't enough. I'm stranded in front of the nation's press and I don't know what I want. I don't know what I should do.

I have never felt so confused in my life.

'Move it!' Hilary's tense undertone makes me jump. I feel like I'm on a conveyor belt. The only way is forward.

With wobbling legs I make my way into the middle of the lawn, where a microphone has been set up on a stand. The sun is glinting off all the camera lenses and I feel half-blinded. I search the crowd as best I can for Nathaniel but I can't spot him anywhere. Trish is standing a few yards away to my right, in a fuchsia-pink suit, and waves frantically. Beside her, Eddie is holding a camcorder.

Slowly I unfold my statement and smooth it down.

'Good morning,' I say into the microphone, my voice stilted. 'I am delighted to be able to share my exciting news with you. After being made a wonderful offer by Carter Spink, I will be returning to the firm today as a partner. Needless to say . . . I'm thrilled.'

Somehow I can't make my voice sound thrilled. The words feel empty as I say them.

'I have been overwhelmed by the warmth and generosity of the Carter Spink welcome,' I continue hesitantly, 'and am honoured to be joining such a prestigious partnership of . . .'

My eyes are still seeking out Nathaniel. I can't concentrate on what I'm saying.

'Talent and excellence!' snaps Hilary from the sidelines.

'Um . . . yes.' I find my place on the sheet. 'Talent. And excellence.'

A titter goes through the crowd of journalists. I'm not doing a very good job here.

'Carter Spink's quality of service is ... um ... second to none,' I continue, trying to sound convincing.

'Better quality than the toilets you used to clean?' calls out a journalist with ruddy cheeks.

'We are not taking questions at this stage!' Hilary comes out crossly onto the lawn. 'And we are taking no questions on the subject of toilets, bathrooms, or any other form of sanitaryware. Samantha, carry on.'

'Unspeakable, were they?' shouts the ruddy-cheeked guy with a guffaw of laughter.

'Samantha, carry *on*,' spits Hilary, looking livid.

'They certainly were not unspeakable!' Trish comes striding onto the lawn, her fuchsia heels sinking into the grass. 'I will not have my toilets maligned! They're all Royal Doulton. They're Royal Doulton,' she repeats into the microphone. 'Highest quality. You're doing very well, Samantha!' She pats me on the shoulder.

All the journalists are laughing by now. Hilary's face is puce.

'Excuse me,' she says to Trish with suppressed fury. 'We are in the middle of a press conference here. Could you please leave?'

'This is my lawn!' says Trish, lifting her chin. 'The press want to hear from me, too! Eddie, where's my speech?'

'You're not making a *speech*!' says Hilary in horror, as Eddie darts onto the lawn with a printed scroll sheet.

'I would like to thank my husband Eddie for all his support,' begins Trish, ignoring Hilary. 'I would like to thank the *Daily Mail* ...'

'This isn't the bloody Oscars!' Hilary looks apoplectic.

'Don't swear at me!' retorts Trish sharply. 'I am the owner of this residence, I'd like to remind you.'

'Mrs Geiger, have you seen Nathaniel?' I look desperately around the crowd for the millionth time. 'He's disappeared.'

'Who's Nathaniel?' asks one of the journalists.

'He's the gardener,' puts in the ruddy-faced guy. 'Lover boy. So is that all over?' he adds to me.

'No!' I say, stung. 'We're going to keep the relationship going.'

'How are you going to do that, then?'

I can sense a fresh interest stirring in the crowd of journalists.

'We just will, OK?' Suddenly, for no reason, I feel near to tears.

'Samantha,' says Hilary furiously. 'Please get back to the official statement!' She pushes Trish away from the microphone.

'Don't you touch me!' shrills Trish. 'I'll sue. Samantha Sweeting is my lawyer, you know.'

'Oy, Samantha! What does Nathaniel think about you going back to London?' shouts someone.

'Have you put your career over love?' chimes in a bright-faced girl.

'No!' I say desperately. 'I just . . . I need to talk to him. Where *is* he? Guy!' I suddenly spot Guy at the side of the lawn. 'Where did he go? What did you say to him?' I hurry towards him over the grass, almost tripping over. 'You have to tell me. What did you say?'

'I advised him to keep his dignity.' Guy gives an arrogant shrug. 'To be honest, I told the guy the truth. You won't be back.'

'How *dare* you?' I gasp in fury. 'How *dare* you say

that? I will be back! And he can come to London—'

'Oh, please.' Guy raises his eyes. 'He doesn't want to hang around like some sad bastard, getting in your way, embarrassing you . . .'

'Embarrassing me?' I stare at Guy, aghast. 'Is that what you *said* to him? Is that why he left?'

'For God's sake, Samantha, give it a rest,' snaps Guy impatiently. 'He's a *gardener*.'

My fist acts before I can think. It hits Guy right on the jaw.

I can hear gasps and shouts and cameras snapping all around, but I don't care. That is the best thing I have ever done.

'Ow! Fuck!' He clasps his face. 'What the fuck was that for?'

The journalists are all crowding round now, hurling questions at us, but I ignore them.

'It's you who embarrass me,' I spit at Guy. 'You're worth nothing compared to him. *Nothing*.' To my horror I can feel tears coming to my eyes. I have to find Nathaniel. Right now.

'Everything's fine! Everything's fine!' Hilary comes thundering across the grass, a blur of pin-stripe trouser suit. 'Samantha's a little overwrought today!' She grabs my arm in a vice-like grip, her teeth bared in a rictus smile. 'Just a friendly disagreement between partners! Samantha is greatly looking forward to the challenges of leading a world-renowned legal team. Aren't you, Samantha?' Her grip tightens. '*Aren't* you, Samantha?'

'I . . . don't know,' I say in despair. 'I just don't know. I'm sorry, Hilary.' I wrench my arm out of hers.

Hilary makes a furious swipe for my arm but I evade her and start running over the grass, towards the gates.

'Stop her!' Hilary is yelling to all the PR staff. 'Block her way!'

Girls in trouser suits start coming at me from all directions like some kind of SWAT team. Somehow I dodge them. One makes a grab for my jacket and I wriggle out of it. I throw off my high heels too, and pick up my pace, barely wincing at the gravel under my soles.

As I reach the gate my heart starts thudding. There are three PR girls standing in a row, blocking the way.

'Come on now, Samantha,' says one, in a nice-cop way. 'Don't be stupid.'

'Let's get you back to the press conference.' One of them is approaching me warily, hands outstretched.

'*Let her past!*' comes a clarion voice from behind me. I look up and to my astonishment see Trish tottering towards me as fast as her fuchsia heels will allow. 'Help me, you fools!' she adds to a posse of nearby journalists.

A moment later the PR girls have been submerged by journalists, pushing open the gate; clearing a way through for me. And I'm out, running down the street, not looking back.

By the time I arrive at the pub my tights have been torn to shreds on the road, my hair has come out of its bun and half fallen down my back, my make-up is swimming in sweat, and my chest is burning with pain.

But I don't care. I have to find Nathaniel. I have to tell him he's the most important thing in my life, more important than any job.

I have to tell him I love him.

I don't know why I didn't realize it before, why I never said it before. It's so obvious. It's so blinding.

'Eamonn!' I call urgently as I approach, and he looks up in surprise from where he's collecting up glasses. 'I have to talk to Nathaniel. Is he here?'

'Here?' Eamonn appears lost for words. 'Samantha, you've missed him. He's already gone.'

'Gone?' I come to a halt, panting. 'Gone where?'

'To look at this business he wants to buy. He left in the car a short while ago.'

'The one in Bingley?' I gulp in relief, still out of breath. 'Could you possibly give me a lift there? I have to talk to him.'

'That's not where . . .' Eamonn rubs his reddened face, looking awkward. I stare at him, feeling a sudden foreboding. 'Samantha . . . he's gone to Cornwall.'

Shock slams me in the chest like a truck. I can't speak. I can't move.

'I thought you knew.' Eamonn takes a step forward, shading his eyes against the sun. 'He said he might be down there a couple of weeks. I thought he'd have told you.'

'Um, no,' I say, my voice barely working. 'He didn't.'

Suddenly my legs feel like jelly. I sink down onto one of the barrels, my head pounding. He's gone to Cornwall, just like that. Without even saying good-bye. Without even talking about it.

'He left a note in case you dropped by.' Eamonn feels in his pocket and produces an envelope. As he hands it over his face is crumpled up with distress. 'Samantha, I'm sorry.'

'It's fine.' I manage a smile. 'Thanks, Eamonn.' I take the envelope from him and pull out the paper.

S
I think we both know this is the end of the line.
Let's quit while we're ahead.

Just know that this summer was perfect.
N

Tears are flooding down my cheeks as I read it, over and over. I can't believe he's gone. How can he have given up on us? Whatever Guy said to him, whatever he thought. How can he have just *left*?

We could have made it work. Didn't he *know* that? Didn't he feel it, deep down?

I hear a sound and look up to see Guy and a crowd of journalists gathered around me. I hadn't even noticed.

'Go away,' I say in a muffled voice. 'Leave me alone.'

'Samantha,' says Guy, his voice low and conciliatory, 'I know you're hurt. I'm sorry if I upset you.'

'I'll hit you again.' I wipe my eyes with the back of my hand. 'I mean it.'

'Things may seem bad at the moment.' Guy glances at the note. 'But you have a fantastic career to get on with.'

I don't answer. My shoulders are hunched over, my nose is running and my hair is falling around my face in lacquered strands.

'Be reasonable. You're not going back to cleaning loos. There's nothing to keep you here now.' Guy takes a step forward and puts my glossy high-heeled shoes on the table beside me. 'Come on, partner. Everyone's waiting.'

TWENTY-SIX

I feel numb. It really is all over. I'm sitting in a first-class compartment on the train to London, with the other partners. It's an express train. In a couple of hours we'll be back. I have a new pair of tights on. My make-up has been repaired. I've even given a fresh statement to the press, hastily constructed by Hilary: 'Although I will always feel affection for my friends in Lower Ebury, nothing is more exciting and important in my life right now than my career with Carter Spink.'

I said it pretty convincingly. I even found a smile from somewhere as I shook David Elldridge's hand. It's just possible they might print a picture of that, rather than the one of me punching Guy. You never know.

As the train pulls out of the station I feel a painful stab and close my eyes for a moment, trying to stay composed. I'm doing the right thing. Everyone's agreed. I take a sip of cappuccino, then another. If I drink enough coffee maybe it'll jolt me alive. Maybe I'll stop feeling as though I'm in a dream.

Wedged in the corner opposite me is the TV cameraman for the news documentary, together with the producer, Dominic, a guy with trendy glasses and a denim jacket. I can feel the camera lens on me, following every move, zooming in and out, catching every expression. I could *really* do without this.

'And so lawyer Samantha Sweeting leaves the village where she was known only as a domestic help,' Dominic is saying into his microphone in a low, TV-commentary voice. 'The question is . . . does she have any regrets?' He gives me a questioning glance.

'I thought you were supposed to be fly-on-the-wall,' I snap with a baleful look.

'Here you go!' Guy dumps a heavy set of contracts on my lap. 'Here's the Samatron deal. Get your teeth into that.'

I look at the pile of paper, inches thick. Once upon a time, seeing a brand-new, fresh contract gave me a rush of adrenaline. I always wanted to be first to spot an anomaly, first to raise a query. But now I feel blank.

Everyone else in the carriage is working away. I leaf through the contract, trying to summon up some enthusiasm. Come on. This is my life now. Once I get back into the swing of it I'll start to enjoy it again.

'From cookery books to contracts,' murmurs Dominic into his microphone. 'From wooden spoons to writs.'

This guy is really starting to piss me off.

I turn back to my contract. But the words are jumbling in front of my eyes. I can't concentrate. All I can think about is Nathaniel. I've tried calling him but he isn't answering. Or replying to texts. It's like he doesn't want to know any more.

How can everything be over? How can he have just *left*?

My eyes are starting to blur with tears again and I furiously blink them away. I can't cry. I'm a partner. Partners do not cry. Trying to get a grip on myself, I look out of the window instead. We seem to be slowing down, which is a bit weird.

'An announcement for all passengers . . .' A voice suddenly comes crackling out of the loudspeakers. 'This train has been rescheduled as a slow train. It will be stopping at Hitherton, Marston Bridge, Bridbury . . .'

'What?' Guy looks up. 'A *slow* train?'

'Jesus Christ.' David Elldridge scowls. 'How much longer will it take?'

'. . . and will arrive at Paddington half an hour after the scheduled time,' the voice is saying. 'Apologies for any . . .'

'*Half an hour?*' David Elldridge whips out his mobile phone, looking livid. 'I'm going to have to reschedule my meeting.'

'I'll have to put off the Pattinson Lobb people.' Guy looks equally pissed off, and is already jabbing at the speed-dial on his phone. 'Hi Mary? Guy. Listen, total cock-up on this train. I'm going to be half an hour late—'

'Rearrange Derek Tomlinson—' David's instructing.

'We'll have to push back Pattinson Lobb, cancel that guy from *The Lawyer*—'

'Davina,' Greg Parker is saying into his phone. 'Fucking train's slow. Tell the rest of the team I'll be half an hour late, I'm sending an email—' He puts down his phone and immediately starts typing into his BlackBerry. A moment later Guy is doing the same.

I'm watching all this frenzied action incredulously. They all look so stressed. So the train's going to be late. It's *half an hour*. It's thirty minutes. How can anyone get so het up over thirty minutes?

Is this what I'm supposed to be like? Because I've forgotten how. Maybe I've forgotten how to be a lawyer altogether.

The train pulls into Hitherton station and slowly comes to a halt. I glance out of the window – then gasp aloud. A huge hot air balloon is hovering in the air, just a few feet above the station building. It's bright red and yellow, with people waving from a basket. It looks like something out of a fairy tale.

'Hey, look!' I exclaim. 'Look at that!'

No one lifts their head. They're all frantically tapping at their keyboards.

'*Look!*' I try again. 'It's amazing!' There's still no response. No one is interested in anything except the contents of their BlackBerry. And now the balloon's soared away again. In a moment it'll be out of sight. They all missed it.

I look at them all, the cream of the legal world, dressed in their thousand-pound hand-made suits, holding state-of-the-art computers. Missing out. Not even *caring* that they're missing out. Living in their own world.

I don't belong here. That's not my world any more. *I'm not one of them.*

I suddenly know it, with the deepest certainty I've ever felt. I don't fit; I don't relate. Maybe I did once, but not any more. I can't do this. I can't spend my life in meeting rooms. I can't obsess about every little chunk of time. I can't miss out on any more.

As I sit there, the contracts still piled on my lap, I feel tension rising inside me. I've made a mistake. I've made a huge mistake. I shouldn't be here. This isn't what I want from my life. This isn't what I want to do. This isn't who I want to be.

I have to get out. Now.

Up and down the train people are stepping in and out, banging doors, hefting bags. As calmly as I can I reach for my suitcase, pick up my bag and stand up.

'I'm sorry,' I say. 'I made a mistake. I've only just realized.'

'*What?*' Guy looks up.

'I'm sorry I've wasted your time.' My voice wavers slightly. 'But . . . I can't stay. I can't do this.'

'Jesus.' He clutches his head. 'Not this again, Samantha—'

'Don't try and talk me round,' I cut across him. 'I've decided. I can't be like the rest of you. It's just not right for me. I'm sorry, I should never have come.'

'Is this to do with the gardener?' He sounds exasperated. 'Because quite frankly—'

'No! It's to do with *me*! I just . . .' I hesitate, searching for the words. 'Guy . . . I don't want to be someone who doesn't look out of the window.'

Guy's face doesn't register an iota of understanding. I didn't expect it to.

'Goodbye.' I open the train door and step out, but Guy grabs me roughly.

'Samantha, for the last time, stop this crap! I *know* you. And you're a *lawyer.*'

'You *don't* know me, Guy!' My words burst out in a surge of sudden anger. 'Don't define me! I'm not a lawyer! I'm a *person.*'

I pull my arm out of his and slam the door shut, shaking all over. The next moment it opens again and Dominic and the cameraman pile out after me.

'And so!' Dominic is murmuring excitedly into his microphone. 'In a shock turn of events, Samantha Sweeting has rejected her glittering legal career!'

I am really going to thump him in a minute.

As the train pulls out of the station I can see Guy and the other partners on their feet staring out at me in consternation. I guess I've ruined all my chances of a comeback now.

411

The other passengers start melting away from the platform, leaving me all alone. All alone on Hitherton station with only a suitcase for company. I don't even know where Hitherton is. The TV camera is still trained on me, and as people pass by they give me curious glances.

What am I going to do now?

'As she gazes down onto the railway tracks, Samantha finds herself at a low ebb.' Dominic's voice is low and sympathetic.

'I *don't*,' I mutter back.

'This morning she was devastated to lose the man she loved. Now she has no career either.' He pauses, then adds in sepulchral tones, 'Who knows what dark thoughts are going through her mind?'

What's he trying to imply? That I'm going to throw myself under the next train? He'd love that, wouldn't he? He'd probably win an Emmy.

'I'm fine.' I lift my chin and clutch my suitcase more tightly. 'I'm going to be fine. I've . . . I've done the right thing.'

But as I look around the empty station I feel slight flurries of panic as I take in my situation properly. I have no idea when the next train will be. I have no idea where I want to go, even.

'Do you have a plan, Samantha?' asks Dominic, thrusting his microphone at me. 'A goal?'

Why won't he leave me *alone*?

'Sometimes you don't need a goal in life,' I say defensively. 'You don't need to know the big picture. You just need to know what you're going to do next.'

'And what are you going to do next?'

'I'm . . . I'm . . . working on it.' I turn and march away from the camera, towards the waiting room. As I near it, I see a guard coming out.

'Um, hello,' I say. 'I'd like to know how to get to . . .' I trail off, uncertainly. Where am I going? 'To . . . um . . .'

'To . . .' prompts the guard helpfully.

'To . . . Cornwall,' I hear myself saying.

'*Cornwall?*' He looks taken aback. 'Whereabouts in Cornwall?'

'I don't know.' I swallow. 'Not exactly. But I need to get there, as quickly as possible.'

There can't be that many nurseries for sale in Cornwall. I'll track down the right one. I'll find him. Somehow.

'Well.' The guard's brow creases. 'I'll have to consult the book.' He disappears into his room. I can hear Dominic whispering feverishly into his microphone, but I don't care.

'Here we are.' The guard emerges, holding a piece of paper covered in pencil. 'Six changes, I'm afraid, to Penzance. And it'll be one hundred and twenty pounds. Train'll be a while,' he adds. 'Platform Two.'

'Thanks.' I pick up my suitcase and head over the footbridge. I can hear Dominic hurrying after me with the cameraman.

'Samantha appears to have taken leave of her senses,' he's panting into his microphone. 'The strain of the situation has sent her over the edge. Who knows what rash move she will make next?'

He *so* wants me to jump, doesn't he? I'm just going to ignore him. I stand resolutely on the platform, looking away from the camera.

'With no address and no back-up,' I hear him continuing, 'Samantha is setting off on a long and uncertain journey to find the man who rejected her this morning. The man who walked away without saying goodbye. Is this a wise plan?'

OK, I've had enough.

'Maybe it isn't a wise plan!' I turn to face him, breathing heavily. 'Maybe I won't find him. Maybe he won't even want to know. But I have to try.'

Dominic opens his mouth again to speak.

'Shut up,' I say. 'Just shut up.'

It seems like hours before I hear the sound of the train in the distance. But it's the wrong side. It's another train for London. As it pulls in I can hear the doors opening and people piling on and off.

'London train!' the guard is shouting. 'Train for London, Platform One.'

That's the train I should be on. If I was sane. If I hadn't taken leave of my senses. My eyes move idly over the windows, at people in their seats, talking, sleeping, reading, listening to iPods—

And then everything seems to freeze. Am I *dreaming*?

It's Nathaniel. On the London train. He's three yards away, sitting in a window seat, staring ahead rigidly.

What – Why is he—

'Nathaniel!' I try to shout, but my voice has turned into a husk. 'Nathaniel!' I wave my arms frantically, trying to get his attention.

'Jesus, it's him!' exclaims Dominic. 'Nathaniel!' he yells, his voice like a foghorn. 'Over here, mate!'

'Nathaniel!' At last my voice is working. 'Na-than-iel!'

At my desperate scream he finally looks up and jolts with shock as he sees me. For a moment his expression is sheer disbelief. Then his whole face seems to expand in a slow explosion of delight.

I can hear the train doors slamming. It's about to leave.

'Come on!' I yell, beckoning urgently.

I can see him getting up inside the train, grabbing his rucksack, squeezing past the woman in the next seat. Then he disappears from view, just as the train starts pulling out of the station.

'Too late,' says the cameraman lugubriously. 'He'll never make it.'

My chest is too tight for me to answer. All I can do is stare at the departing train, moving past carriage by carriage, speeding up, faster and faster . . . until finally it's gone.

And Nathaniel is standing on the platform. He's there.

Without moving my eyes from his I begin to walk along the platform, speeding up as I reach the foot-bridge. On the opposite side he does the same. We reach the top of the steps, walk forward a way and both come to a halt, a few feet apart. My breaths are coming quickly and the blood has flooded my face. I feel shell-shocked and exhilarated and uncertain all at the same time.

'I thought you were going down to Cornwall,' I say at last. 'To buy your nursery.'

'I changed my mind.' Nathaniel looks pretty shell-shocked himself. 'Thought I might . . . visit a friend in London instead.' He glances at my suitcase. 'Where were you going?'

I clear my throat. 'I was thinking . . . Cornwall.'

'Cornwall?' He stares at me.

'Uh huh.' I show him my timetable, suddenly wanting to giggle at the ridiculousness of it all.

Nathaniel leans against the barricade, his thumbs in his pockets, and surveys the wooden slats of the bridge. 'So . . . where are your friends?'

'Dunno. Gone. And they're not my friends. I punched Guy,' I add proudly.

Nathaniel throws back his head and laughs. 'So they fired you.'

'I fired them,' I correct him.

'You did?' says Nathaniel in amazement. He reaches out for my hand but I don't take it. Underneath my joy I'm still feeling unsettled. The hurt of this morning hasn't gone. I can't pretend everything's OK.

'I got your note.' I lift my eyes to his and Nathaniel flinches.

'Samantha . . . I wrote you a different one on the train. In case you wouldn't see me in London.'

He fishes awkwardly in his pocket and pulls out a letter, several sheets long; both sides of the paper covered in writing. I hold it for a few moments without reading it.

'What – what does it say?' I raise my eyes.

'It's long and boring.' His gaze burns into mine. 'And badly put.'

I turn the pages slowly over in my fingers. Here and there I glimpse words that make my eyes fill instantly.

'So,' I manage.

'So.' Nathaniel's arms come round my waist; his warm mouth lands on mine. As he holds me tight I can feel the tears spilling onto my cheeks. This is where I belong. This is where I fit. I finally draw away and look up at him, wiping my eyes.

'Where now?' He looks down over the bridge and I follow his gaze. The railway track extends in both directions, way into the distance. 'Which way?'

I look along the endless line, squinting in the sunshine. I'm twenty-nine years old. I can go anywhere. Do anything. Be anyone I like.

'There's no rush,' I say at last and reach up to kiss him again.

THE END